"Breathe, Ruby..."

"...Breathe through it. Your Dragon is waking up. Bring it in."

"Hurts. Hurts so bad," she managed to say. She thought for sure she was on fire, but he was holding her close, enduring the flames, too. She saw it then, behind her closed eyelids. The Dragon was deep red with streaks of white, its scales glossy. It lifted its head, stretching its neck and releasing a stream of fire from its mouth.

Then she was moving, faintly aware of her skin rubbing against Cyn's. The hunger washed over her in great waves. She pulled him closer, his chest against her cheek, the rub of his sprinkling of hair chafing her jaw.

"Control, Ruby," he whispered, when he should have shouted it.

She shook her head, her mouth sliding against his skin.

He lowered his head, his voice hoarse. "Ruby."

She looked up at him, the embers wild in his eyes, and pulled his mouth down to hers. His hands tightened on her, fingers tangling in her hair. She sucked on his tongue, then nibbled on his lower lip. Things she had never done before, never thought to do.

Hungry...

JAN 1 7 2014

D0711400

DRAGON AWAKENED

A Hidden Novel

JAIME RUSH

FOREVER

NEW YORK   BOSTON

Copyright © 2013 by Tina Wainscott
Excerpt from *Magic Possessed* Copyright © 2013 by Tina Wainscott

Forever
Hachette Book Group
237 Park Avenue
New York, NY 10017

www.HachetteBookGroup.com

Printed in the United States of America

First Edition: December 2013
10 9 8 7 6 5 4 3 2 1

OPM

Forever is an imprint of Grand Central Publishing.
The Forever name and logo are trademarks of Hachette Book Group, Inc.

The Hachette Speakers Bureau provides a wide range of authors for speaking events. To find out more, go to www.hachettespeakersbureau.com or call (866) 376-6591.

The publisher is not responsible for websites (or their content) that are not owned by the publisher.

ATTENTION CORPORATIONS AND ORGANIZATIONS:

Most Hachette Book Group books are available at quantity discounts with bulk purchase for educational, business, or sales promotional use. For information, please call or write:

**Special Markets Department, Hachette Book Group
237 Park Avenue, New York, NY 10017
Telephone: 1-800-222-6747 Fax: 1-800-477-5925**

Prologue

Fifteen years earlier...

Cyntag's phone rang. He set down his glass of whiskey and grabbed the phone. The screen showed a restricted number. His boss.

"Valeron here," he answered.

"I have a sensitive job of an urgent nature."

Guard talk for an assassination to be carried out now. Over the years, Cyn had progressed through the Crescent police agency, going from an Argus to a Vega, the highest classification of officer. It meant taking jobs without explanations, without question... and without conscience.

Cyn grabbed a piece of paper. "Go ahead."

"I'm handing you over to someone else for the details." Of which there would be few.

Another man came on the line. He didn't introduce himself, only gave Cyn ocean coordinates. "There's a yacht named *PHYSIKAL* roughly in that area. Male is a Deuce, female a Dragon. Take out everyone on the yacht. *Everyone*. Understand?"

Irritation bristled, but Cyn kept it from his voice. "As always."

"I've heard much about you, Valeron. Carry out this task and you will be rewarded well."

The phone went dead. Cyn went into his office, pulled out the maritime map from his collection, and pinpointed the coordinates. Far enough out that boat traffic would be minimal at this hour. He headed outside to his back deck, looking at the ocean and orienting his position with his target. A trail of moonlight glistened on the waves like a thousand glittering diamonds, pointing in the right direction like an arrow.

He turned around to take in the warm and welcoming fireplace through the wall of windows in back. More money didn't motivate him, and he was as high in the Guard as he cared to be. What drove him was the thrill of the hunt, the kill...to feel *something* after all this time.

He walked to the seawall, stripped out of his clothing, and dove into the ocean. Water sluiced over his body as it transformed and magick tingled through him. His nose and mouth pulled away from his face, and his lengthening teeth tugged against his gums. His torso stretched, growing large and strong. His tailbone extended, becoming a whip in the water behind him. Scales emerged from his skin, the final transformation to Dragon.

The oceans were vastly uncharted, unmonitored, and mysterious, the last frontier. Emerald Dragons could fly beneath the water, a luxury envied by the other types. Cyn wasn't Emerald by nature. He'd come by the ability in a less than honorable way.

There was nothing like the thrill of gliding free through the water, other than what awaited him. He tuned into his innate sense of direction, shifting south. Fish darted away in crazy zigzags. He skirted the sound of a boat's engine, staying deep. A fish finder might pick up a horse-sized object that the captain would attribute to a school of fish or Goliath grouper.

He came up, saw lights in the distance, then swam close enough to ascertain that the yacht was his quarry. A man and woman sat in the cockpit, though even with his night vision Cyn couldn't see much more than their gender.

His heart beat faster, adrenaline racing through his veins. He submerged again, moving close enough to see the hull cutting through the water. His muscles tightened and released, shooting him toward the bow. He gathered his magick and tore through the hull and out the other side. The impact hurt, bruising and jarring his body, but he powered through it.

Cyn surfaced, only the tip of his snout and eyes above the water. The couple shouted to each other, panic in their voices as they scurried to the deck to see what had hit them. The yacht was tilted, water gushing into the hole he'd created. They were obviously on the run. No other reason for tearing across the ocean at this time of night or to warrant a Guard-sanctioned hit. The targets would immediately suspect an attack.

The man ran down into the cabin. The woman grabbed a rifle and started shooting in a wide arc into the water. She couldn't see him so her shots flew wild. The man returned to the deck carrying a large bundle. Some kind of bomb launcher? But he screamed into the darkness of the ocean, "They don't know anything about this! Leave them alone, please!" He ran to the dinghy and laid his package in it.

Cyn hated when they begged. No matter, he had his orders.

The yacht was sinking fast. The female discharged all her shots, desperately searching the water. Cyn remained just below the surface, his view distorted. She Catalyzed, becoming a Carnelian Dragon. Red, passionate, and pissed, her Breath weapon was a stream of fiery spikes. With her night vision and fine-tuned instincts, she zeroed in on him. Her eyes flared with hatred and fear just before she dove in.

Come and get me, sweetheart.

He'd learned long ago that females, at least Crescent Dragons, were as vicious and capable as any male. He would give her no deference. No mercy. He shot toward her beneath the water, knocking her aside. One of her talons scratched across his scales but not deep enough to penetrate.

She came at him again, her fangs aiming at his throat. His tail whipped out and lashed her side, but she grabbed for him anyway. He let her get close enough to think she had a chance before locking his arm around her neck. Pinned against his side, she kicked and tore at him with her claws. A spray of leathery spines fanned out from the sides of her head, brushing against his face as she tried to thrash back and forth.

Her tail *thwacked* him in the back of the head so hard that he momentarily loosened his grip on her. She pushed off and started to swim away. He grabbed hold of her tail and snapped the bone. She howled in pain as she swam back to the boat and scrambled onto the only part of the yacht still above water.

He climbed onto the back edge right behind her. She

blew fiery spikes at him. He ducked but had little room to maneuver. Fire prickled along his scales, and one spike lanced the unprotected flesh near his eye. He lunged at her, knocking her down and clamping his hand around her snout as she prepared to blow more of that lethal Breath. She kicked, her claws tearing at his scales. He jerked her head back and tore into her throat, finishing it.

Hot blood coursed down his chin. She fell limp and slid into the water with a splash. He followed her down, clamping onto her, Breathing Dragon...taking her essence. It was how he held the power of many Dragon colors. Her Carnelian nature surged through him like a thousand volts of electricity. The water flickered and glowed red as the last of her power transferred to him. She Catalyzed back to human upon death, and he released her to sink to the murky depths.

The ocean suddenly sucked at him as the yacht sank, pulling him down in its current. He pushed away, fighting the vacuum to get to the surface. The far-off sound of an engine caught his ear, the man trying to get away in a dinghy. When Cyn caught up to it, the man leaped into the water. Cyn had no idea what kind of magick the Deuce possessed. He knew Dragon skills by their color, unless they were adept killers who had absorbed their opponents' powers. Deuces wielded all kinds of weapons and abilities, with no indication by their appearance.

The man's hands glowed blue, creating a force field around himself. He sputtered as waves splashed into his face. "We're innocent," he said on a gasp.

"It's not my place to judge." In Dragon form, Cyn's voice was deep and gravelly.

"Please, don't kill my daughter. I beg you—"

Cyn dove through the painful field and cut off the man's words—and his life. He surveyed the area as the man's body sank. No one thrashed in the water. If anyone else had been on board, they were dead, too.

The dinghy kept churning into the night. He grabbed onto the side once he'd caught up and nearly tipped it over as he tried to crawl inside. He Catalyzed to man and pulled himself in. The sight of a blanket wrapped around a sleeping child smacked him in the chest. Ah, the man's daughter. Her feet were bare, nightgown wrapped around her legs like seaweed. Blood marred her temple. Cyn knelt down next to her and found a pulse.

Take out everyone on the yacht. Everyone.

The man who'd given him the order knew the child was on board, knew Cyn was ruthless enough to kill her. He rubbed the back of his neck as he contemplated her. They must have a good reason for wanting her dead. And he *was* cold-blooded enough to carry out any task they required.

Wasn't he?

Chapter 1

———

Present day...

Ah, the smell of fresh paint in the morning.

Ruby stepped out of the office and squinted at the sun reflecting off the windshield of a '57 Chevy. For a few seconds, a bright mark marred everything she saw, including the Gottlieb Grand Slam 1953 pinball machine that was further along in the restoration process. Beyond that, five acres filled with memories of climbing cars, dismantling bicycles, and the sound of her mom calling, "Ruby, get off there. You're going to fall and crack your head open!" To an adventurous seven-year-old: annoying. Now, a sound she'd kill to hear again.

What she didn't see was her business partner. Typical. She stalked across the gravel, searching the sections of vintage toys, old signage, and then Coca-Cola machines for him.

"Seen Nevin?" she asked Jack, her expert on motorcycle restoration.

He nodded toward the back. "Chewing the fat with a friend."

"Augh."

Jack hefted his wrench. "Want me to bust his chops, Miz Ruby? I'll kick his ass all over the place...if you'll pardon my French."

"That's not French," she said, trying to ignore the "Miz Ruby" that he wouldn't stop calling her, along with his flirtatious smile. "Thanks, but he's my problem."

She continued on to Nevin's disorganized side of the yard and found him leaning against one of his junk sculptures, laughing it up with some guy.

"Nevin." She kept her gaze on him, plastering on a pleasant-but-fake smile for his friend's benefit. "Our client is picking up the Wayne gas pump at the end of the week, the one that doesn't look anywhere near ready."

Nevin rubbed his belly where his shirt rode up and exposed pale, flabby flesh. "You're good at finding deals and making old stuff look new again." He gestured to the roof of a 1976 Cadillac Fleetwood he'd fashioned into a table. "How 'bout you do the resto stuff and let me focus on my art?"

"Resto is paying the bills. You haven't sold one piece yet."

"Aw, Ruby, you said business is good. Can't we take it easy for a bit?"

No, she needed to push herself, to fill some need for...something. Her pseudo-uncle Moncrief inherited the Yard, along with her, when her parents were killed in a boating accident fifteen years ago. Because he traveled often performing his magic shows, he couldn't deal with running the Yard. Ruby had sobbed at the prospect of losing the last tangible tie to her mom, so he made a deal with Nevin's parents: a half share for managing it.

After graduating high school, she wrested control from Nevin's father, who proved that being a lovable lackey was in his gene pool. When he passed, Nevin's mom insisted he step in, hoping to give him direction. He'd been one of the early strays Ruby attracted. While she had the kind of affection one might have for a dumb-but-sweet cousin, she wasn't going to let him run the business into the ground like his father nearly did.

The man with Nevin said, "Ruby Salazaar, don't you recognize me?" The wiry guy in a white cotton T and faded jeans gave her an expectant smile. Smoke trailed from the cigarette clamped between his fingers.

"Leo Canton?"

He looked nothing like the Afro-haired kid whose parents were part of Mon's touring troupe. His hair was trimmed short now, round glasses gone. "Been a long time." He approached her with outstretched arms.

She warded him off. "You are *not* going to hug me like we're long-lost friends. Unless you count cutting off my braid and terrorizing me as friendship, which I do not."

He chuckled, dropping the cigarette and grinding it into the gravel with his heel. "You still got a braid." His gaze followed it all the way down to her rear. "The color of honey. You nailed me good after I cut it off. I had that black eye for weeks."

"You deserved every hour of it." She'd pounded him, the rage so overwhelming it scared her. She pointed to the cigarette. "Didn't you see the sign? Anyone who drops his butts has to pick them up and put a dollar into the 'Jar of Bad Behavior.' Which I use for the cat neuter fund." She nodded toward two kittens who were racing over to rub against Leo's ankles.

Leo pulled out his wallet and handed her a fiver. "Still feisty as ever, and a hell of a lot stronger." He had the gall to clamp his hand over her biceps but pulled away at the murderous glare she gave him.

Nevin made a tsking sound. "She hates to be touched, dude. Some guy grabbed her buttocks once, and she dropped him right to the ground. Dude clutched his *co-jones* all the way outta here, yowling like a girl." His pride warmed her heart.

"That doesn't surprise me." Leo slumped back against the car and crossed his arms over his chest. "You did get the best training on attack and evade, thanks to me."

"You mean the Hunter/Prey game you and Jimmy used to force me into playing?" The two would start hunting her, prowling the tour buses or the stage equipment. She was always the reluctant prey. Except something inside her actually liked it while the rest of her hated it.

He shrugged. "We only did it 'cause your uncle paid us to."

"*What?*"

Leo plucked a kitten from midway up his pant leg and set it down. "Five bucks a week. Skills building, he called it."

"You're serious?"

"Your uncle did things to protect you. He was super paranoid for some reason." He peered into her eyes. "You *still* don't..." He clamped his mouth shut and waved as he sauntered off. "Nevin, gimme a shout if you find the part for my truck."

"I still don't what?" she called after him.

"Have a sense of humor," Leo said, though she knew that wasn't what he was going to say.

She pinned Nevin with a glare. "Is this true, about Mon paying kids to torment me?"

He assumed the blank look of the guilty.

Her cell phone rang. "Speak of the devil." She skipped right past *hello*. "Were your ears burning? I've got—"

"Ruby, there's trouble."

"Did you piss off your new neighbors already? I told you not to hang those weird artifacts all over your front porch. Creeps people out."

"No, *big* trouble, ducky. Get over here, quick. There are things I have to tell you, things I should have told you long ago."

Her throat tightened at the agony in his voice. "Be there in about forty minutes."

"Speed."

Speed in Miami traffic. Yeah, right. Especially since a storm had recently passed through, leaving the freeways wet and slick. Which made drivers either go too slow or too fast. The black mass of clouds now squatted roughly over the upscale neighborhood where Uncle Mon lived.

By the time she reached his house, the storm had moved on. Everything glistened from the recent rain. South Florida storms were wicked but brief. Mon chose this area for its secluded lots. Not that fans clamored over him. He had built his fame as a master illusionist overseas. He was almost a rock star in Germany. Deservedly so. Even as she'd watched from backstage, she had never once seen the trick, the hidey-hole, the sliding panel. When she begged to know just one secret, he always said with a conspiratorial wink, "It's real magic, ducky."

Her work boots scraped on the flagstones leading to his front door. Nothing seemed amiss, so his trouble was likely some exaggerated fear spun from his eccentric mind. She brushed past the animal bones, crystals, and silver stars hanging from the porch roof and lifted the knocker. The brass moon banged against the heavy wood door, echoing inside the marble-floored foyer on the other side.

"Uncle Mon?"

She heard a strangled warble that sounded like, "Go!" Which didn't make sense since he'd ordered her to come.

She pushed the door open and stopped cold at the surreal sight of Mon several feet above the floor, his feet dangling. A bolt of green lightning speared him to the wall, right through his chest. She felt encased in a solid block of ice, unable to breathe.

His horrified eyes found her. "G-get...*out*, child."

Run. Obey Mon.

Leave Mon to die from this thing? Hell, no.

She ran forward and grabbed the flower arrangement from the table in the center of the foyer, her gaze on the bolt.

Pain wracked his wizened face. "Don't let it see you."

Which didn't make sense either. She threw the vase with every ounce of strength she could muster. It fell short, but she was already searching for something else before it even crashed to the floor. She had to knock the bolt away from him, but with what? The knives Mon collected that she was never to touch, except for throwing practice.

She ran into the den where several were mounted on

the walls. Two knives slid free of their fancy sheaths in her clumsy grasp. She raced back, skidding to a stop and aligning herself so she wouldn't accidentally hit him. His arms now hung at his sides. His fingers flexed, the only fight he was putting up now.

No.

Before she could throw the first knife, the bolt formed into a ball of light and shot upstairs. Mon fell to the floor in a bone-jarring *thump*, and she threw herself at him, sliding on her knees the final two feet.

"Mon! Talk to me."

She gasped at the hole burnt into his chest, nearly gagging at the smell of seared flesh. His eyes lacked the light of life, dull yet still fearful.

He uttered, "Get out. Will...kill if it sees you." He was talking at least, even if he wasn't making sense.

"Lightning can't *see*. And it doesn't come back. It's random, 'lightning doesn't strike twice in the same place' and all that. I'm calling nine-one-one."

"No." He raised a shaky hand and let it drop on top of hers as it went for her phone. "Can't tell police. Rule Number One."

"Mon, you're in shock."

"Tell them...lightning."

"It *was* lightning. Ball lightning, I'm guessing, which I've heard can act really freaky."

"Not lightning." He took a stilted breath. "Magick."

"An illusion?" But no, illusions didn't inflict mortal damage. He was talking nonsense. "Mon, please let me get you help."

"No use." He sucked in a noisy breath. "Get the envelope I told you about...bottom desk drawer...and go."

She sputtered a hysterical laugh. "Are you crazy? I'm not leaving you."

"Stupid, but not...crazy." He gasped, his hand tightening on hers. "The person who sent it...danger, ducky."

His words sank in. "You're saying someone *sent* that lightning bolt to kill you?" The thought squeezed her throat, especially when he nodded.

"Read my...letter...explains everything." Mon spoke with what looked like every ounce of his remaining strength. "Do not see your grandfather. Too...dangerous."

"Brom's been in that mental hospital in Alaska for years. Wait, are you saying he did this?"

Mon's eyes widened with determination. "Cyntag, he..." He shuddered, then fell limp.

"No. No!" She put her fists on the uninjured part of his chest and pumped. "Come back. Come back, damn it." Even in her disbelief, grief tore at her.

A sound whispered behind her. She spun to find the green ball sailing down the curved stairs and into the den. An acrid smell hit her nostrils. Smoke rolled out of the upstairs hallway, and she heard a *whoosh* in the den. The ball shot back out and hovered a few yards in front of her. She stared at it, almost mesmerized by the green sparks inside—until it came at her.

With a yelp, Ruby ducked as it whizzed so close that she felt a sting on her forehead, then smelled burnt hair. *Her* hair. She grabbed one of the knives she'd dropped as she launched to her feet. It tingled in her hand, emitting faint electrical shocks. She couldn't take even a second to look at it. The ball floated a few feet away, following her movements.

Following her movements?

Like Hunter/Prey. "What are you?" she screamed. *Orb* popped into her mind.

Flames licked inside the den and along the stairway banister. The orb had set the house on fire. Now it wanted her. What the hell?

It zinged toward her, and she threw the knife. It flew faster than she thought possible, stabbing the orb. It shuddered, vibrating so fast that she could barely discern the movements. It disgorged the knife, which disintegrated like friggin' dust. But it had done something. The orb was smaller now. She needed to get the other knife.

The orb flew at her, and she ducked around the backside of the heavy foyer table. Hunter/Prey. It was all coming back. Wood crackled behind her, and smoke filled the house. Noxious fumes tickled her throat, hot and cloying, and she fought the cough burning up her throat.

Flames filled the den now, licking into the foyer as though they were testing the air. She lunged for the other knife but the orb cut her off. It had intelligence, all right. The knife seemed to glow, though it was probably reflecting the green sparks. Or maybe not. Obviously it wasn't a normal knife.

The orb circled the foyer. She could barely see it now because of the smoke and the tears in her stinging eyes. Coughing spasms wracked her body, and smoke strangled the air from her. *Have to get out of here.* She backed toward the door.

The orb flew behind her, sending her jerking forward. Ruby feinted right, then ran toward the kitchen. It beat her to the door. The kitchen was already in flames, but a clear path to the exterior door remained. She took several steps back, facing the orb as it followed. Pretending to head to the front door, she twisted around and slid across the floor toward the second knife. She and Mon had played a form of paintball in his old house, which had marble floors and long hallways. She got good at sliding on the slick surfaces.

The knife tingled again as she gripped it in her sweaty palm. She spun around, searching for the orb. Not seeing it, she ran into the kitchen. Black smoke billowed in the upper portion of the room. The orb hovered between her and the door. The damned thing was keeping her from escaping!

She crouched, but the smoke drew closer to the floor. Soon it would fill the entire room. She readied the knife, held at her thigh and out of sight. One shot. That's all she had because there was no going back in the den. Another coughing fit seized her, and she gripped the edge of the granite counter to keep her balance. All the while, she watched the orb come closer, taking advantage of her weakened condition.

Like a sentient thing. An evil thing.

Sucking in a breath, she snapped upright and threw the knife. Arcs of electricity danced along the blade as it plunged into the orb. While it tried to eject the knife, she grabbed a pot from the hanging rack. Like a baseball batter, she swung her whole body into throwing it. She knocked the orb against the wall and dashed back into the foyer.

Sirens pierced the air. Someone had called the fire department. Thank God.

Or maybe not. Would the orb hurt the firefighters?

She couldn't see it as she dared a glance back while

racing for the door. It flew open, crashing against the wall. Two firemen stood in the opening, clad in protective gear.

"Anyone else in here?" one asked her.

"My uncle!" She pointed, and at that moment, the entire wall where he lay collapsed in flames.

The force of it jerked her backward. No, that was one of the firefighters grabbing her as they retreated onto the front porch. She searched for the orb even as they scrambled to their feet. One firefighter led her farther from the house. She was a limp doll, all of her attention on the hellish nightmare come to life. Flames shot out through gaps in the roof and every window. If she'd still been inside, she'd be dead.

One of the men ushered her to a fire truck. A second truck pulled up, spewing men and equipment. Medics treated the small burn on her forehead, while all she could do was cough and look for the orb.

Had it purposely destroyed evidence? Yes, she was sure of it.

Orb. She'd heard that word before, in the stories Mon created for her when she was a child: a hidden world of magick, with angels and people who turned into dragons. *Magick* with a *k* at the end, spelled differently because it wasn't the illusion type. The sorcerer-like Deuces could make orbs, instilling an intention like spy or fry.

She started shaking with the thoughts and questions bombarding her as she watched streams of water trying to tame the flames. The sounds of pumps, men shouting instructions, and spraying water filled the air. The answers were in the envelope, and it was burning away.

The Book of the Hidden

The white dove's alarmed coos drew Garnet to the window of her turret bedroom. "What's the matter, Opal? 'Tis not like you to be so fitful."

She heard the sound then, far from the usual noises of the immense forest that surrounded the castle. Her gaze riveted upon what looked like black oil running along the ground, pouring around the trees as it advanced. Opal flew off with a distressed warble. Garnet knew of the dark magick in the kingdom, the creatures and dangers hovering beyond the environs of her safe little world. Her parents called it the Hidden.

As it reached the edge of the forest, the "oil" materialized into soldiers, coming faster than any normal humans could. She heard a grunt below her. One of their guardsmen fought a man bearing black horns and armor that resembled the beetles in the garden. Those horns stretched out like snakes and plunged through the guardsman's chest. He dropped with a gasp.

She spun from the window, intending to run to her parents' chamber. Footsteps pounded down the stone floor outside her room, and the door was flung open. Her father was still in his dressing robe, terror on his face. "I have inadvertently brought great peril to our land. You must hide, must—"

A clawed hand reached out and pulled him out of sight. "Leave her be!" Her father's voice echoed in the great hallway.

She ran to the doorway to help him but came up short as the kind of man-beasts she'd just watched below rushed up to block her. They bore blood on their armor, and she knew, somehow, that it was her parents'. And, by the glitter in the men's eyes, she also knew her blood would soon join it.

A scraping sound from the window behind her drew the startled gazes of the men. She dared turn to see what frightened them, these evil murderers. The sight of the creature sliding soundlessly to the floor on its clawed feet stole her breath.

A black Dragon, the size of a large horse, opened its fierce mouth and bared its fangs. It blew out not fire, as she'd read in the legends, but a black smoke that shot toward her. She would die with dignity, she thought, raising her chin. She would not cower, would not—

The stream of smoke passed her, knocking the three men back into the hallway. Their guttural screams echoed in the stone hallway and then grew silent.

The Dragon had saved her from them. Before she could thank it, it rushed forward and grabbed her with its talons. They scratched but did not puncture her skin as the beast pulled her against the cool scales of its chest and flew out the window.

Chapter 2

Despite Ruby's exhaustion, grief and terror kept ripping her from sleep. Well before dawn, she was scouring the Internet for stories about ball lightning. Turned out, ball lightning was a mysterious phenomenon having various shapes and colors. Though it could melt metal, it passed through windows and even screens without causing a bit of damage. It rarely killed a human, and nowhere did she find an account of one chasing down or lancing someone.

And what about the knives that seemed to exude some kind of energy...and affected the orb?

She'd told the lieutenant about the freak bolt of lightning from the storm, omitting most of the bizarre stuff like how it tried to keep her from escaping. Not that he'd have believed her anyway. Mon had said something about magick and Rule Number One, whatever that was.

Had Mon been rambling from shock? He'd been lucid enough to mention the envelope he'd told her to retrieve should anything ever happen to him. She figured it involved inheritance issues or business matters. That he'd mentioned it as he suffered an agonizing death meant it was way more important. Was there a chance it survived? Doubtful, but she had to try to find it. She also needed to find the *Book of the Hidden* that Mon kept in his office. While she had treasured the stories like a chest of jewels as a child, she outgrew them in her early teens and could only remember the essence of them.

The thought of going back to his house chilled her. What if the orb was there or the person who'd sent it? Had it chased her because she was a witness? Probably. How much did this Sin Tag know about her?

She had searched for variations of that name, too, thinking it was a company or government agency. No luck. Maybe SINTAG was a top-secret project and the orb some superweapon. Yeah, that made sense, except...how would her uncle get involved with something like that?

She pulled on old jeans and a T-shirt, stopping short at her reflection in the mirror over her dresser. A lock of singed hair curled in tiny spirals over her bandage. She lopped off the burnt portion, which made one chunk of hair shorter than the rest, so she evened them out.

Ruby called Nevin on the way to let him know she wouldn't be in. She'd given him the freak bolt of lightning story last night.

How did her grandfather fit into this? She had vague memories of awkward conversations with him, a man obviously not used to talking with children. Then waking up at Brom's after the boating accident, a gash in her head and no memory of anything that had happened after she'd been knocked against the cabin's doorframe. Brom broke the bad news about her parents in a pained, soft voice.

She was quickly settled into Mon's life. Neither man would even let her go home to get her belongings. Mon told her that Brom sank into a deep depression and had to go to a mental facility, where he'd been all the years since. From Ruby's memories, it appeared that he'd pretty much gone bonkers.

Her truck rolled to a stop in front of Mon's house. Even in the soft morning light, the house was a horror scene. A firefighter patrolled the edge of the rubble. She didn't want to talk to anyone, but his presence was comforting. The orb had seemed shy, disappearing the moment the fire crew arrived. Still, she searched for it or anything weird.

Its absence wasn't enough to make her feel safe. But her Smith & Wesson was. She pulled it from beneath the seat of the truck. Forget vases and knives. If that thing reappeared, she was shooting it. She hid the gun in the waistband of her jeans beneath her shirt. After making sure the lump at her back wasn't noticeable, she grabbed a couple of garbage bags and approached the ruined house. The stench of smoke filled the air. The firefighter met her halfway, ready to turn her back.

"I'm Ruby Salazaar. The man who...lived here was my uncle."

The firefighter's bloodshot blue eyes made her think he'd been there all night. "I remember you from yesterday. I'm sorry for your loss."

At least he didn't treat her like a suspect. They had

swabbed her hands, looking for accelerants or other signs of foul play. They had no idea just how foul it was.

She could only nod. "I need to see what I can salvage from his office."

The man checked his watch. "We're not supposed to let anyone on the scene for twenty-four hours, but it's getting close. I'll have to accompany you though."

"Great," she answered too quickly.

She took in the house, her throat tightening and eyes stinging. She brushed away hot tears before they could slide down her cheeks.

"Be careful."

She jerked around, thinking the firefighter had seen something.

He nodded to the floor. "You can't tell what's beneath the muck."

"Oh. Yeah, thanks." *Stop acting all scared and freaked out.*

She stepped into the den. First order of business, find that envelope amid unidentifiable mounds and lumps. One was probably what was left of his massive desk. She searched for anything resembling the bottom drawer. All that remained of his files was a wet mess of ash. Paper disintegrated as she pulled things out.

The fireman hovered without intruding. He was probably making sure she wasn't digging up some incendiary device. How would a supersecret government thingamabob set a fire?

She turned to where the bookcase used to be and found burnt framed pictures of both her and the wife and daughter Mon lost years before she came into his life. Book spines, singed covers, ruined pages—she found nothing salvageable. Some of these books had been kept in a locked cabinet, but she'd glimpsed titles with words like *ancient spells* and *alchemy.*

Beneath a slab of wood, she felt a thick leather spine and pulled out a chunk of blackened book. The wood had protected it somewhat, though half the cover and an inch of the outer edge of pages had burned away. She brushed away soot from the tooled lettering.

The Book of the Hid...

The Hidden. She sank to her knees, pressed it to her chest, and whispered, "Thank you, God." She flipped through the pages with trembling fingers, the charred edges crumbling at her touch. A cry escaped her throat. All of the sketches of dragons, Deuces, and angels... gone.

She grabbed another book from the muck that was in worse shape and opened it. The ink was still there. And another. Then she picked up *The Hidden* again. No more girl thrown into a dangerous world, no more Dragon Prince. She recalled her favorite picture of him as he danced with Garnet, spinning her round and round and into his dark spell. Black of hair and heart, he was darkly handsome, with chips of onyx for eyes and his mouth in a permanent snarl. It annoyed Mon that she'd been most fascinated by the villain.

To a girl who'd lost everything, a powerful prince who could whisk a girl out of danger seemed dashingly romantic. Then she'd grown up and discovered there were no princes out there, and men who snarled also bit.

Ruby placed the book in the garbage bag and gave up finding anything else. She headed to the unscathed separate garage and keyed in the code for the door. The front fender of Mon's old Rolls-Royce sparkled as sunlight hit it. She found nothing more than a few tools and some spare parts she'd procured in case he ever needed them.

The car's interior was as immaculate as its exterior. What she did find was his cell phone on the passenger floorboard. The main screen indicated a voice message. She scrolled down his sparse contacts list, finding one that made her heart jump: Cyntag Valeron. Yes, that could definitely be the name Mon had uttered. She went back to voice mail and called in, using the same code that opened the garage door to access his voice mail. *Bingo.*

Her heart seized as a velvety male voice said, "Cyntag, here. I see that you called but didn't leave a message. Have you finally come to your senses, you old bastard? Or is the Dragon beginning to show? I warned that you were playing with fire—literally. Call me. Don't make me track you down."

Dragon? Was that some kind of code? She played it two more times but still couldn't make sense of it. She searched through the call log. First he'd taken a call from Brom. A short while later, Mon had called her and then Cyntag. Cyntag had called back shortly before she'd arrived. He'd tracked Mon down, all right.

If she couldn't go to the police, she had to take matters into her own hands. Someone had to pay for Mon's murder. She couldn't ask Brom, but she needed to find out who this Cyntag was.

She redialed the number. If he answered, she'd pretend to be someone investigating Mon's death.

A woman with a sultry radio voice answered. "Dragon Arts. How may I help you?"

"Dragon Arts?" That word again.

"We're a mixed martial arts studio, with classes in self-defense, cane, jujitsu, and tai chi. I can give you our website address if you want the whole skinny."

"Sure." The woman rattled it off; then Ruby asked, "Does a Cyntag Valeron work there?"

"You could say that, sugar. He owns the studio."

Oh, great. He was probably in top shape and could whip someone's butt without breaking a sweat. But he had access to more powerful weapons than that, like supernatural orbs.

That's all right. I'm going to find out more about you, Cyntag Valeron. And somehow, some way, I'm going to make you pay.

Purcell stepped into the captain's office without knocking. The man bid the person on the phone goodbye and stood. The Dragon bristled at his territory being invaded without diplomacy, especially by a Deuce.

Purcell kept his singed palms out of sight. "Do you remember me? It's been fifteen years since the last time I was in your office."

Recognition clicked in the embers of the man's eyes. "Yes, I believe you were identified as Mr. Smith. What can I do for you?" His words were clipped.

"You sent one of your best Vegas on that assignment for me."

The man's expression shut down. "The yacht."

"Are you sure he completed the assignment?"

"The man and woman were not a big deal, but execut-

ing a child troubled him. That assignment ruined him. He
quit."

"Quit? After how many years on the force?"

"He was a Ward."

An orphan pledged to the Guard. "You're sure he
killed her?" The child named Ruby.

"Yes."

Purcell reached into his mind, just a little. Not enough
for the man to notice. He seemed to be telling the truth.
He was also angry over losing his Vega. The Guard
tapped Crescent orphanages for their most promising
Wards, mentoring them and luring them into service. Perhaps this man was the Vega's mentor. "What was his
name? I want to talk to him."

"We never give out the names of our employees." The
captain's mouth tightened with a hint of smugness. "I'm
sure you understand, Mr. *Smith*."

Purcell reached again, probing for the name now. *Sin*.
Similar to the name he'd overheard in the conversation
between Brom and Moncrief. He knew of a Cyntag, an
old Dragon with a fearsome reputation who had served in
the Guard many years ago. "Is his name Cyntag?"

People usually gave away their answer when you took
them by surprise. The captain shuttered his expression but
not fast enough. "As I said—"

Purcell raised his hand. "I understand. I had reason to
suspect that perhaps he hadn't done his job. But you assure me he did, so I shall consider the matter closed."

His hand was on the doorknob when the captain's
voice stopped him. "Why was it necessary to kill a girl?"

"If we were trying to make it look like an accident, she
would have been a witness to the fact that it wasn't."

The captain gave a quick nod of understanding. "But why would it matter now? If she was alive, what could she do?"

"Loose ends, that's all."

What *could* she do, a girl who had no powers? She could ruin everything, according to Brom's vision. Brom had referred to a granddaughter named Ruby who was destined to save thousands of Crescents. Purcell would not wait another eleven years to accomplish his goal.

His phone rang when he stepped out to the parking lot. His son, who was monitoring the scry orb he'd planted at Moncrief's property. "Yes?"

"The girl who showed up at Moncrief's returned, and you won't believe this—she *is* a Crescent. A Dragon. So she's probably Justin's daughter after all. I suspect Moncrief used a masking spell, which is why we couldn't tell yesterday."

Purcell stroked his trimmed beard. "You are, as always, late with your revelations. I'm sure she's Ruby. You are continuing to monitor the scry orb?"

Darren's silence spoke the anger that the boy didn't have the guts to express. Finally he said, "Of course. She's driving to an area populated with Dragons. Wait. She's pausing in front of a martial arts studio, staring at it like she wants to incinerate the place. The sign says Dragon Arts."

"Keep watching." Purcell disconnected, then made a call that garnered the name of the proprietor. No surprise that it was Cyntag Valeron.

Chapter 3

Ruby sat in her truck across the street from Dragon Arts. She'd changed clothes and done a quick cleanup at home. Even taking that bit of time had stretched her tight. She'd wanted to drive right over and tear out Cyntag's throat.

Those kind of thoughts usually disturbed her, hinting at a primitive violence that reared its head when someone wronged or threatened her. It throbbed inside her, curling her fingers into fists.

Get it under control. This is one bad dude. All I'm doing right now is finding out how bad.

The logical part of her brain added, *A bad dude who possibly has control of bizarre and deadly weapons while you have a gun. Hullo?*

But what else can I do, let him just get away with killing Mon and never know why? No way in hell.

Without that envelope, she had nothing but Cyntag's

name and the schizophrenic thoughts bouncing around in her head.

According to their website, he was teaching a class starting in—she glanced at the clock—one minute. While he was otherwise occupied, she'd snoop and be long gone before his class was over. She had no idea how much Cyntag knew about her. Because she usually wore her hair in a braid, she left it loose and frizzy. Not a big disguise but, at a glance, different enough. She had no intention of him seeing her, but best to be prepared. Which included her gun, the metal cool against the small of her back. She'd found it useful when she started going off-site to look at people's stuff. In a city like Miami, no way was she walking into someone's garage alone and unarmed.

Warm air washed over her neck, and in the corner of her eye, something shimmered next to her. She jerked to the side but saw nothing. All her hairs sprung to attention. It had felt like a breath.

Her mystery rash, which only broke out on the right side of her stomach, burned something fierce. Doctors couldn't figure it out, and she'd tried every kind of medication to no avail. Stress always triggered it.

She stepped into the mid-September heat and humidity. The buildings in this area were old but in good repair. She spotted a Spanish/Portuguese restaurant across the way, and most of the signage was in Spanish with English subtitles. She generally felt like a foreigner in Miami, often one of the few Anglo people at any given location.

She caught sight of her reflection as she approached the glass door: cargo pants, black T sporting the Red Hot Chili Peppers' asterisk logo, and black work boots that protected her feet if something heavy fell on them. The bandage on her forehead, that had to go.

Dragon Arts was first class, with a comfortable waiting area, natural wood floors, and halogen lights in frosted glass cones. A woman about her age, framed by a tattered pirate's flag on the wall behind her, sharpened pencils at a tall reception desk.

Her dark pink lipstick and short, white hair popped against her raven skin. "May I help you, sugar?" The small gold plaque on the desk identified her as Glesenda.

"I wanted to check the place out, see what classes you offered."

She handed Ruby a slick brochure, studying her eyes. "And not listed are…" She did a double take, her eyebrows furrowing. "Well, you can see the listing for yourself."

Well, okay then. Ruby devoured the flier, looking for one thing: a picture of the owner. No deal, same as their website. An Internet search gleaned several articles mentioning Cyntag's name in conjunction with either his studio or some competition a student had participated in, but nothing on Twitter, Facebook, or any other social networks.

Ruby caught Glesenda's eye. "I understand Cyntag Valeron teaches Cane Fighting Level One?" Whatever that was.

Glesenda nodded toward one of the large glass windows. "He's teaching in the Sapphire Room right now."

Ruby wanted to run over and finally put a face to her uncle's murderer. Her breath left her with every step toward the window. A class of ten men of various ages stood in formation as they watched two men spar at the far side of the room. One sported a shaved head, was in his fifties, and weighed about two-fifty. The other—holy Jesus in Heaven. She sucked in air and tried to pull herself together. He was whip-muscular, wearing loose white pants with a tight black sash at his waist, his ripped torso slick with sweat. Gorgeous, dangerous-looking...and the spit-and-polish image of the Dragon Prince. Even down to his dark hair and the exotic slant to his eyes.

He had a tattoo far more fantastic than any she had seen, a dragon crawling up his back. Black and blue wings spanned his shoulders, the tail sliding down his spine to disappear beneath the waistband of his pants. When he shifted, she saw that the dragon's head peered over his shoulder. It looked three-dimensional.

"Yeah, he has that effect on most women." Glesenda wore an amused expression.

Not quite this effect, Ruby bet. Her chest was so tight she had to push out the words. "That's Cyntag, the one with the dragon tat?"

"Sure is. Total hotness," she said on a sigh.

Sure, if you were into men who sent murderous orbs. The hefty guy pretended to sneak up behind Cyntag, who twisted, hooked the other guy's neck with the curved handle of the cane, and sent him flat on the mat in a flash. Unscathed, Hefty jumped to his feet and tried another attack, which was quickly thwarted with a pseudo-whack of the cane to his head. She watched, mesmerized by the stealthy grace of Cyntag's movements, the way his muscles flexed, and how damned fast he was.

"You can listen in, too." Glesenda pressed a button and then ran in five-inch heels to answer the phone.

Cyntag's voice came through the speaker. "The next

counterattack we'll demonstrate is an assailant in a face-to-face assault."

Yes, the low, smooth voice she'd heard on the message.

Ready to take more abuse, Hefty tried to punch Cyntag and ended up with his arm locked behind him and the cane shoving him to the floor.

Cyntag extended his hand and effortlessly pulled Hefty to his feet. "Thanks, Stephen." He raised the cane over his head, which tightened his biceps, and addressed his class. "Looks like a sign of disability or old age, right? If I'm looking for a victim, you're an easy target. Or maybe not. If you've got one of these, you have the ability to fight off an attacker with force. At all times, you can carry a weapon right out in the open, no permit needed."

At that moment, Cyntag started to look her way. Ruby moved out of view, her fingers so tight on the frame around the window that she had to pry them off. Her hands were shaking as she passed the desk where Glesenda was on the phone with someone who was obviously calling in sick. Ruby glanced at a clock. Forty-five minutes before class ended.

She'd laid her eyes on him, all right. What was she going to do about it? The only way to take him out—if she could—was to shoot him from a distance, but that wouldn't glean any answers. She was as desperate for them as she was for revenge. Maybe something here would help.

She passed a sign that read OBSIDIAN ROOM. This room bore no window. Too bad, because disturbing sounds emanated from behind the closed door. She tried the handle, ready to act contrite at interrupting.

Except, no deal. The door was locked. The thumps and

growls coming from within were muffled, as though the walls were somewhat soundproofed. Those primal growls raised chill bumps on her arms. But more than that, they reached deep inside and twisted at her insides.

She rubbed her arms and wandered into the shop, pretending to look at fighting sticks, canes, and uniforms. Until she spotted a closed door with the words EMPLOYEES ONLY on it.

She pushed it open, prepared once again to feign innocence if she found someone on the other side. It appeared to be a break room and, fortunately, vacated. A door at the other end was ajar, and she could see a desk. Maybe Cyntag's office. Inside, a contemporary desk was juxtaposed with more antiques, like framed compasses and maps that looked as though they'd traveled on many a high sea. No pictures of friends, family, or a special vacation. A collection of dragon figurines lined the top shelf of the bookcase, each locked in combat with either another of its kind or a man wielding a sword. Dude had a thing for dragons.

Ruby caught herself scratching the damned rash again and closed the door. She sank into the leather chair at the desk and searched for any clue to who Cyntag was and what he was involved in. Anything incriminating would be documented with her camera phone. She'd rifled through four drawers, finding nothing out of the ordinary, when the door opened. Her heartbeat shot straight up into her throat as she turned.

Because of course it had to be Cyntag standing there.

Chapter 4

———

Cyntag stepped inside and closed the door, his eyes narrowing. Cold dread washed over Ruby. How in the hell had he known she was here? He was supposed to be teaching. And she was sure that he hadn't seen her. She launched to her feet and slid out from behind his desk. Every excuse or bluff fled her mind.

Thankfully he spoke before anything dumb could roll out of her mouth. "Ruby, right? Ruby Salazaar?"

The blood drained from her face. He knew her. *Keep cool and answer him.* She swallowed what felt like a ball of sand.

No. Yes. What's it to you? What came out was, "Yeah?" *Brilliant, Ruby.*

He stepped forward, reaching for her. Her street-smart instincts kicked in. Mon had taught her to look for a defensive weapon in her surroundings. At the yard, she could always lay her hand on a shard of metal or a screwdriver.

Her fingers touched a silver letter opener as he brushed past her and plucked a cell phone from the desk just as it began playing Queen's "We Are the Champions." He ignored the call, and the song stopped.

Since she already had her hand on the letter opener, she went with it, pulling it out of the leather cup and rubbing the curves of the silver dragon handle. "It's beautiful. Very detailed, even down to the talons." She wasn't used to going for the gun; if she had, she'd have blown it for sure by overreacting.

What's wrong with you? Cool and calm, calm and cool.

Not working. Her rash felt as though it were on fire.

Cyntag eyed the letter opener, obviously nobody's fool. "And very sharp. I'll take that." He tugged it from her reluctant grasp but didn't return it to the cup. "Moncrief finally sent you to me then?" He glanced around. "He didn't come with you?"

"He's dead." *Which you know, considering you killed him.* The words burned up her throat and singed her tongue. The rage, she could hardly hold it back.

Cool and calm, calm and cool, damn it.

His eyebrows, shaped like sleek raven's wings, settled into a furrow. "Moncrief is dead? How?"

"You sent an orb, some kind of lightning thing, to kill him. Don't play dumb with me." The words boiled out. So much for cool and calm. "He said your name. I asked him who had done it, and on his dying breath, *he said your name.*" Now she'd accused him. He would have to act, defend…or kill her. She pulled the gun from her back and leveled it at him, because the latter option was most likely.

An odd expression flickered across his face. "Ruby, what are you doing?"

Losing her mind, that's what. Her heart thudded roughly in the area of her diaphragm, which was weird because that's not where it resided. She grabbed his phone and thumb-dialed her number with the same hand that held it. Her brief outgoing message played, then the beep. She shoved it toward him with her other hand. "Say your name and admit it. Admit you had him killed."

He was eerily cool, the way she should have been. "I didn't kill Moncrief."

"He said you did."

"I don't think he said that, Ruby." God, the way he said her name, slow and smooth, like thick honey. "You obviously saw an orb kill him. You were upset, scared. Like you are now."

She pushed the gun closer. "I'm not *scared*. I'm pissed. I know how to use this. I hit the center of the target nine times out of ten."

"Impressive. Are you shaking like this while you're aiming?" In a flash, he turned her around, shoved her arm aside, and tightened his grip on her wrist. His arms encircled her, his bare skin brushing against her arms.

A sharp click, then another, and the magazine dropped to the floor. "Is there a round in the chamber, Ruby?" his voice rasped close to her ear. "I don't want to hurt your wrist, but I will if you don't answer me."

"No round."

He flicked the safety anyway. "Then I suggest you release the weapon, and we'll continue this conversation in a more civilized fashion."

The gun fell from her hand, thudding on the floor. He took the phone from her other hand and disconnected, then set it on the desk. Finally, he released her. She moved as far from him as she could, rubbing her wrist.

He casually leaned back against his desk. "What exactly did Moncrief tell you about me?" Cyntag had a deliberate way of speaking, properly enunciating each word.

"I only know your name because Mon said it as he was dying."

That seemed to surprise him. "You know nothing about me?"

You're the Dragon Prince. Yeah, that would sound logical. Not that anything about this was logical. "I heard the message you left him. The police have it, by the way." She glanced at her wrist, even though she wore no watch. "They'll be here any time to question you."

He pinched the bridge of his nose, hopefully buying her bluff. "What did you tell them about the orb?"

"Everything."

Worry tensed the corners of his mouth. "The regular police?"

"Of course, what other—oh, I'm sure they contacted the FBI, the ATF...if an agency has initials, they're involved. They—"

"Describe the orb." *Still pretending he knew nothing about it, huh?* "It set the house on fire?"

"Yes, and how might you know that?"

His nostrils flared. "I smell the smoke on you. Tell me what happened."

She intended to give him a cursory description and had to hand it to him, like an investigator, he extracted every detail from her. He even looked angry when she talked about how it blocked her escape.

"You must have been terrified." *Was he gloating?*

"I was too busy trying to save my ass to be terrified."

"Nobody saw it but you, right?"

"No, it hid when they arrived and"—she glanced toward the door—"someone should be here by now. The investigator warned me not to come on my own, but I wanted to talk to you first. Tell me why you killed him. Off the record."

He didn't look as though he were buying her bluff one iota. He walked to the window, placing his hands on the glass and letting out a long, frustrated breath. Instantly, fog steamed around the perimeter of his palms and long fingers. "You did not tell the police about the orb because they would think you were crazy. You're smarter than that."

She inched toward the door.

"*You* may think you're crazy." He shook his head. "Old bastard wouldn't listen to me. Thought he was invincible. When I saw that he called, I hoped he'd come to his senses, but he never called back."

She reached for the door handle, and suddenly Cyntag stood there, his hand tight over hers.

"You're not going anywhere."

"How…how did you do that? I didn't even see you move." She tried to kick him in the groin. Another dumb idea, considering what he did for a living.

He didn't hurt her, not much anyway. He did, however, pin her against the door, his thigh pressing the offending leg tight. His hands gripped her wrists and held them at her hips. "That is not a wise thing to do."

Panic, and something she couldn't name, fluttered through her at the feel of so much man and heat so close to her. She coaxed her bravado from where it had scurried and lifted her chin. "Afraid I'll hurt you?"

"Once my instincts are triggered, it's hard to stop. I'm sure *I'll* hurt *you*. As of right now, I do not wish to do that. That may change as days go by."

"*Days*?" Fear coiled around her chest. "What are you going to do, keep me...hostage?"

He let her question hang for an agonizing moment, as though he were considering it. God, had she given him ideas? He said, "Not entirely." That did not sound good, but before she could get too freaked out about it, he continued. "Your uncle and I did not share a warm and loving opinion of each other, but I didn't kill him. Do you know why I would not harm one hair on his head?"

She wanted to believe that the guy whose hard, muscular body pinned hers against the wall and who could no doubt break her neck with a flick of his fingers hadn't killed her uncle. "I'll play your silly game. Why didn't you kill him?"

He gave her a chastising look. "Because his death puts you in danger, and I am your sworn protector. Moncrief had your best interest at heart, but I told him it was a bad idea to try thwarting nature. And fate. I have gone on with my life and hoped he made the right decision. But if he's dead, I am now saddled with a neophyte who has no idea the danger that stalks her, the world into which she was born, or her own powers. So believe me when I say, I would not wish death on him."

He stepped back enough so she could escape from the

heat of his body. Except her knees buckled, and she had to lean against the door for support.

She stared at him. "Do you know how friggin' crazy that just sounded?"

He shook his head and looked up to the ceiling. "So much to learn. So little time to do it. Such a buffoon."

"You're calling me a *buffoon*?" And who used that word, anyway?

"That remains to be seen. I meant your uncle. He left us in quite the mess."

This conversation wasn't going in any direction she could follow. "It's been lovely, but I need to scream now. I mean, go now." She reached for the door handle, and he closed his hand over her wrist in a firm grip.

Which again put him in close proximity. "The orb that killed Moncrief, you saw its power?" His voice was soft and deadly.

"You're threatening me?"

"Enlightening you. You put a gun to my chest. If I could make an orb, wouldn't I have used it against you then?"

Well...yeah.

He continued. "And, in fact, I've had you under my physical control twice. I could crack your neck like this." He snapped his fingers.

Hadn't she thought the same thing?

"And I did not. We need to find out who did kill Moncrief though, because he or she may well be after you, too."

Ruby tried to pull away but he maintained his hold over her hand. His black-and-blue dragon stared at her, almost as mesmerizing as the man himself. She dragged her gaze to his. "Why would someone want to hurt me? Obviously Mon was involved in something dangerous, but that has nothing to do with me."

"We don't know why Moncrief was killed. At the least, you're a witness. Reason enough to make sure you don't blab your mouth about killer orbs."

She could swear the dragon blinked. That Cyntag had the tattoo, the dragon decorations, and that he looked like Mon's Dragon Prince was a bizarre coincidence. But no less bizarre than the rest of this encounter.

Cyntag released her and leaned against the door so that it would be impossible to open it wide enough to slip out. *Okay, let's not freak about being trapped in here with the crazy dude.*

He assessed her with his dark gaze and then skimmed his hands down her shoulders and arms like he would with, say, one of his students. The action held no sensuality, no sense of impropriety, and yet, his hands left a heated imprint on her skin.

"At least you're in good shape. That will help." He nodded to the gun on the floor. "You came to take me down for killing your uncle. Because he uttered my name on his dying breath." Amusement glittered in his eyes. "You, a mere girl, would take me down."

"I'm not a *girl*, and don't underestimate me."

"I admire your bravado. You'll need that. Still, you must never walk into the enemy's den without knowing anything about him."

"To be clear, I came here to snoop, because that was the only way I could find out more about you. The gun was for protection, just in case. You were supposed to be busy teaching your class." How had he known she was there?

"*To be clear*, if I was your enemy, you would be dead now. Moncrief wasn't naming his murderer. He was trying to send you to me because, as his life ebbed, he knew I was your only chance of surviving." In a voice under his breath, he added, "I'm sure he loved that." He picked up the letter opener from his desk and ran his finger down the edge. "You want his murderer to face justice, do you not?"

"With every cell in my body."

"Good." He held the opener out to her, handle first. "Take it."

She did, feeling the warmed metal against her palm and the curves of the dragon.

He raised his arms out to his sides. "If you're sure I killed him, go ahead then. Take your revenge."

She squeezed the handle and stared at a chest that looked so hard she wasn't sure the tip would penetrate. He was taunting her. Daring her. She pressed the tip to the molded pec over his heart, just below the dragon's mouth, and met his gaze.

"Could you do it, Ruby? As tough as you like to appear, could you sink a sharp object into someone's flesh? It's harder than you think. Physically and psychologically, even when you feel justified. Could you handle the feel of warm blood gushing between your fingers and down your arm?"

Every bit of the rage she felt since seeing the bolt piercing her uncle's chest rushed in around her. "Yes."

"Good." He paused, staring into her eyes in a way that twisted her stomach. But nothing like his next words did. "You've felt it, haven't you, a rage so hot and fierce that you believe you *could* take someone's life? Even though that sane and civilized part of you abhors that ferocity, a darker part craves it." Her denial withered on her tongue. He didn't press her because he seemed to know she had. "Have you ever killed someone?"

She wanted to say *one or two* but somehow she knew he'd spot her lie. "I threatened someone. And I would have gone through with it, too, if he hadn't paid for the merchandise." She could hardly push the words out of her dry throat.

Nevin hadn't bothered to check the slip of paper the hulk of a man waved in his face, and off the restored motorcycle went—without getting paid for. When she'd hunted the man down, he dismissed her as a mere girl. She threatened the creep with bodily harm—oddly, not with shooting him but tearing out his throat. He must have sensed her suppressed violence, because he paid on the spot.

"Killing is not easy to do," Cyntag said. "And should never be done out of rage."

"Are you speaking from experience?" It sure sounded like it.

His mouth twitched ever so slightly. "I don't think we should go there just now."

Which meant they'd go there later. And that she was right.

Cyntag smelled of earth and fire and—where in the hell were these thoughts coming from? His energy and heat pulled at her. Were his eyes glowing? She swore something flickered in them, just for a second.

He nodded to the point of the letter opener. "Why are you hesitating?"

She took a step back, bringing the opener to her side.

"Because I can't be sure you did it." He was right. If he was Mon's murderer, she'd be dead.

"Very good. You put logic over your anger. As opposed to when you pulled the gun on me or tried to crush my balls. Never let your emotions drive you."

"I'm not a rash and emotional person. Then again, I don't usually watch someone I love die or get chased by a supernatural ball of fire."

He leaned against the door again, though she couldn't be certain it was to block her escape. He looked so relaxed. *Yeah, as relaxed as a lion.* "What do you know about the Hidden?"

"It's a fairy-tale world my uncle made up for me. How do *you* know about it?" She couldn't imagine Mon sharing that with this guy. Or anyone, really.

"Tell me about this world."

"Seriously?"

"Yes, seriously."

Fine, she'd humor him. "Centuries ago, there was this Atlantis-like island in the Bermuda Triangle called Lucifera that was governed by gods of Dragons and magick. Because of the weird energy that comes from crystals found deep within the Earth's surface, along with a planetary alignment and a solar storm, some of the gods were able to take physical human form. They succumbed to human emotions and, as Mon put it, 'fell in love' with the people. What he meant was that the gods got with the humans, because they created children. They were called Crescents because they inherited a sliver of their sire's godly nature."

He dipped his head in confirmation. "Legend has it that three gods realized procreating with humans wasn't a good idea. An angel, a Dragon, and a Deuce formed the Tryah and incited a war in hopes that the Crescents would kill each other off. It escalated into a magick war."

"Alrighty then, glad you cleared that up for me."

"Happy to do so. Go on, let's see if you've got the rest of it right."

Feeling like a schoolgirl being tested on history, she found herself striving to recall the details. Which was ridiculous, since it was a friggin' fairy tale. "The war ended up destroying the island and forced the humans to the mainland. The naughty gods were trapped in a state of limbo between their plane of existence and the Bermuda Triangle."

"That's right. What else was part of Moncrief's Hidden?" he asked.

"Monsters, demons, elves, that sort of thing, but only Crescents could see them. That's why they were considered Hidden."

"Was there no Cyntag in the stories then?"

She wanted to laugh, of all the conceit. "No." Her gaze slid to the dragon figurines. "There was a man who looked like you, but he was only known as the Dragon Prince. He kidnapped a young woman and seduced her to darkness. They fought a great evil together, but he was basically an arrogant butthead, and she ended up killing him."

His upper lip twitched, not quite a sneer but close. "Seduced her to darkness, hmm? And did this woman have a name?"

"Garnet." Mon's sketches of her had reminded Ruby of Alice from *Alice in Wonderland.*

Cyntag slowly nodded. "I suppose he was trying to

prepare you in his feeble way, giving you the truth without telling you that it was, in fact, true. Except the Dragon Prince would never kidnap anyone. How do I know? He based the prince on me, I'm sure, though I am no prince."

"*That* I can believe."

He very nearly smiled that time. "You never made the connection between Garnet and Ruby both being red gems?"

"Of course. I figured since he wrote the stories for me, he gave the girl a name similar to mine. *Stories* being the key word there, as in make-believe, fictional. Come on. Gods? Dragons?"

"You *are* the girl in the story. When you reached puberty, you should have been initiated into your full power. Moncrief could not do that because he's not the same type of Crescent as you. You were supposed to move in with people like you to learn their ways. I swore to your grandfather that I would train you, prepare you, and be your protector. But Moncrief wouldn't cooperate, stubborn old goat."

He looked up at the ceiling and rubbed the back of his neck where his black hair curled in damp spikes. "You would have been so much easier to deal with then. Malleable. Impressionable. I can see you will be every bit the pain in my ass that your uncle was."

"You mean I would have been brainwashed." *People like you*, he'd said, as though they were in some cult. "You just wanted some young girl under your spell. Ew, you wanted *me* under your spell."

He gave her a look that reeked of disdain. "I would only want a grown woman under my spell. I consider you far too young for me. And, beyond that, not my type."

"I'm twenty-four years old. And you're what, thirty?"

His mouth turned up in a slow smile. "I'm two-hundred-and-sixty-something, but thank you for the compliment."

"Hah, funny. Look, I really must be going. I've got employees expecting me back at work. Strong, big, muscular employees." Well, Nevin counted as big, anyway. "Let's just forget this little misunderstanding." She grabbed the gun and magazine and tucked them separately into her waistband. *See, no threat at all.*

"Ruby, you don't seem to get that everything changes now. First, I need you to understand what you're dealing with. Your uncle kept you in the dark, one of those bad decisions based on emotions."

"Mon was the least emotional person I ever knew." He'd taught her to release her emotions by pounding on something rather than crying.

"As a master of illusion, he revealed only what he wanted you to see. He was a magician in the truest sense of the word. He used his magick for fame and fortune, which is generally frowned upon, but it helped that he performed in Europe. Did he ever reveal to you how he performed his illusions?"

"No. Well, he did say it was real magic. When I was a child, I believed him. As I got older, I knew there had to be tricks. I saw those shows where the guy betrays his fellow magicians and reveals how the popular tricks are done. I figured it was something like that. Wait a minute. You said danger was stalking me. Why would someone harm me?"

"Where do I start?"

"There's a *list*?"

"First it was from the people who had your parents killed."

"Killed? Mon said it was an accident, that the authorities thought their boat hit something out in the ocean and sank."

Cyntag shook his head. "Someone ordered their deaths."

"That's as crazy as everything else you've said. *More* crazy."

"We decided to let everyone think you died, too. Did you ever wonder why Moncrief adopted you so quickly, changed your last name to his, and took you out of the country? It was too risky for Brom to raise you since he was a blood relation and easily connected to you. Moncrief had lost his wife and daughter years earlier, and Brom knew he would do good by you. His most important illusion was hiding that you hold magick."

He slowly waved his hand in front of her face, his eyes staring straight into hers between his long fingers. "Crescents can identify one another by our eyes. Some are icy glitter, some swirling mist, and others burning embers."

Her heart hitched. Hadn't she thought she'd seen a glow in his eyes? She looked again but couldn't see it now.

He lowered his hand. "Moncrief cast an illusion spell to hide the magick in your eyes. You looked like a Mundane, a regular human. Now that he's gone, the spell is wearing off. Soon it will be obvious to every Crescent who sees you."

She walked over to a gilt-framed mirror on the side wall and stared at herself. No glow. He was full of it. "I don't see anything like what you described."

"Because you cannot *see*." He came up behind her.

"You have not been Awakened. Crescents are initiated in a ceremony at thirteen, when their powers begin to appear. It's similar to those of many native tribes to celebrate a coming of age. But much more comes with being an Awakened Crescent."

Thirteen. She remembered a gnawing hunger deep in her belly and vivid dreams filled with colors and longing and...dragons. That's when the damned rash had popped up, too. Different than what she heard other girls her age going through. Not that she was around many with whom she could compare notes.

She hadn't wanted to kiss boys—or girls—or wear makeup or go shopping. She wanted something she couldn't define. Drinking, partying, working her ass off, nothing sated it.

Cyntag brushed her bangs from her forehead, his thumb grazing the skin near her burn. "The orb did this?" She nodded, and anger shimmered over his face. "Unacceptable."

"I thought so."

He'd said it as though the attack on her was a personal affront to him. *Like he owns you.*

"Right now you're like a baby chick fallen prematurely from the nest, without feathers developed enough to fly from danger or any way to fight enemies. Unable to even see them. You might get a glimpse now and then, but that won't be enough."

"You're saying I have powers?" Could her disbelief be more clear? "Can I make one of those orb-lightning-bolt things?"

Another twitch of a smile. "Sorry, no. However, you are much more magnificent than mere magick."

"I'm magnificent. Yeah." She couldn't help but glance down at herself. "Fine, how do I get... what'd you call it? Awakened?" *Let's play along.*

"Considering the circumstances, only I can awaken your powers."

Did his arrogance know no bounds? *Dumb question, Ruby.* "What do I have to give you for that?"

"You assume there's a price?"

"There's always a price." She could see that he had one, too.

He stepped closer, again breaching boundaries. She wouldn't move away. If only she didn't have to look up at him. Even though she was five foot eight, he was way taller. His heat reached out, beckoning her. She stiffened her stance. The dragon tattoo eyed her, but no, she did *not* see it move.

He waited until she drew her gaze back to his face. "The price is that once you see, you can never go back to being blind. Once you know, you can never forget. Once you experience your true nature, you can never ignore it."

"Ignore what?"

He released a breath. "We'd better start with the small stuff."

The Book of the Hidden

The Dragon Prince stood before Garnet as a man now, though she knew the dark beast lurked inside him. His hair was so black that it was nearly blue where shafts of sunlight fell upon it. Eyes just as black, eternal wells where shadows dwelled beyond her ken. In the days since she'd come here, she had watched intruders try to storm his stone castle high on a mountaintop, watched him and his army of Dragons knock them back. Had they been her people come to rescue her? She did not know.

He had summoned her to a room of colorful marble and glittering chandeliers for their first real meeting. The kind of sitting area where one entertained important guests.

He sat like a king in a tall-backed chair of rich tapestry and carved wood. "Welcome to my castle, Princess. I hope you find it to your liking, as you will dwell forever more with me."

"You cannot keep me here as a prisoner." But he could. She saw in his eyes that he could do whatever he wished. "Why? Why did you save me, only to enslave me?"

"Your destiny lies with me. When you come of age, you will become my wife."

He turned into a Dragon and approached her. She stood tall and strong even as her knees quivered. He opened his mouth and released a dark mist that enveloped her. She tried not to breathe, sensing the magick in it. The spell.

Finally her lungs burst, and she sucked in the mist. She felt it slide down her throat and change her very cells. Like the New Year's fireworks, flashes of images blinded her. Dragons, small and large, bright and dark, filled her mind.

"What have you done to me?" she screamed, trying to push away the images.

"You are mine, and so you must become Dragon like

me. You'll have time to embrace your magick, to see the wonder of what you now are."

She felt it inside her, the coiling energy of something foreign and dangerous. "You are evil! I will never be your wife, never!"

She ran, but there was no escape. This castle, like herself, was a jewel set in the middle of treacherous thorns. So she went back to the only sanctuary she knew: her chambers. She hurried to the window, far above the ground, and let the sun warm her cheeks while the breeze chilled the tracks of her tears.

A flutter made her eyes open. "Opal!"

The dove landed on the sill, stepping onto Garnet's finger as easily as before. It rubbed its cheek against her palm, the heartwarming gesture it had done from the first time it landed on her hand. "I must not be too much a monster if you still come to me." She nuzzled the bird. "Or have you come to remind me of who I really am?"

Chapter 5

⌒

Cyntag opened the door, leaned out, and yelled, "Allander!"

He held it open for several seconds, watching her for some reason—probably to make sure she didn't dash out—and then closed it.

"What does that mean?" Probably some Spanish word meaning *Bring the knives; we have dinner.*

"This would be much easier if you trusted me," he said, moving up beside her.

She leaned away, narrowing her eyes. "*What* would be easier?"

He released a resigned breath. "Exactly." Then he pulled her against his hard body, one arm across her chest, the other on her forehead.

She jerked, but his hold was as tight as a locked seat belt. A seat belt with muscles. "Let me go! You want me to *trust* you, then you grab..." The rest of her words disintegrated as she stared at...she had no idea what it was, only that it hadn't been there a moment before: a creature only two and a half feet tall, skin burnished red with a pointy face and black hair as wild as a flame. It perched on the corner of the desk.

Cyntag continued to grip her, though it wasn't necessary. She'd stopped struggling.

"What...is it?"

"That's Allander. He's a salamander."

"Doesn't look like any newt I've ever seen."

"Not an amphibian-type salamander. He's a fire spirit. An Elemental. Didn't Moncrief include them in his stories?"

"He had fire, water, earth, and spirit faeries and elves." Anything else she remembered fled her mind as she stared at Allander.

The creature lifted his lip in a snarl, revealing cat-like teeth.

"They don't like being stared at," Cyntag murmured, guiding her to the mirror. Her gaze zeroed in on him first, his sharp features and then his dark eyes...except they weren't dark. An ember like the flame atop a candle flickered in their depths, just what she thought she'd glimpsed.

"Your eyes..." Hypnotizing, tugging at some deep part of herself...

"Look at yourself, Ruby."

The sound of her name, blanketed in the richness of his voice, shuddered through her. She pulled her gaze to her reflection and gasped. "My..." A flame dancing in an unseen breeze, in *her* eyes.

Movement at Cyntag's shoulder caught her attention. The dragon—the friggin' dragon tattoo—ran its tongue across its upper lip.

Overwhelmed, she pushed away and turned to face him. No embers in his eyes, no moving tattoo, and no whatever-the-hell that thing was sitting on his desk. She searched her reflection. Just her hazel eyes, wide and unsettled. She didn't even think about it, just reached out and ran her fingers over his tattoo. His skin was warm but otherwise felt normal.

You're touching him.

Yes. Soft, smooth skin. Hard muscles.

She blinked and jerked her hand back. "What did you do to me?" She ran to the desk and patted the place where the creature sat. Nothing.

"I lifted the Veil so that, through me, you could see the Hidden. It's all here; you just can't see, as I explained." He ran his hand down her arm, twining his fingers with hers, and stretched her hand toward the empty space. Except it wasn't empty, because she felt the skinny arm of the creature. Parchment skin, short, coarse hairs. "Now you can feel it."

He released her, and she pulled her hand back. She stared at her tingling fingers as she rubbed them together, then at the desk. "It's still there, right this second?"

"Allander, light the candle...please. They don't speak, but they insist on respect. It's not always reciprocated, but Allander has been with me for many years. We have an understanding." He nodded for her to look at the candle, because her attention was riveted on him. The flame came to life.

He leaned back against the edge of the desk. "Have you ever seen something in the corner of your eye, only to look and find nothing there? Or heard a sound somewhere in your home but couldn't find the source? How about the ubiquitous missing sock or keys that aren't where you left them?"

He tilted his head toward the invisible being. "Elementals, usually. They're in the non-physical plane all over the world, but we can see and touch them because of our own otherworldly essence. Some are mischievous, others a nuisance, and a few dangerous. A lot of what's considered poltergeist activity is either their doing, demons, or Deuces."

Something in the corner of her eye? "Sometimes I see shadows move among the parts in my resto yard, but I can never find what causes them." No, no, no, this couldn't be real. She focused on his last word, remembering it from Mon's stories. "Deuces who make orbs?"

"Most can make orbs of some kind, some more deadly than others. I need to find out if there's a select group of Deuces who can make the kind of orb you saw. That will help us narrow down who could have sent it, at least a little."

"*Us?*"

"You and I have a lot of work to do before someone comes after you again."

"Like hell I'm working, or doing anything else, with you. I need fresh air." She grabbed at the candle, snuffing out the flame and sniffing the black wax. "You've got some kind of hallucinogenic substance in here. Or somewhere."

"Those weren't hallucinations, Ruby."

"Stop saying my name like...that." She reached for the door, amazed when she turned the knob and stepped into the hallway without his hand clamping onto her. She didn't dare look back. Everything he'd told her, everything she'd seen, bounced around in her head like a hundred rubber balls.

Glesenda watched her stalk past with a puzzled expression. Outside, sunlight beckoned, and people walked past the studio, nice, normal people.

Don't turn around. Just keep going.

Cyn watched the girl walk so fast down the sidewalk that her ass swished provocatively back and forth. He had sensed Ruby, or at least sensed the presence of an unknown Crescent, in his studio. That she'd ducked out of sight when he looked up fired his instincts. He'd followed her scent to his office. Her accusation about Moncrief's murder shocked the hell out of him. He pulled on the shirt he'd grabbed in his office and slid into his shoes.

Glesenda followed his gaze. "Who *is* she? There was something odd about her. I thought I saw a flicker in her eyes, and then it wasn't there. I was about to mention the Dragon training room but stopped myself." The flame in her eyes danced. "If she's a troublemaker, I can take care of her."

He shot her a derisive look. "Pull back your fangs, woman."

She *hmphed* and crossed her arms over her chest. "Fuddy-duddy. Don't worry, I won't eat your little friend. Wouldn't want to risk your wrath." She studied him for a moment. "Your eyes are flickering something fierce. Been a long time since I've seen them do that. And over a girl who dresses like…I'm not even sure how to categorize her style. Grunge? Thrift store?"

He watched Ruby cross the street, or try to, between cars. "I'm not attracted to her." Though she had an intriguing mouth, with her upper lip a bit wider than her lower lip, wide jaw line, and strong chin. The sass that came out of her mouth was more interesting than annoying, for the most part. She would learn to respect him. "You're going to see a lot of her. She's a new Crescent."

"New, at her age?"

"Long story. I expect you to help her however you can. She's got a hell of an adjustment period coming."

Glesenda's eyes widened. "You mean she doesn't know—"

"She has no idea."

Ruby glanced back, blinking when she saw him at the door watching her. She gave him a look that probably equaled the finger and got into her dark blue truck. He pushed the door open before Glesenda could grill him further. The flow of traffic forced Ruby to wait before pulling out of her spot.

She also had no idea that a demon sat in the passenger seat of her truck. Whoever had sent the orb was wasting no time in trying to take her out. His Dragon clawed at him, its protective instinct pushing to Catalyze.

You know better. Not in public.

He ran to his '57 T-bird as Ruby peeled away from the curb. The demon turned to him, its red eyes flaring, its lip curling with victory. A humanoid demon, it took the shape of a person, but with brown skin and ears that pointed up like horns.

Hell. The damned thing was gloating. Cyn despised the humanoids only second to harbingers. He pulled into traffic as the truck moved out of sight. He tried to pull around the cars between him and Ruby, but traffic gave him no break.

He took the chance on a small gap, passing one car at the cost of a blaring horn. The demon watched him, its hand on the back of the bench seat like it was Ruby's date. It couldn't materialize, bound by the same rule as Crescents: never reveal your presence to Mundanes. It could, however, kill her right there, depending on how much evidence and chaos it was willing to cause. Demons weren't known to be subtle. Those rare cases of spontaneous combustion and one-car accidents? Usually demons.

"Damn it." His Dragon strained now.

Cyn thought about pounding his horn to get her attention, but she'd likely drive away faster. He passed another car, narrowly missing a collision with an oncoming garbage truck. Now he was one car behind hers.

The demon leaned close to Ruby's neck, flicking its long pointed tongue toward her skin. She brushed at her neck, glancing over but obviously seeing nothing of the menace sitting right next to her. All the while it looked at him.

He thought she might go to her restoration yard. He knew where that was. Despite reluctantly agreeing to Moncrief's plan, he'd checked on the girl from time to time to see if the spell had broken yet.

The demon waved its long fingers as Ruby cleared a traffic light. The light skipped from green to red, making the driver in front of him slam on his brakes. Cyn's bumper tapped the rear of the car, but he was already looking for a way around. Ruby's truck turned right one block ahead. Short of running down people on the sidewalk, Cyn could do nothing but wait. He gripped the steering wheel so hard it began to crack.

He had to get to Ruby. The moment the demon had her alone, it would all be over.

Chapter 6

Sed, the demon, followed Ruby into a building that was identified as a library. She asked the person behind the desk where she could look up old newspaper articles, then followed his directions toward the back.

The place was not very busy. He searched for Crescents, who would be able to see him. A Deuce was checking out. Sed ducked behind the aisle as the man left. A handful of Mundanes. Easy to dispense with.

That was what had gotten him into trouble in the first place, relegated to a prison on the Dark Side. He had been sprung to carry out a task, the kind he most enjoyed.

The object of his task took a seat in the back of the building, the perfect location. If he could get rid of the rest of the inhabitants, he would be done and allowed to play as his reward.

Mundanes couldn't see him, but they could feel him. Sed moved up close to one male who was reading at a table. *Mmm, would love to eat him, torment him.* All he was allowed to do was send him a feeling of dread.

The man shivered and looked around. He closed his book and left. Several others were just as easily dispensed with. Some took the time to check out, while the more sensitive ones left their stacks of books behind.

Now, the workers. Sed made two of them violently ill by flooding them with negative energy. They staggered out, sure there must have been something toxic in the coffee they had shared. One became unaccountably angry and stormed out. Which left the man who appeared to be in charge, and who was accountably angry that his entire staff was gone. He did not respond to the demon's emotional blasts because he already held anger and hopelessness.

He reached for the phone and looked at a list of names and numbers. Before he could call replacements, the demon reached into the man's chest and squeezed his heart. He gasped, shock on his face.

The demon inhaled his pain. *Die, Mundane. Die by my hand, and no one will know any better.*

The man dropped to his knees and collapsed, claimed by the heart attack. Sed ran to the door and locked it just as someone approached with a stack of books. The woman tried the door, peered in, and then dropped the books into the metal bin. The demon thought about sliding his hand out of the rotating bin and grabbing her. How amusing it would be to see her expression of horror.

Alas, he had to follow the rules if he hoped to gain freedom. He flicked off the light switches at the front and made his way to his target. The one he *could* torment.

Ruby's brain was literally buzzing. *Hah, I knew he put some funky drug in the air.*

Except that didn't explain the killer orb. That was no hallucination, nor was Mon's death. And she didn't feel high or dizzy or otherwise altered. Her rash was flaring big-time though.

She'd barely taken time to enjoy the smell of the books, a scent she found oddly comforting, on her way to the bulky machines at the back of the building. Why had she never thought to look at the old newspaper stories dating back to the time of the boating accident?

She stopped at the headline: FAMILY PERISHES AT SEA.

This was it. To the side was a picture of all three of them, posing at what looked like a picnic. She plunged in. Her father was obviously doing well in whatever job he'd been working on—something to do with physics— as the boat was described as a yacht. The Yard certainly wouldn't fund such a thing.

The press played it up as another mysterious Devil's Triangle disappearance. Investigators speculated that it was either an accidental explosion, rogue wave, or pirates.

The *family's* disappearance. It hit her then, that she was included in the missing. There was no mention of her rescue. At the time, she was Ruby Winston. Mon adopted her and, as Cyntag had pointed out, immediately changed her name for some legal reason she had never questioned.

Because he was hiding you?

She'd been a distraught nine-year-old and had just gone along: name change, Mon's move into a new neighborhood, and his continuing touring, coming back to Miami every two weeks but leaving again soon after. The way he'd set up the Yard so it wasn't in her name until she turned eighteen. It also explained why she couldn't get her belongings or visit her friends. All those things she'd accepted and forgotten about. Until now.

It also explained why her grandfather kept his distance, something that had always hurt. But that would mean Cyntag was telling the truth. She flipped through the follow-up articles and was even more stunned: her father painted a villain, having sabotaged the physics work he had been doing at SUNLAB. One theory was that he'd stolen his research to sell to the highest bidder. Another was that he'd gone on a rampage before taking his family to sea to their deaths.

The man she remembered was kind and soft-spoken. Never once had she seen him lose his temper, and, God no, he wouldn't have killed his family.

So the alternative was…someone had killed her parents. All these horrible allegations were a setup to cover the murders.

She sat back in the chair, feeling so cold she was shivering. How *had* she survived? She remembered being on the boat, the jarring thud that knocked her out. The next thing she knew, she was at Brom's, about to get the worst news of her life.

As she absently rubbed her neck, she realized she was still feeling the weird warmth. She searched for nearby vents. Except it was summer and the heat wouldn't be on. Something odd prickled through her. This library branch was a small building, but it was eerily quiet. Though sunlight came through the windows near her, the interior looked dim. The electricity hadn't gone out, or the micro-fiche machine would have died.

Earlier she'd heard a couple of thumps and someone coughing violently, but now she heard nothing but a low-level hissing. She lurched to her feet. Danger bristled up the back of her neck. Her rash felt as though it was liter-ally on fire.

A shadow moved in the corner of her eye. She twisted to the right. Nothing. Or maybe it *was* something, like that creature in Cyntag's office.

She reached for the gun she still had tucked into her waistband, keeping it down as she walked to the middle of the library. The fluorescent panels were dark, yet lights twinkled from a computer behind the checkout desk.

Not one person in sight. She raised the gun, ready to shoot. Something knocked it out of her hand, sending it skidding across the carpet. Something she couldn't see.

Hell.

Hot breath pulsed against her neck. She spun around, banging into the end of a book aisle. The gun lay only a few feet away, but what good was the damned thing go-ing to be if she couldn't *see* what threatened her?

You cannot see . . .

The shadow moved again. She strained her eyes, trying to discern an outline, anything. It, whatever it was, shoved her. She felt pressure against her upper chest a second be-fore she tumbled backward to the floor.

It wasn't small like Allander.

A book toppled from an upper shelf, landing several feet in front of her. She scrambled to her feet, eyeing the door. *Not again.* As she dashed toward it, something hot pushed her from behind. She kept her balance, darting down the aisle to the checkout desk and coming to a bone-jarring halt. A man lay sprawled on the floor, his hand clutching his chest. His face was frozen in an expression of pain and shock. She knew, even without checking, that he was dead.

The sound of metal rattling against metal pulled her attention to the front door again. Cyntag! Trying to open the door that was obviously locked. Could she really be happy to see him?

Arms—at least that's what they felt like—wrapped around her. She dove forward, out of the thing's grasp. It pushed, sending her rolling across the hard, carpeted floor. Even with the room still spinning, she could see that Cyntag wasn't at the door any longer.

Maybe she'd imagined him. But she sure as hell wasn't imagining this thing. No, she wasn't that crazy. She held her hands aloft, ready for anything. Hunter/Prey. Was this what Mon had prepared her for?

A crashing sound drew her attention to the back door flinging open. Cyntag shoved the door closed, his hard gaze on something to the right of her. Of course, *he* could see it. And from the expression on his face, it wasn't good.

She ran toward him, definitely the lesser of two evils. He moved in that preternatural way, suddenly beside her with his arm protectively across her as he faced...well, nothing.

"Who sent you?" he asked it. "Who released you?"

"What is it?" she whispered, though she didn't know why. The thing could no doubt hear her.

"Humanoid demon."

"What does it look like? How big is it?"

Cyntag didn't take his eyes from it, or where she guessed it was. "You don't want to know."

"Yes, I do. Lift the Veil like you did at your office. I need to see what I'm fighting."

His hand slapped over her forehead. Oh, God, he was right. Just the sight of it turned her stomach. Its eyes glowed red, like the embers of hell. Its skin was a bit like the Elemental's, only earth brown and mottled like water-stained leather. Its nails were like something out of a Freddy Krueger movie.

Books rained down on it. Though they fell right through its body, it flinched in pain and looked up. One of those Elementals sat atop the shelf, its heart-shaped face tight with anger as it pushed down more books.

The demon reached toward the creature, its arms stretching like rubber. The Elemental tried to duck away, but those arms looped around it and brought it down to the demon's level. The Elemental screamed and then fell silent as the demon tore its head off with teeth as sharp as its claws. The demon dropped its body and focused on them again.

The Elemental had been trying to help. Outrage filled her, and she tore out of Cyn's grasp, only to lose sight of the demon that, in a moment of insanity, she thought she could make pay. Something clamped onto her sides, two hands, she guessed by the claws that dug into her. A rush of heat washed against her side as she tried to pry those hands off her. Faintly she could see the shadow of the demon only inches in front of her. Suddenly the hands released her and something came between her and the demon.

Something big, black. With scales. Spines that fanned

back over its head. And fangs like a saber-toothed tiger's.

The room spun as she staggered back and held on to the edge of a bookcase for support. Cyntag no longer stood there. What *was* there stole her breath away.

A dragon. A friggin' dragon.

"Get farther back, Ruby."

Cyntag's voice came from the dragon. Had it eaten him? His pants lay in a heap, his shirt tattered on the floor.

Maybe it had.

Blue spikes studded the dragon's spine between two wings tucked against its back. It spun around, eyeing something behind her. She could only stare at the beast, larger than a horse. The dim light shimmered across its scales as it moved. It lunged forward, expelling sinuous black smoke. She saw the outline of the demon in the smoke, its long arms snaking toward the Dragon's muzzle.

The Dragon thrashed its head back and forth, knocking into the rows of shelves and sending them crashing down. She was leaning against one of them, so she snapped out of her terror and moved before she went down with it.

She felt the creepy heat again, the breath she'd been feeling since leaving Mon's house. That thing had been with her the whole time. Fear and revulsion rolled through her. The Dragon's head lunged toward her, freezing her as glistening fangs came close.

Though terror should have claimed her as the dark blue eyes of the beast held her gaze, she felt a longing ache. *The Dragon Prince.*

It turned, its teeth snapping at the demon that was now obviously near its tail. That tail whipped around, knock-

ing a cart several yards away and scattering the books
it had contained. The Dragon snapped at the demon that
must be climbing up its back by the way the spines were
bending. If only she could see the damned thing. The
Dragon threw itself at another shelving unit, obviously
trying to dislodge it. Suddenly, the beast's head pulled
back at a painful angle.

Do something!

Where was her gun? She couldn't see it among the
piles of books. Frantically she started digging through
them, gratefully wrapping her fingers over the cool metal.
She aimed just above the dragon. The demon felt the
books when the poor creature dropped them. How about
a bullet? She jerked with the release, holding strong. The
bullet hit the wall a short distance away.

Something sucked the air from her lungs, like a vacuum hose shoved down her throat. She dropped to her
knees, gasping and clawing at her throat. What was the
demon doing to her? Not strangling her, because she
couldn't feel its hands.

The Dragon bumped her, throwing her to the side and
ending the horrible asphyxiation. She struggled to her
hands and knees, hearing the sounds of battle just out
of sight. Then the roar of an explosion. A puff of black
smoke rose to the ceiling. Her ears rang in the sudden
silence. Who had won? Or, gawd, had they both com-
busted?

Cyntag stepped into view, wearing his white pants and
holding the tattered shirt. "We have to get out of here."

She got to her feet, scooping up her gun with shaking
fingers. "You're a...were a..." She rubbed her forehead.
"I've gone bonkers like my grandfather."

Cyntag took her hand and led her through the wreckage, commenting on neither of her statements.

She glanced back to where the Elemental had died. "Is it there? The creature who died?"

He paused. "Yes. Its body will fade away." He tugged her out the broken back door to where an old black Thunderbird was parked at an angle.

"Are you all right to drive?" he asked. "You need to follow me back to the dojo. We have a lot to cover and not a lot of time to do it."

"I can drive. I'm crazy, not handicapped."

"You're not crazy. You're just part of the Hidden."

Smoke curled up from his untouched cigar as Purcell watched the demon he'd summoned get crushed. Through a scry orb, Purcell had watched Ruby go to Valeron's dojo and then storm out a short time later. Valeron had followed and sabotaged the perfect kill opportunity. Now Purcell watched the Dragon snatch up the orb. The window through which he could watch snapped closed, leaving him in the dark room.

Valeron was still protecting Ruby. It baffled Purcell that someone would put their life on the line for a virtual stranger. He would not even do it for someone he knew well. Taking risks for a god was a different matter, of course.

That Fallon, Deuce god of nature, had approached Purcell for assistance was both humbling and gratifying. Most Deuces brave or desperate enough to appeal to a god had to perform a ceremony with magick-infused driftwood. In this case, a god needed him. It still awed him, even after all these years. He had failed because of Justin, but he would not let Fallon down again.

Fallon had opened the portal to the Dark Side and made the proper introductions. He had then left the door open so Purcell could access it on his own if it became necessary. That door, like a holographic image floating in his living room, was unnerving. Purcell detested having to use it again, but demons were a weapon that could not be traced back to him. Like the scry orb, the portal was round and hovered a few feet away from him.

The Demon Master appeared in the window. If Purcell passed him on the sidewalk, he might think the Master a surfer. His blond hair looked windblown, his skin tanned, eyes a brilliant blue. Purcell didn't know if it was a façade or if he was a different sort of demon altogether. He had no interest in asking.

"You're back," the Master said, sounding none too enthused.

"Indeed. The demon failed, losing its life to a Dragon. I'm afraid I'm in need of more."

The Master showed no sadness at the loss. "How many?"

"Three, maybe four, just to be certain. They seem to be easily defeated by this particular Dragon."

Purcell suffered the Master's silence for several long moments. Finally he said, "I shall see what is available. And willing."

A dark shadow moved behind the Master, and a scream like nothing Purcell had ever heard pierced the air just before the window closed. Purcell knew little about the Dark Side, only that it was in a plane of existence similar to where the gods were trapped. Most Deuces did not have the courage, nor the connections, to contact the plane populated by demons and other creatures Purcell had only glimpsed in the background. It was, as the name implied, dark and flat, the way the landscape appeared during a full moon.

Demons sometimes escaped the Dark Side on their own and roamed the Earthly plane, but most were controlled by the Master. Those that got out of control were imprisoned.

The window opened again. Several dark faces lurked behind the Master, their silhouettes etched against the grim landscape.

"I have four that are willing to do your bidding for some bloodlust sport. One is a harbinger."

"It will work into my plan."

"Do you agree to the Three Tenets?"

"Yes," Purcell said. They were his responsibility, and he would pay the price should they expose the Hidden. He would supervise them and send them back or terminate them if they broke out of his control. And third, he accepted the danger inherent in dealing with demons.

This was the part he despised. The demons scrambled through the window, their clawed feet scratching on the wood floor as they gathered in front of him, their temporary master. The harbinger had taken the appearance of a homeless old man. The others looked as terrifying as the first one he'd taken custody of.

"I have two targets, both Dragon." He summoned the illusion of Cyntag's and Ruby's faces. "He is a powerful Obsidian. The girl is not as strong."

One demon narrowed its red eyes at the image of Cyntag. "He is the one who took out Sed?"

Purcell hadn't known the demon's name. "Yes. He murdered your comrade. Perhaps your friend?" Better to motivate them with revenge.

The demons laughed, a sound like someone shaking a bag of glass bottles. One said, "That asshole? We were happy to hear of his death."

A second one said, "But we hate Dragons even more. We don't need revenge to juice our bloodlust."

Could they read his mind? Purcell pushed past that disturbing thought. "You may take them out in any way that you'd like, provided it doesn't compromise Rule Number One. Eliminate anyone who might help them. Or gets in the way."

The demons nodded their understanding, releasing hisses that might be glee. Purcell brought up an image of the dojo and turned to the harbinger. "You, hang around this establishment and watch for our targets. You three, remain close and wait for my order."

Now for the worst part. Purcell held out his hand to form the psychic bond. Their dry hands clasped his, and he felt the tips of their claws press into his skin.

The harbinger bared its teeth in a smile. "Till death do us part."

The Book of the Hidden

The day of her eighteenth birthday dawned bright. Garnet had been here five years, with freedom to come and go within the confines of the castle and its grand gardens.

She had a nanny and teachers, the finest of meals and entertainments. The best part was that she had not seen much of the Dragon Prince, who dined with her every now and then and asked after her welfare as though he cared. The real prison was the spell he had cast upon her—the Dragon that resided within her clawing to be let out.

A quick knock on her door startled her out of her thoughts. It was her lady-in-waiting, who looked as though she were bringing bad news.

Gwendolyn gave her a tremulous smile. "Happy birthday, Your Highness," she said with a bow. "It is time. The Dragon Prince has told you, yes?"

"Told me what?"

"That you and he are to marry today. A small ceremony, just the staff. He wishes for me to ready you." She pulled a basket filled with flowers from behind her back. "For your hair. He loves it long, you know."

"No, I don't know. I know nothing of him. Which is fine with me."

"You will know much after today." Gwendolyn's face blushed. "The stylists will be here soon, to do your hair, fit you for the dress, and make up your face. You are pretty now, but you will be a vision soon."

Hours later, Garnet was finally alone again. The dress was as heavy as her fate. She hardly recognized herself in the mirror's reflection, with her curled hair adorned with petals and flashing with crystals. How would she feel when her Dragon was released? She knew little of the process, only that she would be Awakened in a ritual. Had she been born with the Dragon inside her, she would have Awakened at puberty. The prince assured her that he would personally train her to master it. He promised he would help her to find the beauty of it. Garnet highly doubted the latter.

She wandered to her window, where she dreamed of going home. Opal flew down and landed on her finger. The dove rubbed her palm with its cheek, touching her heart with the familiar gesture.

"Have you come to wish me a happy birthday? The only person who shall be happy today is the prince, for he will get his way." She narrowed her eyes, the first smile in weeks gracing her lips. "Or maybe not completely."

She settled Opal on the sill and pulled out the sewing kit from beneath her bed. She filled her days with creative projects, like sewing dresses for Gwendolyn and the other girls who'd never owned anything pretty. The prince supplied everything she asked for, even the expensive lace and ribbons.

Garnet turned to the mirror again, feeling a fire inside her she had not felt for so long. She spent the next hour tying her wedding dress into odd configurations, tucking in the sleeves and adding a neckline that covered her décolletage. She cut her hair and twined dead roses into what was left, thorns and all. She dabbed Earthen behind her ears, a healing mixture that smelled of mold.

Garnet expected the prince to be furious. And welcomed it. His staff was up in arms once they saw her, fighting her to fix her modifications. She assured them that she would tell the prince she alone was responsible.

She did not expect to be taken in by his handsome visage as he waited at the front of the small church. One of the prince's best soldiers escorted her down the aisle, his nose wrinkling at the smell of her. He backed away, tak-

ing on the same look of fearful anticipation everyone else had as they awaited the prince's reaction.

He took her in with a hint of shock in his onyx eyes and a twitch at the corner of his mouth. Then he threw his head back and laughed. His people joined him, ready to mimic his every reaction. The priest hesitated until the prince said, "Please proceed. I cannot wait to marry my rebellious and creative bride-to-be."

Why wasn't he angry? She'd humiliated him. Taunted and defied him. He acted as though she were indeed the beauty he'd intended. He had bested her again.

Their hands were bound, binding her heart as well in a choking hold. When the priest decreed that he could kiss his bride, the prince claimed her mouth the way he had claimed her. He whispered, "Now you are officially mine," and then turned to the crowd. "I present your new queen."

The prince led her down the aisle and accepted many well wishes from people who both feared and revered him. A carriage took them to the great hall filled with music and the aroma of sumptuous foods. Someone announced them as husband and wife as they entered to great applause, and the prince led her to the center of the dance floor.

The music started, and he pulled her into his arms. The spell of him wrapped around her, like the Dragon spell. He spun her around and around, blurring everything but himself. His body felt strong and warm as he held her close, amusement glimmering in his eyes. Her mind screamed a warning, even as her heart softened and inexplicably strained toward him.

He drew his finger down her cheek. "You have fire.

Spirit. This is good, as you will need it. For it is time to Awaken your Dragon. A great darkness comes. A prophecy brought me to you before the Shadows would have killed you. Now it also brings the Black Doom. We are destined to fight it together to save mankind."

Chapter 7

It had been fifteen years since he'd had to be familiar with the nuances of Deuce magick, but Cyn knew someone who could corroborate his suspicions. As he drove, he initiated a call on his Bluetooth system, one of the many things not original in his car. "Kade, it's Cyntag Valeron. I need some info on a rather nasty orb. I've never seen one like it."

"Did you piss off a Deuce?" Kade laughed, because it wouldn't be the first time.

"Not me, a...friend." Presumptuous, but how else to categorize her? He described the orb, remembering how Ruby had tried to hide her terror when she'd told him about it.

"Star orb," Kade said after a long whistle. "Powerful. They're hard to shake. But you obviously have a witness who got away. He must be clever. And damned fast."

"Sure is." He felt an odd surge of pride. "Can you tell me who might have the ability to make one?"

"Only an early generation Deuce." First Gens, the original offspring, were the most powerful. Every subsequent generation lost some of the strength of their powers. "You're probably looking at someone in the first three or four generations. The problem is, as you know, they've taken on layers of identities by now. There's no way to know."

As Crescents got too old to be alive, as far as the Mundane databases were concerned, they had to arrange for their deaths and take on a new identity.

"Yeah, and they don't exactly go around advertising it either. What can you tell me about star orbs?"

"They take a lot of work and fry your palms, from what I understand. The good news for you is that whoever sent it won't be able to conjure up another one for a day or so."

A small relief there. Cyn didn't have to tell Kade that anything he said would remain confidential, and that worked both ways. They'd shared a few secrets over the years when they worked together at the Guard, done things that would forever remain between them and the men they'd taken orders from.

"Can whoever sent it see through the orb?"

"Yes, and they can direct its actions. If someone sent a star orb after your friend, he means business. Your guy better watch his ass."

More like *he* was going to have to watch *her* ass. "That's what I was worried about. Thanks for the information. I'd love to catch up, but I've got a situation here. I'll be in touch soon." He disconnected.

Now that Ruby was on the move, she should be safe until another demon picked her up. How much did the murderer know about Ruby?

At a red light, Cyn pulled on the extra shirt he kept in the trunk, a necessity for Dragons. In the rearview mirror, he saw Ruby brushing her hair from her face every few seconds, eyes wide as she glanced at the passenger seat. Her skin looked as pale as alabaster. She was holding on by a thread. He needed to get her into the Obsidian Room, where she could release the tension and fear inside her. She had to get up to speed pronto and Awakened soon after. No time to be gentle about it.

The light turned green and he went straight. He glanced back. "Hell." She had taken a sharp right and sped out of view.

Ruby hightailed it to the Yard where things were normal and safe, where she could forget that she'd been attacked by a demon she couldn't see and *had* seen a guy turn into a dragon.

Maybe, just maybe, she wouldn't totally freak out. Hell, even the ordinary sound of a plane flying overhead had her shrinking in fear. If only her rash would stop flaring. Nervous perspiration dampened her collarbone and neck as she drove through the gate and got out of her truck. She came to a standstill in the central corridor of the Yard, feeling lost.

"Hey, Miz Ruby, sorry to hear about your uncle."

She started as Jack came up and gave her a hug. Thankfully his lanky arms went around her shoulders and nowhere near the bulge of metal at her waist. She cleared her throat and moved back. "Thanks." His expression of sympathy vanished, morphing into bewilderment.

Assuming it was about the injury on her forehead, or per- haps some new one, she waved it away. "I'm fine, just a small burn."

"Your...eyes."

Bloodshot? No doubt. Or maybe her pupils were di- lated. Did that happen when you went crazy? Jack was the coolest, calmest guy she knew—well, until she'd met Cyntag. Which meant there was something really wrong with her eyes. "What about them?"

His voice lowered, and he glanced around as though to make sure no one was nearby. "Miz Ruby, you're a Cres- cent. But you weren't a Crescent when you hired me, and you weren't even one yesterday. How..."

The memory of the embers in her reflection shot to mind. Not a hallucination if Jack could see it, too. Wait a minute. He was talking about Crescents. Jack, who did not know Mon, could not possibly know of his tales. She gripped his arm and stared into his eyes. There, just for a second, a spark like she'd seen in Cyntag's eyes.

"Tell me what you see, Jack."

"Embers. But...I don't understand."

"Believe me, you're not the only one."

He grinned, shaking his head. "I knew there was some- thing about you, Miz Ruby."

Something about her. She stumbled away, her chest so tight she had to pound it.

Nevin walked out of the building where the gas pump was being restored, his face pinched. Leo stepped out next to him, and he looked even more tense.

"Ruby, can we talk to you?" Nevin asked, his voice squeaky like it was when he was about to tell her he'd bungled a project.

She robotically followed them into the building where Nevin closed the door despite the warmth inside. Leo's arms were straight down at his sides, hands clenched as though he was ready to tackle her. Her body stiffened in response.

"Ruby, did you kill your uncle?"

Had she seen a mist in Leo's eyes? Was she friggin' seeing things everywhere now? Could she be swept up in a full-blown schizophrenic hallucination? Which was preferable to this all being real, because there were pills for that.

"I tell you about your uncle paying me to toughen you up, you hightail it out of here, and then your uncle dies in a fire." Leo's voice softened the way it might if he were talking to an insane person. "I know you were upset, but I want you to think about what happened. Did you go a little crazy? It's okay, Ruby. You can tell us."

He thought she'd killed her uncle.

She laughed, a sound that probably corroborated his suspicions because it came out a hysterical cackle. He started to reach for her shoulders, like he was going to restrain her.

She saw the mist swirl again, and before he could reach her, she screamed, "You're one, too! I can't believe this." She grabbed Nevin by his shirt and wrenched him to within an inch of her nose. "What about you? Do you have anything in your eyes? Glows, flames, mists—"

Leo's arm went around her waist, and he hauled her out of the building as though she were a piece of metal ready to be soldered. Sideways. She kicked and punched him, but he didn't set her down until they were outside. He waved off Nevin, who looked as though she'd smacked him.

When they were some distance away, Leo set her on her feet and threw his hands up to ward off the fist she was pulling back. "Nevin's not one of us," he gritted out. "Rule Number One, Ruby!"

Not one of us. Then Leo's admonishment about Rule Number One registered, the same thing Mon had said.

"Back away from her. Now."

The authoritative command came from behind her and made Leo automatically step back. She knew that voice before she even turned. Cyntag looked like a ninja warrior in his white pants and tight black shirt, so out of place, so larger than life that she hoped *he* was a hallucination. Unfortunately he looked real, from the way the material hugged muscular thighs all the way to the sun reflecting on his dark hair.

She jabbed her finger at him. "You, get away from me. I don't know what the hell you are—"

"I'm what you are, Ruby."

"No." She shook her head hard. "I am not a…" She let the word *dragon* trail off.

"Who the hell are *you*?"

She spun to find Jack drawing up, his shoulders wide and hands fisted. His body tensed even more when he met Cyntag's gaze. The two did some kind of male posturing thing, clearly sizing each other up. Jack was a teenager's wiry kind of muscular. Cyntag was bigger and buffer, and held an energy that just felt more dangerous. Jack appeared as though he might combust on the spot.

Cyntag looked lethally relaxed. "I'm Cyntag Valeron. You don't want to mess with me."

Jack's jaw tightened. "Well, I sure as hell ain't gonna let you come in here and harass Miz Ruby."

Taking Jack's cue, Leo stepped forward. "Me either. I'm an old friend of hers. I think she may be in trouble, and none of this concerns you."

Even with two against one, Cyntag didn't appear as though he were going to back down. "*Miz* Ruby's business is my business. She *is* in trouble, big trouble. I'm her sworn protector, so she's my responsibility."

She held her hands up. "Whoa, whoa, whoa. I'm not his"—she turned to Cyntag—"your responsibility." God, she hadn't been someone's responsibility since she turned eighteen and took control of the Yard. She looked from Jack to Leo, neither of whom seemed baffled by Cyn's assertion. "Come on, you can't know about this sworn-protector business."

"It's an honor thing," Jack said. "You promise to take care of someone at any cost."

"It was used more often in the olden days," Leo said. "Back when there *was* honor. Or so I've been told ad nauseam by my parents."

"I swore it to her grandfather," Cyntag said. "Brom Winston."

"Brom?" Leo said. "Isn't he the dude who predicted the island would sink? He was like Noah, told everyone to build boats and saved a bunch of our ancestors. And he was only ten years old or something."

Cyntag nodded. "Yes, that Brom Winston."

Her grandfather, Brom Winston? Then the rest of what they were saying hit her. The island sank. *Our ancestors.* Ruby staggered, because she couldn't deny it any longer. Mon's fairy tales...weren't tales.

Though both men clearly weren't comfortable around Cyntag, she sensed their deference to him. Or maybe a fearful respect. Either way, the subject of Brom calmed the edge in Jack's body language.

Cyntag stepped up to her, forcing Jack to move back. "Ruby has to go away for a while. I suggest you take a few days off until we figure out what's going on. There might be some dangerous visitors looking for her."

She shook her head. "What? No, I've got projects, commitments..." The words died in her throat. *Visitors as in demons.* This was real. Crazy, insane, but real. The demon killed that man and that poor little creature. It might hurt these people. Cyntag met her gaze, nodding as he saw understanding dawn. He'd been real, too, with scales and fangs and deep blue eyes. An honest-to-God Dragon. She turned to Jack. "Take a vacay."

Jack said, "I can protect you, Miz Ruby." He nodded to Cyntag. "I mean, you don't even know this guy, do you?"

Cyntag walked over to the Harley and ran his hand over the freshly painted tank. "Nice job, kid." A compliment, yet she knew the word "kid" was meant to establish a hierarchy. "Have you been trained to fight?"

"Enough to fend off the occasional punk-ass trying to assert his dominance." Jack glanced at Ruby. "If you'll pardon my French."

She shook her head. "It's fine."

Cyntag seemed to be assessing Jack. "But you've never Breathed Dragon."

"No, sir. But I could." His shoulders widened. "I sure could if I had to."

"What's Breathing Dragon?" Ruby asked.

"Later," Cyntag said.

That didn't sound good, but she didn't need to know *more* crazy stuff.

He met Jack's gaze again. "Ever tangled with a Deuce-made entity or demon?"

"Couple of times. Had a feud with a Douche neighbor." Jack glanced at Ruby. "Sorry, Deuce. Nothing that would kill me but a real pain in the ass. Literally." He patted his butt, then blanched as he looked at Ruby again. "If you'll—"

She held out her hand. "I can handle curse words. Like *holy shit*, how the *hell* did I get myself into this crazy-*assed* situation?" She gave him a forced smile.

Cyntag's mouth quirked but he maintained his serious expression as he turned to Jack. "I appreciate your dedication and loyalty, but you're still in school, aren't you?"

"Yeah. I'm in my last year, and then I'm joining the Guard."

If that was meant to impress Cyntag, it didn't seem to. "You go to the Dragon Academy?"

"Yes, sir."

"Finish your schooling before you start throwing yourself in battle. If you stick your snout into this, I'll have them pull your ass from the program."

Jack's jaw tensed, obviously taking the threat seriously. "Yes, sir."

Cyntag gave him a nod. "Let's clear out, Ruby."

"Nevin," she called to her partner, who lingered a short distance away with a worried expression that turned even more apprehensive when he looked at Cyntag. "We're closing the Yard for a few days." He wouldn't mind that part. "And no, I didn't kill my uncle. But whoever did might come here. I don't want to take any chances."

Nevin walked closer. "Wait a minute. Are you saying it was...murder? Have you talked to the police?"

"I can't tell you everything right now." Or ever, but she'd have time to come up with some plausible story. Well, she hoped she did. "And we can't tell the police. Just go home and be safe."

"But—"

"Go, please."

When he left, Cyntag raised one raven eyebrow. "He accused you of killing Moncrief?"

"I did," Leo said. "Well, not accused exactly," he added quickly. "Questioned."

"I was a little mad when I left to see Mon." Why hadn't Mon told her all of this? On top of everything else, she felt like an idiot.

Cyntag rested his hand on Leo's shoulder. "This does not involve you. Leave."

Leo nodded, then wandered over to Jack.

"Ready to talk now, Ruby?" Was Cyntag just a tad bit smug or did he always look so sure of himself? "In a reasonable manner without weapons and accusations? And in private?"

No, she wasn't ready to talk and be reasonable, especially not in private. She wanted to run screaming into the night. Only she couldn't, and it was daytime besides. "Fine."

"At my dojo. It's considered a safe zone."

"No, in my office. That's my safe zone." She led the way, arms crossed tight over her chest. Let him follow.

"You know you can't stay here."

"I've got records to grab, so I can let the customers who are coming in over the next few days know...What do I tell them? 'Can't work on your vintage soda cooler because someone's trying to kill me. Hope you can be patient.'"

"I wouldn't tell them that."

"I was kidding!"

Cyntag glanced at his watch. "You have a little time to grab the things you need. But not much."

He put his hand at her back and guided her onward. She stepped into the cool, dark office. No one had been in to turn on the lights. She didn't bother to do so either, finding the dimness more comfortable. This time they were in her territory, and she was in control.

He set a gun on the desk and walked over to the window to peer out.

She patted her back. Nothing. "How'd you *do* that?"

"One of the skills you learn at the Guard is to quickly disarm anyone who's potentially dangerous."

Did that mean he saw her as dangerous? Remembering their encounter earlier, she decided probably not. "You mean the National Guard?"

"No. Our Guard is the police force that governs Crescents. They report to a council called the Concilium, comprised of members of all three classes of Crescents."

Cyn surveyed the yard outside again, seeing the three men he'd just met talking and glancing toward the office, no doubt discussing him. Two of them were young Crescents, full of the piss and fire he hadn't possessed in decades. Crescents aged slowly, but one benefit of taking Dragon power was that it slowed the process even more.

Cyn turned back to find her pulling folders out of a filing cabinet drawer. "Do the three guys out there work here?"

"You're interrogating me."

He lifted a shoulder. "It's my nature. I need to know who's in your life."

"Was that supposed to be an apology?"

"I don't apologize."

She stared at him, and he could tell by the spark in her eyes that she was considering defying him, or maybe making him wait for an answer to assert some sense of control. Fine, let her have it. It might be the last time she felt in control for quite some time.

Her muscles relaxed, the defiant spark dimmed. "Jack Aster works here after school and weekends."

And he had a crush on Ruby.

Cyn glanced out the window. "He's close to storming in. Wave at him, let him know you're fine."

She narrowed her eyes again, most likely at the order, but gave Jack the universal OK sign. She crossed her arms over her chest and tilted her head at Cyn. "Happy?"

"Yes. I don't want to have to kill him."

"You're kidding, I hope."

"What about the other two?"

She paused, probably realizing he hadn't answered her question. "Nevin is my business partner. He didn't have that"—she wiggled her fingers in front of her eyes—"flicker. Leo said he wasn't one of us."

"He's a Mundane, a regular human. And Leo's the one who was manhandling you?" Cyn's Dragon had bristled at the sight of the man's arm around her waist, the rough way he was carrying her.

"I don't know what that was about. Leo came in looking for a part yesterday, the first time I've seen him in eight years."

"That seems odd, him showing up the day your uncle is murdered. He's a Deuce, but not powerful enough to make a star orb. That's the kind of orb that killed your uncle."

She swallowed hard. "How can you tell what he is?"

"Deuces' eyes swirl like fog."

Her face paled as she shifted her gaze from the Yard to Cyn. "Your eyes had embers, and so did mine when I saw them in the mirror. Dragon eyes are like embers. No." She shook her head hard, making her hair float out like a cloud. "Magick being real, I'm just beginning to grasp. Big ole lizards with talons and wings and scales, well, I saw that. But that *I'm* one, no friggin' way."

"What about the protected—or, rather, kidnapped—Garnet in Moncrief's stories? Didn't she turn into a Dragon?" Surely he would have accurately portrayed Ruby.

"The Dragon Prince put a spell on her that made her go Dragon. When they fought, they became savage beasts, with drool dripping out of their mouths. And they smelled like dirty socks. But in reality she was a Deuce."

Something like a growl emanated from his throat. He swallowed it back. "Nice of him to portray us that way." Moncrief not only hated Cyn, understandably, but also he disdained Dragons in general. Neither surprised Cyn, but the man should have kept his prejudices out of the stories. After all, Ruby was Dragon, too.

"We're not lizards." He gave a quick, disgusted flick of his head. "Or snakes with legs. Yes, we have scales, but we're hot-blooded. Our eyes are more catlike, and so are our bodies."

"But that's how Chinese Dragons are portrayed. Or is it Japanese?"

"That's just a reflection of a particular culture. Every ancient culture seems to have seen an actual Dragon. Pictures, carvings, and descriptions go back millennia.

I'm guessing that the Dragon gods showed themselves to early peoples in different ways."

Ruby raked her long hair back, holding it away from her face. Her thick bangs came halfway down her forehead, just above that burn. "I'm not a Dragon. I'd know a thing like that."

"You do know, Ruby. You've felt the power, the violence. You just didn't know why."

She shivered, her eyes wide as she stared at nothing in particular. "Those times I wanted to tear someone's head off..."

He felt an odd urge to pull her into his arms and smooth her hair back, clearly imagining the strands sliding against his skin, remembering the heat of her body against his. Bad idea to let those kinds of thoughts curl through him like a stream of smoke.

He gentled his voice instead of giving into his urge, much safer. "Ruby, you change into a Dragon. A powerful, gorgeous—"

"Stop." She slapped her hand on his chest. "Stop telling me that, and stop saying my name like..."

"Like what?"

"It sounds so...intimate."

Her hand felt warm on his chest, even through his shirt.

"I don't mean to say it like that." Relief crossed her face but disappeared at his next words. "But we *are* going to be intimate in the next couple of days." He clarified. "I have to give you a crash course on being Dragon."

He saw the toll this was taking on her, the twine of grief, fear, and confusion in her eyes. For a moment, he got caught up in all the different hues of greens and browns in them. Her eyelashes were long, and because she wore no makeup, he doubted she used one of those torturous-looking devices to curl them.

She appeared surprised at the sight of her hand on his chest, as though just realizing it was there. He pressed his hand over hers before she could pull it back. "I'm sorry about Moncrief, sorry that you're being thrown into all this." And most of all, sorry that he'd taken so much from her.

No apologies, remember?

He'd never thought about the families of those he'd been ordered to take out. His superiors at the Guard had bad or dangerous people killed. Or so he'd thought until he'd seen that girl in the dinghy.

This girl.

Her chin trembled as she stared at his hand over hers. "Don't say that," she whispered.

"Don't say 'I'm sorry'?"

Her body leaned toward him, and he had the urge to pull her the rest of the way. She needed comfort, probably needed to feel safe, even for a moment. He wasn't good at comforting, but he could improvise just this once. She leaned closer yet, as though he were a magnet pulling her toward him.

He brushed a stray hair from her cheek. "It's okay to break down, scream, cry, whatever. You've been through a lot." He couldn't imagine having to assimilate this all at once. "You're an innocent."

The protective side of his Dragon pushed against his hard exterior again. She *was* innocent, but she wasn't a child. That interesting mouth of hers, the swell of her breasts, reminded him of that. Much better to think of her as the untrained Dragon that she was. His responsibility, nothing more. He took a step back.

So did she. "That demon in the library, was it there to kill me?"

"Yes. Deuces can summon them to do their bidding."

"Could Brom summon one? Just before Mon died, he told me it was dangerous to see him."

"Brom is a powerful Deuce, and yes, he probably could, but he wouldn't harm you. Moncrief's warning means Brom is somehow involved in this."

Her eyes widened. "*He* killed Mon."

"I don't think so. They're best friends, have been for centuries. I'll find him."

"But Mon said—"

"I can deal with dangerous. What we don't know is whether you're a target because you were a witness to Moncrief's death or if there's another reason." He saw the fear on her face. Good. She needed to be afraid. But she also needed to be strong and ready to fight. He changed tack. "I can stash you away in a safe house and find out who's behind this."

He saw his words prickle at her. The little girl vanished, and the woman who'd held the gun to his chest stepped into her place. Perfect.

"I'm not hiding. I want to find out who killed my uncle." She curled her hand into a fist. "I want them to die."

He tried to stifle his smile and the pride it would reveal. "Then you'll need to be Awakened."

"Into a Dragon." Her bravado wilted. "I'll become what you did at the library?"

"Yes. The next time you face a demon, you'll be prepared. You'll at least know what you're dealing with."

"And see it. The only thing scarier than seeing you as a Dragon was *not* seeing that thing."

She was getting it. "But know that Awakening will be intense and painful. Training will be the hardest thing you've ever done." Before he thought better of it, he reached out and brushed his finger against her cheek. "I'll be with you every step of the way."

She stiffened at his touch. "Why does that not comfort me?"

He pulled back, irritated that he'd let himself go soft. "Then here's something else for you to focus on: when we Catalyze to Dragon...we do it naked."

The Book of the Hidden

Garnet faced the Dragon Prince on the immense lawn behind the castle, the sun glistening on the dewy grass. Her gaze darted all around, looking for a way to escape despite the guards positioned all around them.

"Don't be afraid," he said.

He drew his hands up, and in unison with his movements, the force of the beast rose within her.

"No!"

The rush of wind in her ears drowned out the word. No, not wind, but a change in her body, her very essence. She fought, her soul scratching and clawing against it. But when the mist cleared and the deafening sound quieted, she stood on four legs, not two. She took herself in, seeing the long snout growing out from her face, the talons on her hands, the red scales shimmering in the sun just as the dew had.

No, no, no! Her soul cried out at the ugly armor, and she closed her eyes and looked upward, pleading for the gods to kill her.

Something cool rubbed against her neck, startling her. A Dragon with scales black and blue like the heart of midnight, eyes holding the flicker of a flame within. The Dragon Prince.

He rubbed his head against her cheek. "You will get used to it."

"And what of the smell?"

He shrugged, or she thought he did. "You'll get used to that, too. And the drooling. Yes, we are ugly, horrid beasts, but we are the strongest of all." He nipped her, though she barely felt it through the scales. "Show me that spirit, love. Fight me with all you have so I know where to start."

He dared call her 'love'! She spun around and knocked him to the ground with her tail.

Chapter 8

Ruby sat in the passenger seat of Cyntag's T-bird, *The Book of the Hidden* on her lap. "I don't remember anything in Mon's stories about them being naked." She absently scratched at her rash.

"As you know, he took some liberties with the truth. For instance, was I drooling? Did I smell like"—his nose twitched—"dirty socks?"

"No."

He was gorgeous as a Dragon, if you were into that sort of thing.

She blinked. God, she was. She remembered feeling a powerful draw to him, or at least some part of her did.

Her Dragon.

God.

She ran her hands across the pages, forcing those thoughts away. "There were beautiful illustrations here. Since the fire, they're gone."

"Moncrief probably created them with magick. Just

like the spell he put over you, the stories disappeared, too."

No, she didn't want to think about never seeing the illustrations or his beautiful writing again. She tried to remember the main story line: the Dragon Prince kidnapping Garnet, but saving her as well, imprisoning her, casting the Dragon spell, training her. There were similarities in the story and what had happened so far.

Think. Think about the rest of it.

Something bad was coming. Something they had to fight together.

She turned to Cyntag, trying not to get caught up in his profile, the natural pout of his lower lip, the bump on his nose that spoke of a break in the past. He looked aristocratic, regal. Even as Dragon, actually. His eyelashes were thick but not feminine. Yeah, he was total hotness.

Uh, not getting caught up in his profile, remember?

"You said Brom can tell the future?"

"Yes."

"Could Moncrief?"

"Not that I know of. His skills ran toward creating illusions, like the pictures in the book and his magic tricks."

So the parallels with the story were a coincidence and not a foretelling of the future.

While Cyntag drove, he kept watching the rearview mirror as well as their surroundings. She knew he wasn't watching for traffic but for horrid creatures.

Speaking of… "When you were at the Yard, did you see any of those things you said were all over, like the one in your office?"

"A couple, yes. One stayed close to you. A fire Elemental, like Allander."

So ironically, she *wasn't* crazy because the monsters and creatures were real.

"I could see Leo's and Jack's Crescent eyes. Why couldn't I see this Elemental?"

"Your ability to see the Hidden isn't consistent because you haven't been Awakened yet." He pulled down the street on which his dojo resided, driving slowly. Odd, since he'd been driving fast the entire way.

"Get down," he said.

"What?"

He placed his hand against her head and pulled her toward him. In that second before her cheek was on his hard thigh, she saw an old man sitting on a bench in front of the dojo.

"One thing we need to get straight right now, Ruby. When I tell you to do something, you do it. You don't question or hesitate." Tension vibrated in his voice. "You just do it." He took a corner sharply. "Now you can get up," he said in a very deliberate voice because the moment he'd lessened his pressure on her, she'd snapped upright.

"What the hell? You can't just shove me around—"

He grasped her face with one hand, pulling her close. "I am the difference between whether you live or die. You don't have to like me. In fact, disliking me would probably be better in the long run. But you have to obey me, which means trusting me."

"You have to earn someone's trust."

"We don't have time for that." He released her. "Did you see the old man on the bench?"

She rubbed her cheeks where his fingers had dug in. "Yeah."

"Not an old man. A harbinger demon. One of the few that can be seen by Mundanes, which is why they take a disguise. And they can take any disguise. But we can see the shadow around them that signals what they are." He pressed a couple of buttons on his phone. "Dragon Arts," the DJ-smooth voice said through the car speakers.

"Glesenda, there's a harbinger outside the door."

"Oh, shit. What are you involved in—it's that girl, isn't it?"

He slid her a look. "It's not her fault, but yes, it wants her."

"Can I play with it?" Glesenda's eagerness permeated her words. "I can draw it in. What's the girl's name?"

"Ruby Salazaar, and I'm not a girl."

Glesenda laughed. "Ooh, baby, you *are* a baby. Cyn, you got your hands full with that one."

He sighed. "Indeed. Go ahead, lure it into the Obsidian Room. Call if you need me. Have fun." He disconnected.

"You're going to let her fight that thing by herself?"

"Glesenda can hold her own. She's a hundred and forty years old, so to her, you are a child."

"You're really...what'd you say, two hundred years old?"

"Two hundred fifty or sixty something. After a while you tend to lose track. Once you're Awakened, the aging process slows down. You'll look like you're in your mid-twenties for decades." His mouth stretched into a sort-of smile. "If I can keep you alive that long. That will depend on you."

"On whether I obey your every command."

"Exactly."

She flopped back against the seat, arms crossed in

front of her. "There's a reason I'm my own boss. I never had a lot of rules to follow growing up. Dad was busy with his science stuff, and Mom was busy with the Yard. I don't take orders well." Ever since losing her parents so suddenly, being in control of her life was paramount. Now this arrogant man-Dragon was insisting she follow his every order without question. He was right though. She needed him. And when he'd held her face and harshly ordered her to obey, she thought she saw a speck of fear in his expression. Fear for her safety.

"Everything in your life is about to change," he said, getting onto one of the interstates. "*You're* about to change. I suggest you put aside your stubbornness and pride. Neither will serve you well right now."

"This sucks, you know. Totally reeks of suckiness. The suckiest ever."

Another twitch of his mouth. "Whining won't serve you either."

"Well, I deserve to whine. A little."

The coil of edgy energy she felt coming off him when he'd driven past the dojo was gone. He leaned back in his seat, his left hand draped over the top of his steering wheel. On the underside of his arm was a scar that looked like an elongated *V*.

"Where are we going?" she asked.

"To my place. I have a soundproofed room there, too."

"It's not a castle, is it?"

"My castle, I suppose. The Dragon Prince had a castle?"

She picked up the book, which had slid to the floor when Cyntag manhandled her. "Yes, where he kept her prisoner." Panic speared her as she recalled her fears when he'd caught her in his office. "I can leave your house whenever I want, right? I won't be a prisoner." Reading about Garnet's imprisonment had always given her a claustrophobic feeling.

"You may leave. But only with me."

Augh. He did sound like the Dragon Prince.

He took an exit and drove through one of the many not-so-nice areas. Bars on the windows of businesses, people loitering outside. The area was run-down and dirty. Soon, though, they were downtown, passing through the touristy area where the cruise ships docked.

As they continued, they passed a park and several marinas, definitely a nicer area. The cars were fancy and expensive, the kind she usually only saw at the resto Yard in a decimated state. Coral Gables maybe. She didn't venture toward the coast much. A lot of the houses were Mediterranean or Spanish style, all large with yards filled with flowers and trees.

"Won't this bad person who sent demons know where you live?" she asked.

"Not easily. It's hidden, too, under layers of corporations. When you're as old as I am and you hold power, others want it."

"They...*want* it?" He paused, and she knew he was considering whether she could handle whatever it was. "Just tell me. It can't be any worse than anything else you've told me...or that I've seen." She hesitated. "Can it?"

"Dragons can take the power of another Dragon."

She snorted. "Well hey, they can have my power."

"You have to die first."

"Okay, maybe not."

"It's called Breathing Dragon."

"That's what you and Jack were talking about. But that's murder."

"Long ago, the Concilium decreed that no Dragon should kill for the sole purpose of attaining another's power. It works as well as the Mundanes' laws about murder and theft does."

"Oh, great. So there might be people after me just for my power."

"The good thing is that you'll have little, at least in the beginning. You're a mere morsel." His gaze drifted down her for a second.

She felt a shiver move across her body. "That is not comforting, not that you're a comforting kind of guy." But he'd brushed her hair from her face, said he was sorry. And she'd nearly let herself fall against him. *Idiotic thing to do.*

"I'm not here to comfort you, Ruby. I'm here to train you to defend yourself. To teach you to fight. And to keep you alive."

She didn't want to be a morsel. "But that's not why I'm being targeted now, is it?"

"No, a Deuce cannot take your power. As soon as we get you up to speed, we're going to find out what the hell is going on."

He pulled up to a gated entrance. Thick, green hedges blocked the view of what lay beyond a bit more effectively than the detailed iron gates that slowly opened. She'd refinished a set of gates like these years ago for one of her regular customers. Cyntag's were even more ornate, topped with spikes that discouraged someone from climbing over.

Her chest tightened as he drove up to a beautiful home,

a mixture of contemporary design and wood. Everything was going to change. *She* was going to change.

Once they were done pulling her luggage through a spacious kitchen with dark wooden floors and matching cabinetry, he said, "I'll make lunch, and then we'll get started."

"I'm not hungry."

"You'll eat. After Awakening, you're probably not going to feel like eating for a while."

"Great, knowing that will help my appetite."

She was too worked up to even appreciate two stories' worth of ocean view beyond a wall of windows. A curving staircase, a bridge over a pond surrounded by plants, and water drifting beneath a piece of solid glass to the pool out on the patio.

He passed the stairs and opened the door into the short hallway just beyond. "You'll stay here for as long as it's safe. Take a minute or two to settle in, then meet me in the kitchen."

"As long as it's safe?" She paused in the doorway. "I thought this place was hidden."

"The thing about the Hidden is, we're never really safe. As strong as you are, there is someone stronger. As clever as you are, there is someone more clever. And as hidden as you think you are, someone will find you. They know about me, obviously. If someone has the right connections or the right magick, they'll find where I live. Which is why we don't have much time."

She stared out the huge glass doors at the sparkle of sun on the choppy waves and felt as though she were slipping beneath them. His finger on her chin startled her.

"I can be easy on you, at least in the beginning. If you need that."

She stepped away from the way his touch felt electric on her skin. The way his low, soft words washed over her. "No, don't be easy on me. These people killed my uncle. And are trying to kill me. I don't want easy."

"Good girl. See you in a few minutes."

Damn it, he'd manipulated her again.

Chapter 9

⌒

Can we turn the lights down?"

Ruby followed Cyntag into a windowless room the size of a tennis court.

He stripped off his shirt and tossed it to the floor. "I forget, you still have the modesty of a Mundane." He strode to the control box near the door and dimmed the lights.

The halogen lights honed the planes of his cheeks and angles of his jaw, razor sharpening the cut of his muscles. The mirrors on two sides of the room created infinite versions of him. Cyntag, everywhere she looked. She scratched at her stomach again. Damn rash was worse than ever.

"You have an itch," he said, and she swore he meant *that* kind of itch. Which she did not have, thank you very much.

She waved her hand dismissively. "Psoriasis, the doctors think, though they've never given me anything that relieved it."

"Show me."

"You're used to ordering people around, aren't you? Of course, you're a sensei or whatever, with classes of rapt students following your every command." And probably women falling at his feet.

"True. Your point?"

"Would it kill you to *ask*?"

He seemed to consider it. "No. Show me the rash. I'm not morbidly curious. I think I know what it is."

With a roll of her eyes, she unbuttoned the lower part of her shirt and lifted it.

He knelt down to get a better look. The feel of his fingers brushing her skin startled her.

"Cyntag—"

"Call me Cyn."

Cyn, which sounded like "sin." Figured. Because with him kneeling in front of her, his dark hair catching the dim light, bare shoulders gleaming... *whoa. Cut that shit out.* "Well, Doctor Cyn, what is it?"

Though his hair was straight, a few locks had minds of their own, curling in various directions. She had the insane urge to run her fingers through what looked like silk.

He rose. "Dragon rash."

"Huh?"

"Started when you were about thirteen?"

"Yeah."

"Kicks up when you're stressed. I bet it was driving you mad when I Catalyzed—turned Dragon—in the library."

"Well, yeah."

He stroked his own dragon tattoo. "It's the part of you that's Dragon. And it's literally itching to come out."

"It sounds like there's a creature inside me. I'm having flashbacks of that *Alien* movie when the baby alien bursts out of that guy's stomach."

"It's not like that. It has no physical form outside of you."

Her eyes widened. "I'm going to have a tattoo like that?"

"It's not a tattoo, but it passes for one. It's just below your skin's surface." He wrapped his hand around her waist where the rash was. "We hold the essence of our Dragon inside us. Though we are mostly human, the Dragon is all animal. Once Awakened, it will pull at you to release it. To act on its impulses."

She lifted her face to his, feeling the heat from his body, from his words, envelop her. "Impulses," she heard herself repeat.

His fingers tightened on her skin, and he lowered his mouth just a little closer to hers. "It responds to stimuli like food, conflict...lust. When it wants something, it will goad and seduce you. It speaks to you telepathically, simple words like *mine* and *want*." He let those words sink in.

And they did, like warm honey soaking into her skin. "Mine," she repeated, feeling it thrum through her. "Want."

"Mmm-hmm. And *hungry*."

"Hungry," she said, spellbound.

"And not for food." His voice grew soft and low, his eyes hooded. "You'll feel it through your whole body, hear the siren song in your mind."

Yes, she heard it, felt it. Her body began to sag toward him, wanting to feel him against her. The spell! Just like the spell the Dragon Prince wove around Garnet. Ruby stepped away, pulling down her shirt. "It sounds like being possessed."

He ran his hand back through his hair and cleared his throat. "It can be if you let it get the best of you. The Dragon has no reasoning skills, fears no consequences. If we let it control us, *we* pay the consequences."

"Oh, great." She realized she was scratching again. "The rash has been a lot worse since... well, since I've been around you."

"Your Dragon is responding to mine. It aches to be free. That's why I have this room, so I can let the beast run. I created the Obsidian Room so others can release it safely."

Yes, something inside her *was* responding to him. She studied his tattoo, remembering how it had blinked when he'd done that Veil-lifting thing at his office. "I saw your Dragon move."

He walked to a cabinet built into the far wall. The pants he wore reminded her of karate uniforms she'd seen, only the material was soft and did amazing things for his ass. It didn't hurt that he had a fine one, combined with the walk of a man comfortable in his skin. No matter what skin that was.

"They can move, but they won't crawl off you or down your leg or anything. Mostly they keep an eye on things."

If only she could go back to the time when she thought it was mystery eczema.

He set several thick, short candles on the floor against the back wall. She wondered if he'd Breathe on the wicks to light them, but no, he used a lighter. Could he Breathe fire? Could she?

He turned on a stereo system and cranked what sounded like old rock and roll. She had a fleeting thought to run, get the hell out while she was still normal and human and...

You're not normal. Never were.

"Have any Red Hot Chili Peppers in there?" she asked instead, hearing a quiver in her voice.

"Nope. I tend to like the classic rock and metal music. Elvis was all right, but I started really enjoying music in the sixties and seventies."

He was around when Elvis got his start. Wow. Just...wow.

"So my parents were Dragons?"

"Your mother was Dragon. Moncrief, your grandfather, and your father were Deuces. Descendents inherit only one aspect. Generally, the different types of Crescents don't intermingle, but love doesn't always make sense." He let his gaze settle on her for a moment before his expression reverted to the business at hand. "Time to start. You need to submit to me. To my will."

She anchored her hands on her hips. "Oh, this is the part where I would have been more malleable had you gotten your hands on me when I was thirteen."

"I wasn't 'getting my hands' on you."

"I didn't mean it that way." He probably wanted a woman more experienced in the ways of Dragon. And likely other things. "But I'm not submitting to you."

He put his hands on her shoulders. "Ruby, as your sworn protector, I will lay my life on the line for you." His words shivered through her because she heard the devotion in them. "But you have to do your part. You have to grow into your strength and power and out of your tough façade."

"What do you mean, façade?"

He drew his finger from her shoulder to her collarbone, where he made tiny circles. "Your real strength lies here, in your Dragon. I'm your way of reaching that."

She so did not like needing him. "I am tough. I didn't crumble in fear when that damned orb was chasing me or when I saw a friggin' demon."

Damn it, his smile reeked of patronization. "You are tougher than most would be in your position. Now you have to get tougher."

"I get images of you forcing me to kiss your boot." Her eyebrows furrowed. "Or someplace even more degrading."

His mouth twitched. "Interesting image. The more degrading place."

She slapped his finger away. He laughed, irritating her even more because he never reacted the way she expected. Reminding her of the Dragon Prince on his wedding day.

"I don't need to force you to do petty acts to assuage my need for dominance. Submitting is an act of strength, not weakness. In the beginning, with your Dragon Awakened, it'll feel like riding a bucking bronco. Hold on tight. I'll be Dragon, too, and if I need to, I'll hold you down. Or knock you on your ass. I won't let you hurt yourself, or me, if you're out of control."

All her life she'd done everything to be in control. Never drinking to excess, not doing drugs, being her own boss. Now she might lose it completely.

Her throat felt as though she'd swallowed sand. "How do I become human again?"

"You will it. You're the master. I suggest you remove

your clothes now and set them in a neat pile so you can get to them easily when you Catalyze back. I'll cover my eyes." He gave her such a condescending smile that she narrowed her eyes. He chuckled. "You have fire. Good. You'll need it."

Déjà vu smacked her in the chest. She'd heard those words before, before the Dragon Prince enabled the spell. More bits were coming back—because they were living them.

He removed his pants and set them with his shirt. Not a speck of modesty. She watched him walk away, the candlelight gilding his glutes, and when he started to turn, she glanced down. Did he have to be achingly beautiful?

He faced away and covered his eyes with one hand. Her gaze drifted down wide shoulders that tapered to a narrow waist, his exquisite ass, and then strong legs dusted with hair as dark as the hair on his head. And the Dragon climbing up his back. Her gaze drifted to the mirror's reflection where she could see the front of him. His closed eyes and strong chin, the Dragon watching her...

"Ready?" he asked.

She started. "No." The word snapped out of her mouth, only because she'd been gawking. She put her clothes in a pile far from his. After arranging her hair to fall over her breasts, she said, "All right."

He turned around to face her. "I've been to a lot of ceremonies. Each teenager has a family member who triggers the Awakening. I will act in that role. When you Catalyze for the first time, it will be intense. Painful." He must have seen her trepidation at those words. "I know you can handle it, Ruby, because you're meant for this. And I've been told you're quite tough."

"Hah hah." He still said her name in that sultry way, wrapping his voice around it like a coating of melted chocolate.

He placed his hands on either side of her face and brought his mouth toward hers. Her body wanted to fall toward him the moment his mouth settled over hers, but she remained on her feet.

Heat tore down her throat, lighting every vein on fire. Her body jolted with pain as fingers of flame reached into her extremities. Her rash felt as though it were tearing away from her body. She screamed, blindly reaching out and digging her fingers into his shoulders. He pulled his mouth away but jerked her against him. She gasped, her body shivering.

"Breathe, Ruby. Breathe through it. Your Dragon is waking up. Bring it in."

"Hurts. Hurts so bad," she managed to say. She thought for sure she was on fire, but he was holding her close, enduring the flames, too. She saw it then, behind her closed eyelids. The Dragon was deep red with streaks of white, its scales glossy. It lifted its head, stretching its neck and releasing a stream of fire from its mouth.

Then she was moving, faintly aware of her skin rubbing against Cyn's. The hunger inside, God, the hunger washed over her in great waves, and she no longer dug her nails in to fight against him. She pulled him closer, his chest against her cheek, the rub of his sprinkling of hair chafing her jaw. She ached to pull him inside her.

"Control, Ruby," he whispered when he should have shouted it.

She shook her head, her mouth sliding against his skin. Her breath came in shallow pants, her hands moving over his back.

He lowered his head, his voice hoarse. "Ruby."

She looked up at him, the embers wild in his eyes, and pulled his mouth down to hers. The need to taste him, to feel his mouth on hers again, overcame her. Her tongue sought his, dancing, sparring. His hands tightened on her, fingers tangling in her hair. She sucked on his tongue in an incredibly phallic way, then nibbled on his lower lip. Things she had never done before, never thought to do.

Hungry...

Yes, hungry for Cyn, for his touch. For the way his mouth devoured hers now. This overwhelming desire was something so new, so foreign, yet she embraced it. She flattened her body against his, wanting to feel all of him. His hands moving down her back, pulling her closer against him, his arousal a hard shaft pressing into her solar plexus, sent an inferno roaring through her. It stripped her humanity and left her...Dragon.

She opened her eyes and felt completely different, dense and brimming with power. Like Garnet, she saw the snout—her snout—growing out from her face. Standing in front of her was the black and indigo Dragon, nostrils flaring as it faced her.

"Ruby, are you okay? Talk to me."

She nodded, feeling the weight of her head. "I...think so." She looked down. Her chest puffed out in shiny scales of red. She lifted her hand, starting as it flexed its talons at her command. Then she lost her balance and stumbled.

He was beside her, holding her weight for the few seconds it took to regain her footing. That hot, hungry part of her reacted to his closeness, and she heard it emit a growl deep in her chest.

"Watch it, hot stuff," he said. "Maybe I didn't make it clear that the Dragon part of you is very horny."

"That would have been nice to know." She had ravished him. The memory of it should have embarrassed her, but it excited her instead. She wanted more of him, his skin against hers, his—

She moved away from him, overwhelmed by his heat, and, damn, the hunger for him. Her Dragon wanted his Dragon bad. *Focus on me, not him, silly beast.*

She lifted her hand again, this time ready for the shift in weight. "I'm a friggin' Dragon."

His chuckle was soft and low. "Indeed you are."

Another wave of energy hit her, and it was exactly as he'd described, like holding on to one of those bronco things in a country bar. She felt the energy of the Dragon, separate and yet connected to her. She raced around the room, a wild freedom soaring through her.

Then it hit her. She also felt complete. The emptiness she'd suffered from most of her life was gone. It had been her Dragon, hungry and waiting within her. The power! She inhaled it with her soul. She was strong, and magnificent, and everything Cyn said she was. She caught sight of her reflection, the elegant lines of her body, the spikes along her back and the regality of her face. Orbs schmorbs. She'd much rather be Dragon.

She turned to look at her tail, circling to watch it slide behind her. With her will, she flicked it. Wiggled the tip. Then she allowed herself to meet Cyn's eyes, taking him in in a whole new way. No, her Dragon was taking him in, soaking in his beauty, responding to his power.

"Focus on learning, Ruby." He nodded toward the far, blank wall. "Try to Breathe your fire at the circle in the middle."

"Circle?" She squinted and saw the tiniest speck.

No problem. She inhaled and Breathed out. One small spark eked out and then died.

He laughed. She shot him a—well, she thought it was a dirty look—and faced the speck again. Breathed again. A few more sparks came out.

Cyn stepped up beside her and shot a stream of smoke right to the target like an arrow. He looked at her, a blatant challenge.

She faced the speck and spit again. "It's harder than it looks."

"Your Breath is your most valuable weapon. Try again."

She focused on the speck again. This time a stream of sparks shot almost all the way to the wall.

"Good job. Keep at it until you hit it."

The power that rushed through her very soul was intoxicating. She blew out again, hitting the wall but nowhere near the target.

Power.

Finally. But hungry.

The thought surprised her because it wasn't hers. The idea of an independent entity inside her startled her, even though Cyn had warned her.

This time her Dragon blew out the spikes and hit the target.

"Ruby, your Dragon is taking over. Remember, use your will."

She heard Cyn's voice from what seemed like far away, even though she saw him from the corner of her eye.

"Ruby, come back to human. Now. I remember how seductive the Dragon can be when you're not used to it. Come back."

She shook her head, only it wasn't her doing the shaking. She'd lost control. Seductive, yes, and scary and exhilarating, all at once. Her Dragon did not want to obey Cyn, and it sure as hell wasn't going to listen to her. It ran, dragging her along with it.

"Damn it," Cyn muttered somewhere behind her. "Back," he ordered. "Now!"

Her Dragon dodged him like a playful puppy. Panic prickled at the edges of her soul. What if she couldn't regain control?

Cyn slammed her to the floor, pressing his weight down on her. Her Dragon body struggled, whapping him with her tail, hard enough to knock him off balance. She leaped to her feet and ran, turning in time to see him unleash a cloud of black mist that shot right at her. She felt her body fly to the side, hitting the wall. And then nothing.

Chapter 10

———

Cyn watched Ruby morph from Dragon back to woman, her body sprawled on the floor. She'd landed on her side, hair spread wildly all around her. He knelt down next to her and checked her pulse. Racing, no surprise.

His fingers remained at her neck, because for some reason he couldn't pull them away. She was out cold. He tapped her cheek. "Ruby. Wake up. No time for slacking."

She murmured but didn't begin to revive. He allowed his gaze to drift over her shoulder, her waist, where he saw the outer edge of her new brand. He continued to the curve of her hip and toned legs. She wasn't a child, much as he'd like to see her that way. Should see her that way. He had no right to look at her and feel a stirring anywhere.

There wasn't much that aroused him anymore, though he did enjoy the sensual pleasures of life. Right now his body had decided that the sight of her was one of those pleasures. He stood, cursing softly, and dressed.

Ruby flexed her fingers, then opened her eyes the very moment he pulled on his pants. Her gaze went right to him, and she came back to herself in that moment. Flames danced in her eyes now, even as they widened with embarrassment. She sat up and pulled her bent knees close to her, tucking in her feet for as much modesty as she was going to get.

He turned away, picking up her pile of clothing and handing it to her behind his back. "Look at your stomach."

He heard her soft intake of air. "The rash, it's…"

"Your Dragon."

"You looked," she said, the accusation clear.

"I couldn't see it. Wrong angle."

The silence told him she was wondering what he *had* seen. He heard the shuffle of clothing being pulled on. "I wasn't able to get control over it." Anxiety permeated her words. "It took over, like you said it might."

"You'll get the hang of it."

"No, I'm not doing it again. You can turn around now." She brushed her hair from her face, and he could see fear in the tight lines around her mouth.

He stepped closer, resisting the urge to brush the stray lock of her bangs back in place. "You have to Catalyze again and practice gaining control."

She shored up her shoulders. "That's one thing you can't make me do."

"I know it scared you—"

"It didn't scare me. It freaked me out, like I'd been possessed." Her cheeks reddened, clear enough to see even in the soft light of the candles. "And speaking of, that thing we did, that I did…to you…" She rubbed her fingers across her mouth. "I've never done anything like that in my *life*."

"Interesting that you'd fixate on that over everything else you just went through."

"I think that bothered me more. I feel like I don't know myself anymore, like I no longer have control over every aspect of my being."

"The Dragon is a sensual creature, and it ignites your own sensuality. You'll get used to that, too."

"I don't have any sensuality to ignite. Why are you smiling at me like that?"

Hmm, he did have a smile on his face. "Because I know that you do now. Let me see your tattoo."

She lifted the bottom of her shirt, exposing her long waist and the new Dragon peering at him. It spanned from her ribs to below her waistband.

"Beautiful," he said, drawing his finger down the line of its back.

She froze for a moment, her eyes widening at his touch. Then she moved away, looking anywhere but at him. He noticed she said nothing about the pain she'd endured. Hadn't whined or complained about any of that. Only the kiss bothered her enough to mention.

His Dragon tingled at the memory of her mouth on his, her tongue sliding against his. Sucking on his. Igniting something inside him, too.

Forget it. You know damned well we can't—I can't let that happen again.

She turned to face him. "I can feel a soft electrical current going through me. Is that normal?"

No, it's this crazy chemistry between us. Then he realized what she probably meant.

"I'm so used to it I hardly notice. What you're feeling is the *Deus Vis*, literally the god force. That's the weird energy, as you put it, that emanates from the crystals that formed the core of Lucifera. It's what throws off compasses and electrical equipment in the Devil's Triangle. Some people believe Atlantis is out there because of that energy. After our people came to Florida, they discovered that leaving the Triangle weakened them. If they couldn't get back, they withered away. Our god essence needs the *Deus Vis* to survive. That's why Moncrief had to come back to Miami every two weeks."

"It just keeps getting weirder and weirder." At least she didn't look distressed. More like grimly resolved.

He tuned in to the energy around him. "What's not normal is the slight fluctuation you'll feel if you're sensitive to it. Solar storms affect the *Deus Vis*, even the flares that precede it. You've probably heard the Mundane scientists talking on the news about the large storm that's predicted to erupt tomorrow. They're worried about possible interruption of power grids and GPS when the wave hits Earth two days later. Crescents feel it in our bodies."

"Yeah, they showed a video of the sun's swirly red spots."

"Those 'swirly red spots' are the flares."

She made a face at him. "Why do you do that, repeat what I say with this patronizing tone?"

"I assure you, I don't mean to…patronize you."

"Augh." She threw her head back. "I'm sure you don't." She gave him a look that indicated her sarcasm. "So will this wave hurt us?"

"It mostly affects people who are already weak. We might get tired, irritable."

Her expression grew somber. "The newspaper articles I read at the library speculated that the boating accident was due to the Triangle's weirdness. Well, they had the weird part right anyway." She grew silent for a few seconds, her frown deepening. "They made my father out to be some whacked-out bad guy."

"All I know is what Brom told me. He saw a vision of mass death because of something affecting the *Deus Vis* and knew it was connected to a project your father was working on. Justin was secretive about the project, but it appears that Brom's warning was a wake-up call. Days later, Justin sabotaged his work and went on the run. For that, he was executed."

Ruby swallowed hard. "Why kill my mother? She wasn't involved in any project."

Looking back, Cyn now saw a Dragon fighting to protect her young rather than a villain. The memory stabbed him harder than any of her fiery spikes ever could.

Ruby pointed to herself. "And they wanted *me* dead. Me, a kid!"

"The assassin was probably ordered to take out everyone on the boat so there would be no witnesses."

"Who gave the order?"

Cyn's chest tightened. He had to be careful. There were things she couldn't know yet. She would hate him, would never work with him. He wanted to tell her as much of the truth as he could, though, so she would understand.

"It came through the Guard."

"What kind of police agency has *assassins*?"

"Our government and police force are primarily in place to keep the balance between the different classes of Crescents and to enforce Rule Number One."

"Mon mentioned that, and so did Leo. What is it?"

Cyn leaned against the wall. "Never reveal your magick. If the Crescent is found to have revealed the Hidden out of recklessness, he or she is terminated. If it was an accident, and the Mundane can't be memory wiped, he dies."

"So the Guard goes around killing people?"

"Not always. Generally they act in a right and just way."

Ruby's expression crumpled, creating a dimple at her cheek. "How is killing a child just?"

"That's obviously what the assassin thought."

"He was someone you worked with, wasn't he? I want his name, damn it."

"His name is not important. He was doing his job, nothing more. If he'd refused, someone else would have done it. Someone ruthless enough to complete the task."

She rubbed her fingers across her mouth, deep in thought. "I guess I should be thankful that he wasn't completely ruthless. Still, he killed an innocent woman. Maybe an innocent man. I want to know who he is, to have a face and name to focus my hatred on."

"You'll have your chance to confront him. But now we focus on you." He would tell her, when the time was right. Let her vent, gouge his eyes out, whatever she needed to do. Maybe it would make him feel better, too. But not before he trained her.

She stepped closer, her gaze on his. "Promise?"

"I promise."

"All right." She pressed her fingers together, a dangerous glint in her eyes. The same glint he'd seen when she held the tip of the letter opener to his chest.

Something about her fire ran through him like a flame across a thread. He had felt nothing in decades. *You can't afford to feel something for this girl.*

His cell phone rang from its place inside the cabinet. His first thought was Glesenda, but he didn't recognize the number.

"Hello," he answered, unwilling to give out any more information until he knew who was on the line.

"Cyntag, it's Peter Fernandez," the familiar voice said. A voice he hadn't heard in probably twelve years, the last time his mentor and former boss had tried to get him to return to the Guard. "Can you talk freely?"

Cyn glanced at Ruby, who stood near the line of candles running her fingers across her tattoo. "Half moon." How easily the code words came back.

"Understood. I'm giving you information at great risk. The mission that caused you to resign."

Cyn's whole body stiffened. "Yes?"

"The man who issued the assignment came in this morning."

"Name?" His voice gave away his tension, making Ruby glance up.

"*Smith.* He inquired about the officer who carried out the hit, if I was sure he had, indeed, carried it out. I assured him that he had but would not give out his name. He mind-probed me and said the first name of the Vega officer. Correctly."

"I see."

"*Did* the officer carry out the entire task?"

Ruby now stood before him with curiosity in her hazel eyes. No doubt piqued by his terse responses and the fact that they gave away nothing. "As far as you know."

Fernandez cleared his throat. "That's what I was afraid of. We should talk."

"I'm afraid I can't help you with that." Another call beeped in. Glesenda. "Thanks for the heads-up. I've got to take this call."

"I need you, darlin'," Glesenda said without preamble.

"Be right there." He disconnected. "Get your shoes on. We've got to get to the dojo."

He was halfway through the house when he realized Ruby wasn't moving as fast as he. Soon she'd feel the speed and energy of her Dragon even while in human form.

"The demon?" she asked, catching up quickly.

"Glesenda needs us. Which means things are seriously screwed up, because she never asks for help."

The Book of the Hidden

Garnet woke to the trembling of the castle's walls. Thump. Thump. Thump. The prince leaped from the bed and ran to the window, she at his side.

"Am I having a nightmare?" she asked, staring at the three-headed monster that crushed the forest and flattened the hills as it stalked toward the castle.

"No, it is the Black Doom." He gathered her face in his hands. "It's what we've been preparing for."

He'd trained her ruthlessly, loved her fiercely, and, under his spell, made her love him, too.

They turned Dragon together, flying out a window

large enough for their exit. Dragons, Deuces, and the few angels that resided within the castle came out, ready to defend and fight.

Opal darted in front of the monster's eyes to distract it, but the horrible beast swatted her, sending her crashing against the trunk of a tree. Her limp body landed on the ground in a feathery heap. Garnet let out an agonized cry. Anger filled her with its power, and revenge sharpened her senses. She and the prince pounded the monster, weakening it enough so that an angel severed one head; then a Dragon severed another.

"We must fight it together," the prince told her. "Use our Breath to incinerate it."

She inhaled, as he did, and expelled a Breath filled with spikes and venom. The monster roared and knocked the prince directly into the path of their combined stream. Her own lance of fire cut into him like a sword, making him arch in pain. The monster grabbed the injured prince in its huge fist and crushed him, letting him drop to the ground. Like Opal.

With his death, the spell wore off, and Garnet dropped, too, no longer Dragon. She had no time to mourn or to ponder the loss of the beast inside her. Once she had come from magick. Now she would conjure the power she needed. As the monster reached for her, she created an orb of fire and threw it. While the others distracted and pounded at the monster, it was Garnet who had to defeat it. Garnet alone, she realized, looking at the broken body of her husband.

And so she threw orb after orb, but none did more than singe the monster. Then she had an idea, one that came from her Deuce instincts. She created an orb that looked like a pearl and sent it floating toward the monster. It stopped warding off its enemies and stared at the luminescent orb that very gently landed on its finger. The monster tilted its head as it brought it closer, smiling at its beauty. And when the orb exploded, so did the monster's head. Its body fell with a force that cracked the castle walls. The castle's residents applauded and begged her to stay as their queen. But this place of beauty had been her prison long enough. It was time to return to her kingdom and find out what was left.

Chapter 11

I want you to stay in my office."

Ruby flinched at the order as Cyn drove. Though he appeared calm, she saw the flames darting in his eyes.

"What? You're the one who's always goading me to jump in, to not be afraid. Like hell I'm going to hide out in your office. The demon's after *me*."

"Which is my point. You're not ready to fight as Dragon yet. I don't know what we're walking into."

"I can use my fire Breath to hurt the demon, right?"

"Ruby, you're not listening to me. You are not ready, and if I have to focus on keeping you under control or out of danger, I'm not watching my own back, or Glesenda's."

Ruby crossed her arms over her chest. "You're saying I'll be more of a distraction than a help."

"Exactly."

"But I—"

"No."

"I—"

"Remember, Ruby, you follow my orders."

She let out a huff. "Remember, Cyn, I didn't agree to that." She hated the thought of being a liability. Truth was, she probably would be. She could throw knives and shoot guns, but this was a whole new arena. "What was the first call about? You got all tensed up, and from what I've seen, that's unusual."

"Later."

"I really hate 'later.' It's never good."

He didn't deny that, watching the road ahead. Damn.

"You'll see everything now. That will help. But always keep Rule Number One in mind. You can't give away the Hidden."

"I know, I know."

He parked at the curb and jumped out. She met him as he came around the front of the car. The harbinger demon wasn't out front. Cyn pushed open the door, holding it for a second while he scanned the lobby.

Glesenda stood at her post behind the desk, talking to a man about their classes. All seemed normal, except her eyes flared something fierce. The man's, as he turned to follow Glesenda's dire gaze, did not.

Mundane.

Not so mundane, the four demons lounging in the lobby. Three of them were humanoids, she thought Cyn had called them. One stood at Glesenda's shoulder, licking at her ear. She flicked it away, trying to appear normal. Another was involved in a stare-down with Allander, the Elemental Cyn had shown her earlier. The harbinger lounged in the waiting area eating from a dish of hard candy. Suddenly, all four demons focused their creepy red eyes on Ruby, making her take a step closer to Cyn without even thinking about it.

She felt her Dragon stir against her skin. God, that was weird. Okay, not as weird as, say, four demons looking like they couldn't wait to sink their fangs into her.

Glesenda gave the man a genuine smile. What self-control. "We're about to close, but you're welcome to come back tomorrow, try a class even." She came around the desk and put her hands on his shoulder to guide him to the door.

He gestured to the same room where Ruby had first seen Cyn. "Can I watch—"

"Sorry, that's a private class."

One of the humanoids slid up to the man, reaching its rubbery hands toward his neck. Ruby started forward. Cyn grasped her wrist, mouthing *Rule Number One*.

The demon gripped the man's throat, its long fingers digging in. On the way to the door, the man tugged at his collar, obviously feeling it. Ruby strained forward again, and Cyn jerked her back.

"But we can't…"

Her words lodged like sharp rocks in her throat at his fierce look. As the demon and man passed Cyn, he swiped at the demon. It fell back, releasing its hold on the man. He quickly left, obviously feeling something ominous here.

Cyn locked the door, and Glesenda made her way over, the demon still close by.

She nodded toward the room. "Class full of Mundanes."

"Yeah, I thought so," Cyn said.

"One demon, I could handle. Two, doable." Glesenda

flicked the one whose long, pointed tongue was reaching for her ear like a snake. It flinched.

Another one moved closer to Ruby, and Cyn snarled. It backed up, but not much.

He said, "They know we can't Catalyze." His hand still holding Ruby's, he led them back to the Obsidian Room.

Obsidian, like the kind of Dragon Cyn was.

"I thought this was a safe zone," she said, meeting the gaze of the demon who followed close behind and trying not to shudder in revulsion. That's what it wanted, she realized, to toy with them.

"It's a courtesy rule that churches and other designated places like this are considered safe. That no one should enter with violent intent. Whoever's behind this doesn't feel he has to obey the rules."

Allander followed them, making to grab at the back of one of the demons.

"No," Ruby said, remembering that poor creature at the library. She shook her head. Allander paused, its brows furrowing. "Please don't get involved."

"Ouch!" Glesenda whirled around and stomped on the foot of the demon who'd scratched her, looking like she was stamping a bug. The demon backed away, hissing. Four blood-red lines materialized on her arm.

Cyn opened the door to the mysterious room. It looked like the one in his home, but the walls were padded. Like for crazy people.

Which she now was.

No, you're just part of a crazy world.

She followed Cyn's lead, filing to the side against the wall. Glesenda locked them in, the *click* tightening Ruby's chest and clawing at her throat. The demons were now locked in the room with them. Good for the Mundanes. Bad for the Dragons.

Cyn stripped out of his clothes and faced Glesenda, who was doing the same. "She's not ready for this. She's newly Awakened with one short session of training. I was going to send her to my office, but leaving her alone doesn't seem like a good idea now."

"I am ready," Ruby said, realizing she, too, would have to strip.

"I can take her out of here," Glesenda said. "But that leaves you alone. Even *you'll* have a tough time dealing with four at once. So no, not doing that. She'll have to hold her own. I'll watch her back."

"I'm right here," Ruby said, shoving down her pants and kicking them aside. "Don't act like I'm such a neophyte that I can't even hear you. I can handle this, now that I see the damned things." They were all looking at her. *I'm their target.* She pulled off her shirt and bra.

Then all hell broke loose.

The first demon launched at her, the others following. Cyn shoved her to the side and Catalyzed. She hit the floor as Glesenda, already a deep yellow Dragon, blocked another demon. Ruby's Dragon strained to be released, and then she Catalyzed. Power surged through her, along with a general pissed-offedness. Like hell they were going to keep her out of the fight when the damned things wanted *her*.

A *smack* drew her attention to a demon flying through the air right past her. It hit the wall and slid down, grimacing in pain. Then it jumped back to its feet, no worse for wear. Cyn's Dragon sent a burst of black smoke at the horrid thing. It dodged it, then reached for Cyn with its unearthly long arms. Cyn shot it again, the smoke like an arrow this time. The damned demon was fast, but not fast enough. Spike after spike lanced the demon's shoulder, its leg, and finally plunged into what might have been its heart. It dropped to its knees where a final arrow disintegrated the creature.

Fight. Kill.

Would she ever get used to hearing a separate entity inside her?

The harbinger still looked like an old man, but it sure didn't act like one. It leaped high into the air, aimed at her. Claws sprouted from the toes of its bare feet, claws that slashed down her scales. She bumped it, sending it skidding across the floor. It darted for her tail, and she remembered how the demon in the library had gotten hold of Cyn's neck by skittering up his back. She lashed just as it reached her tail, leaving a welt across its face.

It lifted its upper lip, revealing an even set of pointed teeth. She sent a blast of fiery Breath at it, burning off its clothes and pushing it back. Before it circled back to her, she flicked a glance at Cyn, who was facing off with another demon. He lunged, his fangs cutting into the demon's shoulder. It screamed and shot away, dark red blood pouring from the wound. Immediately it readied itself to attack again.

The third demon jumped on Glesenda. She whipped her spiked tail up and lanced it as it scurried along her back. It screamed, falling to the floor where it gained its footing and darted forward to bite Glesenda's leg.

Ruby's focus shifted back to the singed harbinger, its mouth curled in a macabre smile. Naked, it looked less human and more demonic. Its corded thigh muscles tightened as it readied to launch at her.

Ruby acted first, charging with her teeth bared. It stood defiantly until a second before she would make contact. Anticipating that it would dart to the right, she changed direction. Her teeth connected with flesh. It howled in pain. Before she could go for another attack, its rubbery fingers clamped her snout closed. She jerked her head back and forth, but the thing clung like a leech. Even crushing the demon between her and the wall didn't dislodge it, though the attempt gave her a screaming headache.

The harbinger's claws slipped beneath her scales, stabbing her flesh. A roar bellowed out of her, pain and rage, and this time she slammed the thing against the unpadded door. It fell to the floor, and she bashed her hand down on it. Her talons sank into its flesh all the way through to the floor. It screeched and wriggled and then bit her wrist so hard that she had to pull back as pain radiated up her arm. The demon bounded to its feet again.

Damn it, they were as hard to kill as cockroaches. A black arrow streamed past her to the demon, which dodged it by a hair. Cyn's arrow hit the wall and left a seared mark that smoked. The demon raised its hands, razor-sharp talons ready to slice. Its eyes shifted from her to Cyn, who had come up beside her. She heard Glesenda still fighting but didn't dare take her attention from the demon in front of her.

"Ruby, back up. I'll handle this one."

I want it.

Her Dragon took over, lunging at the demon. Her fangs sank into flesh. Its claws ripped the delicate skin around her nostrils. Warm blood gushed down her mouth and tasted of copper. Her blood. She fought through the pain, tearing into the demon, hardly able to hold on to her own creature.

"Damn it, Ruby!"

His long, elegant neck flashed in front of her, and then his gleaming white fangs as he snapped the demon into two pieces. Its eyes widened in shock at the dark blood pouring out of the lower half of its battered body. It fell to the floor and disintegrated.

She felt blood pouring from her nose and the sting of a hundred razor blade cuts. Her Dragon's rage at Cyn, for taking her kill, suffused her more than the pain. Was the red she saw her blood or her rage?

"Get control, Ruby," he said in a low voice, his fiery eyes holding her gaze.

The bucking horse threatened to explode into a frenzy. *Back down!*

She fought it, pulling the reins. Her Dragon started to throw her soul back, as it had in Cyn's room, and she struggled to overpower it.

Got...you.

It bucked again. *Or not.*

A weight pressed her against the wall, all heat and muscle and Dragon. Her Dragon pushed against the invasion of her space. With a burst of power, she wrested control, barely holding on.

"Got it," she said, her vision clearing. With a final gasp, she stepped fully into her body. Cyn was about to crush her. "Get off me."

The regal face, only inches from hers, assessed her. "Yeah, that sounds like Ruby." He finally released her.

"Learn how to command your Dragon before you get yourself or someone else killed."

He moved toward Glesenda, who was fighting what Ruby realized was the last demon. It was trying to get around the yellow Dragon, eager to sink its fangs into Ruby by the fierce look in its eyes.

"Glesenda, Ruby, Catalyze back to human, get dressed, and leave. I'll deal with this one." Cyn stepped between the demon and Glesenda, who immediately obeyed the order.

No. Her Dragon again, being stubborn. Or was that her own voice?

Everything inside Ruby rebelled at leaving Cyn to handle it, but if he had to restrain her again, that would leave both of them distracted, just as he'd said.

Damn it.

Ruby inhaled deeply and focused on being human. She fought the Dragon that hungered to fight. *Human. Now.*

The struggle for control reminded her of the wrestling matches she'd watched on television once in a while. She conquered the impulse and found herself human again. No time to revel in her victory. She pulled on her clothes as Cyn blocked the demon from slipping around him with a whip of his tail. He was right; she still had a lot to learn. He had a few scratches, and she was battered and bleeding. Dizziness assailed her.

Glesenda grabbed her arm, pushed Ruby out of the room, and locked the door behind her. Ruby's lips tickled, and she scratched, only to feel the slipperiness of blood. It covered the tips of her trembling fingers.

Glesenda was already on it, shoving what looked like

the contents of a whole box of tissues at her. "Hold this over your nose."

"Where are we going?" She felt even dizzier as the woman rushed her outside into the late afternoon.

"Apartment, upstairs right here." She gestured to the upper floor at the end of the shopping plaza.

An older man stepped into their path, his white hair and beard a tangled mess. His eyes pleaded with her, and she thought he was a homeless person. He wore the creepiest shawl she'd ever seen, brown and fuzzy and— oh, God, not a shawl but a demon growing out of the man's body like a strangler fig. Her stomach lurched because, in that moment, she recognized the face from her distant memories. Her grandfather.

He reached for her, uttering a strangled sound that might have been a groan or a word. Her Dragon responded to the threat, vibrating with the need to Catalyze.

Not here.

She jerked away before Brom could touch her.

"Go, go," Glesenda said, shoving her past the man.

Ruby glanced back as they ran down the sidewalk, dodging people who had no idea what they were looking at, other than a homeless man with mental issues. Brom watched her, his expression stark.

Glesenda unlocked an exterior door and tugged Ruby into a tiny foyer with an elevator and a wall of mailboxes. Ruby nearly tripped on the stairs, her knees so weak she could barely lift her feet high enough to clear the treads. A short run down the hall, a second to unlock a door, and Ruby was ushered into a neat, small apartment.

"Sit." Glesenda shoved her down onto a chair and went to the kitchen. She returned a moment later with a damp washcloth, which she used to wipe the blood from Ruby's nose. Ruby gasped at the pain that was settling in now that her shock was wearing off.

The door burst open, and Cyn rushed in, his gaze going right to her. "I've got her. Get back to the dojo before the class gets out. Clean up the blood all over the floor."

Glesenda nodded, releasing the cloth to Ruby before dashing out. Cyn closed the door behind her.

Her blood. But the pain and the thought of her blood on the floor wasn't as horrifying as what she'd seen. She clutched Cyn's arm. "Brom! Did you see him?"

His eyebrows furrowed. "No. Where?"

"Right out there on the sidewalk. He tried to grab me! He's behind this. That's why Mon warned me about him."

Cyn knelt down in front of her, pulling the washcloth away from her nose. He pressed his fingers around her nose as he examined her and then gently pressed the cloth back as more blood kept pouring down. "Are you sure it was Brom?"

"Of course I am. Well, pretty sure. I haven't seen him in fifteen years."

"That's my point. But considering Moncrief warned you about going to him, maybe he's back in Miami. Did he say anything?"

"No, only made some kind of grunting sound." She shivered. "And he was part demon."

That snapped his attention to her eyes. "Part demon? Describe." When she did, he said, "A parasitic demon. Ruby, I need you to Catalyze."

"Here? Now? But—"

"Your nose is torn in half, the cartilage crushed." He stilled the hand that automatically went to verify it.

"Don't. And you're losing a lot of blood. Didn't you hear yourself slur just now? As Dragon, you'll heal faster."

It was bad. She felt the throbbing pain of it, but Cyn's words caved her in. "I want to see—"

He wrapped his fingers around hers and tugged her to her feet. "Come to the bedroom."

Had she not been bleeding all over, she might have wondered at the alternative meaning of those words. And just to illustrate how dizzy she actually was, some part of her got excited by that prospect.

He helped her settle onto the three beds all pushed together in the center of the room. "Do I want to know what this room is used for?" she murmured.

"For healing. Like now." He turned around and waited.

Oh, yeah. Get naked. She pulled off her shirt, the tears and blood splattered all over it turning her stomach. *Let's not get sick now. This is bad enough.* She summoned the Dragon, feeling the surge of power, the need to *do* something.

Cyn, still human, pressed her down. "Lie still and heal."

"You like being bossy, don't you?"

His mouth quirked. "I like being obeyed. There's a difference."

She snorted, a puff of smoke coming from her mouth. He sat on the edge of the bed, his shirt unbuttoned and bloody. Also her blood. He examined her body, his fingers sliding against her scales. As hard as they were, she could feel his touch as though it were on her skin.

"What's a parasitic demon?" she asked, needing something else but the pain and his touch, wildly different sensations, to focus on. "Is it something Brom summoned?"

"Doubtful. From your description, it sounds like he was trying to tell you something. That demon was sent to make sure he couldn't. It insinuates itself into the throat of the victim, preventing him from speaking. Like a parasite, it's damned hard to get rid of."

A cold wave swept over her, and she curled up and started to shiver. A dripping sound made her look down and see her own blood splattering the sheets.

Cyn stripped out of his shirt and then shucked down his pants, and if she weren't feeling so very light-headed, she'd have thought... what? That he was being presumptuous? More arrogant than she'd even thought, thinking he could take advantage of her now? Or that he was so damned beautiful, she could barely put together any other thoughts.

Yeah, that one.

He Catalyzed, the mattress sinking under his weight as he climbed onto the bed with her. "You need a boost. You're still losing a lot of blood. Dragons can channel their energy to help heal another Dragon." He hovered over her, his mouth next to hers.

She moved closer to him, seeking his warmth. Only that. Not the raw energy of his Dragon, his sensuality as it filled her, coiled through her very being. Her Dragon— yes, *her* Dragon now—drew toward him. She could no longer fight it, closing her eyes and drifting into chaotic dreams about demons and Dragons.

The dreams went on for what felt like hours. No more demons, only two Dragons sparring and then nuzzling each other. In the way that dreams morphed without logic, she was human again, she and Cyn standing naked, still rubbing against each other. Her hands were on him, sliding across his skin. It was so real that she could even feel the slight bristle of the hairs on his thighs and then the firm skin of his ass.

Her eyes snapped open. And there it was, her hand trailing over the curve of his bare ass to the dip of his lower back. And like in her dream, they were human again, still on the bed. He lay facedown, eyes closed and head turned toward her. She was on her side facing him, her leg bent so that her knee pressed against his thigh. They were lying that close, like lovers, with his hand draped over her waist.

Her heartbeat bounced, and she swallowed hard. Was the jolt she felt because they were naked in bed together, man and woman? Dragon and Dragon? Her body felt alive in a way she'd never experienced before. Her Dragon shifted on her skin, as though it were trying to reach out to him.

A soft smile played on his lips. Oh, man, cold busted. She pulled her hand back, ready to come up with some plausible reason for why she was stroking him. Except he wasn't opening his eyes. And wouldn't you do that if you woke to someone touching you?

Which meant he was still asleep, having a nice dream of his own if that smile were any indication. She let herself sink back into that hazy state, easy enough when he was slowly brushing his fingers back and forth on her skin.

Mine, her Dragon purred as Ruby soaked in the sight of him. Hunger rumbled through her the way it had during her Awakening. Hungry for Cyn. The memory of attacking him when she'd Awakened didn't seem so shameful now. No, more like arousing. He had definitely been aroused, and she wondered if he was now.

She kept stroking his back, soaking in the sight of him. The heat tingling beneath her fingertips traveled to the vicinity of her chest…and lower. His olive-toned skin contrasted with the white of the sheets. He was so friggin' strong and gorgeous that she could hardly blame herself for wanting him. For touching him when he was asleep. She wasn't even a lustful person, too self-protective to let herself ache for something she couldn't have. Definitely not the kind to be touching a guy in the throes of sleep.

What she should be doing is getting off the bed and putting on her clothes. That's what a sane, logical Ruby would do. Except his hand moved up over her ribs, and his thumb grazed her nipple, which nearly made her gasp. She swallowed the sound because she did not want the moment to shatter. He let out a soft murmur, tracing circles that curled her toes.

His hand moved to cover her breast, squeezing softly as his thumb continued stroking her nipple. Which, it seemed, had a direct line to the place between her legs that now throbbed. Oh, boy. She was getting in deeper and deeper, and when he woke—

He slid his hand to her back and pulled her right up against his body, tilting himself up so that she was snuggled between him and the bed. Oh, yeah, he was definitely aroused. He nuzzled her neck and inhaled softly. "Ruby," he said in a thick voice.

Now the way he said her name fit the situation. He was dreaming of her, of touching her and holding her like this. This was definitely a dream, even if she wasn't exactly asleep. But she was lost in the fantasy of it, him wanting her. His whole body was wrapped around her, powerful and yet gentle.

When she pressed against his erection, his eyes opened. She saw the moment he realized this was reality, as he took in their intimate position. He disentangled and got to his feet, scrubbing his hand through his hair. "Sorry. Dreaming."

Oddly, she didn't feel embarrassed at her participation or desperate to pull the sheets over her body. She gave him a tremulous smile, unable to keep her gaze from flicking to his pelvis. "A very interesting dream obviously."

He stretched, flattening one hand over his erection. "Clearly. Christ, I haven't had a dream like that in ages."

"You said my name."

A small tremor shook him, though his expression remained passive. "You must have misheard me." He pulled a pair of pants from a drawer in the dresser and slid into them.

No, she was quite sure he had murmured her name, but she wasn't going to press the issue. He did not want to admit that at least some part of him wanted her, and he was probably right not to. Getting sexually involved would complicate their relationship. She definitely didn't need a complication like Cyn.

She pulled the sheet around herself. "How long have we been asleep? It's dark out." Only the light on the nightstand illuminated the room. She sought out a clock and gasped. "Hours."

"It's been a busy day. I haven't had two altercations in one day in decades." He rolled his shoulders, his muscles flexing with the movement.

She reached up to her nose, gingerly touching it. "Still tender, but it feels like it's in one piece again. Even the blood's gone."

"I cleaned you up after you fell asleep." The image of him tenderly cleaning her while she slept stole away any response she might have. He looked at her over his shoulder. "You managed your Dragon well in there. But don't get cocky. This time you got your face split. Next time could be worse." He balled up his bloody shirt and tossed it into a small garbage can. "Speaking of things splitting, I keep extra clothes in the car, at the dojo, and here, in case I don't have time to disrobe." He nodded to her bloodied pile of clothes. "Or if you get injured."

He opened a couple of other drawers and extracted a shirt and pants. "You're roughly Glesenda's size. When she came up and checked on you, she said you were welcome to use her clothes."

Apparently Ruby was as deep a sleeper as Cyn could be. She caught the clothing he tossed to her. "What do we do next?"

"We go to Brom's and find out what the hell is going on with him."

Chapter 12

Cyn drove to Miami Beach, where Brom had lived all those years ago when he'd brought Ruby to him. He hoped that, like many Crescents, Brom had stayed in one place. He glanced over at Ruby in the passenger seat of his car, running her fingers along the dash.

"Beautiful car. What year is it?"

His Dragon pulled against his skin toward her. *Want.*

He rubbed his shoulder. *Submit. Not yours.* "Fifty-seven. Saw it in the showroom and couldn't resist." He'd felt passion then, at least he thought he did. One decade ran into another, the fire for life ebbing with them.

"Did you buy it new?" She rubbed the bridge of her nose. "God, what a question. But you did, didn't you?"

"Back when they made real cars. When Miami was much smaller, a tourist and retirement destination. When life was interesting."

Waking up to find her in his arms had been mind-blowing. The fact that she'd been a willing captive was even more interesting because he was pretty sure she hadn't woke the moment he had. In his dream, she was stroking his back. That's how it had started, but he was a bit muddled on what was real and what was not. Did she normally have a man in bed with her to stroke? He doubted it, or she would have mentioned him by now. He thought of the young Dragon at the Yard who desired her. Ire prickled through him, which was ridiculous because he had no use for those kinds of feelings. Especially where Ruby was concerned.

Ruby who was not a girl. The red shirt molded her chest, and hell, he'd seen enough of her to know her curves were all woman. Had, in fact, felt those curves, or at least he had a vivid dream memory of squeezing one of those delectable breasts, feeling the peak stiffen. His fingers flexed at the thought.

Had she even noticed that she moved differently now that her Dragon was awake? That her hips swayed and confidence injected her with sensuality? *He* shouldn't be noticing.

"Why isn't life interesting anymore?" she asked.

He trained his gaze on the road ahead, always a good idea when driving in Miami. "When you've lived as long as I have, there isn't anything else to do. I've fought, killed, nearly been killed. I've lost friends, lost the freedom to fly, to be Dragon. You get to a point where you don't care about anything."

"Even staying alive?"

He shrugged. "As long as I don't die because some damned demon or Dragon got the best of me." The upside to not caring was that he didn't have to fear losing anything. Or anyone. The downside? Not caring about anything. Or anyone.

"Dragons can't fly? We have wings."

"It's against the law now. In the 1700s, when I was born, Miami was largely unpopulated by Mundanes. It wasn't until the 1870s that developers came in hordes. During the population booms, we only flew in the dark, soaring through the night skies with the glitter of stars and moonlight on our scales. With the development of satellites and radar, airplanes and cameras, we can't take the chance anymore. Can you imagine those videos up on YouTube?"

Younger generations didn't know the singular experience of soaring through the night sky, the wind tugging at their wings. A shame. Then again, it was probably worse to know a pleasure one could no longer experience.

Yes, much worse.

His gaze went to her mouth, and he remembered how it had felt on his. Another pleasure he could not have again.

She faced him, her head tilted as she studied him. "You care about flying. I heard something in your voice. Emotion, nostalgia, longing."

"Your imagination."

"Yeah, right. So what if Crescents did come out of the closet, so to speak? Rule Number One seems pretty severe to me. And very restrictive."

"Before Miami was populated, the Crescents didn't hide their powers. A group of settlers pretended to be our friends, but one night they ambushed Crescents in their own homes. They killed over a hundred of us before they were stopped."

"That's terrible."

He only nodded, not letting himself go back to that dark, moonless night. "The Concilium has discussed it over the years, but ultimately the Rule has remained. People are afraid of what they don't understand. Especially when it's dangerous."

"I guess they'd get pretty freaked out to learn that there are Dragons among us. I sure did."

How far she'd come. "That call I took earlier was from my former boss. The man who ordered your family's murder just contacted him, suspicious that the assassin did not complete the assignment. Somehow Mr. Smith"—his expression told her it was the anonymous kind of Smith—"has figured out that you're Justin's daughter, alive and well. Which confirms for me that he's the one who sent that star orb. His target was Moncrief, but he could see you through the orb. The question is, why did he go after Moncrief to begin with?"

"Mon's phone showed a call from Brom a short time before he called me to come over. And he did warn me that seeing Brom was dangerous."

"So maybe Mr. Smith was spying on Brom and heard whatever it is that's brought him back to Miami. He couldn't kill Brom so he sent a parasitic demon instead. He does kill Moncrief because he knows too much. And that could be why you're a target, too." The thought of them hunting her tightened his chest. "But why is he trying so hard? It's not like you've gone to the Guard or Concilium to report anything."

She gripped the door handle. "If I get my hands—or talons—on him first, I'll kill him."

"Remember what I said about letting emotion drive you. I've seen revenge backfire when fury gets the best of someone."

As they drove through Brom's old neighborhood,

Ruby did a double take at a man walking his dog on the sidewalk. "That man was a Crescent. I saw that mist swirling in his eyes."

"They tend to congregate in the same areas, like the Cubans, Haitians, and any peoples of a different culture do. For us, it lessens the chance of accidentally exposing our magick to a Mundane. And minimizes people wondering why you don't age."

"Why did your former boss call *you*? Why not call the assassin?"

"He figured I might know where he is."

"What is he like? A vicious killer. Cold. A Dragon, right?"

"Yes to all the above." He slowed down in front of a gated entrance similar to his. "Crescents also value privacy. Many of us bought our properties before the big boom. We've had a long time to cultivate hedges and other privacy measures."

"I vaguely remember coming here. Mon was usually here, too."

Cyn drove past the closed gate and pulled in to a public beach access. "We'll come in from the back. Just in case." He reached beneath the seat and pulled out an ornate wooden stick that was about a hundred years old.

"What's that?" she asked as she got out.

"Walking stick."

It didn't have a hooked handle like a cane, only a rounded knob at the top that was a perfect fit for his hand.

She came around and met him at the front of the car. "I saw you teaching cane fighting. I've never heard of that."

He flipped the stick and pressed it across her collarbone. "I want to teach you some of the basics. It's a great weapon, one you can take everywhere."

She plucked the stick from his grip, hefting it in her hands. "Why would I want to use this when I can become a snarling beast with fangs?"

"Because you can't do that just anyplace. Even in the dark there's a chance of being spotted."

They walked toward the beach, and she ran her fingers down the length of the stick. She might as well have been stroking him again because he could *feel* her fingers. But it wasn't his back that he wanted her to touch.

Maybe she was thinking the same thing because she abruptly handed it back to him. "We're not ugly. You were right; we're magnificent. If I don't say so myself."

He smiled though she couldn't see it. "Indeed. There's a rocky history between Deuces and Dragons. The fighting goes back to the gods, who argued about who was the first to hold magick and whose magick was better. They see us as drooling, stinky beasts, and we see them as pompous douche bags." He didn't pardon his French.

"Is that why Mon hated you?"

"Part of it." He found it almost impossible to deceive her. What the hell was wrong with him?

Moonlight shimmered across the water, calling him to fly. He'd fallen a step behind her so he could keep an eye on anything that might sneak up on them. Their feet made *shush-shush* sounds as they trudged through the thick sand. Ruby had braided her hair though he liked it better loose. The braid probably represented her need for control and order. And her hair *was* pretty wild. He could easily imagine his fingers tangled in it as he tugged her closer. He remembered burying his face in it, smelling the apple scent of her shampoo. He shifted his gaze seaward again because looking at Ruby in the moonlight called to him even harder than the prospect of flying did.

Not her. Anyone but her. Because he would make good on that promise and introduce her to the man who killed her parents.

She followed his gaze to the waves rolling in only a few feet away. "You were a pirate, weren't you?"

Her question surprised him. "Why do you ask that?"

She stopped and faced him, and the moonlight kissed her cheeks, casting her eyes in shadow. "The pirate memorabilia you have all over your dojo. If you're that old—"

"I'm not old enough to have been a pirate. They were in the area in the sixteen hundreds to the early seventeen hundreds, right around the time I was born. But my Spanish ancestors were. I've tracked down some of the booty they availed themselves of."

"A pirate heritage. Figures."

"Why do you say that?" He forced himself to continue walking, digging the stick into the sand.

"It fits you, that's all." She fell into step beside him. "Dark, dangerous."

Murderer.

A few minutes later, Cyn pointed to one of the homes. "This is his place." It was hard to miss the stained glass windows, even in the dark. "Quiet. Whoever put the parasite on him could be here waiting. Once we're in the privacy of the yard or the house, you can Catalyze if necessary."

She followed him up a trail toward the sixties-era house, with its slanted roof. Moonlight spilled onto the concrete deck but left shadows behind the many plants. A dim light was on inside the house, and music floated through the air. His nostrils flared as he sensed the area. He picked up nothing human, Crescent, or magick. He broke one of the rear windows and pulled open the door.

"It's clear."

She grimaced. "Smells musty. Did he really go crazy? He looked crazy." Revulsion reverberated in her voice.

"After your parents died, he went crazy with grief. With impotency." He flicked on a light switch.

"He had ED? Do I really need to know this?"

He laughed despite himself. "I forget that word is now used for sexual issues. It's damned irritating when society changes what a word means. Gay. Bitch. Ass. Somehow they gained different meanings." He opened the fridge, finding no stores of food. "Imagine having the power to see the future and then not being able to save those who mean the most to you."

"Leo said something about him saving a bunch of people."

Cyn nodded. "His failure to save Justin and your mom pushed him over the edge."

"And sent him to a mental hospital. I never heard from him, not even on Christmas or my birthday."

And that hurt. He could hear it in her voice. "But now you know that he was actually trying to protect you."

Her pained expression softened. "Yeah, I guess you're right."

He moved through Brom's house, small by beachfront standards. Most homes of this era had been razed and replaced by ostentatious monstrosities. Some of the old Crescents relished the past and kept them as they were.

"What the heck?" Ruby said behind him, as she must have also seen the claw-foot tub in the middle of the formal living room. It was filled with water and a large glass prism.

"Brom had this set up when I brought you to him all those years ago. When he saw the vision, and your father didn't want to believe it, Brom insisted they consult a guy Justin befriended at college. Jay had figured out a way to see the *Deus Vis*. Normally it looks like ribbons shifting like kelp in a gentle ocean current. A solar storm will make it fluctuate, so it's less stable. But Brom said when he checked it, the ribbons were vibrating so hard they were almost breaking apart. He called it fracturing."

Cyn picked up the long black light on the floor and flicked the switch. He held the light over the surface, bringing ribbons inside the water to life. Disintegrating ribbons. "This is why Brom came back. He must have had another vision about the *Deus Vis* fracturing, returned to Miami, and put this together to confirm it."

Ruby stared at the ribbons. "So whatever my father was doing all those years ago is happening again."

"Looks like it. Mr. Smith wanted to make sure Brom couldn't stop him this time."

She met his gaze across the tub. "This is what keeps us alive, right? So if these ribbons fracture, a lot of people could die."

He snapped the light off. "Will die."

Suddenly this was bigger than Ruby, demons, and Moncrief's death. They remained there for several seconds as that sank in.

Finally she blinked and looked down, then reached for

a journal that was lying next to a pen. She flipped through the pages. "It's blank, like Mon's book. Does this mean he's dead?"

"Moncrief's book was created with illusion. It looks like Brom was writing in this." Cyn searched the pages with his hands. "I feel magick. He's hidden whatever he wrote. Did Brom try to touch you?"

"Yes." Her mouth twisted in disgust. "He reached out like he was going to grab me."

Yeah, she must have really thought he was mad. "Brom can impart his visions to others through touch. That may be the only way he can communicate with us. We need to find him." He grabbed his walking stick. "Let's go."

They headed back down the beach, and once they were a distance from the house, he called Kade. "It's Cyntag. Apologies for calling so early in the morning. I require your Deuce expertise. I've got a book I need deciphered."

Kade's voice was husky with sleep. "Is it in code?"

"It's hidden. It belongs to Brom Winston."

"*The* Brom Winston?"

"Yes, and you didn't hear that name from me."

"You taunt me, Cyntag. You know I can't resist all this secrecy."

He chuckled. "Yes, I do." He slid a glance to Ruby. "I hear I'm a master manipulator, as a matter of fact."

Kade's low laugh rumbled over the phone. "Oh, yeah, I gotta hear this."

"Where can we meet? Like now."

Once he'd made arrangements and disconnected, Ruby asked, "Can you trust this guy?"

"We worked together in the Guard for a long time. Serving in the Guard is like being a cop or in the military. We've covered each other's asses, kept each other's secrets, and saved each other's lives. He's still there, so we haven't had much to talk about since I quit. So the answer to your question is: mostly."

"Why did you quit? Seems like you were in it a long time."

Careful. "It was time to do something else. I'd lost the fire."

"That's sad, a Dragon who's lost his fire."

Her words burrowed into him like a drill aimed for his heart. "It's just the way of it, Ruby. The longer you've lived, the more you've seen, the less you care. You've got a long way to go before you start feeling that way."

She touched his arm but quickly let her hand drop. "I wasn't worried about it happening to me. I was thinking of you."

The breeze toyed with the strands of her honey hair that had escaped the braid. He resisted the urge to twine one around his finger. His Dragon strained, pulling him toward her. *Want.*

He held strong. *No.*

Something about her sparked his soul, the first time he'd felt such a thing in...he didn't even know how long. She, of all women. Talk about karma.

He smacked the walking stick into his palm, feeling the sting of it. "Don't feel sorry for me." The words blasted out like bullets. "Don't feel anything for me."

The Book of the Hidden

Garnet returned to her castle at last, accompanied by Dragons to keep her safe on her journey. She had left her home a girl and returned a woman. A fighter. A widow. The Dragon Prince's spell must still dwell inside her, as his death was an ache in her soul.

As they neared, they were met by a band of villagers who shared terrible news. Much of her kingdom was held under the dark reign of the Shadows, even though their master was dead. Now Garnet and those who would fight beside her would banish them.

The word spread through the hovels and exile camps throughout the woods that the princess had come back to save them. Garnet gathered an army of Dragons and Deuces. Elves and fairies joined, too. One fairy, Emerald, took the form of a dove. Had her beloved Opal been a fairy all along? This dove would spy on the castle and report on the enemy's movements.

Emerald brought back both intelligence and the horrors of what was going on at the castle. The Shadows were killing Dragons and using their power to create a new master. And even worse, children were being sacrificed for their purity and innocence.

Garnet and her army readied a plan to take back the kingdom...

Chapter 13

———

Ruby and Cyn walked down a long dock, searching for the right slip number. Boats—scratch that—yachts lined either side, some occupied if the lights inside the cabins were any indication. A dog barked as they passed a sailboat.

She inhaled. "The smell of the sea and lapping sound of the water brings back good memories." Until that last hurried night when her father had gone on the run.

Cyn blended into the night with his dark hair and clothing. They'd stopped at his house to wash up and gather what they'd need in case Mr. Smith found where Cyn lived. She'd brought *The Hidden* to see if this Kade could resurrect that, too.

It was now a little less of a god-awful hour of the morning, nearly five o'clock.

"Here it is," Cyn said, coming to a stop in front of a vintage beauty fully ablaze with lights. Polished chrome reflected them like starbursts.

"The Guard must pay pretty well." It wasn't a huge boat, maybe the size of the one her dad bought right before the accident.

"When you get to the top, as a Vega, it does. Not like how the Mundanes pay the people who protect their citizens." He stepped easily onto the top of the edge and jumped down, then held his hand out for her.

She could handle climbing onto a boat, but refusing would make her seem churlish. Except as his hand enveloped hers, her knees actually went weak, which put her off-balance when she stepped down and fell into him.

"Sorry," she said, her hands automatically bracing herself on his hard chest.

His fingers tightened on her waist like an involuntary reflex. They both froze, gazes locked. The embers in his eyes danced, and she had a feeling hers were, too. She knew she should step back, oh, about now. And he should be letting her go. Neither of them were moving. She felt dizzy, then realized she hadn't taken a breath since his hands had gone around her. His mouth opened, as though he were going to say something. Or lean down and kiss her.

Yes, kiss me.

Oh, jeez, that was her command, not the Dragon's.

"Whoa, who's getting hot and bothered on my boat?"

They spun to see a man who was jumping down from the roof. He chuckled, low and genuine. Cyn didn't refute the fact that they were getting hot and bothered so she didn't either. The two did the manly kind of hug, shoulder to shoulder while patting each other's back. Kade was cast in silhouette, so all she could see of him was the outline of tousled wavy hair.

"Come on in." Kade waved for them to follow him into the cabin. "Thought this might be the best place to meet for unofficial business, and I happened to be staying the night here anyway."

Cyn looked around. "Suits you."

"There's nothing like being rocked to sleep. It doesn't hurt that the chicks dig it."

Kade assessed her the moment she stepped inside, his moss-green eyes revealing his curiosity about her role in all this subterfuge. They also revealed the swirling mist that marked him as a Deuce.

He thrust his hand at her. "I'm Kade."

His hand was strong and calloused and didn't give her the jolt Cyn's hand did. "I'm—"

"Garnet," Cyn said.

"Nice to meet you, Garnet." Kade slid a smile to Cyn. Yeah, he got it. At least Cyn hadn't called her Ms. Smith.

Kade didn't need a yacht to impress the chicks. He looked like a guy who owned a sailboat, a surfboard, and probably a Sea-Doo or two. His sun-burnished hair even appeared wind-tossed, though that was probably because they'd roused him from sleep. He didn't look like a police officer, that was for sure.

Cyn chuckled, tugging on Kade's flowered shirt. "Going Jimmy Buffett?"

"*Someone* was always haranguing me to get a life outside the Guard." He raised his arms out. "This is it."

That's when Ruby saw the dagger tattoo on the inside of his right arm, the sharp tip at his wrist. An elongated *V* with curved lines at the top was incorporated into the hilt. For Vega? More interestingly, the tattoo shimmered with magick, though it didn't move like the Dragon did. Her gaze went to Cyn's forearm, realizing that the faded scar there matched the design of Kade's *V*.

Cyn picked up some paperwork on the table, shaking his head as he tossed it down again. "Still working on your off time."

"But I do have a beer *while* I'm reading over the case notes."

"I appreciate you seeing us like this." Cyn handed him the book they'd found at Brom's. "Is there anything on these pages?"

Kade flipped through them, flattening his tanned hand on one every now and then. The fog swirled blue and gold in his eyes, and a glow emanated from his hand. "Yeah, but it's fighting me."

"'It'?" she asked, checking to see that the book was still just sitting there.

"The magick Brom used to hide his words is strong. Deciphering it is like holding quicksilver. I'll try picking up his state of mind while he was writing."

He closed the book and his eyes, his square chin lifted. "He wrote this in a frenzied state. A while ago, twenty years or more. It took a few days to get it all down. I can feel his impatience, his confusion over the visions." He opened his eyes. "Seers get bits and pieces, at least what I've heard."

"So he's not dead?" Ruby asked.

"Not that I can tell."

Cyn leaned against one of the cabinets. "Can you bring out the text?"

"I haven't done anything like this in years. Remember the Deuce who was killing all the psychics? He kept a diary, and he hid the entries with a similar spell. I can unlock the spell, yes. It's set at the beginning of the book when the Seer starts writing it. Unlocking it reveals the text in the same timeline that it was written. The murderer killed a psychic every week, then wrote about all the juicy details. Once I unlocked the first entry, I had to wait a week for the next one to appear. It's a wait-and-see process. You want me to start?"

"Ten minutes ago," Cyn said.

The corners of Kade's mouth turned up in a smile he aimed at Ruby. "Pain in the ass, isn't he?"

"You don't know the half of it. Well, maybe you do, if you worked with him."

"Skip the commentary," Cyn said, not looking amused.

Kade dropped into a chair at the tiny table and opened the cover of the book. He closed his eyes again and pressed his hands to the exposed pages. This time they glowed a brilliant blue, spreading out from his fingers until it covered the entire book. He spoke words she didn't understand, until she heard Brom's name, and then more unintelligible words. The whole book glowed now. She hoped it wouldn't burst into flames.

Her heart gave a jolt to find Cyn watching her. He didn't shift his gaze away as she'd expect a man caught to do. Of course, Cyn wasn't just any man.

The glow dissipated, and Kade opened his eyes. The page beneath his hands was still blank.

"Didn't it work?" she asked, coming closer.

He flipped the first page, revealing scrawly writing. She sat down at the table.

Cyn came up behind her. "If this is a vision of the future, it's not written in stone, right?"

"No, like any foretelling, it portends the likelihood of

the future given the intentions and events in motion now."

She could feel Cyn's tension, and his heat, as he leaned over her shoulder to study the writing. "Whatever this says is open to interpretation. Remember that."

"Yeah, okay." What was he so tensed up about? And why was he so close, getting her Dragon vibrating? The citrusy scent of his soap tickled her senses.

She pointed to a line. "There's my name."

Kade gave Cyn a sly glance. "Thought your name was Garnet."

He met him, look for look. "It is."

She pulled her attention back to the book. "Something about the Dragon...specifically you, Cyn, coming in and saving me. Sweeping me away at the moment of danger. Well, you didn't do that when that orb was chasing me around."

"Whoa. She's the one who evaded the star orb?" Kade said, amazement in his voice now.

Her gaze went to the dagger tattoo on Kade's arm. "When I was fighting the orb, I used a couple of daggers in Mon's office. They felt...well, now I'd say magickal. Like a current of electricity."

Kade nodded. "Sounds like they were charged with magick. Did they help?"

"Both times I hit the orb, it seemed to shrink."

"Damn, you hit a star orb twice? You're good."

"She got lucky. Don't encourage her," Cyn said.

Kade assessed her with a spark of admiration in his eyes. "Why not? Give the girl some credit. Takes some skills to survive one of those." He looked up at Cyn. "Hell, my friend, you've got your hands full, don't you?"

"You don't know the half of it."

She wondered if Cyn did that to other people, too, mirroring their words back.

"If you'll recall," Cyn said, now talking to her, "I did sweep in and save your pretty little ass in the library."

Her mouth dropped open at both his assertion and his compliment. She clamped it shut again. "Yes. Yes, you did." She turned back to the page. "Here it says, 'hide her away,' or at least I think it does. And then 'awaken.' So far, it's on target with what's happened."

"What did you save her pretty little ass from?" Kade asked.

"Demons," they both answered at once.

Kade grimaced. "Fun."

Cyn braced his hands on the table. "Summoned by the same Deuce son of a bitch who sent the orb, I'm guessing." He tried to read farther down the page, pointing to the words *Justin's work*. "He's underlined it."

She flipped the next pages but found nothing else. She looked at Kade. "We have to wait for the rest?"

"For however long it took him to write it down. There's not a lot here, I can tell you that. A few pages."

She got up and grabbed the larger book, setting it gingerly on the table. It reeked of smoke. "Can you bring back the words in this book? My uncle used magick to create beautiful fairy tales for me. Now they're gone."

He waved his hand over the leather cover, tilting his head as he sensed for the magick, she guessed. "Is he dead?"

She nodded, still having trouble saying that he was. She'd hardly had time to mourn the loss of him.

Kade shook his head. "When a Deuce creates illusions,

they die with him. It doesn't always work with demons that are summoned, unfortunately, or tulpas."

"Tulpas? What are those?"

"Later," Cyn said, picking up both books. "Time to go."

"Later. Always later." She looked back at Kade. "They're not good, are they?"

"She's newly minted," Cyn said at Kade's confused look. Apparently she should know all this. "Don't ask. It's a long story."

"In other words, *later*," she said to Kade.

Kade chuckled, but his expression quickly grew serious. "Sounds like you're in dangerous territory."

"You don't know the half of it," Ruby and Cyn said at the same time. He shook his head and headed to the door. "Have you felt any change in the *Deus Vis* lately?"

"Yeah, the solar storm flares are kicking in. It'll get worse once the winds hit, Crescents getting irritable, others getting weak. Nothing we can't handle."

Cyn didn't contradict that last statement. He clasped Kade's hand. "Thanks, I appreciate the help. And the confidentiality."

"This isn't going to put me in a position to lie to my superiors or give you away, is it?" Kade asked, following them out the door. "You know what I went through. I can't do that."

"No one should connect you to me."

Kade put his hand on Cyn's shoulder just before he could follow Ruby onto the deck. "You ever going to tell me why you quit so suddenly?"

She paused at his low voice, wanting to hear the answer, too.

"All I can say is, trust your gut above all else. If it doesn't feel right, it's probably not."

"I'll keep that in mind." Kade didn't look any happier with that non-answer than Ruby was. "Be careful," he called out as they left.

She waited until they neared Cyn's car before reaching for his forearm. "You had the same tattoo Kade has. *V* for 'Vega,' I presume."

He watched her trace the lines. "Yes, they use magick ink, inscribed by a Deuce with that particular skill."

"But yours is faded."

"They use magick to take it away, too, when you leave."

She saw the shadows in his eyes. "Come on, tell me. Why did you quit?" When his expression hardened, she said, "Oh, wait. I know. Later."

That actually got a smile out of him.

Cyn's body was plastered to her backside.

It wasn't an altogether bad feeling.

Okay, it shot heat through her, little electrical sparks down to areas that hadn't felt anything like that before meeting Cyn. And her Dragon was writhing in pleasure, which felt weirder than anything else.

They were in his workout room, and she was supposed to be learning how to fight with the walking stick. His arms were around her as he showed her how to position her hands on the stick.

"Hold it firmly, hands roughly shoulder width apart," he was saying just above her ear.

She didn't mean to, but she leaned slightly into him, her eyes closing for a second. Something about his body enveloping hers, the strength of him, made her feel safe. She'd never needed to feel safe before, never had a guy act protectively on her behalf. She was too tough to need a guy's help. Until now. And somehow Cyn and his protector role aroused her, too. *Get hold of yourself.*

She focused on their hands, side by side on the carved wood. "Like this?"

"Perfect." The word rumbled next to her ear. "You have excellent posture, shoulders even and up, body straight."

She swore her Dragon purred in response. Something had changed in the way she moved. Subtle, but definitely different. Since she'd Awakened, she had gained an awareness of her body.

And with sexy-as-sin Cyn around and half naked, another part of her body had awakened, too. Because for an old man, he totally rocked.

Without saying a word, he'd pulled into a music store on the way back and bought her a Red Hot Chili Peppers CD, which was now playing.

Her Dragon sighed.

"Okay, Ruby, pretend I'm an assailant who's come up behind you. If you're not expecting it, you'd have the stick down like this." He guided the stick so the tip hit the floor, molding her hand over the smooth top of it with his. "The instant my arms go around you, bring the stick up and hit me in the neck. The element of surprise only lasts a second or two, so capitalize on those seconds." He clamped his arms over her shoulders.

The problem was that it felt so good she didn't want to make him move away.

"Ruby? Attacking you, remember? Don't worry about hurting me. I'm tough." He was real tough, not her bluff tough, she realized.

She pulled up the stick, stopping it when it touched his neck. Then she twisted out of his grip and brought it to the side of his head, feeling like a baseball batter.

He didn't even flinch or try to stop the movement. "Good job. Do it again."

They worked for another hour, and she was glad he'd made her fortify herself with eggs and toast when they'd returned to his house. He taught her some general moves, for those times when she couldn't Catalyze and now, when she didn't have the stick. They moved past the Chilis back to the music Cyn had loaded into his music system, and Robert Plant, lead singer of a group called Led Zeppelin, belted out about needing a whole lotta love.

Which she really did not need to hear with Cyn periodically pressing some part of his body against hers.

She faced him, blocking his attempts to grab her. "So is this what you would have been doing if Mon had brought me to you when I was thirteen?"

"Yes. At the dojo though, in a class."

She knocked his hand back, hearing their flesh collide with a loud *smack*.

Her eyes met his. "And now I get private lessons."

He merely grunted in response, then lunged forward to grab her. Remembering the move he'd just taught her, she grabbed him back. Which, unfortunately, knocked them both off-balance. He tried to right them, she overcorrected, and down to the wood floor they went, her on the bottom.

He braced himself with his hands to keep from falling on top of her, which left him hovering over her. "It would not be effective to have the demon land on top of you."

He didn't get up, even though she could see the strain of his arm muscles as he poised over her like he was going to do a push-up. She could feel his heat, and more so, the heat in his gaze as his eyes locked onto hers. He lowered his mouth, so subtly she might have imagined it. Her body strained to meet him halfway. God, her Dragon was going nuts.

He suddenly stood, reaching down to help her to her feet. He'd been about to kiss her. So why hadn't he? She had to get a handle on her disappointment, and the fact that her disappointment meant she wanted it, too.

He released her hand the moment she'd gained her footing. "Now we do some Dragon work. I don't know how much time we're going to have here, or if we'll get back to the dojo. Still need candles?"

Oh, yeah, a challenge. She saw it in the glint of his eyes. "Yes." She had to stop letting him manipulate her.

He had a lazy sway to his gait as he walked over and lit the candles. She hit the lights, plunging the room into a den of candlelight.

"You're going to have to grow up and get over the candles," he said as he returned.

"In case you haven't noticed, I am grown up." She pulled off her shirt and tossed it to the floor, her gaze on him.

He paused, embers flickering in his eyes. "Ruby, don't do that."

"Do what?" She pushed down her pants and kicked them off.

"Play the seductress. This is not the time nor the place for it."

She laughed, more of a sputter. "Me, a seductress? You're kidding, right?" Like she could seduce a man like him.

He did not seem to share her amusement. Or her disbelief. "Look at yourself."

She found her reflection, taking in the cant of her hips and the swell of her breasts because of the way she stood straight and confident. The soft, undulating light played over her skin. "I'm..."

"Beautiful."

She met his gaze in the mirror, her heart thudding at the way he'd said the word, the way he'd meant it. "I was going to say different. I feel different since you Awakened me."

"It's the Dragon. They're very sensual creatures, and now that sensuality flows through your veins."

Yes, it did.

"So that's why I threw myself at you?"

"The only reason."

"Then why did you kiss me back?"

He shrugged. "Caught up in the moment. Let's get to work."

She Catalyzed. He shucked his pants and became Dragon, too. She charged him, eager to release some of her pent-up energy. If she battered him a bit, all the better, since he was the source of it. She rammed into his shoulder, bouncing back because he didn't budge.

"Give me what you got, Ruby."

Sheesh, even in Dragon speak, he could say her name like that. She faced off with him, figuring out her next angle of attack. He lunged beneath her, lifting his head and sending her rolling down his back. She landed off-balance but bounded up quickly.

"Good recover," he said.

He swung his head around and pinned her against his shoulder. "As Dragon, your throat is your most vulnerable area. There's a kill spot just beneath your chin where the scales are thinner. Our enemies know this. Never let anyone near your neck."

Ruby knocked him back, freeing herself. She swung her tail at him, and he blocked it. The firelight shone and danced on his scales, making him as gorgeous as Dragon as he was as human.

"Do Dragons have sex?" she asked. "I mean, they seem..."

"Horny?"

"Yeah, pretty much."

He leaned forward, as though to nuzzle her neck, and then thumped her instead. "Watch your neck. Dragons would have sex if we let them. It's one of the reasons you have to be in control before you can even think of finding a mate. You can't let your Dragon go humping another Dragon. They'll kill each other. Not intentionally, but throw claws and fangs into a frenzied mating ritual"—he shook his massive head—"dangerous as hell."

She felt the shiver shimmy all the way down her body. *No Dragon sex for you.* Because Cyn's Dragon had some razor-sharp talons and killer teeth.

Curiosity got the better of her. "Dragons have mates?"

"Like all beasts, they seek the right mate. If there's genuine affection between two Dragons who partake in lovemaking, the beasts take it as being mated for life. They don't understand the complications that go with human relationships or concepts like irreconcilable differences."

They moved in a circle around each other, closing in until they were neck to neck, cheek to cheek.

She found herself playfully nipping his neck. "Sorry, that was my Dragon, not me."

He nuzzled her, an evocative growl coming from his mouth. With what looked like some amount of effort, he pulled back. "Ditto."

Against her will, she stepped closer to him again. "Our Dragons seem to be hot for each other."

"Dragons have no sense of right and wrong, only of what they want. Mine doesn't give a damn that you're off-limits. Time to Catalyze before they get the wrong idea."

Suddenly they were human again, side by side, their bare skin pressed together. Their gazes locked. She came to a stop, her chest so tight she could barely breathe. He, on the other hand, was breathing deeply.

"Except it doesn't go away when the Dragons do," she whispered.

"No, it doesn't."

He clamped his hand at the back of her neck and jerked her toward him, covering her mouth in a hungry kiss. She responded, desire exploding inside her. She was no accomplished kisser, but her mouth seemed to know exactly what to do, her tongue dancing and sparring with his the same way they'd just done as Dragons.

She nestled closer against him, threading her fingers into his silky hair. She slid her hands across the width of his back, the heat of his Dragon tingling on her fingertips. Like the night before, she followed the lines of his spine down to the dip of his lower back, over the curve of his ass.

He let out a soft groan, running his hands down her collarbone and squeezing her breasts. She moved into his hand, craving more of his touch. His slightly calloused palms created delicious friction on her skin. She pressed her thighs closer to his, feeling the light sprinkling of coarse hairs against her legs. She clutched at him, pulling him fully against her so that she felt the full length of his erection like a steel rod against her stomach.

Yes, yes, want—no need—to feel you. All of you. On me, in me.

He moved his hands to her ass and pulled her closer yet, as though he'd sensed her desire. His mouth left a wet trail down her neck, making its way slowly down to her nipple, which ached for his touch. She let out a small gasp as his tongue circled and tickled and flicked. And as he moved to lavish the other breast with the same attention, his hand cupped her mound and moved in lazy circles.

Warm satisfaction rolled over her. His fingers parted her folds and stroked the slick skin on either side of her throbbing, swollen clit. He dipped his finger into the well of her entrance and used her own wetness as he slid over and around every inch of her. Little mewling sounds she'd never uttered before came out of her mouth as his finger slid inside while he caressed her nub. And then he covered her mouth with his as she gasped, her orgasm rocking her.

She caught her breath, not easy as he continued kissing

and caressing her, and wrapped her fingers around his erection.

"Ruby," he said on a groan, rubbing his mouth back and forth across hers. He took a shuddering breath and stepped back. "I can't let this happen." He released her, still shaking his head. "This isn't right."

She was dizzy at the flip of emotions, trying to gain her balance both physically and mentally. "It felt pretty right to me." But then she remembered something he'd said earlier. "You said I was off-limits."

"You are." He grabbed up her clothes and shoved them at her. "I'm..." It was the first time she'd seen him truly thrown off. "I'm your sworn protector, and you're in a vulnerable place right now."

She tugged her shirt over her head. "Me, vulnerable? Did you see me kicking that demon's ass?" Oh, no. What if he was just using that as an excuse? "No, don't explain. It was obviously just Dragon lust. You made it clear that I was too young and not your type." She hoped he would negate that and look at her the way he had when he'd said she was beautiful.

He kept his expression carefully masked, his voice even when he said, "You are too young. Definitely not my type."

"So you agree that this"—she gestured to indicate the electricity between them—"is only because of our horny Dragons?"

"Yes."

"Nothing to do with Ruby wanting Cyn. Or...Cyn wanting Ruby?"

"Nothing at all. Once we're done with this, and we're apart from each other, you'll forget all about me."

Which meant the opposite was true as well. He would forget about her. All righty then. *Get that through your head, Ruby. He doesn't want you.* Even as he was doing everything in his power to keep her safe. "Why did you swear to become my protector? That's some serious business if it means laying your life down for someone."

The heat in his expression was gone, but his Dragon was flexing its talons and looking at her as though it would eat her. And not in the bad kind of way. Her own Dragon responded, aching to reach out to him.

Stop it.

"You were an orphan like me."

"You're an orphan?"

"You needed a Dragon to guide you, teach you. Since my organization made you an orphan, I accepted the duty to be that Dragon." He obviously didn't want to go into his own past, gliding right over it.

She remembered his expression when he'd told her about the massacre. "Your parents died during the Mundanes' ambush, didn't they?"

He hesitated before answering. "Yes."

"Tell me."

"I was sleeping on my parents' bedroom floor after having a bad dream. I woke to gunshots, and by the time I got up, the Mundanes were already running down the hall. My mother took her last breath as I gripped her hand. My father could only blink as blood poured from his head. The Mundanes ducked into each of our rooms, splattering the beds with gunshots, and then moved on to the next house. My brother was dead. I would have been, too, if I'd been in my own bed."

He had kept emotion from his voice, but she saw it in his eyes. "I'm sorry," she said, knowing better than anyone that no words could ever soothe the past.

He walked to the cabinet to turn off the music. "Get a shower. We're going to see another friend of mine. I'll fill you in on the way."

Chapter 14

Purcell lit a cigar and settled at the desk in the lab to study the latest solar event alert from the Space Weather Prediction Center. The experts had been warning about the solar maximum for months now, the peak of storm activity that occurred every twelve years. Two smaller eruptions had already passed the Earth with little effect, but the one that had just erupted was supposed to be a three or four out of five on the NOAA Space Weather scale. It would affect the Earth's magnetic field in two days when the coronal mass ejection hit.

That's what he was counting on.

But he had learned in the more than three hundred years of his life not to count on anything. Not on the company of his first two wives, whose lives had been cut short. Not on the fidelity of his third and final wife. He had lost two of his offspring during the earlier, violent years of Miami. By the time his remaining son was born—if he was, indeed, his biological son—Purcell had stopped caring about much. Darren had been simpering and desperate to please, going into physics just to make his father happy. As in everything else in his life, Darren was only average in his efforts.

Darren wasn't naturally inclined to the sciences, but he'd tried. His biggest achievement was introducing Purcell to his brilliant friend. Justin had an amazing idea about creating portable *Deus Vis* so Crescents could leave the Field for extended periods of time. He only needed funding, a facility in which to work, and privacy. Purcell offered him all for a cut of the tremendous profits they would reap. Perhaps Miami would be less crowded and less dangerous if Crescents could leave. Gone were the days when they numbered in the hundreds, when the different classes remained separate rather than interbreeding and muddying the purity of their bloodlines.

Justin's goals centered on offering freedom rather than gaining notoriety or profit. Purcell suspected Darren garnered a sense of importance from being associated with the project.

When Justin's last version disturbed the *Deus Vis,* he took a step back to re-evaluate his process. Fallon had felt the disturbance on the godly plane and saw it as a way to gain their freedom. That he and the other two gods in the notorious Tryah needed Purcell was an even bigger rush of power. Suddenly Purcell was infused with a higher purpose. Not only helping gods but also finding a more permanent way to clear out many of the Crescents. He had used financial incentives, including a yacht, to push Justin to continue. Brom's vision of mass death proved that they were on the right track, but it frightened Justin into destroying all of his research and prototypes.

Purcell got to his feet and wandered through the lab. Graphs, charts, years of work to re-create Justin's research. Once they'd begun disturbing the *Deus Vis* again, Purcell planted a scry orb at Brom's house in case the old Seer got another vision. Good thing, too. It had followed Brom to Moncrief's house, where he elaborated about his vision of doom returning and that Ruby could thwart them. Brom told Moncrief that he must prepare her to save Crescentkind. Purcell knew only one girl named Ruby, and she was supposed to be dead.

The door opened, and Darren stepped inside. "Please tell me that Ruby's been dispensed with."

Purcell shook his head. "The demons failed."

"*All* of them?"

"They have not reported back, and driving past the dojo revealed nothing out of the ordinary. I suspect this Cyntag Valeron is the problem. He's protecting her, probably out of duty because he killed her parents." Purcell huffed in impatience. "He's in the way."

Darren settled his glasses firmly on the bridge of his nose. "So we kill him, too."

"Clearly that won't be easy. He is old and fierce, a former Guard Vega. Our best bet is to get the girl alone. I am unable to create another star orb just yet." He held up his palms, still singed. "The good news is that my sources have ferreted out Valeron's home address."

He stroked his beard, staring at a chart. "Once we kill her and Valeron, we will have no more obstacles. The parasitic demon will make it difficult for Brom to alert anyone else, especially with only two more days left."

"Father, since I'm the one who constructed the reactor, I'd like to keep it here so I can continue to work on it."

"I feel better with it in my possession."

Darren's laugh was shaky and bitter. "Do you really think I'll snap and destroy everything like your boy wonder did? After all the work I've put into it?"

At least his son had moments of assertiveness. Darren took after his mother, unfortunately. Her whininess and manipulative nature had pushed Purcell beyond his limits one day, and she met the fiery side of an orange orb. His son had married a similar harridan. Freud could no doubt explain why.

The worst part was that this harridan was a Dragon. Darren had gotten drunk and had sex with Magda. Then she'd turned up pregnant, and Darren thought he was doing the right thing by marrying her. Even after Magda lost the baby, Darren hadn't divorced her. He'd gotten caught in the trap of wanting to please her, and fulfilling her wish to have a baby was his biggest goal. Purcell had made sure that never happened, though neither knew of his magick manipulation.

"I trust you. What I don't trust is the ability to get more demons. Once word gets out that the ones I've brought here have been killed, they might not be so happy to oblige. But I have another idea, a creature I haven't implemented in a long time." His mouth curved in a smile. "A creature I can have some fun with." He settled in to watch through the scry orb waiting by Cyntag's black car.

When Cyn walked out of his room, a duffel bag thrown over his shoulder, he searched for Ruby. His Dragon sensed hers, drawing him down the short hall like a bloodhound. She was inside his cells now, permeating his blood.

He rapped on the bedroom door. "Ready? We need to get to my friend's."

"Almost. You can come in. *If* you think it's appropriate."

Yeah, she was miffed. That was much better than naked and in his arms.

Says you. His own thoughts this time, taunting him the way they had all through his shower.

He pushed open the door to find her sitting on the bed looking at Brom's book. Not even glancing up at him. She thought he didn't want her. He released a soft sigh as he watched her. *You don't know the half of it, sweetheart.*

He'd never lost control with a woman before. Hell, he'd been minutes from hoisting her up, wrapping her legs around his waist, and driving into her. He had experienced lust, sure, but never this uncontrollable urge to claim her, take her…cherish her. Even worse, despite what he'd told her, those urges didn't just come from his Dragon.

She had one leg tucked beneath her, nervously twisting her braid and making a concerted effort not to look his way. "Another page of his notes appeared."

After being numb for so long, why did this inexperienced woman whom he could not possess have to be the one to awaken *him*?

Yes, he'd felt an awakening, too, when she pressed her mouth against his.

Need.

Yes, she did need him. To train. Protect.

We need her.

Cyn shut out the Dragon's nonsense. "What does it

say?" he asked, resisting the urge to lean close enough to see the text.

Her voice was somber. "He's written our names, underlining them like he did with *Justin's work*. It says I...need you."

Cyn swayed for a second. "Who else is going to teach you the necessary survival skills?" He gestured to a sketch of two stick figures, a swirl around them. "What's that supposed to mean?"

"I think...it's us dancing." A sense of disbelief tainted her voice. "Yeah, don't see that happening. And here, where the stick figure that's supposed to be you says, 'You have spirit, Ruby. You're going to need that.' You said it to me, and the Dragon Prince said it to Garnet. Garnet's father did something to cause the evil beings to overrun the castle. Just as they were about to grab her, the Dragon Prince swoops in and takes her to his castle." She tapped the book. "Mon's main story was based on *this*."

At least there was nothing here about how her father and mother had died. "What happens in Moncrief's story? What's she going to need spirit for?"

She rubbed her temples. "The prince trains Garnet, Awakens her, and then they fight a monster. It kills her precious bird...like the demon killed the Elemental at the library." That made her brow crease in a frown.

"You said Garnet kills the prince."

"Not on purpose. He accidentally ends up in the stream of their Breath. The Dragon spell wears off. Garnet has to fight using magick, because she's really a Deuce. She defeats the monster and saves her kingdom. It used to annoy Mon that I wanted him to bring the prince back." She snorted. "No wonder."

"Why did you want him back? You made it sound like he was arrogant and annoying."

She gave him an assessing look. "In some ways, yes. But he was alluring, protective, and he loved Garnet. And despite everything, she loved him back."

Those words trickled through his veins. "Moncrief clearly elaborated on Brom's vision. We've not seen a dove. There are no castles. Dragons don't drool or smell. So unfortunately we can't rely on his prejudiced version."

"Not 'unfortunately.' The prince dies, after all. Did Mon hate you that much?"

"We had no use for each other. Like many Deuces, he disliked Dragons in general. Given his version, he wished you were a Deuce, though he obviously loved you." He rubbed his hand over the page of Brom's book. "The real vision is in this."

Before their eyes, another few words appeared: *Ruby's destiny.* Also double underlined.

Cyn leaned closer. "He must have given this to Moncrief to translate for you, and he did it in the form of fairy tales. He figured if you weren't Awakened to Dragon, he could thwart fate."

She stared at the words. "My destiny." She stood, searching his eyes. "What is my destiny?"

"To face a monster, hopefully in a metaphorical way. To slay the person or people who ordered your parents' murder."

"With you. Because I need you."

The way she said those last words tightened his chest. He had to force his gaze to their names on the page, linked with the plus sign. "For now."

Her expression hardened. "Don't worry. I have no intention of clinging to you."

"I have a prophecy for you, Ruby. You will be the one to walk away from me."

"Why do you say that?"

"Trust me on this. Remember, when our Dragons are pulling toward each other, you will walk away and never look back."

Confusion creased her face. "Because I finally get my fill of your arrogance and the way you've shuttered your heart and cloaked your feelings?" She studied him, the hardness in her expression gone. "I've seen the wild flicker in your eyes, Cyn. I know you haven't buried your feelings completely. You don't have to be bored and alone." She turned away from him, tucking the book into her bag. "Just saying."

It wasn't his Dragon who ached at those words. He had found the perfect woman, the one who could bring his passion back to life...who had definitely brought his body back to life. And he couldn't have her. Fucking karma. Fate. Destiny, whatever.

He glanced at his watch. "We'd better go. Grayson's a busy man."

She hefted her bag, following him out. "Does this Grayson work for the Guard, too?"

"He has nothing to do with the government, which suits me just fine."

"Is he a Dragon or a Deuce?"

He led the way through the house toward the garage entrance. "Neither. He's a Caido."

"Mon didn't have any Caidos in his stories."

"He had angels, right?"

"Yeah, but he didn't have a lot to say about them, only that they had a weapon that looked like some kind of light."

"Legend has it that Luca, the supreme god of Lucifera, sent angels to police the situation after the gods became physical. They became physical, too. I imagine it was hard to resist temptation with gods partaking of carnal pleasures all around them. The angel/human offspring are called Caidos, which is 'fallen' in Spanish. They tend to keep to themselves for good reason." As she started to open her mouth to no doubt ask why, he added, "Which I will not divulge."

"Not even later?"

"Not even then."

"Do they have wings?"

"Sort of. Like our tattoo that becomes Dragon, their tattoo becomes wings. Not feathers though. More like energy."

She shook her head, her eyes wide. He enjoyed her reactions. Everything was old to him, but it was new to her, whether beautiful or terrifying. "What you do need to know before you meet Grayson is that he's a very old and powerful Caido, so don't piss him off."

"Now why would I go and do that?"

He raised his eyebrows. "You have a way about you."

She narrowed her eyes at him, probably ready to say something acerbic. But she may have remembered some of the things she'd done, because she only said, "I promise I won't hold a gun to his chest."

"That's a start." They walked into the garage, and he popped the trunk, then took her bag and set it inside. "Not that you'd survive a second after that. The only reason I didn't wipe you was because I knew who you were."

"Awfully nice of you." The sarcasm melted away. "Though now that I know what *you* are, I feel quite lucky." She meant it.

"Caidos are also sensitive to emotions, so try to keep yours tamped down. The emotional Dragons—Citrines and Carnelians—are particularly troublesome, and you, Ruby, are a Carnelian. And don't get caught up in the Thrall."

"The Thrall?"

"People get mesmerized just looking at them."

She leaned against the passenger side of his car. "So I should restrain myself from drooling, as Dragons are apt to do."

He laughed, because damn it, she had a way of making him laugh like no one else. "Yes, please." His humor died quickly. "There's one more thing you should know about Grayson. He doesn't like Dragon women."

"Why not?"

"A female Dragon captured and tortured him for years. I think the experience warped him."

"Oh, goody. Some guy who can probably incinerate me with a look." She gestured to her clothing. "But I'm the least seductive person around. Well, not *the* least certainly, but still."

He got in the car and, when she got in, said, "Don't underestimate your seductiveness, Ruby." She had other effects on him, too, besides making him laugh. A deep wanting. Throbbing ache. Effects he also hadn't experienced in decades. Or longer. He tended to lose track.

She closed her door. "He tolerates you then? I mean, not because you're...intolerable or anything. Well, you can be. But you being a Dragon and all."

He simply smirked at her and backed out of the garage. Once he'd closed the door, he sensed their surroundings. "There's magick in the air."

"Oh, *now* you're being romantic?"

"Not that kind of magic." He got out of the car and fought the urge to Catalyze. Even though his yard appeared private, he couldn't take a chance that some Mundane gardener was trimming bushes or that someone on a boat was out there with binoculars.

He saw the orb skitter across a branch just as Ruby, who'd gotten out of the car as well, said, "Are you hunting bugs again?"

"Scry orb." His Dragon led him to a large banyan tree at the corner of the property.

"That's what you killed in the back of my truck, right? The spy orb?"

"Exactly. Which means Smith has found my home."

"Oh, great."

He climbed the tree from the back side and spotted the orb perched on a branch. He needed to grab it before it flew away and would then follow them. Obviously sensing his magick, it crept down one of the many roots that grew from the branch back to the ground. Cyn reached down and snatched it, crushing it in his hand with both force and magick. "Let's go, before he shows up to pay us a visit."

Thirty minutes later, Cyn pulled into a guest parking spot at the Raphael high-rise. Ruby pulled her long braid over her shoulder and stroked the length of it as she looked at the sign. "Hah. The Raphael. I get it. So, what are we seeing this guy about?"

"Grayson is going to take you back in your memories

to the night your father went on the run. Maybe you heard something that might help us."

Cyn had only told Grayson that he didn't want Ruby to go any farther than the moment of impact. He didn't want to take a chance that she'd seen him and buried the memory. He wasn't ready for her to leave him yet.

Because you want her.

I don't want her out there alone.

"Cyntag Valeron to see Grayson Winters." He showed his ID.

The man checked his screen and gave him a nod. "He's expecting you. Go on up."

The elevator automatically took them to the twenty-first floor. The mirrored walls reflected Ruby to infinity, the back of her braid trailing down to the top of her waistband, her shirt not quite meeting it to reveal a slice of her skin. Her gaze met his in one of those reflections, jolting his heartbeat. He was glad the door slid open at that moment.

Grayson was already waiting, filling the doorway with his muscular bulk.

"Good to see you, my friend. I appreciate you doing this." Cyn made the introductions.

Grayson gave Ruby a nod. "Would you like a drink or should we get right to it?"

"Let's get right to it," Ruby said, rubbing her hands together in what Cyn thought was a nervous gesture.

Grayson motioned for her to sit on the leather couch and then sat across from her on the thick glass coffee table. "I'll need to put my hand on you to establish a connection."

Ruby nodded, her gaze on Grayson. "You can touch me," she said in a soft, inviting voice. Her head tilted, and her mouth curved in a smile. "Your eyes are beautiful, with little sparks like frost."

Even his tough little Ruby wasn't immune to the Thrall. Well, not *his* Ruby.

Cyn's Dragon clawed at his skin. *Mine.* Its tail swished down the center of his back.

Back off. Not ours.

Grayson's big hands rested on Ruby's shoulders. "That's right, just relax." He turned to Cyn. "Dial back the territorial feelings."

Ruby blinked, coming out of the spell. "You can pick up his feelings? *Territorial* feelings?"

"Surely Cyn told you about the whole Dragon-beast territorial thing, especially considering what I'm picking up between the two of you."

Cyn kept his expression neutral. "I'm her protector and teacher, nothing more."

Ruby hitched her thumb toward Cyn. "What he said."

Grayson took in their earnest expressions and shrugged. "Look, you don't have to pretend around me. I pick up feelings; I don't judge them." Grayson focused on Ruby again. "Go back to the memory you want to explore. I'll be there, but try not to pay attention to me. It'll yank us out of the memory."

Ruby sank against the back of the leather couch as her eyes closed. She was tough on the outside, but Cyn sensed something could shatter her protective shell and crumble her. He drew closer and watched as Grayson put her into a hypnotic state. What exactly was Grayson picking up from him? What Cyn felt for Ruby was foreign, like the rash she had described, an itch somewhere deep inside him.

"Daddy, what's going on?" she asked in a little girl's voice. She listened, as he must have given her some explanation for their last-minute trip.

"Who's he on the phone with?" Grayson asked in a soft voice a minute later.

"Darren, his lab partner. We go to their house a lot. They sometimes have me over so my parents can go out on a date." Ruby smiled. "Magda, his wife, says I'm her surrogate daughter. She pretends I'm her daughter sometimes."

Cyn moved closer yet, eyeing Ruby's tensed hand on the couch. He had an insane desire to hold it. *Resist.*

Ruby frowned. "But Daddy's wigging out, telling Darren, 'Brom was right. What we're doing is dangerous. I've destroyed everything. I'm taking my family and leaving.' I can hear Darren yelling, but I can't hear what he's saying. Then my mom's taking me down into the cabin, telling me it doesn't concern me."

Cyn said, "That's enough, Ruby. We've got what we need."

She shook her head. "I need to see more. Maybe I saw the man who murdered my parents."

"All you'll see is the Dragon. That won't be enough to identify him."

Cyn's chest tightened, drawing Grayson's attention to his pain. The frost glittered in his eyes. He knew Cyn played the part of an assassin during his tenure as a Vega. He'd probably figured out why Cyn didn't want her to go too far.

Grayson removed his hands from her shoulders, and Ruby snapped out of the memory.

"Why did you break the connection?" she asked Grayson.

"I can only hold on for so long."

Poor Grayson was picking up Ruby's disappointment and Cyn's tangle of emotions. Hopefully he also sensed his gratitude.

To make sure, he gave Grayson a subtle nod. "I told Ruby I would introduce her to the Vega who was assigned to kill her parents. But right now she has to focus on what's important, like saving her life."

She pushed up from the couch, her mouth in a pout. "I just wanted to see him, a tiny glimpse."

Cyn led Ruby to the door, turning to Grayson. "Thank you for your help."

"Anything for a friend." Grayson's eyes narrowed. "You've changed since the last time I saw you, what, five years ago. You were easy to be around. You're not anymore."

Hell. Before he'd been flatlined, emotionless; that's what Grayson was saying. And now? It was probably best that Cyn didn't know.

"That too will change." After Ruby stalked out of his life.

"What did that mean?" Ruby asked when they were once again closed inside the elevator. "Why aren't you easy to be around anymore?" When he didn't answer, she got right up in his face. "Is it because the previously unfeeling Cyntag Valeron has feelings now? Feelings he's afraid to admit?"

She had no idea the courage it took him not to act on those feelings, and yet, she called him a coward. He steeled that courage and pushed out the words, "I have no personal feelings for you."

The elevator door opened, and they walked out to his

car in silence. She leaned against her door, facing him. "So you would have no problem if I, say, approached Grayson for a date. You were right. He's friggin' gorgeous and—"

Cyn reacted before thinking, grabbing her wrists and pinning them against the car. "Don't do that."

"What? Make you jealous? But you have no feelings for me, so you couldn't possibly get jealous." She raised her eyebrow, an impudent spark in her hazel eyes. "Or could you?"

"You're trying to rile me up so I'll expose my feelings? Is that what this is about?"

"Yes." She glanced down where he held her wrists. "I'd say it's working."

Damn, but she had him twisted up inside. He leaned so close that their noses almost touched. "Ruby." This time he could hear that intimate tone she'd been accusing him of.

"Yes, Cyn."

"Don't toy with my Dragon. Trust me, you will not like the price."

Chapter 15

What *was* the price of toying with Cyn's Dragon? Ruby wondered as he drove like a maniac through the city streets. He'd cranked the stereo, and a rock band was singing about being bad company. That fit Cyn right about then, so she decided to back off from provoking him further. The price might be crashing the car.

Cyn was cool, calm, inured to things that would freak out others, like, say, demons, or a woman holding a gun to his chest. So inciting a reaction in him satisfied her on some deep level. Ooh, how he'd gotten pissed—no, territorial—when she'd talked about Grayson. Sure, the Caido was gorgeous, but Cyn was the man who did it for her.

What was the deal with her Dragon Prince? Well, not *her* prince.

"What's this Darren's last name?" Cyn asked.

"I can't remember. They were simply Aunt Magda and Uncle Darren, though I knew they weren't real family. I'd hate to think he's Mr. Smith."

"He's the one person who might know what your father was doing."

"Or not. I can remember Darren's snide comments about my father being secretive about his work. It seemed to really bother him."

"Right now he's the only lead we have. If he isn't behind this, maybe he can shed some light on the people behind the private lab they both worked for."

"Let's go by the Yard," she said as they approached one of the nearby exits. "I don't have a lot of things from my childhood, but I do have pictures of my parents. I'm pretty sure Darren and his wife are in them. Maybe there's a last name on the back. And I'd like to eyeball my place, make sure everything's all right."

"That place means a lot to you, doesn't it?"

"It's my life, my livelihood. Where I spent time as a kid when the world was good, and where I grew up and learned responsibility. And it's my one link to my mother." Damn, her voice had quivered. "This Mr. So-called Smith knows about the Yard, no doubt."

Cyn must have picked up on the emotion in her voice because he gave her a soft smile and switched lanes to take the exit. "Which is why we have to approach it very carefully. We have to assume something's waiting for us. You can sense magick, if you tune in to it."

"So we can tell if there's a demon lurking around?" There was some relief in that.

"Yes, but there are ways to mask it, too. And some aspects of the Hidden don't give off a signature."

"Yeah, that's great."

As he pulled onto another road, she said, "Yesterday you advised me to never kill out of high emotion. You described the feeling of someone's blood gushing over your hand as something you knew firsthand." She'd been holding a letter opener to his chest. It seemed surreal now, and so long ago. "You said we shouldn't go there then. Can we go there now?"

He looked like he was going to say no, but he released a breath instead. "Being in the Guard is like being in the military. Sometimes it's kill or be killed."

"What kind of people did you have to kill?"

"Those who violated Rule Number One. Crescents who succumbed to the lure of their magick, which means they lose their conscience and start using their powers for bad. Demons. Dragons infected by Red Lust."

"What's that?"

"Remember when I told you about Breathing Dragon, how Dragons can take each other's power? When I healed you, I Breathed out, sending my essence into you. If you kill a Dragon, you can Breathe *in* their essence and assimilate their power. You have to be very careful if you manage to kill an old soldier like me. Take more than you're ready for, and Red Lust throws you in a bloodlust frenzy."

"Oh, boy, that sounds like fun. Think I'll pass on that whole Breathing thing."

"No, take the power, if it comes to that. You need all you can get." He drove slowly past the Yard, doing that magick-sensing thing probably.

She tried to see past the sentimental aspect of the Yard and focus on anything out of the ordinary with her sixth sense. It was her ordinary sense of sight that zeroed in on the gap in the front gate, right next to where she'd hung the CLOSED FOR A FAMILY EMERGENCY sign she'd made before they left. "Someone's here."

She could *feel* Cyn's energy snap tight. Weird. He pulled way off to the side and killed the engine.

She whispered, "Demons don't have to unlock gates, do they?"

He shook his head.

"Maybe we'll get lucky enough to find the Deuce behind the demons."

Cyn's eyes flared with bloodlust as he searched the Yard beyond the fence. "I hope so."

Anyone—or any*thing*—could hide behind the thousands of items in the Yard. Her projects and investments and splurges, like the fifties toy car, could all be harboring some evil being. She and Cyn slid through the gap and walked side by side down the center of the Yard. Ruby found the old Dodge Dart and then the owner of said car, Nevin, who appeared to be painting his Cadillac Fleetwood table. She sighed in relief at the same time that Cyn muttered, "What the hell?"

"I know, it's shocking to see Nevin working when he's supposed to be taking time off." Except Cyn hadn't meant that kind of *What the hell?* because he didn't know Nevin was a lackey.

Which meant he was referring to something else.

Nevin walked out of the booth several yards away, pulled down his respiratory mask, and called out, "You startled me." He wore the same relieved smile she'd sported a moment before. "I came to pick up something and didn't see anyone here. Figured it'd be okay if I worked on my Caddy table." His smile drooped. "Why are you looking at me so strange?"

Not at him but at someone peering above a stack of flattened cars a short distance behind him. A stack more than ten feet tall. Ruby automatically clutched Cyn's arm. "What is it?" she whispered. All she could see was the top of a head with wild brown hair and a hint of eyes.

Cyn was laughing, only it wasn't an amused kind of laugh. It was one of those *I can't believe it* kind of laughs, which she knew was not good. "A tulpa. I can smell it from here. Damn, I haven't seen one of those in years. Get rid of the Mundane."

"A...tulpa?" she spat out on a vehement whisper. "You didn't tell me about tulpas!" She vaguely remembered Kade mentioning the word, and Cyn telling her "later."

"It's one of those things that doesn't emit a magick signature because it's not real."

The ten-feet-plus-tall human-looking creature stepped out from behind the stack of cars. Two cats scattered, but the tulpa thankfully paid them no mind...because it was focused on her.

"It looks like a kid!" Ruby whispered. "A huge, demented girl with *pigtails*!" She forced a smile as Nevin approached, but her gaze was on the tulpa. "Nevin, you have to go now."

He wiped his arm across his sweating brow. "I will, as soon as I'm done. I get it now, why you're all excited about seeing something go from junky to shiny and pretty. This is gonna look so cool."

The tulpa pushed a stack of carburetors Nevin had been talking about welding together as an art form. He spun around as the stack crashed to the ground, his mouth gaping.

Could he see the tulpa?

"Holy heck in a handbasket, what—" He spun back to Ruby. "Did you see that? The whole stack just tipped over. What if someone had been standing beside it? You were right, Ruby. I should have done something about that before now."

And that answered that. Nevin walked toward the stack. Ruby tugged at his arm the same way her Dragon tugged at her to Catalyze. "Nevin, it might fall more. Don't go near it."

She looked up, *way* up at the tulpa. The "it" she was really talking about smiled down at her. There was something oddly familiar about that smile. It wore no clothes, its body a vague mass of flesh-toned substance. And yes, it smelled like a sponge that had been sitting in dirty water for weeks.

The tulpa sniffed at Nevin, then flicked his head. Nevin stumbled at the impact, his hand to his head as he looked for what had hit him. "What was that?"

Ruby hauled him backward. "Remember when I said there might be trouble? Well, there's trouble."

He rubbed his head, confusion on his face. "Is that what hit me? What knocked the carburetors down?"

"Yes." She led him to his car, looking back to see Cyn standing between her and the tulpa, trying to keep it back. In human form, he didn't have the power he would as Dragon. "Nevin, you really have to leave now."

"Should I call the police?"

"No, definitely not. I don't want to involve you. And I don't want you hurt."

He looked pained, glancing over her shoulder at Cyn. "Ever since that guy came on the scene, you've been acting weird."

She wanted to laugh. Ever since Cyn arrived, she *was* weird. "Trust me, it'll be okay. Go. Bye."

He got into his car and pulled toward the gate. Cyn was throwing things that were awaiting restoration at the overgrown girl. A kid's bike bounced off the tulpa's hip. A Sunoco sign hit the tulpa's arm and made it frown. He was goading it, leading it farther back into the Yard. Away from the fence where someone could see them Catalyze, she suspected.

"What kind of world did I end up in?" she muttered, locking the gate behind Nevin's car and turning to join Cyn.

He was now in Nevin's territory, which meant general chaos. Stacks of parts, walls of crushed cars ready for scrapping. She circled around the edge of the Yard and came up behind the thing. She gave him a nod. He was safe to Catalyze. To be clear, she did.

So did he, his scales shimmering in the late afternoon light. Cyn lunged forward lightning fast, taking a bite of the tulpa's flesh, then another.

"Ouchie!" The tulpa swiped at him, missing by a fraction. "Bad Dragon!" it shouted, shaking its pointed finger. Just like a kid. It turned as Ruby crept up from behind and kicked a stack of cars, sending them crashing down. Ruby scurried back.

"Tulpas are Thoughtforms," Cyn spoke as though he were merely conversing with himself. "Not terribly smart but capable. Created by a powerful mind, given an agenda that they're pretty single-minded about. But they like the killing part."

"It looks weirdly familiar."

"It's you, Ruby, at the age you were when Mr. Smith had your parents killed. Sick bastard must have gotten it from the newspaper article. He's trying to screw with us."

"Ohmigod, I see it now. My hair. My eyes. How am I supposed to kill *myself*?" she squeaked. Yeah, it definitely screwed with her.

"Don't let it mess with you." Cyn approached, drawing its attention. But he looked as disturbed by the image as she was.

The tulpa picked up one of the carburetors from the pile and threw it at him. Cyn rolled out of the way, and it reached down for another one. Ruby took advantage of its distraction and started to jump on its back, but it turned toward her. The damned thing threw that carburetor at her. Ruby ducked behind a rusty Ford truck with an inch to spare. She actually felt the air as it whooshed past and crashed into something behind her.

"Ruuuuby," the tulpa called in a singsong voice, "come out and play with me."

It started to pick up the truck—the whole damned truck—when it spun around as Cyn obviously attacked. The truck dropped back down again, narrowly missing Ruby's foot. She scooted out and jumped onto the tulpa's back, plunging her talons into what felt like rubbery flesh. As long as she didn't look at it, she could kill it.

"Naughty Dragons!" it shouted, slapping its hand behind it and flattening Ruby.

Cyn swung his tail in an arc and stabbed the tulpa's stomach. It wailed in outrage and thrust its hand toward him, knocking a stack of flattened cars so hard that the stack started to fall. Ruby screamed as cars rained down on Cyn.

Before she could think to help him, a hand slammed down on her. The breath left her lungs as she fell to the ground, landing on her back. The tulpa lifted its foot and stomped down right over Ruby. She could do nothing but hold her talons as stiffly as possible, making herself into a big sandspur. The foot came down and jerked back up again, followed by a childlike scream.

Ruby had still suffered the brunt of the pounding, her body aching as she tried to get up. The tulpa clutched its foot and hopped over to a flattened car. Ruby saw the cars shake as Cyn tried to free himself. The tulpa smashed the pancake down on top of the moving piece.

"Bad tulpa!" Ruby shouted, pulling herself to her feet.

The tulpa scrunched its face up. "No, *you're* bad!"

Ruby needed to keep the tulpa's attention while Cyn tried to extract himself from the pile. In giving the tulpa her childhood look, Smith had also given it a child's behavior.

Ruby countered with, "No, you're bad."

Was Cyn trying to extract himself? Or was he badly hurt? She flicked her gaze behind the tulpa, seeing a Dragon's hand reach up and grab on to the edge of a car. When the tulpa followed her gaze, Ruby rushed forward and sank her teeth into its leg. Bad idea, though, as it kicked in an attempt to throw her off. She clutched the thick stalk with her talons until a big hand grabbed hold of her and plucked her away from its leg.

The tulpa lifted her to within inches of its face—Ruby's face—and scowled. Then it spun as Cyn obviously did something to it. Suddenly Ruby found herself the battering ram as she rushed down and smashed into him. They both tumbled to the ground in a heap of arms and legs and tails.

"You all right?" they both asked.

After giving each other a quick nod, they got to their

feet and faced the tulpa. It was picking through a huge pile of various parts, grabbing up a handful of fenders and throwing them at Ruby and Cyn. Like a child in a temper-tantrum frenzy, it kept scooping up headlights, rims, and pieces of jagged metal and hurling them.

Cyn pulled her behind a Corolla as a crumpled motor-cycle came flying at them. The car shook with the impact. He popped up and tried to send a deadly trail of black smoke at the tulpa but had to duck again as a tire sailed toward them. "We need to split up and attack from two fronts. If you can distract it like you were doing earlier—"

"When I was being crushed and grabbed and stomped on, you mean?"

"Yes, that was perfect."

"Really? That's what you want me to do?" With a growl of indignation, she waited for the next deluge and then darted out as the tulpa grabbed more ammunition. She launched up, as high as she could go, swearing she felt her wings unfurl for a second. As the tulpa turned back for another throw, Ruby hit its neck and held on. The tulpa tossed the handfuls of junk at Cyn before it reached for her.

He sent a stream of smoke at its stomach, and she felt the blast vibrate right through the tulpa. "Ow, tummy ache!" it cried out. When it smashed into a stack of crushed cars, Ruby took the brunt, feeling the sharp metal scratch across her scales.

"You're in the wrong place!" Cyn called. "I can't hit the target with you wrapped around its neck."

She tightened her grip as it took several loping steps toward the two-story metal warehouse. "I need to train. Just tell me how to kill this thing!"

It bashed her into the side of the building, and she had no choice but to let go. She slid to the ground with a hard *thump*.

"Not like that," Cyn called.

She sneered at him. "Smart-ass."

He sent a stream of black smoke that wrapped around the tulpa's neck. While it grappled for the stream, she tore at its ankle, sending it off-balance and toppling to the ground. It made an even bigger *thump* as it hit. Cyn tussled with it, like a rodeo stud with a calf, working that stream of smoke as he pulled closer.

"Get back," he said, his teeth gritted with effort.

He yanked and severed the tulpa's head. What looked like black oil poured out of the gaping hole of its neck and down its body. Then the whole thing shuddered and disintegrated.

Ruby dropped to her knees, exhausted and aching, automatically Catalyzing back to human. "That was fun." She looked at the mess the tulpa had left, and a laugh-hiccup sound came out of her.

"You okay?"

She pushed up, to prove that she wasn't a simpering female, and brushed off the dirt. She winced at the bruises and cuts. "I'm fine. I held my own, didn't I?" Damn, why'd she have to add the question?

"You did."

"We fought well together. I wasn't a handicap."

"No, you weren't."

And damn but she thought she saw pride in his eyes. "Any other information you'd care to share about creatures we might encounter?"

"Magick has no boundaries, no end. You would run

screaming into the night if I told you everything about our world at once."

"In other words, later. And you know what? At this moment, later is okay with me."

He was already walking over to where they'd dropped their clothing. She followed, seeing his injuries. Nothing too serious, most having started the healing process within seconds. Beyond those bruises, he was breathtakingly perfect. He walked without shame or self-consciousness, his shoulders high, his ass tantalizing.

"*Ruby?*"

The sound of Nevin's voice, filled with shock and a hint of accusation, floated from a distance. Where, she now saw, he stood at the gates watching her and Cyn retrieve their clothes.

She slapped her shirt against her chest. "Oh, great."

"This is when the clothes shedding can be tricky," Cyn said to her, pulling up his pants in one slick move. He moved in front of her, blocking Nevin's view.

"Fire ants," Cyn said to Nevin.

Ruby blinked. "What?"

"Fire ants all over us," Cyn clarified to both of them. He shrugged. "Had to shed the clothing because there's nothing worse than fire ants up the crack of your ass. Wouldn't you agree?" Because he sounded so unruffled, and snapped his shirt out while seeming to inspect it, Nevin had no reason not to believe him.

"You're good," she said in a low voice before taking the opportunity to dress behind the shield of his body. "And I thought I was a great bluffer." Not one logical reason for standing there in the Yard naked with Cyn, a man she'd met just the day before, came to mind.

"Yes, I am."

She met Cyn's gaze at those sultry words, feeling an answering spark in her eyes, and forced herself to look Nevin's way. "Please, go."

"I was just worried. What happened with the trouble?"

"This doesn't concern you. And don't come back until I call you." Why'd he have to become industrious *now*? "I'll explain everything…somehow," she added in a whisper.

Nevin gave her a wounded puppy look before turning away.

In an even softer voice, Cyn said, "You have to cut ties with him."

"I know. He could get hurt if something else waits to attack us here."

"And having a Mundane in our lives is dangerous for us, too. Rule Number One."

She bit her lip as she watched Nevin walk to his car. "I've complained ever since learning that I had to share ownership of this place with him. He couldn't balance a budget if his life depended on it. But now his life depends on me cutting him loose, separating the businesses."

"You care about him," Cyn said, heading toward the office building.

"I do. He's a stray, like I was once a stray. I have a soft spot for them." She leaned down to pet one of the kittens that was crouched between two coolers. It hissed and ran away, sinking her heart. "Must be spooked because of the tulpa. Red, it's okay. Come here."

The cat was looking at her, its fur raised. Then it shot away and disappeared among the cola coolers. Her shoulders drooped. "Now the strays don't even want me."

"Don't take it personally. Cats freak out around Dragon energy." He smoothed his hands over his hair, then pointed to one of the Elementals hiding behind a hubcap propped up against the fence. "That one seems to like you. He was following you around the other day." He curled his fingers in invitation, and the Elemental slowly emerged. "He's a fire Elemental, like Allander."

She knelt down as the creature with the red-tinged skin and large eyes took tentative steps toward her. "You said they don't talk. How do you know Allander's name?"

"Just pick a name. He'll tell you if he likes it or not."

She tilted her head. "Hmm. How about...Ziggy?"

It made a face that actually looked like a grimace. Cyn's expression wasn't as subtle.

"Fine. Fergus. How about that?"

The frown relaxed, and its eyes twinkled. Her heart lifted. She'd lost her cats, but maybe she'd gained an Elemental.

"As much as I hate to interrupt this touching moment..."

She shot him a look. "I've lost my uncle, my livelihood for now, and my identity as a normal person living in a normal world. So finally I've found a creature who likes me." She lowered her voice to a growl. "Give me a friggin' minute."

Chapter 16

⸺

Ruby led the way upstairs to her apartment, digging into her pocket for her keys. Home. The thought of being inside filled her chest. She pushed open the door, but Cyn stepped in front of her before she could go inside.

He flicked on the light. "I don't feel any magick, but I'm not taking any chances. Demons don't give off the scent of it either."

"Tulpas sure do. That must have been where Mon got the dirty-sock smell idea."

"No doubt." He took in what she knew was an eclectic décor, then opened her bedroom and bathroom doors. "Looks clear." He paused by her kitchen table, which was actually a 1950s Coke cooler with a glass top. Inside were some vintage Coca-Cola bottles. "I remember when they looked like that."

"I keep forgetting how old you are."

He took in her walls covered in framed posters, pausing at the SANITY IS OVERRATED one featuring a hamster that looked like it just came out of the dryer.

"These are my demotivational posters. They make me laugh. Want to see the one that reminds me of you?"

"Do I?"

"Be brave." She steered him to the one with Captain James T. Kirk's smug smile and the caption: I'M SORRY, I CAN'T HEAR YOU OVER THE SOUND OF HOW AWESOME I AM.

He wrinkled his nose. "You're so very funny."

"I can donate it to your dojo. I think it would look good in the lobby. We could superimpose your face over Kirk's."

He'd thrown on his shirt but hadn't buttoned it. So when he stepped in front of her, trying to intimidate her with his faux annoyance, all she saw were his perfectly formed pecs, a hint of the Dragon, and the hollow at the base of his throat.

He looked at her with eyes aflame. "Trying to antagonize me, are you? You do realize I could eat you for lunch?"

She cleared her throat, heat stealing up her neck as she met his gaze. "I'm not afraid of the big, bad Dragon."

Well, she was a tiny bit afraid of its ferocity and hunger beating a pulse within her. And the way she could feel the same emanating from him. The combination of dangerous, deadly, and sexy, those hints of his compassion...intoxicating.

"You should be." He slid his hands up her shoulders to her neck. "I could break you with a twist of my hands."

"Impressive." She mirrored *his* earlier use of a word for a change. She placed her foot on top of his, bracing her hands on his hips for balance. "And I could crush those tiny, delicate bones on the top of your foot."

"That could be painful."

"Work boots. Thick heels."

It was hard to sound threatening with the tremble moving through her at the feel of his thighs touching hers. His body heat enveloped her, shooting fire through her veins and making her Dragon tingle.

"Dangerous," he murmured, his thumb stroking her neck.

"Yes, I am, and I was even before I could turn into a beast. I could crush your balls." She drew her knee up the inside of his thigh but stopped short of contact.

The corner of his mouth twitched. "I've heard you can hit the bull's-eye on a target nine times out of ten, too."

"I can. But I'm not shaking like this while I'm aiming." God, she *was* shaking, too, trembling with need to feel his skin, to taste him. She grabbed the sides of his shirt and yanked him close, trailing her mouth along his collarbone, dipping her tongue into the hollow at his throat. When his fingers slid into her hair, she pulled out the ponytail holder and started loosening the braid. He finished the process and buried his face in her hair, inhaling softly.

He whispered her name, both agony and raw desire in that word, and claimed her mouth. She ground her body against his, wanting to sink into his flesh...wanting him to sink into hers.

"Cyn..." Yes, he was sin. She tunneled her fingers through his silky hair and then drew them down his back. His Dragon stirred, too, shifting against his skin.

She felt his hunger for life, for the fire he'd been miss-

ing for so long. Felt it in the way he ravaged her mouth,
the way he held her tight against him. Felt it as his hands
slid beneath her top and hungrily roamed over her bra. He
walked them several steps back until they came up against
the wall and ripped off her shirt altogether. She tore away
her bra, desperate to feel his touch. He squeezed, kneaded,
and then his mouth moved down her neck and covered one
nipple. His tongue felt exquisitely gentle and overwhelm-
ingly intense all at once. Her Dragon thrashed in pleasure,
filling her with heat. She dug her nails into Cyn's shoulders, feeling herself spiral away.

More, more, more.

She twisted so that his back was against the wall, pushing his shirt over his shoulders until it fell to the floor. Her
body pressed close to his, and she followed the faint trail
of hairs that led down to his waistband. She took her time
working her way back up again, closing her lips over his
nipple. Gawd, she'd never been so famished for a man before. Never been wanton like this.

He braced her hips, thumbs rubbing beneath the
waistband of her cargo pants. Pants that were too tight
now, too restrictive. He ran his hand over the front and
slid down between her legs. Even with fabric between
his hand and her flesh, hot pleasure washed over her.
And eager need. Too much between them. She unbuttoned her pants and pushed them and her underwear to
the floor before stepping out of them. As though sensing
her need, he nestled his fingers in her hair before sliding
between her folds. She was so worked up that just that
touch made her quiver.

He lifted her as though she weighed nothing and carried her to her bedroom. He nipped at her neck and tossed

her on the bed, taking her in with wild eyes that looked part human, part Dragon. When he came down on top of her, his mouth found hers again. He slid his arm beneath her, holding her body against his. Like he couldn't get close enough to her. She knew exactly how he felt. His thigh braced against hers, and his heat enveloped her. The energy of his Dragon thrummed through her, infusing her with a sexuality she'd never felt before.

Maybe it was just Cyn.

Definitely it was Cyn.

She put her hand on his face, feeling the slight bristle of stubble. He met her eyes, his glassy. He was as lost as she, finally surrendering to his desire for her. Something inside her shifted, deepening from lust to more. "Is this all Dragon, Cyn?"

He shook his head without even thinking about it. "It's us, Ruby. All us."

She smiled, his admission filling her with the courage to speak the emotions that were revealing themselves. "I want to make your life interesting again. Let me give you my passion and awaken you like you did me. I want to make you care again."

He curled his fingers over her hand. "You already have."

Then why did he look so serious when she couldn't stop smiling? Maybe this was a monumental admission for him. Then she would go one step further. "You're the first man I've ever wanted to give my heart to. And the thought of that"—she shook her head, laughing nervously—"is scarier than it was when I was facing my Awakening. But I managed that. I think this will change me, and I can manage that, too."

"Ruby, I can't—"

She pressed her finger to his mouth. "Don't say you can't do this. Being my protector doesn't exclude you from loving me. I'm not a child. It's not our Dragons, as you just admitted. There's no reason we can't act on our feelings."

He sat up, tension in his expression. "There is a reason we can't act on this."

She snapped her fingers as a thought occurred to her. "Condoms. To be honest, I'm not used to having to think about protection. So we don't go all the way. Because I think you know this is more than sex."

He got to his feet and paced by the bed. "That's the bigger problem." He paused at the sight of a framed picture on the dresser of her with her parents, then turned those dark eyes on her. "I can't keep my distance from you, an intolerable weakness on my part."

She sat back on the bed, her hands braced on her thighs. "You said surrendering was strength. And that's what you just did, surrendered to me. And I surrendered to you. It was a beautiful thing."

His expression spoke not of beauty but pain. "I promised I wouldn't touch you, no matter what my body—and my Dragon—wanted. That was hard enough. But now..."

"Now what?"

He rubbed his forehead. "I can't let this happen until you know the truth about me."

So this was about him. She came to stand in front of him and touched his arm. "I know you've killed people, that you're a...bad dude. That doesn't matter to me."

Her touch seemed to hurt him. He glanced at her hand

and then squeezed his eyes shut. "It was me, Ruby." He met her gaze. "I was the one ordered to assassinate your parents."

The words settled in like spikes, making her drop her hand and clutch her chest. "You..."

"I was the Vega they tapped because they knew I was ruthless. They didn't tell me there was a little girl, only that all the people onboard were to be terminated. I knew nothing about the targets—"

"'Targets.' Targets? They were my *parents*!"

"They were targets to me. When you take these kinds of assignments, you can't make it personal."

She felt as though she'd been dunked in ice, the air leaving her lungs in a painful whoosh. She stalked into the living room and got dressed. The buttons on her shirt were missing so she held it together with one hand. He'd followed her out, but she spoke before he could say anything.

"But it *was* personal. They were people. Son, daughter, parents to a girl who needed them." Heartache crushed her chest. She faced him, trying not to see the man whose face she'd just tenderly touched. Making herself see a cold killer. "Tell me. Tell me all of it."

"You're sure you want to—"

"Yes." The word came out brittle and harsh.

"I rammed the boat and disabled it. I've killed enough Emerald Dragons to take on the ability to swim like they do. I took on your mother first. She fought well, though I now realize it was a mother's protective instinct that drove her the most. But she was no match for me." He spoke in a low monotone, now as emotionless as he'd been before.

Parts of Ruby's heart broke away at the mental picture. "How? Exactly how did you kill her?"

"She lunged at me, getting close enough for me to lock my arms around her neck. She tore at me, but she couldn't move her head to use her fangs. So she used her tail."

Ruby felt a glimmer of pride at her mother's ability to fight someone like Cyn. "Did she hurt you?"

"Yes. Enough to nearly free herself. I broke her tail."

The blood drained from her face. "Go on."

"She swam back to the sinking yacht and managed to get onto the part that was still above water. I climbed up, too, and she shot me with her fiery spikes. Nearly blinded me. Something you should know, Ruby. Our eyes are vulnerable, as is the flesh around them."

She crossed her arms over her chest. "Noted. Continue."

"I grabbed her snout, keeping her from Breathing out. Then I pulled her head back and ripped out her throat."

He'd held back nothing, cold bastard. No, he wanted her to hate him, she realized. Something else occurred to her. "Did you ... take her power?"

He nodded. "It's customary."

She clutched her stomach, feeling it spasm. He started to reach out, probably an involuntary reaction. She batted his hand away. "What about my father?"

"We can finish this later."

"No, now. There won't be a *later*."

"That's why I didn't tell you before. I didn't want you to stomp off in some rage before you were ready to defend yourself." He gestured between them. "I never intended for this to happen. I was supposed to be your protector, nothing more. Every time we touch, it becomes harder to pull back. This time I knew I couldn't stop."

"So it wasn't that we were going to have sex that forced your confession." She reviewed the now painful conversation in her mind. "It was that I was going to give you my heart. And that was too much." When he didn't deny that, she shifted her focus back to the dark truth he'd revealed. "Tell me what you did to my father."

He trained his gaze to some point beyond her. "While your mother kept me preoccupied, he got you into the dinghy. With his last breath, he tried to keep you safe." He seemed to sink back to that moment. "He said something about them doing something dangerous. That he was just following orders. Then he pleaded with me not to kill his daughter." He rubbed the bridge of his nose. "I was following orders, too. I cut his throat. Then I looked in the dinghy and saw you."

She took a step closer, her hands fisted at her sides. "Why didn't you kill me?"

He met her angry glare. "You were an innocent. For the first time, I purposely failed a mission." His mouth tightened. "And no, I didn't get a pat on the back. I quit."

"Because you lost your killer instinct?"

"No, I lost faith. You have to trust those in control, especially in the kind of work I did. Once I lost that trust, I was done."

He'd quit over it. Saved her life at great risk to himself. *No, no, no, keep your anger. Think of what he took from you.*

It wasn't only his betrayal that hurt. It was how alone, utterly alone, she was now. She had come to see him as her ally. And more. He'd taken that away, too.

He touched you, kissed you, knowing what he'd done. Bastard!

She hit him in the chest, her tears blurring the stony look on his face. "You wouldn't have taken an assignment like that if you weren't a cold, heartless person. And I bet... I bet you enjoyed it, didn't you? Killing them made you feel something."

"Yes, it did. The hunt, the kill, is an adrenaline rush." Even now he wasn't softening the truth.

"Damn you!" She hit him again, hearing her fist *smack* against muscle.

"Control your rage, Ruby." He didn't flinch or move back, nor did he give away any hint of the pain she was inflicting. Did he have any emotion or regret about what he'd done? Not by the passive expression on his face.

She laughed, tears salty where they gathered at the corners of her mouth. "Control my rage. Yeah, someone as cold and ruthless as you could say that to me."

"Hit me if you want. But be in control."

"Even now, being my teacher. How quaint, the man who killed my parents is the man who would teach me. *Awaken me*." She spat out those last words because he'd awakened her in more ways than one. The anger took her like a wave, thrusting her up high and out of control. She threw herself at him, her words unintelligible as she pounded at him. *She* didn't even know what she was saying anymore. Finally, drained, tired and aching, she slid to the floor. She was that girl again, learning that her parents were dead, that she couldn't go back home.

He didn't try to comfort her, which both hurt and relieved her. She would have thrown off any show of solace. Or any apology, as if that would make a difference.

She used the couch to push herself to her feet when she finally got herself together. Her shirt gaped open, and she didn't even care. She avoided looking at him. "I want Mr. Smith dead."

"We'll make him dead."

"*I'll* make him dead."

Ruby turned to leave, but Cyn grabbed her by the shoulders, pulling her to within an inch of him with his iron grip. All she could see was his chest, red where she'd pounded him, streaks where her nails had scratched.

"Ruby, look at me." His dark eyes, the embers jagged, bore into hers. "You showed your strength when you didn't give away that a tulpa was standing next to your Mundane friend. Use that strength, that restraint, now. You need me. I know you hate that, but you need me if you want to make these people pay."

"I don't need you," she gritted out.

"Remember what Brom's visions showed."

The book. She needed to see if anything new had materialized on the pages. He wouldn't let her go, proving that he was stronger than she could ever hope to be. "You lost control just now, Ruby. That's dangerous. I let you go off on me; your enemy will not. He will take advantage of your lack of focus and kill you. Master your emotions."

He let her go. She stalked outside to the car, seeing him follow in the corner of her eye. She forced herself not to look at him, walking around to the passenger side but stopping short at the sight of the man hunched there, waiting for her.

Brom. With his demon parasite, if Cyn was right.

Out of instinct and fear, she backed away with a yelp. Brom reached for her, his eyes wide in desperation. The demon reached, too, with long spindly fingers.

She backed into a hard body.

"He wants to touch you, to show you," Cyn said, his hands bracing her shoulders. "I've never heard of a parasite transferring to someone else, but I wouldn't let it grab on to you. It's there to keep Brom from speaking mostly."

She shuddered at the sight of its "roots" sinking into Brom's throat. God, this was sick, crazy sick. "Can't we kill it?"

"No, because we'll kill Brom."

Cyn grabbed her wrist and jerked it toward Brom's wavering fingers. She struggled, but it was too late. Brom's hand clamped over both hers and Cyn's hands. She jerked with the impact of the images that bombarded her mind: people collapsing, gasping for air, writhing in pain. Children crying as they clawed at their parents' sleeves. Jack, right there at the Yard, stumbling against the Harley. Leo falling to the passenger seat of his car, driving right into the side of a building. Glesenda and others dropping at the dojo. Oh, God, a whole class of kids staggering, falling to their knees as they called for their mommies. The vision panned out, showing people falling all over Miami.

She saw a flash of her and Cyn fighting together, and then the vision disappeared. Brom had backed away. The parasite's hand was nearly touching hers.

Cyn pulled Ruby closer, his arm going over her shoulders. "Brom, what can we do to help you? I don't know much about parasitic demons."

Brom shook his head and made those horrible sounds she'd heard earlier. "J . . . J . . ."

"Justin? Is that what you're saying?" Ruby asked.

The parasite tightened its hold around Brom's throat, cutting off even those words. And then they both simply disappeared.

"What happened?" Ruby asked.

Cyn swiped his hands through the area where Brom had been standing. "The demon either cast an illusion of invisibility or took him somewhere else. I don't feel him so I'm thinking it's the latter."

She kept staring at the place where Brom had been. "Those pictures, people dying."

"That's the future," Cyn said. "And we have to stop it."

We. She and Cyn. *No.* She pulled the book out of the car, set it on the hood, and opened it to the sketch that was supposed to symbolize her and Cyn. Mon had translated it to a dance. Like she would dance with Cyn.

She turned to him. "Mon knew what you'd done. That's why he hated you, isn't it?"

Cyn nodded. "Brom understood that I was only a weapon, and he was grateful that I saved you. Not so Moncrief. We didn't have the kind of history Brom and I had."

"Of course Mon wouldn't want to turn me over to you when I was thirteen. You're the reason I was orphaned!"

She saw a fleeting shadow of regret. "He found that problematic, yes."

"Problematic." She laughed at the absurdity of Cyn's understatement. She couldn't bear to look at him another moment, turning the pages instead. But she couldn't not look at him. "You tell me to put aside my emotions, control them. That's easy for you to say. You don't have any." The acidic words tingled on her tongue. "Do you?"

She wanted him to admit that he did.

"No."

But she heard it, a sliver of rawness in the word. Grayson had picked up his feelings, though he hadn't said exactly what those feelings were. And she had seen Cyn's surrender. Even if he wouldn't admit it.

She wouldn't kill him. *As if you could*, her inner voice taunted. She would simply walk away from him, because the thought of that obviously caused him distress. Probably because it would compromise his role as her protector.

The thought empowered her. For about two seconds. She wasn't experienced enough to handle demons and tulpas and God knew what else would appear. She did need him, damn it. And it wasn't only her life at stake here. So she would focus, just as he said, until they killed Mr. Smith.

There, that's being logical and in control of my emotions.

No matter what, she would not let her anger or her heart soften to this cold killer. She turned back to the book. The word *Doom* had appeared since the last time they'd looked. "Mon called the three-headed monster in his fairy tales Black Doom. All those people dying, that really is doom."

"And your destiny is to stop it."

She walked back to the Yard, intent on finding out Darren's last name.

Cyn's footsteps were soft on the stairs below her. She had wanted her parents' killer. When she reached the top of the steps, she turned back to him.

"Thank you for not . . . for stopping when you did."

A clear lance of pain crossed his expression. "I shouldn't have let it get that far between us. Another example of letting emotions overrule logic."

"What emotions? You just said you feel nothing."

His mouth tightened, revealing his lie.

"Tell me, Cyn, what emotions *do* you have as far as I'm concerned? Am I this obligation you carry because you made me an orphan? Because I'm a helpless newbie? Or were you just horny?"

"It was part Dragon. The rest…doesn't matter. Not anymore."

She turned and went inside, pulling out the box of pictures Mon or Brom had managed to take from the house. She dropped to the floor and dumped them out to search through them faster. Seeing those pictures of happy times tore at her heart.

"Here they are." Ruby held up a picture of the couple who had been so close to her family. Whose house she remembered spending so much time at. Darren was a plain-looking man, wearing thick glasses and a warm smile. His wife was nicely dressed and wore lots of jewelry. Other photos showed the couples in Halloween costumes and sharing a Christmas meal.

Ruby rubbed her finger over the photograph. "I wondered why they, of all people, didn't come to see me after the accident." It had made her feel as though there was something wrong with her or that maybe people blamed her. Now she knew better, but to a grieving kid who'd lost everything, it made perfect sense.

She turned the picture over, finding their names marked through in black. "Sweeney." The name came to her, dredged from memory. "I'm pretty sure it's Sweeney."

"Good job," he said, and she realized she was looking at him, sharing the triumph of remembering.

She got up and turned on her computer, staring at the

screen as it booted up. Her Dragon, the traitor, pulled toward Cyn.

No. Not him, she told it.

But it purred. Purred!

Well, hadn't Cyn said they were fueled by instinct and lust? That was for damned sure.

She clicked on several links, but they weren't the Darren she looked for. "There's not much on the Internet about him, other than a bunch of those find-a-person sites."

The sound of cell phone keys beeping had her turning around. Cyn stared at the floor as he waited for someone to answer. "Hey, it's Cyn. I need you to look up a Deuce named Darren Sweeney. Find out everything you can about him."

While he waited for the person on the other end to retrieve the information, his gaze drifted to the pictures. One was of Ruby as a child, hugging a dog. He shifted his entire body away, and then she heard someone talking. Cyn said, "Great. And when you get a chance, could you look up a defunct lab called SUNLAB? I need to know who owned it. Thanks." He walked to the computer and gestured for her to move so he could sit down.

"Please, be my guest." Damn it, he should be contrite, not silently ordering her around. Why wasn't he trying to prove he wasn't coldhearted and ruthless? Or begging her forgiveness?

Would you forgive him?

Hell, no.

He went to one of the map sites and typed in an address. "Darren's a Deuce, which fits our profile. He's been married to Magda for thirty-two years, no children. And he's self-employed, lists his occupation as a physics research consultant." Cyn was zooming in on a house with the satellite view. A separate building sat several yards behind the residence. "Maybe that's where he does his research."

She twisted the fabric of her shirt. "It hurts my stomach to think that Darren could be behind this."

He gave her a sympathetic look. "He's the one person we know about who was involved in your father's work. And who could reasonably replicate it. Before we approach him, we're going to do a little investigating. We wait for them to leave and then we find out what kind of physics research he's doing."

"How are we going to do that when neither of us is a physicist?"

He got to his feet. "We take pictures, and we grab anything else we can get our hands on and bring them to someone who is."

Chapter 17

Darren's house was no mansion on the water. Still, it was nice, so his consultant services obviously earned him decent money. As with most Crescents' homes, tall, thick hedges surrounded it.

Cyn had parked in a church lot with a view of the entrance. He'd verified their presence inside, so now it was a matter of waiting for them to leave. Which gave him too much time in this small space with Ruby.

That was the problem with getting emotionally involved. It made you do ill-advised things, like nearly making love with the woman whose parents you killed. He had been involved with women before, but he kept everything on the surface. Ruby had burrowed beneath his skin. Burrowed deeper than that, if he dared to contemplate.

He didn't.

She'd talked about giving him her heart. That's the part that killed him, that had broken through his haze. It was bad enough that he'd been about to take her body.

His Dragon responded to her pain. It tugged at him to reach for her, to say whatever he could to make it right. Nothing would make it right though. He'd committed the ultimate sin, taken everything from her. No matter that it was on someone else's orders, he had their blood on his hands. Then he'd let things get heated between them, a bigger sin in his mind.

Heated. His Dragon snorted at the downplayed word.

Cyn had wanted her, every cell of her, even her soul. He'd drowned in his emotions the moment he buried his face in her neck. So he deserved the sting of her nail marks, the bruises from her beating.

Ruby settled into the seat, her arms crossed in front of her. In a monotone voice, she asked, "What's the plan?"

"I have to figure out where you play into this."

"I'm not hiding here in the car."

Cyn braced his hand on the side of her seat, only inches from her. "I would never expect you to hide, Ruby. But remember, as much as you might hate me—"

"I do hate you. There's no 'might' about it."

"As much as you hate me"—he shoved the words out, each one lodging in his throat—"I have your best interests at heart. Don't disobey my orders just to spite me. You getting killed *will* spite me. But is that worth it?"

She blew out a breath. "I'm not going to cut off my nose to spite my face, if that's what you're worried about. I might need you in this fight, but I don't *need* you. There's a difference."

He focused on Darren's house again. "Understood. We're going in as soon as they leave. I don't want to approach him until I've had a look at what he's up to." He settled back in his seat. "Rest, Ruby. It might be a while."

She leaned her head back, pressing her fingers over her closed eyes. He took in the creamy skin of her neck, his hunger increasing. Not sexual hunger, which would be much easier to handle.

Damn.

He closed his eyes, too. When he woke, several hours had passed. Dew covered the windshield and hood of the car. The sky was gray, hinting at the coming dawn. He checked on Ruby to make sure she was still there, even though she couldn't have left the car without him knowing.

She was curled against the seat, deep asleep. He was sure it was only relief, but he felt an overwhelming desire to touch her, comfort her. Like the innocent girl he'd found in the dinghy, she reached places in him he didn't know existed. He had no idea how to comfort anyone. No one had comforted him when he'd lost his parents.

He sat watching her for almost an hour. Oh, he tried to look elsewhere, anywhere, but his gaze kept going back to her. Movement beyond her caught his attention. A car pulled out of Darren's driveway, two people inside. He wanted to follow, but he needed to get into the workshop more.

"Ruby."

She woke with a start, her eyes heavy as she took in her surroundings. He could see the moment reality dawned when a hardened expression replaced her dazed confusion.

He reached for the glove box and removed a small leather kit. "They just left. Let's move."

They walked casually down the street and then disappeared from view once they headed down the driveway. He led the way around the back to the windowless workshop. The door was solid metal with multiple dead bolts. No sign of an alarm system or magick. He went around to the back and found another secured door. After checking to make sure no one could see them, he picked the lock and pushed the door open. He stripped, ready to Catalyze if necessary before stepping inside a lab. They found tables with papers and a whiteboard covered in calculations he had no hope of interpreting.

Ruby took it all in with an odd expression. "I used to see these kinds of calcs in Dad's home office. This is a chart that tracks solar storms. The peaks seem to correspond with this other chart, though I can't figure out what it represents. Wait. I recognize this." She held up a metallic object about a foot long. "My father had something like this at his lab." She held it out toward him. "Feel it."

His fingers brushed hers as he touched the cylindrical piece. It pulsed with an energy he thought was *Deus Vis*. "This could be it."

"So whatever my father was doing, Darren has recreated it."

"And it took me *years*," a bitter voice said from the doorway. "After he went crazy and destroyed everything."

They both spun to find Darren and Magda. The aura that had obviously kept Cyn from sensing them fell away. Cyn held the device down and out of sight.

"Because he knew it was going to hurt people," Ruby said, her voice amazingly even. "And you had him killed for it."

Cyn came up beside Ruby, ready to step in front of her if necessary. *Good girl, Ruby. Stay calm.*

But she kept talking, emotion now leaking into her voice when she said, "You used your connections to have us all killed. We were your friends. You used to babysit me."

"My connections." Darren's smile seemed almost wistful before it disappeared. "Your father should have thought of that before he ran off with years of research. Research to which I contributed. He was clearly planning to profit—"

"That's the story you told everyone else," Ruby cut in. "I know the truth."

"You're right. That was the for-public-consumption version. The truth was your father had finally figured out how to accomplish his lifelong goal, and he wasn't about to heed Brom's warning to destroy it. He took everything and went on the run. I couldn't let him endanger people by continuing his project."

Cyn's eyes narrowed. "That's what you told your connection at the Guard, that Justin was dangerous."

Darren merely said, "He couldn't be allowed to harm others."

"Why didn't you simply have him arrested? Why kill all of us?" Ruby asked.

"Not knowing how much your mother knew, or how much you had overheard, made it necessary to eliminate everyone. It was nothing personal."

"And you couldn't leave witnesses who would contradict the accident story," Cyn added.

"Nothing personal?" Ruby turned to Magda. "You were our friends. I was your surrogate daughter."

Magda's shoulders stiffened. "Friends? No, we socialized because Darren wanted to feel that he and Justin were a team, equally responsible for the project's progress. Spending time with your family was excruciating. Justin spoiled your mother rotten. If Leah so much as whispered some wish, he made it happen. Even getting her pregnant the first month they tried. And don't think that she didn't rub it in my face that her husband got all the glory and money from SUNLAB's financial backer. And yes, you were a substitute for the daughter I couldn't have, but after a while it became too painful to spend time with you. I didn't want you dead, but it was not my decision to make." Her hard eyes flicked to Cyn. "You know that you're allied with the man who killed your parents, don't you?"

Ruby flinched. "He's better than the person who ordered their deaths."

Cyn was glad Ruby hadn't found out like this. It was too late for Magda to drive a wedge between them.

Ruby faced Darren. "What you're doing is threatening the safety of every Crescent, including children."

"And you base this on Brom's warning? Do you really believe that crazy old man?"

Cyn crossed his arms over his chest. "Obviously you do. You set a parasite demon on him to keep him quiet." The pieces began to fit together. "You were expecting Brom to return when you started fracturing the *Deus Vis* again, probably put a scry orb on his house. It followed Brom when he went to Moncrief and told him about his prophecy and Ruby's part in it. That's why you're so determined to kill her."

Ruby turned to Cyn, her eyes wide. Then she turned back to Darren. "You had Mon killed because he knew too much."

Darren's face was rigid. "And you made it easy by showing up. If only you'd died easy."

That's when Ruby's control finally snapped. She Catalyzed, but Magda was faster, pouncing before Ruby could tear at Darren's throat. Cyn tossed the device beneath the table and let his Dragon loose. He meant to block Magda, but Darren hit him with a ball of energy that washed over him like an electrical shock.

Ruby took the hit from the Citrine Dragon, whose mouth had closed over Ruby's neck. They both hit the floor.

Darren sent another orb at Cyn that threw him against a cabinet. He pushed through the pain, shaking from the effort. The waves obliterated his view of Ruby, as though he were underwater. All he could see were blurry figures.

"Stinger, Ruby," he managed to say. He hoped she remembered his lesson on what powers the different Dragons possessed.

Magda's tail lifted up to lance Ruby, who dodged out of the way. Ruby lunged, and Magda howled in pain, blood oozing from beneath some of her scales.

Still reeling from the two orbs, Cyn didn't have the wherewithal to move out of the way as a different orb came his way. It enveloped him, like one of those bubbles from a kid's plastic bottle. It didn't break when he tried to puncture it. He jerked his talons back from the sticky shell.

He inhaled but found he couldn't draw enough Breath to generate his smoke. Darren approached him, hands out as he kept the bubble going. "And you have been a real pain in our ass, too. Ruby would have been taken care of long ago if it weren't for you. What is it about this girl that weakens you, powerful and ruthless Vega? Women aren't worth that kind of sacrifice. All they do is nag and demand and harass, and nothing you ever do is good enough. But you're going to die for one of the insatiable bitches."

Magda lifted her head at words spoken with a bitterness as powerful as his damned orb. Ruby took advantage, scraping her talons across her opponent's vulnerable eyes. Magda screamed, trying to brush away the blood that dripped into her eyes.

Fueled by anger, Cyn drew enough strength to inhale and shoot out a stream of black smoke. It penetrated the bubble and looped around Darren's neck. The bubble broke as Darren's concentration did. He then created some kind of magick to disintegrate the rope of smoke. It loosened as Cyn lunged at him. Darren lurched to the side, and Cyn's fangs ended up only grazing Darren's side. Still, blood gushed through the tear in his shirt. Darren put his hand there and lifted red-smeared fingers, shock on his face. Maybe it was deeper than Cyn thought.

The bastard threw another orb, knocking Cyn against the wall. Magda's tail whipped back and forth as she blindly aimed for Ruby. Ruby blew out a stream of fire that singed the scales down Magda's side. She screamed and lurched. Her tail hit Ruby, jolting her with poison.

Cyn tried to get to her as she fell with a gasp, but Darren surrounded him with another bubble. Remembering when he'd been caught in one of these before, Cyn got the bubble rolling toward Darren. The bubble collided with him, sucking Darren in, too. Cyn pinned Darren down, then turned to Ruby.

She was struggling to stand as Magda jabbed her tail wildly into the air. Magda kept wiping away the blood, but she couldn't keep her eyes open for more than a second. "I'll find you," she growled. "Even if I can't see you, I will find you." She moved closer to Ruby, who was beginning to convulse from the poison. It was attacking her nervous system. The more hits Ruby sustained, the less control she would have.

Darren shoved his hand against Cyn's chest, sending a current like those shock paddles. He fell back but had enough mind to kick Darren as he did so. The man's head hit the corner of a table, and he slumped to the floor. The bubble disappeared.

Ruby was on her feet, wobbling as she evaded the tail with the pointed black stinger. If Magda sank the tip into Ruby's heart, it would all be over. Every time she moved, Magda followed. The sound of Ruby's tail sliding over the floor was giving her opponent the audio clues she needed to track her.

"Pick up your tail," Cyn hissed, drawing Magda toward him and away from Ruby.

Ruby pulled up her tail, narrowed her beautiful, fiery eyes at Magda, and whacked her with it. The Citrine Dragon fell to the floor but bounded to her feet.

Another bubble orb flew past Cyn, missing him but enveloping Ruby. Darren's voice was strained but loud: "I'll hold her 'til you get there."

Ruby struggled against the confines of the bubble as Magda limped over. Her tail twitched like a cat's, readying for its fatal task. Cyn knocked her back with a wall of smoke, and he heard her choking and gasping. The room filled with it as he let it expand. Ruby was protected in the bubble, but her expression held fear as she watched.

"It's just me," he told her as he used his senses to track

the Deuce. The scent of Darren's blood filled the air, inciting his Dragon to bloodlust.

Go for it.

Cyn could make out Darren's outline. The man was trying to wave the smoke away, but it was thick. Cyn took Darren by the throat. His scream was cut short as blood spurted from his neck. His hands fell slack, and his dead body hit the floor. Cyn cleared the air in one long Breath. Magda was feeling along the floor, only a few feet from Ruby, who was now free of the bubble. Magda squinted through her blood, seeing her dead husband and then Cyn.

"Bastard!" she screamed, but instead of rushing at him, she took off toward the open doorway. She paused there though, and Cyn moved in front of Ruby. Now human, bloody, and stooped over, Magda smiled eerily as she flipped a switch that was high up on the wall and ran out of sight. No lights went out.

"Get out!" Cyn said, snatching up his clothing in one hand and Ruby's arm in the other. They shot through the doorway seconds before the building exploded. The force threw them several yards away, where they landed in the grass, naked and human.

He checked Ruby, relieved to see that she was stunned and bruised, but all right.

She pointed at the fiery building. "That thing we found, the one that's messing up the *Deus Vis.*"

"Gone."

He shoved the shirt at her as she got to her feet. He slid into his pants, and they pushed their way through the hedges into the yard next door. The sounds of alarmed voices filled the air, and Cyn pulled Ruby out of view just as someone came running out of the house. Her body slammed into his, and he held her fast for a moment, soaking in the feel of her. Once the people ran out of view, she jerked away.

Smoke billowed into the air, filling it with the acrid scent of chemicals. They kept close to the hedges and made their way to the street. Sirens signaled coming police vehicles.

Cyn assessed her, his shirt coming down to her upper thigh. "Stay here in the shadow of the hedges. You're not indecent, but you'd definitely attract attention. I'll bring the car up, and you can jump in."

Pink light streaked across the sky now. He crossed the street, probably looking like a man sneaking out of his married lover's house, and got into his car. A quick U-turn, and Ruby stepped into the car. Cyn turned down a side road just as two cop cars raced past.

She held her body stiff, shoulders straight. "They tried to kill me. They were our friends, and they were going to kill me just to protect his project." She stared straight ahead, her eyes vacant. "She blew up the lab. Just...blew it up, probably to destroy the evidence. She was hoping we'd be gone, too. Maybe she was the supportive dutiful wife, trying to protect her husband's reputation. Not to mention her own."

"Maybe." Cyn let Ruby talk it out.

"*Mr. Smith* is dead. It's over." A tremor vibrated in her voice. "No more d-demons. Or t-tulpas. Just Magda. I can handle her."

Not if he could help it. "Yes, you can. You did well. You put your emotions aside and fought logically. That's what kept you alive."

"I don't need emotions. I don't want to feel anymore."

He fought not to touch her, tightening his fingers on the wheel instead. "Don't do that. Because once you bury them, it's hard to bring them back. And you don't feel anything, not joy or excitement or real desire." *Until someone special comes along and rocks you out of your numbness.*

And now he was feeling pain he told himself he'd never experience again.

They drove in silence, except for Ruby's occasional soft gasp as she tried to rein in her reaction to the adrenaline. He had to hold back words of comfort, because he knew she wouldn't want them.

"Do you feel my mother's energy?" she asked. "All those Dragons you killed and Breathed, can you feel them?"

"No, it doesn't work like that. If you kill Magda, you have to catch her essence at the moment of death or within seconds of it. Get nose to nose with her and Breathe deeply. Your Dragon will know what to do from there. If she's either old or murderous, you might be overwhelmed by the power you inherit."

"I'll keep that in mind."

Twenty minutes later, he pulled up to the gates of the Yard. He opened the trunk and pulled out her bag. She took it, hefting it over her shoulder. Her eyes were devoid of anything when they looked at him. He had mastered that lack of emotion for most of his life. So why did hers gut him?

Her gaze drifted to his bare chest, probably to the bruises and scratches she'd inflicted. Only then did he see some flicker of something, though he couldn't figure out what it was.

"Do you want to hit me again?" He remembered the fire in her eyes when she'd talked of killing the man responsible. That was better than the deadness in them now. He spread his arms as he'd done in his office after handing her the letter opener. "Get it out of your system."

She raised her eyes to his. "I don't want anything from you. I don't need the Dragon Prince anymore. I can handle myself, my power. I never want to see you again."

Why did it feel as though she'd plunged that letter opener into his chest? He forced himself to nod, putting his mask in place. "Be safe, Ruby."

He didn't leave as she turned away, punishing himself by watching her. She went in, relocked the gate, and walked into the Yard. Even when she was out of sight, he couldn't seem to move.

The sense of loss acted like the poison in a Citrine's tail, working its way from his legs, up to his chest, his throat, pounding in his head. He realized he hadn't breathed in a long time, maybe the whole time she'd been out of his sight. He leaned his forehead against the edge of the roof, grimacing from a pain he'd not felt before. His fingers even hurt. He realized he was gripping the metal and released them. Eight small dents marred the surface.

He pushed himself to get into the car. Then he had to force himself to drive away. He had a Dragon bitch to hunt down. He was still Ruby's sworn protector, even if he never saw her again.

Friggin' Hidden. She was done with it.
Friggin' Cyn. She was done with him, too.

Ruby dropped her bag on the floor and sank down next to the pile of photographs. She hated him. H-A-T-E-D him. "I hope you're hurting, Cyntag Valeron. I hope you are suffering at least a fraction of what you've put me through."

Then why does your heart ache?

She'd fallen in love with the man who'd murdered her parents. That was bad enough. The worst part was she still wanted him. *I suck.*

She could smell his scent, his essence permeating her. Well, of course, she was wearing his shirt! She wrestled out of it and threw it across the room. The pictures on the floor were of happier times, and yet, now she knew her father had been doing something that endangered people. Had he known before Brom warned him? Had he resisted destroying his work at first? She would never find out.

She stumbled into her bedroom, catching her reflection in the mirror over her dresser. Her beautiful red Dragon seemed to be looking at her with sympathy.

"I'm stuck with you, aren't I?"

It shifted, the tip of its tail wiggling.

"I guess I can live with you." She pointed at it through the reflection. "But you can forget the black Dragon. Forget any Dragon. If I can't date . . . Mundanes, then I'm not interested in dating. I was doing fine before. I didn't need a man in my life then, and I don't need one now."

Something thrummed through her though: need, desire.

"Stop it." She dropped onto the bed. Emotional and physical fatigue, along with a night in a car, caught up to her. She was bruised, achy. Achier in her heart than in her body.

She tried to recall Mon's fairy tale, how Garnet had gone on after the Dragon Prince died. Sleep claimed her as the final battle played out in her mind. A sound scratched at the outer edge of her dreams.

Probably nothing. Or Fergus. She sank back into sleep.

The Book of the Hidden

Garnet and her army bided their time, gathering intelligence on the comings and goings of the Shadows and where they had stationed guards. Her heart ached at learning how many of her people had died, how many were now slaves to the Shadows. Thinking of her slain husband and Opal, her fury grew.

More refugees joined them. Their army gathered, timing their attack for the end of the guards' shift, when they would be the most tired, but before the new shift arrived. Each troop brought their particular skills to battle as they rushed forward. The Deuces pounded the Shadows with fiery orbs. She'd told the Dragons how the prince had defeated the Shadows when he had rescued her. She fought, too, cutting down monster after monster as she remembered how they had killed her parents. The battle raged for hours, and eventually they brought down the Shadows and their ruler.

In the aftermath, she was heralded as a savior, more beloved than any queen. She helped clean the rubble, restoring her castle and the kingdom to a semblance of its former beauty.

A fortnight later, she stood at the Great Room's window, looking out at her lands. A dove alighted on her finger, rubbing its head against her palm. She knew all would be well.

Until the next battle...

Chapter 18

Purcell held Magda as she sobbed in his arms. She'd collapsed the moment he'd opened his door, and he'd barely managed to guide her to the living room. Her broken report about what had happened at the lab was slowly seeping into his brain. First, how this would set them back. Second, that Darren was dead. And Purcell had never once thanked him for his work, praised him for his accomplishments. Guilt lanced his grief.

"You should have alerted me when you knew Cyntag and Ruby were outside your house. I could have helped."

Magda loosened her grip on him and sat up straight on the couch. "I told Darren we should let you know, but he wanted to handle it himself. He always felt inadequate. I probably didn't help, comparing him to Justin years ago. To you. I think he needed to prove himself. But Darren doesn't have the magick you do. He did his best, but in the end, it wasn't enough. My fighting skills are a bit rusty, I'm afraid. I wasn't enough either."

"You destroyed the lab."

"I couldn't defeat them, nor could I run off and leave them there to take evidence. I felt it was the only solution, and I thought it would kill them." She let out a ragged sigh. "But they escaped."

Purcell nodded. "I suppose it was the best decision in the end. But Justin's early prototype was there."

She shook her head. "I didn't see it or I would have grabbed it. I assumed it was here."

"No, I only have his second, smaller prototype." The only two things that Justin wasn't able to get his hands on that fateful night. Early attempts, they didn't pull in *Deus Vis* but did hold minute amounts of it. Darren had been using them to re-create Justin's work. "I'm glad I didn't give into Darren's whining about leaving the actual reactor at the lab."

"He was angry that you wouldn't let him keep it, seeing it as proof that you didn't trust him. But you would have been proud of him. He fought well. And he hid your involvement, taking responsibility for everything."

Purcell rubbed his fingers across his lips as he considered that. "So Ruby and Cyntag might think they've thwarted me and destroyed everything." Maybe his son was smarter than he'd given him credit for.

"Ruby knows that Cyntag killed her parents. I was so hoping to break that news to her, since I couldn't believe she would work with him if she knew. She's angry at him over it though. Her eyes flamed when I mentioned it."

Purcell ran his fingers down his beard. "A wedge between them may give us an opening. If we get rid of her, he may back down."

She twined her fingers in her hair, her mouth stretching

into a frown. "He won't. I could see his devotion to her. He'll come after us even harder." She stared at nothing for a few moments before focusing on him again. "But revenge won't be his only motivator. Thanks to Brom, they must know the consequences of our success."

Purcell reached for the cigar that he'd set in the ashtray when Magda had banged on his door. "I have an idea, but it will mean widening the circle of the Chosen." And inviting another Dragon in, not something he was fond of doing. Purcell figured about fifty people could survive on the *Deus Vis* the reactor emitted. There were not many vacancies left.

She gathered his free hand in hers. "Am I still one of the Chosen?"

Her fear of being excluded shadowed her eyes. And filled him with a rush of his own power. *He* got to play god, in a way, choosing other early generation Deuces and esteemed members of the Concilium or Guard, along with their select family members.

He patted her hand and pulled out of her grip. "Of course." She didn't know that she was the only Dragon thus far, and only included because of her affiliation with Darren. But Purcell would live up to his word. The Deuces he had chosen were purists like himself. None would be mating with Magda.

She stared past him, wiping away her tears. "The last thing Darren said..."

"Was what?"

Her smile was as vacant as her eyes. "That he was willing to die for me. That's the kind of man your son was."

Purcell couldn't imagine his son being so noble. "You should return to your home. I imagine both the Mundane and Crescent authorities will be investigating. We'll come up with a story. You were out, your husband was concocting something in his lab and accidentally blew it and himself up. Who knows what kind of crazy thing he was working on? You don't, certainly. You can play the grieving and shocked woman well enough. After all, you did a good job just now."

They'd saved thousands of Crescents. Cyn should feel good. Relieved. Well, if he could focus his thoughts on all that and not Ruby. Of course, that would be easier if he wasn't patrolling the road that the Yard was on.

He picked up his cell phone and fought the urge to call Ruby's number. Instead, he called Kade. When he didn't answer, Cyn called another Vega he'd served with.

After Parker answered and Cyn identified himself, he said, "It's great to hear from you, but I can't talk right now."

Cyn could hear noise in the background. "You wouldn't happen to be investigating an explosion, would you?"

"Yeah, I sure am. An outbuilding, blown to bits. You know something about it?"

"All I can say is look closely at the woman who lives there."

"She just returned from an errand and found this. She's all broken up but she's cooperating. We're questioning her now, but she claims to have no idea what her husband was doing when he blew himself up."

"I'd detain her for as long as you can. Check out her story."

Cyn signed off. Ruby should be safe for a little while at least. As exhausted as he was, an uneasiness twisted his stomach. Once Magda was taken care of, he would have no reason to contact Ruby again. The thought burrowed into his chest.

He called Glesenda. "Hey. Everything normal?"

"We don't have any uninvited guests hanging around, if that's what you mean."

"I'm not coming in today. See if Dave can teach my cane class this afternoon."

"Is it because of that chick? And the demons?"

"No, that's over. We took care of the guy behind the demons, and the *chick* is not in my life anymore." He felt a stabbing pain at those words.

"Too bad about the chick. She fired you up. It was good to see you like that."

He grunted in response.

"But," she continued, "there's no need for a substitute teacher. Six of the students have canceled, along with a bunch for the other classes. There's some bug going around. I even feel run-down, and I never get sick."

"Have any Mundanes called in to cancel?"

"Hmm. Now that you ask, no, only Crescents. Pretty strange, don't you think?"

He couldn't tell her that everyone would be feeling better soon without explaining, so he said, "Go ahead and close early, get some rest."

Which is what he should do. The uneasiness was getting stronger, though, and his Dragon was downright agitated. Something didn't feel right.

In Brom's prophecy, and thus Moncrief's stories, Garnet and the Dragon Prince defeated a huge monster. And he and Ruby had—the tulpa. In Moncrief's version, the Dragon Prince died, but that was obviously his spiteful addition. Garnet had returned to her kingdom to find it still under siege by the Shadows. From Ruby's description, they sounded like demons. Garnet and her army went on to defeat them and all was well.

All did not feel well here. If something was truly wrong, Brom should be sensing it. Demons were supposed to return to the Dark Side if their summoner died. Any demons here to do Darren's bidding should be gone. Including the parasitic demon. Cyn headed to Brom's and took the back way in again, getting no answer when he called Brom's name. As he entered the house, he saw no sign that the man had been back. But he did see that the ribbons were still fracturing.

A beep caught his attention, and he followed it to an answering machine. The loud deep voice sounded familiar. "Hey, Brom, it's Jay. I've got some elements to try based on the new information you gave me. I'm going out to the edge of the Sanctum's Field where the *Deus Vis* is similar to Miami's to run some experiments. Since that's in the wilderness, I'll be out of pocket until tomorrow tonight. Hopefully I'll have an answer, because if you're right, we've only got until sometime tomorrow to figure this out."

Jay. Sanctum. Cyn knew exactly who he was, and it made sense that Brom had consulted him again. According to the date and time on the phone, Jay had called this morning. Cyn programmed the number into his phone and headed back to his car, his mind spinning. He needed to find out what Brom had told Jay. And he needed to find Magda and get his hands on whatever was fracturing the *Deus Vis*. It obviously wasn't destroyed.

No demons.

Those words flashed in his mind as his feet sank into the sand on the way back to the car. He tried to figure out why it bothered him. No demons should be a good thing. In fact, it had been great that Darren hadn't summoned any to help during their final altercation. And *that's* what bothered Cyn. Someone who could summon demons possessed stronger magick than bubble orbs.

Had they killed Mr. Smith? Cyn needed to find out for sure. His former boss and mentor would be heading to work about now. Maybe Cyn could catch him.

Fernandez was, indeed, walking to his car, wearing his dark blue suit, a travel mug in hand. He was already watching as Cyn's car pulled down the long drive. No doubt he recognized the car.

Fernandez set his mug on the roof and waited for Cyn to get out and walk over. "Everything all right? No, I'm assuming not, since you're here. Not to mention that you look like hell."

They shook hands, and Cyn smiled. "I earned it. I have a question, off the record. What did Mr. Smith look like? A general description will suffice."

Before Fernandez could say anything, the front door opened, and Celia stepped out. "Cyn! I thought that was your car." She was still wearing a robe, her complexion pale. "It's been so long."

"I'm sorry about that. I wish I had time to visit."

Her wistful expression tightened his chest. Ward orphans, back before they created institutions for them, were taken in by a Guard officer and his family. Similar to foster care, only there was a solid commitment to raise the child, train him in the Crescent ways, and then push him to join the Guard. When Cyn had quit, he'd had to quit them, too. He couldn't take the chance of inadvertently revealing the truth about why he left. But he did stop by from time to time and always sent cards and gifts.

She waved away his words. "I can't anyway. I've got the flu."

The flu. Like all those other Crescents. "Good to see you, Celia. I hope you feel better."

When Celia closed the door, Fernandez turned his troubled expression back to Cyn. "Smith. He looked older, which means he's old. Early generation Crescent, I'd guess. White hair and neatly trimmed beard. Distinguished, typical Deuce coolness. Arrogant. You want to tell me what's going on? Maybe I can help."

Darren wasn't Mr. Smith. Which meant Mr. Smith was still alive. Still out there hunting Ruby. Cyn called out, "I have to go," as he ran to his car. He tried Ruby's number, but he didn't expect her to answer if she knew it was him.

He jumped in his car and tore away to the Yard.

Something was forming on the page of the open book in the female Crescent's living room. The demon watched for a moment, feeling the magick in the book prickle across its skin. A three-headed monster appeared line by line. Very small stick figures were next, standing in front of the looming monster.

Selwig closed the book and searched the living space. It liked going through her things. What joy, tormenting Crescents by moving their things around, punching them in their sleep and creating mystery bruises. But it was not

here to have innocent fun; its mission was even more ex-
citing. The demon didn't like Dragons, having seen his
comrades slaughtered by them over the years. Now, fit-
tingly, this demon had been freed from prison to kill one.

A song began to play. Selwig followed the sound to a
flat square sitting on the table. The screen read CYN. The
song ended. It followed the scent of the woman to the
open doorway. She lay sprawled on the bed, naked.

A demon of sin would do other things to her. Being
a harbinger was much better, with the ability to take any
kind of physical form.

A fire Elemental tried to dart past, but Selwig stomped
its foot and stopped the pesky creature. Its gaze flitted to
the woman's sleeping form. Ah, so it meant to warn her.
The demon bared its fangs. The Elemental did, too, but it
recognized it was way outpowered and backed away.

The woman stirred and rolled to her side. A second
later, her eyelashes fluttered open. Selwig took form and
approached her.

Chapter 19

Purcell walked into Captain Fernandez's office, once again without knocking. He pasted on a pleasant expression, even though the dark-haired man scowled at the sight of him.

"Captain," Purcell said in greeting, closing the door behind him and strolling behind his desk to look out the window.

Fernandez bristled at the invasion of his territory. "What do you want now?"

"Have you noticed that a lot of Crescents are feeling under the weather? You've no doubt seen that several of the secretaries' desks are vacant this morning. Due to the same *bug* that your wife no doubt has."

The captain's desperation and fear was clear. "How did you—"

"Only it's not a bug. It's a disruption of the *Deus Vis*."

Purcell turned, seeing that the man's hostility was replaced by interest. And fear.

"Already? But we're just seeing the effects of the smaller flares. We aren't supposed to feel the big storm they've been hyping up on the news for another day or so. The Concilium advised the Guard and our medical staff that Crescents might feel more than the usual ruffle of the *Deus Vis*, but nothing severe."

"That's what they're telling you. I am willing to share the truth under the confidentiality of the Guard's Silence Credo."

"You're not Guard."

"Details." Purcell smiled. "Call in your secretary. I overheard her telling one of the other ladies that she was going home after lunch."

While he did, Purcell pulled out a cloth from his pocket that held the small prototype.

Marie came in, her complexion pale, eyes dull. Hardly a flame flickered in her eyes. "Yes, sir," she said, her voice lackluster, too.

Purcell flicked on the reactor and took her hand in his. "Dear, you look positively ill."

"Oh, you shouldn't touch me. I'm..." She blinked. "Sick. Or was sick. That's weird. I feel better." The color was returning to her face. "You're a healer?"

"In a manner of speaking," Purcell said.

She squeezed his hand. "Thank you. Thank you so much." She turned to Fernandez. "The open cases summary is almost done. I'll start working on the expense reports." She spun and left, closing the door behind her.

"Your wife could feel better, too, just that fast," Purcell

said, reaching into Fernandez's mind and feeling his profound relief at that thought.

"What do I need to do?"

A sound. Her phone ringing. Ruby rose slowly to consciousness. Who would be calling? The clock indicated she'd only been asleep for a short time. Not long enough. The ringing stopped. She closed her eyes again. Whoever had called could wait. Probably Nevin, who was no doubt dying of curiosity.

Her Dragon clawed at her, like an insistent dog needing to go out. She groaned, rubbing her tattoo. "Don't tell me I have to let you out to pee."

It nudged her. "Later," she said, then grimaced at the word. Something small landed on the bed, like a drop of rain. Then another. She opened her eyes when one landed an inch from her nose. A red M&M.

She jerked to a sitting position and searched her room. The Elemental stood in the doorway holding a bag of M&M's. "Fergus, what are you doing?"

A cat jumped on the bed.

She sighed out loud. "Oh, just one of the kitties."

Except the kitties were freaked out by her now. And the reason they were freaked out pushed hard against her, urging her to Catalyze.

So she did.

And the kitty turned into a demon.

"Holy hell."

She was pretty sure it was a demon, though it looked like a man. Sort of. Its skin stretched unnaturally across its cheeks, and its eyes were solid black with a white retina. That he wore clothing, baggy jeans and a white T-shirt made it seem more surreal. And oddly, even creepier than the subhuman demons. Now she saw the shadow Cyn had mentioned. A harbinger then.

"No. This is supposed to be *over*," she said.

It giggled. "Nope, not over, dearie. Play with me. My name is Selwig."

Was Magda behind this? But Dragons couldn't summon demons.

Selwig reached toward her in some kind of weird gallant gesture, and she bit its hand. It hissed at her, or maybe it smiled and air leaked out between its rubbery lips. Either way it sent chills scurrying across her scales.

"Ooh, playing hard to get, are you?" it said, now definitely smiling.

"Very hard to get." She shot out a stream of fire spikes.

It ducked out of the way, but the skin on its arm bubbled in the heat. "Thanks, dearie. I needed a tan."

"Then allow me to oblige." She Breathed out again, obliterating the demon in a fireburst. When the flames cleared, its entire body was charcoal.

Selwig surveyed itself. "I bet you're a terrible cook." It disintegrated into a pile of ash that re-formed into a creature that just plain looked demonic. "Maybe you'll like me better this way."

"Dark green skin, bald head, and those mesmerizing eyes. How can I resist?" She Breathed flames again, but he danced out of the stream.

"Think I'll go rare this time." God, it was having fun, giggling, moving its hips back and forth as it taunted her. A moving target.

She narrowed her eyes and sent another blast, singeing its arm. It blew on the smoking skin in quick bursts. Before she could nail it again, Fergus jumped on its back. "No!" she shouted, as its small but razor-sharp talons sank into the demon's shoulder. Selwig reached back with a growl, but Fergus jumped off in the nick of time. Before she could send another Breath, the demon flew at her, clamping onto her neck and sinking its teeth into her.

She tried to wrench it off, but it grew spikes that lanced her hands. Blood dripped from her palms and fingers when she jerked them back. She had to get this thing off her. Its fangs pierced through her scales and into her muscle, close to the kill spot Cyn had described. Pain shot from the puncture right up to her head. She thrashed, smashing it against the wall again and again until the leech fell onto her dresser. It leaped to the chair. She banged her fist down on it, cracking the chair but missing the demon that had jumped away.

"What, no more giggling?" she asked. Her reflection in the mirror showed a trickle of blood down her neck.

"No, now you're just pissing me off."

Fergus darted forward and took a nip before the demon could spin around to face it. While they sparred, she crept up behind Selwig and lunged. It morphed into a dragon, nearly as big as her.

What the hell?

Well, of course, if it could look like a cat, it could look like her. Exactly like her, other than the white eyes. It rushed forward and rammed right into her, sending her tripping over the broken chair and onto the floor. It lunged down toward her, and she snapped at its snout with her fangs, drawing blood. Selwig jumped up and landed on top of her before she could move in the crowded space. It now had the weight of a dragon, nearly cracking her ribs. She threw it off, sending it crashing into the dresser. Pain rocketed through her body as she tried to get up.

Hunter/Prey. She needed to get the demon off guard. Fergus waylaid Selwig, then paid the price by being tossed across the room. Ruby remained on the floor and tried to look terrified.

Selwig came close, eyeing her throat. "Well, dearie, this has been fun, but it's time for me to end this dance." The demon flexed its fingers, readying its sharp claws to finish her off.

"No," she pleaded. "Please."

The moment it leaned close, she clamped her mouth around its neck. Her fangs sank through skin, muscle, then crushed bones. Black blood squirted. Selwig screamed in agony. Its body sagged and then it evaporated in a puff of dust. She jerked upright and searched the floor. Nothing remained to re-form into anything else.

Fergus jumped up and down and made happy sounds. Before she could even sigh in relief, magick prickled through her. She whipped around to the doorway of her ruined room, feeling the spikes on her back rise.

Cyn stood there, feet spread, body rigid, as though ready to Catalyze. But he was very human. He slowly clapped his hands together. "Very nice. My student has learned well."

She remained Dragon, adrenaline coursing through her, hoping to use it to intimidate him into going away. Of course, he didn't. She thrust her head at him, snarling, nudging him hard enough that he had to take a step back to keep his balance.

He didn't look the least bit intimidated. In fact, he reached out and stroked her cheek, as though she were a horse. Damn it, her Dragon purred, leaning into his touch.

Ruby Catalyzed to human and changed into the first shirt and pants she could find in the debris. "How did you know I wasn't really injured?"

"I could sense your energy. You looked afraid, but you felt pissed off."

"It's disturbing that you can feel me like that." She narrowed her eyes. "I thought this was over!"

His tight, stretchy shirt molded to his chest as he lifted his hand to the room. "It's not, as you can see."

"But why? How? We killed Darren, and Magda can't summon demons."

"We assumed that Darren was the mastermind. But something didn't feel right. I went to Fernandez, my former boss, and asked for Mr. Smith's description. Not Darren. So it appears that we're stuck with each other for a while longer."

"But I handled the demon all by myself."

"You did indeed. It was gratifying to watch." The embers in his eyes flickered. "Deeply satisfying, in fact." He blinked, dousing the embers. "Unfortunately, when this one doesn't report back, Smith may send more. You're not equipped to handle more than one yet. We do this together, just as Brom's prophecy says."

With an impatient huff, she stepped over the broken pieces of her chair and pictures on the way to the living room. The demon had been through her things, moving pillows and even the coffee table. She found Brom's book in a different place than where she'd left it and opened it to the latest entry. "There's a new picture. Oh, great, a big monster with three heads. So that part of Mon's story wasn't his literary license."

Cyn leaned over her shoulder. "And both of us fighting it."

His heat called to her Dragon, drawing her to lean back against him. *Stop it! Bad Dragon.*

She felt it snort, a really odd sensation.

Want.

The worst part was she wasn't sure if that last sentiment was hers or her Dragon's. She snapped the book shut and shoved it into her bag. "What kind of monster is that? Another tulpa?"

He was right behind her, his feet light on the stairs as they went down. "Nothing I've ever seen. I suppose a Deuce could make a tulpa that looked like that though."

They approached the fence, and Ruby grabbed the lock, which was still intact. "How did you get in? And how did you know a demon was here?"

"I climbed over." He showed her the scrapes on his hands from the barbed wire coils at the top of the fence. "As soon as I discovered that Mr. Smith is still out there, I knew he'd be targeting you again."

She relocked the gate once they'd passed through. "Just because I'm going with you doesn't mean I've forgiven you."

"Understood."

She slung her bag in the trunk he opened for her.

"More bad news," he said as they pulled onto the road. "The *Deus Vis* is still fracturing. Whatever is causing it wasn't in that lab. It's beginning to hit Crescents hard. How are you feeling?"

God, it really wasn't over at all. Panic squeezed her throat. "I'm tired and achy."

"Like the flu?"

"Like I've got demons and tulpas trying to kill me." *And a Dragon tearing up my heart.* "I figured it was everything I've been through lately." She remembered the images Brom had flashed into their minds. "People are still going to die."

"Yes."

"Kids. Grandmothers. Us. What about the Elementals?"

"They don't require *Deus Vis* to survive."

She felt some relief, but it was small consolation. "What do we do? How do we stop it?"

His cell phone rang. "Fernandez," he said to her and answered it. She couldn't hear what the man was saying. "No," Cyn said, glancing at her. "Okay, I'll be right there." He disconnected. "He says he knows what's going on."

"Could he be in on it?"

"I considered that when I went to see him this morning, but I doubt it. I've told him very little, for his protection and ours. As in any large agency, there's the possibility of corruption at the upper levels."

He took an on-ramp and merged with the flow of traffic on the interstate. "I'm meeting Fernandez at my house."

A short while later, he took an exit leading to southeast Coral Gables. "Hungry?"

"Famished."

He pulled into the parking lot of a small café. "This is one of my favorite places. Spanish food."

She got out, and the scent of garlic and tomatoes wafting through the air unleashed a growl from her stomach.

"Mr. Valeron, good to see you," the host said when they walked inside, giving her a nod, too. "Welcome." He had olive skin and dark hair like Cyn, and his eyes flickered in the Dragon way.

The place was quaint. Murals depicted cozy scenes with what she guessed were Spanish homes and balconies.

Cyn ordered for them, which would have been annoying except she didn't know what some of the dishes on the menu were. An array of plates were delivered soon after, including one filled with baby octopi. Ugh. The array was colorful though. She ate the things she recognized, olives and cheese, chorizo sausage, and slices of beef.

"Ruby, remember how I'm an arrogant ass and want you to obey me?"

The olive she was chewing went down like a rock. "Yeah…"

"I don't want you coming in with me. I'd like to say I trust Fernandez. He and his wife raised me after I was orphaned. That's the way being a Ward worked in the old days, if you had no family to take you in."

She didn't want to know about how he'd lost his parents, how he had no family. "But?"

"I can't completely trust him."

"So I'm hiding in the car?"

"No, I want you nearby so you know what's going on. We'll walk through the neighbor's yard. They're up north for the summer, so the house is closed up. I've got a boat off the side dock. Duck down there. Ready?"

"As I ever will be."

He stood and dropped some bills on the table. Once

outside, he walked to the passenger side and peered into the car first. "Rule of thumb when being hunted by demons: always check your vehicle before you get in. Not a bad idea anyway. Miami has its share of ghouls of the Hidden and the Mundane variety."

He was still teaching her. It should annoy her, but somehow it had the opposite effect. Their gazes locked, and that sexuality curled through her. She could feel the heat of the sun on her back, and his heat from where he stood inches in front of her. "Cyn..."

She tried to dredge up something angry or cold, anything to put distance between them. All she felt was a draw to him, even knowing what he'd done. She ached to feel his hand on her, even just to brush a strand of hair from her temple.

"Ruby, don't look at me like that. Because it makes me want to do this." He did touch her, stroking his fingers along her jawline.

She batted his hand away. "Damn it, we aren't supposed to be here again. Together. Feeling like this. You were supposed to be—" She cut off the words.

"Feeling the ache of you turning your back on me?"

"Yes, I wanted you to feel even a fraction of what you caused me to feel. But you can't feel, can you? That's what you said, anyway. Tell me I was only a moral obligation to you. A few moments of lust." She lifted her chin.

"You like to hear the raw truth, don't you, Ruby?" As though he'd read her mind, or maybe her energy, he did brush a stray strand of hair from her forehead, trailing his fingers across her brow. "Are you sure you want to hear it this time?"

"Yes." She braced herself for his cold, harsh words.

"Watching you Awaken woke up a part of myself I didn't know existed. It was more than you growing into your Dragon's sensuality. It was how your spirit touched me so deeply that I could not stop myself from wanting you. I told myself it was just sexual attraction. But when you told me I was the first man you wanted to give your heart to, I realized what's between us was much more. And that I wanted you more than anything I've wanted in a long, long time. The only way I could keep from violating my moral code was to tell you the truth. Watching you walk away cut so deep, hurt so much, I actually looked for blood on my shirt. Now I feel such a deep emptiness, it's like my insides have been sucked out. Does that fill your need for revenge?"

She swayed, forcing herself to breathe. Every word had twisted so tight around her heart, lungs, her entire body. She felt the truth in words filled with pain, saw it in his eyes. Her voice sounded hollow when she said, "That should do it."

He opened the door for her and said, "Let's see what Fernandez has to say. Maybe we can finish this now, and you can walk away again."

Chapter 20

⁓

Ruby was glad for the silence in the car as Cyn turned onto his street. She was waiting for the satisfaction over his admission. It should be coming any second now. But it didn't, because she was suffering, too, though she'd die before admitting it.

What astounded her was that he didn't appear to be in pain. He could mask it so well. What else did he hide from her? From himself, for that matter?

He parked in the driveway next door and killed the engine. "I want to get you into a hiding spot before I meet Fernandez. Mr. Smith could be watching."

He led her around orange and grapefruit trees to the ocean that sparkled in the midday sun. "We're going to climb down there and take that ledge over to my dock."

The ledge was made of broken concrete close to where waves splashed. Bracing himself on the edge of the seawall, Cyn stepped down and gained his balance, then looked at her. She followed suit, mirroring his movements as he scooted along the ledge, hidden by the seawall to anyone who might be lurking around Cyn's house. His property was on a point, the dock on the side that faced across the canal to another house. The other side looked out to open ocean. She eschewed his offered hand and stepped onto the dock, crouching down as he did.

"Wait for me to get you. If there's trouble, you'll have to determine whether it's better to get involved or stay hidden. For instance, if I'm killed straight out, there's no point in jumping in. You'll only die, too, because if someone gets the best of me, you have no chance." He took his phone from his back pocket and placed it in her hand. "If that happens, wait until they leave and find Kade. Or Grayson."

She put her hand to her chest as she watched him head back to the car. The thought of his dying made her heart hurt. It was only fear of being on her own, right?

It seemed like forever before she heard his voice, carried on the breeze. "We're safe to talk out here. My neighbors are gone for the summer. Lately I don't like being in closed spaces."

Ruby dared peek just above the wall. The other man was dark-haired, too, but shorter and stockier. Cyn positioned himself so that the man's back was to her. His gaze flicked to her before focusing on Fernandez again. "What's going on?"

"Mr. Smith came to see me again. He said you're harboring a woman who has been trying to sabotage his efforts to save as many people as possible from the *Deus Vis* fluctuations."

"It's not the fluctuations that are threatening us. It's that our life force is actually breaking up. I'll bet he didn't tell you that he's causing the fracturing. Brom Winston saw the devastation his project would cause. That's why Justin sabotaged the project, and why he was executed."

Fernandez shook his head. "Mr. Smith told me how he hired Justin to come up with portable *Deus Vis* so Crescents could leave the Field. How the device he engineered exacerbated the fluctuations of the solar storms that were hitting at the time. And yes, Brom did warn him, but Justin ignored those warnings. When Mr. Smith talked of shutting the project down, Justin took all of his research and the device and went on the run to continue his experiments. *That's* why he was terminated."

Fernandez clearly believed the story Mr. Smith had fed him. But Ruby didn't.

Cyn didn't either by the hard edge to his next question. "So why are we experiencing this extreme disruption now? Did he have an answer to that?"

"It's a huge solar storm. You've heard it on the news, physicist Michio Kaku talking about the way it might affect electricity and satellites. It will affect Crescents in more devastating ways. Mr. Smith has a device that holds *Deus Vis* and will feed a select number of Crescents the energy we need. The woman is trying to destroy this device. We'll all die." Fernandez's words grew raw with emotion. "Celia is already ill, as you know. Those who are weakened are feeling it first."

"Who chooses the ones that benefit from this supposed device?"

"The Chosen are based on their value to Crescent society. My wife, I, and you, Cyn, we'll all get the energy. But only if you turn over this woman to my custody."

"And you trust a man who won't even tell you his name?"

Fernandez nodded with conviction. "I've seen the device revive my flagging secretary."

Ruby went cold. She was a bargaining chip. Cyn lived if she was taken into custody. She knew he'd never hand her over.

"I'm not turning her over."

Fernandez's shoulders slumped. "I'm sorry, Cyn. I can't let my wife die."

Ruby tensed, ready to come out and fight. Especially when a man stepped out from the hedges. He looked to be in his sixties with a trim beard and expensive-looking clothing. She held her position because she didn't see any weapons or demons. In fact, his hands were held at his sides in almost a surrender style.

"Cyntag Valeron," he said in a strong voice. "We meet at last."

"We haven't met, since I don't know your name." Cyn, always smooth and in control. His body language, though, was poised for action. His hand flexed behind him, a message to stay put.

"I mean you no harm. You or the girl."

"Those demons weren't exactly benign messengers."

"My son, Darren, went overboard. I didn't know he'd gone to such extremes. I am Purcell, by the way."

He was Darren's *father*?

"Listen to your former mentor, Cyntag. What would I have to gain by causing the death of so many Crescents? Do I look like a diabolical mass murderer? I am, in fact, a savior. While the Mundanes have been preparing to protect power grids and global communications satellites, the private lab I've been funding has invested years of research to figure out how to protect Crescents. The problem is that there are just too many. When the coronal mass ejection arrives, many will lose their connection to the *Deus Vis* and their essence will wither. And they will die."

"Why not warn the population?" Cyn asked. "They could leave the Field for a time. Surely the fluctuation will not last for more than two weeks."

"First, how would we get all of this across in a secretive manner? Then, can you imagine the panic that would ensue? It's unfortunate that many will die. You remember during the Cold War when a nuclear attack seemed imminent? The U.S. government built fallout shelters for their high-ranking officials. It's logical to protect those who can rebuild society. I am willing to ensure that you and yours are included in the Chosen. But you must give me something in return."

Cyn fisted his hands at his sides. "I'm not handing over Ruby."

"Ah, you care about her."

"She's been through enough. You had her family murdered."

"But the girl was not harmed, due to your... compassion."

"I wasn't *harmed*?" Ruby exploded from her hiding place, rage heating her cheeks, and her Dragon. "You killed my family! My uncle! And you've been trying to kill me."

Cyn gripped her arms as she tried to pass him and face the man who had taken so much from her. He held her fast, whispering her name in a warning tone.

Purcell didn't look the least bit afraid of her. "The

blame lies squarely on Brom's head. He is quite mad, you know. He accused Darren of re-creating the fluctuation and then stormed off. Darren sent a scry orb to follow him, worried for his safety. Brom told Moncrief about his vision, that you would follow in your father's insanity and sabotage everything we've worked for. Darren would not let that happen. He acted rashly, without consulting me. I apologize for the trouble he has caused."

He apologized. *Apologized* for killing her uncle!

She crossed her arms over her chest. "A demon tried to attack me *after* his death."

Purcell's mouth tightened. "A demon that continued to fulfill its obligation." He met Cyn's gaze. "You killed my son, because he acted recklessly." His cold eyes shifted to her. "Your father died for the same reason. Enough people have perished. Now we must focus on saving those we can."

Rage trembled through her body, making Cyn squeeze her shoulders.

Cyn's voice was rigid when he asked, "Won't it be odd when thousands of people die for no apparent reason?"

"Of course. The CDC will be desperately searching for the killer pathogen that will seem like the avian flu panic all over again. But it will be over before they can even begin their research. You, Cyn, are—were—a Vega, the most capable of Guard officers. We could use your help." He looked at Ruby. "You will be spared, too, if you cooperate."

Purcell turned to Fernandez. "Show them your bracelet."

He did, plucking at a leather band. Purcell pulled more

bands from his pocket. "I will give you four of these. When the lack of *Deus Vis* becomes too much to handle, the Chosen will be called to a central location, where we will ride out the storm. Like a hurricane shelter." He held out the bands. "Do we have a deal?"

Cyn gave her shoulder another squeeze. "Deal. We'll cease and desist." He couldn't be thinking of trusting this guy!

Purcell's steely gaze shifted to her, and she felt an odd pressure in her head. "I know you doubt me," he said, as though he'd read her mind. He had, she realized. "But with your comrade on our side, you haven't a chance of succeeding. Cyn, when you or Ruby start feeling ill, call Fernandez. He'll have instructions by then."

Fernandez approached Cyn. "I'm sorry I set this up." He watched Purcell's retreating back as though he were afraid the man would disappear.

Cyn narrowed eyes that showed his sense of betrayal. "Set *me* up. This could have gone much differently."

"I can't lose her, Cyn." The man's voice bled with regret. He ran across the lawn to follow Purcell.

As soon as he was out of earshot, Ruby asked, "We're not really—"

Cyn shook his head, answering and cutting her off with the same movement. He motioned for her to follow him to the T-bird. As soon as they pulled away from the house, Cyn instructed his cell phone to dial Grayson.

His deep voice boomed over the speakers when he answered. "What's up?"

"I need a Leap to Chena. I'll fill you in when we get to your place." He disconnected.

"Who's Chena? And what's a Leap, and why does it

make my stomach knot up even more than it already is? Don't you dare tell me 'later.'"

He slid her a slightly amused look. "Chena is a what, not a who. It's a town in Alaska, one of the few places where pockets of *Deus Vis* can sustain Crescents."

"*Alaska*? Are we running off to save our asses? Or are you running off?"

"Ruby, you've got to stop letting your emotions drive you. Back there, bursting out like that could have gotten us killed." He released a breath. "You really think I'd leave you to save myself?"

She settled back in her seat. "No."

Cyn pulled into the high-rise's parking lot and started heading to the entrance. "Maybe Purcell's telling the truth, and this disturbance is a natural result of the impending solar storm. My gut says it isn't."

"If he's right, my father was either crazy or greedy. My gut says it's not true."

"Your gut or your heart? You must be able to tell the difference."

She recalled the memories Grayson had revived. "I remember my father telling Darren that what they were doing was dangerous. That's why he destroyed everything. He wasn't a man intent to run with a moneymaking device, but one in fear for the safety of his family. And all Crescents. My gut says that in the end, he did the right thing."

Cyn nodded. "Trust your gut always. Trust your emotions never. Going to Alaska is about getting answers. Jay Caruso's had a fascination with the *Deus Vis* ever since he went to college with your father. When Brom had his vision fifteen years ago, he called Jay, whose idea it was to use the prism to see the *Deus Vis*. Jay is a permanent resident at Sanctum, the Crescent sanctuary where Brom went. When I was at Brom's earlier, there was a message from Jay on his machine. He's running experiments based on something Brom just told him. We're going to find out what that something is." He ran his hands lightly over her shoulders and down her arms. Her body stiffened, and he pulled back. "You're going to need a coat."

Even that casual touch sent his energy into her body. "I can get one at the airport."

"We're not going via plane. We're going via magick."

Chapter 21

Cyn outlined what they knew while sitting at the bar at Grayson's. Grayson took a generous drink, obviously feeling the emotions zinging between Cyn and Ruby. "There was something on the news this morning about an uptick in people getting the flu. I don't feel it, but I'm old. I'll take you and come when you're ready to return."

"I understand." For Cyn, Sanctum was a place of healing. For Grayson it was probably a reminder of why he'd needed healing.

Grayson slammed down the rest of his drink, setting it on the counter with a *thud*. "Ready?"

Ruby slid from the stool and grabbed the coat Grayson had borrowed from the lone female Caido in the building. She'd taken the whole Leap thing pretty well. Of course, compared to demons and finding out you were a Dragon, Leaping was pretty tame.

She put on the coat, then grabbed a small bag. Cyn had

nothing but the clothing he wore and a long black leather coat.

Grayson stripped out of his shirt. Their "wings" weren't the Mundane's vision of the feathery kind. Even so, they still tore through clothing—and hurt like hell if his grimace was any indication. Ruby stared as he came around the bar, trying to see his back. She didn't get a chance. He put his big arms around both Cyn and Ruby. "You'll feel light-headed, light-bodied. It'll pass." In a flash of white, Cyn felt the very sensation Grayson had described.

Seconds later, they stood outside the remote commune known as Sanctum. A sign gave the impression that it was, indeed, some kind of private mental facility. Beyond the utilitarian entrance lay beautiful landscaping and buildings.

Cyn turned to Grayson, who was also taking in the place. "It calls to you already, doesn't it?"

Grayson said, "Yes, which means it's time to go." In a flash, he was gone. Here, among only Crescents, no one had to hide their magick.

Ruby held out her hands. "I can feel a difference in the energy here. Is that what you mean?"

"Sanctum has an odd mix of natural magick and strong *Deus Vis*. You can see the aurora borealis here year-round, where it's usually only visible in winter months. It's a bit like the Thrall. The broken come here to heal, to become whole again. And you never want to leave."

Now Ruby's hazel eyes had the same effect, holding him in a different type of thrall. "Sounds like you've been here before." She tilted her head, seeming to look right into his soul. "What did you need to heal from?"

"My life. My past. I made a little girl an orphan. I quit the only career I'd ever known. I gave up a lot for the Guard, and I caused loss and suffering in the name of duty. I ended up staying for a year. This place held me as a willing captive." She was looking at him as though *he* were an angel. "Don't let it suck you in."

Ruby blinked at the directive. "No, of course not."

He called Jay's phone but it went right to voice mail. "Jay, this is Cyntag Valeron, a blast from the past. Listen, buddy, I'm here at Sanctum, and I need to talk to you as soon as you get back. It's about Brom." He disconnected. "I'm going to get a room so you can rest up until he gets back."

"I could use a hot shower. But what about you?"

"Don't worry, I won't be around." He looked at the familiar buildings and landscape, his soul taking comfort in just the sight. "I'll give you some quiet time."

Ruby took in the landscape as they headed to the lobby, her face lit with enchantment. "I haven't seen mountains for years, when Mon dragged me all over Europe on his tours."

Her nose was pink, the freckles across her cheeks standing out even more, and her delight filled him with some emotion he dare not name. Or acknowledge.

The woman at the front desk greeted them with a demure smile. "May I help you?"

Cyn pressed his hands on the granite counter. "Do you have a cottage available for the night?"

She clicked on the keyboard. "You're in luck. I have one left but only for tonight. Starting tomorrow we're fully booked with a waiting list. People are panicking about the solar storm, thinking the stronger *Deus Vis* here will save them."

It might save them from far worse than the fluctuations of the storm. "We'll take it." Cyn handed her his credit card.

Ruby tossed her bag over her shoulder as they headed out of the lobby a few minutes later. "Where did Brom stay when he was here?"

He pointed to a building behind the one they'd just exited.

She stared at the three-story building for a moment, her expression pensive. "Now that one looks like a mental health facility. It's even got gates around it."

She continued down the winding path the clerk had highlighted on the map. He followed a couple of feet behind her, watching the way her braid slid back and forth with her movements. Remembering how he'd loosened it and buried his face in her hair. He stifled a sigh.

Some of the people they passed bowed in greeting, wearing the baggy cotton clothing Cyn remembered well. One man whispered, "Namaste."

"Now it's looking like a monastery," Ruby whispered.

"It can be monastic if that's what you need." For Cyn, this wasn't only a place of healing but of penance. He had lived like a monk in one of the many cottages scattered over the property, allowing himself little pleasure and no luxuries. His pace slowed, memories of walking down paths of sharp rocks barefooted to ground himself in his body, the hot springs in caves and cold showers outside the meditation hut, all coming back.

"Is that what you needed?"

"I had to come to terms with the fact that I'd killed a lot of people in the name of right." He came to a stop at the edge of the labyrinth, short evergreen hedges that followed the concrete path in a round maze. In the center sat the meditation hut. "And that maybe it hadn't always been so right after all."

"*Brother Cyn?*" The words, dripping with incredulity, made them both turn at the man approaching.

He smiled at the sight of his sponsor and clasped the hand offered with both of his. "Brother Cameron, good to see you."

Cameron was another old Dragon, though he only looked to be in his fifties. The bowl haircut made him appear even younger, the fringe of brown hair straight across his brow like a mod sixties haircut. He looked beyond Cyn to Ruby and said, "Did you bring us another lost soul?" He clasped her hands with both of his, giving her a warm smile. "Welcome, dear."

Ruby glanced at him, then back to Cam. "I'm not lost." She turned to Cyn. "Who else did you bring here?"

"Brom. I knew it was what he needed when he was falling apart."

Cam nodded. "He stayed for a long time. Many people find they stay much longer than they intended. And that they are more lost than they realized."

"We don't have time to stay, unfortunately," Cyn said. "We've got a problem in Miami, something I hope Jay Caruso can help us with."

Cam gave Cyn a look that meant he was assessing him right down to his soul. "Maybe that's why you *think* you've come." He gestured to the hut. "Please avail yourself of our facilities. It looks like you could use them." Compassion tempered his knowing smile. "You, too," he said to Ruby. "There's a women's and men's side for the springs and showers. The outdoor shower in the garden is open to both genders, so knock before opening the gate."

Ruby turned to Cyn. "I'll find the cottage and meet you there later." She took the map and gave him no choice by heading off.

"I'm here if you want to talk." Cam gestured to the hut. "Otherwise, please . . ." He left Cyn to his thoughts.

Cyn didn't want to talk. What would he say, how he'd caused Ruby the most pain of her life and was selfish enough to still want her? He walked along the circular pathway and ended up around the back of the hut, where a small stone garden and thick hedges surrounded the outdoor shower.

He went inside to the men's section and pulled out the pants and wrap shirt most of the residents wore. He flagged down one of the employees and asked about getting his clothing cleaned and delivered to the cottage. Then he wrapped a towel around his hips and walked outside.

It was warm for this time of year, about fifty-five degrees. He knocked at the gate, and when no one called out, pushed it open. Just the sight of the tiny garden infused him with peace. He took it in for a few minutes before turning on the shower. Jets of cool water raised a slew of goose bumps on his skin. He relished the discomfort, along with the numbness that followed as he washed his body and hair.

He was the lost soul.

Staying lost would be the best thing. Since Ruby had come into his life with her fire, he couldn't numb himself anymore. He lifted his face into the stream of spring water and hoped it would cleanse all thoughts of having her from his body, his mind.

Ruby let the hot water pound her body and soothe her aching muscles. For the first several minutes, she found herself continually looking out through the clear shower curtain, imagining a sound or a shadow.

Psycho, anyone?

Except that movie didn't have demons and tulpas.

She leaned against the tiles, pressing her cheek against the cool ceramic. She *was* a lost soul, fighting her own emotions with an aching heart. She'd accused Cyn of following orders to kill out of ambitiousness, but she'd seen his loyalty to others. His loyalty to her despite her anger.

Think with your gut.

He followed orders because he had placed his faith in the Guard and, in particular, the man who had raised him. And if she were to concede that maybe her father was good despite his blind ambition, she had to see why Cyn had done the things he had. Not blind ambition, but blind faith.

Deep inside him, he held goodness.

She dried off and dressed, disappointed to find the cottage empty. Where was he? She put her hand to her Dragon. *Find him.*

Her Dragon jolted at the command like a dog released to find a treat. She followed her instincts to the meditation hut. No surprise. He'd looked at it with the longing of a man who needed solace.

It was late afternoon, though the sun was still high in the sky. She followed the labyrinth, walking into the sanctity of the octagonal building. The blinds let in dim sunlight, the only light in the open room. No chairs, only mats and a few people sitting in lotus positions. None were Cyn.

She wandered through some of the other gardens, finding most of them empty. The sound of running water on the other side of a thick hedge caught her attention. She followed it to a wooden gate. A waterfall? She opened the gate and froze.

She'd found him all right. He stood naked beneath a showerhead, his hands braced on the wall, facing away from her. His head was bowed, as though he were in pain. She automatically put her hand to her throat, feeling it tighten and go dry all at once. Why was he showering out here? Goose bumps covered him. The lack of steam coming from the water made her realize it wasn't warm either.

His position reminded her of someone under arrest. She shivered, wondering if he'd done this before. Atoning for the people he'd killed. For her parents.

His wide shoulders tapered down to narrow hips, to a tight ass made even tighter because all his muscles were clenched. The body of his Dragon trembled, its wings shrinking close to its body. A tremor passed through him, making him flex his fingers.

She approached slowly, her heart as tense as his muscles. The Dragon's head turned and looked at her. It seemed to be pleading for her to stop its torture. She reached through the water and ran her hand down his back, over the lines of the Dragon's body. He didn't jerk, making her wonder if he'd known she was there all along. Of course, no one snuck up on Cyn.

He, in fact, did not turn to her but flattened his hands against the walls. "Ruby, what are you doing?" His voice was hoarse. From cold or something else?

"I could ask you the same thing."

He turned to her then, and she saw turmoil in the embers of his eyes. "T-taking a shower."

"Mmm. A cold shower in the cold air."

The water *was* cold, already numbing her fingers. They remained on the indent of his lower spine, where the Dragon's tail dipped to his tailbone. Droplets sprayed her like ice chips. She'd forgotten to put on her coat.

"It f-feels good," he said.

"No, it doesn't." She reached for the shower to turn it off, but his hand clamped over hers, still fast despite how numb it must be. It felt like a glove of ice.

"Ruby, I'll meet you back at the cottage later."

She ran her other hand back up to his shoulder, now half in the shower's spray herself. "I forgive you, Cyn."

He didn't seem to register her words, staring fiercely into her eyes.

"I forgive you." She placed her palm against his cheek. "For killing my parents."

He shook his head. "No, you don't get to f-forgive me."

She arched her eyebrow. "I can do what I damn well please." He gave her the expression he wore whenever she questioned a command. "You don't get to tell me what to do on this one."

He gripped her wrist as though he were going to pull her hand away. But he held fast. "I don't want your forgiveness."

"You do want it. You just don't think you deserve it." All those words he'd said to her earlier tore at her, how he wanted her, how the thought of not having her hurt so badly he thought he was actually bleeding. "You do deserve forgiveness. And me."

He groaned, so obviously fighting what she was offering. She stepped fully into the stream with him, pressing her body against his. His Dragon became a deeper, more vivid blue. He resisted, remaining stiff as she kissed the Dragon through the water, up his pecs to his collarbone.

"It's the magick here," he said on a raw whisper. "I warned you—"

"It's not magick. It's everything about you, Cyn, your honor and loyalty, and even the fact that you're resisting for *me*. But all I want is you." She kissed the place beneath his jaw as he stared at the wall with the ferocity of his resolve. She wrapped her arms around him, continuing to kiss the bristle at his chin.

He broke, burying his face in her neck and pulling her so close that her body was crushed against him. "Ruby," he whispered, the one word a plea, a thank you, and a declaration felt by her Dragon.

Mine. His.

She nodded, tilting her head back and relishing his surrender. She dug her hands into his hair. "Come back to the cottage. Let me warm you up."

He held on for another second before releasing her and shutting off the water. His hair stuck out in wild strands, but his eyes entranced her. That was where the magick was.

He grabbed the towel on a shelf but wrapped it around her, carefully drying her even as he trembled. "Let me get another towel," she said, searching for a door to inside the building but finding none.

"I'll put this on." He pulled on the sort of garb she'd seen some of the other residents wearing.

She took his cold, stiff hand and led him to their

cottage. As soon as she closed the door behind them, she went to the bathroom and got a towel. He'd already stripped out of the now wet clothing. His Dragon shifted, its eyes as fiery as its human's.

She removed her cold, wet clothes under his watchful eye. As though she were the most gorgeous, sexy woman in the world. She did move with a new kind of sensuous grace now. It coursed through her as she approached him with a dry towel. She dried him the same delicate way he had done for her, rubbing the towel over his hair and mussing it even more. He took the towel and tossed it aside, tilting her chin up and taking her mouth. His hands pulled her close, one tangling in her hair, the other sliding down her backside.

Despite the cold, he was fully erect, pressing into her stomach. His tongue slid against hers, brushing the edge of her teeth, and she found it hard to focus on all the different sensations rushing through her. She was no longer cold, not with the heat of his hands, his body on hers.

He maneuvered her to the bed, sliding down with her and kissing her as though he couldn't get enough. In between kisses, he said, "Ruby, if I make love to you, my Dragon will consider you mine. I didn't get a chance to tell you that part. Your Dragon will consider me yours. It's—"

She gripped his face, touching her nose to his. "My Dragon already has it in its head that you're mine. Ours. Whatever." She kissed him hard, pulling him down so she could feel the weight of him on top of her. She sank into the soft mattress under him, feeling fully encompassed. For so long, she was the tough one, or so she thought. Now she gave in to his strength.

Need.

Not only her need, but also her Dragon's. Its craving roared through her, nearly sweeping her away. She held on to control, even as its heat licked through her.

Cyn rolled them to the side and nibbled down her neck, sliding his hands around to cup her butt and pull her tight against his pelvis. He met her eyes before kissing her again, wrapping his body around hers.

She pushed him back onto the bed and straddled him, breathless at the sight of his naked body against the moss-green sheets. She leaned down and kissed his beautiful Dragon, feeling its heat beneath her lips. Her Dragon stirred where it touched the side of his stomach.

He caressed her breasts, rubbing his thumbs over her nipples. He'd said he wanted to get lost in her, and she knew the feeling of that madness. She left a trail of kisses across his ridged abdomen and then along his shaft and the velvety tip. He let out a sound between a growl and a sigh that made her smile just before she took him into her mouth. She stroked, licked, sucked, feeling his thigh muscles tighten beneath her hand as she brought him to the brink of orgasm.

Not yet, baby. I have other plans for that big erection. Like burying it inside her.

She worked her way back up, slowly, and then wrapped herself over him. His arms slid around her, squeezing her tight against him for a few moments. Then he rolled her over and ground her into the bed, nudging her thighs apart with his knee. He bowed before her, dipping his head between her legs. She didn't know which was more provocative, his bowing or his mouth covering her throbbing clit. His tongue danced and flicked and made her arch in pleasure. Then a wave washed over her, and she writhed at the overwhelming sensation rocketing through her. When he made her come a second, and then a third time, electric shocks coursed through her body.

He sat up and pulled her onto his lap, facing him, encircling her waist with his arms. She eased onto him, glad he'd readied her as the length of him pushed inside her. And in the way her Dragon had filled an emptiness she'd harbored since adolescence, Cyn filled her soul. She'd never had sex in this position before and relished how close she was to him. He lifted her butt, his hands firm and warm over the cool skin, and held her aloft so she could move against him.

She wrapped her legs around him and kissed him. He devoured her. His intensity shot from a slow easing in to flying. He gripped her as though he'd never let her go, invading her mouth the way he invaded her body. And hers welcomed, no craved, that invasion. Her Dragon responded, pulling her into an intensity that equaled Cyn's. She sucked on his tongue, bit his lower lip, and nipped his neck.

He had awakened her, as a Crescent and a woman, and she felt both aspects as they moved together in a heated frenzy. Then he rolled her over, lifted her legs, and placed pillows beneath her butt. Was it her Dragon that made her grasp his cock and draw it back, desperate to have him inside her again? Sometimes she didn't know where she ended and the Dragon began.

He thrust alternately shallow and deep, stroking his fingers across her already sensitive nub. This time her orgasm started deep within her core, spiraling through every cell in her body before bursting to the surface.

"You're beautiful when you come," he said on shallow breaths.

"Mmm," was all she could manage as he drove faster and faster into her.

He threw his head back, eyes closed in pleasure, and let out a roar that sounded like, "Mine."

Mine, her Dragon answered back.

Cyn throbbed inside her, and her own body seemed to pulse in an answering rhythm. She watched him revel in the sensations, and then he buried his face in her neck and squeezed her close. She closed her eyes and sank into the feeling of being possessed. Claimed.

Cyn lay down beside her, still intimately joined with her. "I like your hair loose like this." He pulled it over her shoulder, coiling a lock around his fingers, then tugging her close for another kiss.

She rested her cheek on his chest. "Just like the Dragon Prince."

He drew lazy circles on her back. "Too bad he dies in the end. I'll bet they could have been happy."

"Very, very happy."

Her body sated, fatigue now set in. She dozed, for how long she didn't know. When she woke, Cyn was watching her with sleepy eyes. He smiled at her, and the sight filled her heart.

"Let me show you the lights," he said, his voice husky.

"Mmm, you already did."

His chuckle reverberated through her. "I mean, the aurora borealis. I heard one of the guys say that because of the impending solar storm, the lights are more spectacular than ever."

"And leave this bed?"

But it was clear that he wanted to show her a different kind of magic. She eased up on her elbows and searched for the clock. She'd been asleep for three good, deep hours. "I'm starved."

"We'll eat, take in the lights, and then maybe we'll have time for more of the other kind before Jay gets back."

After dinner, Cyn led her up a dimly lit trail to an area where a few benches were situated to look over a small valley. A couple of people were there, but she could barely see them.

He led her to a bench, dropping down onto it and pulling her down on his lap. His arms encircled her, his chin resting on her shoulder as they sat in silence. The feel of his body against hers made her more content than she'd ever been.

Her Dragon purred. She purred, too.

"There," he whispered, pointing toward the right of the star-glittered sky.

She saw the first ribbon undulating in a vibrant green. It swirled around, rather like the fog in a Deuce's eyes, and then disappeared. Another wave of lights flickered like miles of blue fire. She inhaled deeply at the magic of it, the surreal beauty. He squeezed her tighter, sliding his hand beneath her shirt to rest against her stomach.

"Incredible," she whispered. "Like ghosts dancing in the sky."

"Yes, incredible." She heard the awe in his voice, too, the reverence.

When she turned, he was looking at her.

The Book of the Hidden

Garnet angled her body into the warm spring. Hedges all around the castle garden afforded her privacy, but it wasn't her nudity she worried about. It would not do for her staff to hear their queen crying. Even seven months after his death, her heart ached for the prince who was dark of hair, but not so dark of heart.

Ribbons of magical lights danced like ghosts and fairies in the night sky. As steam wafted up from the water, she prayed again for the end of her heartache. It wasn't good to steep herself in such sadness, but she mourned silently now, her tears dropping into the water some believed to be magickal.

A rustle in the bushes drew her attention to the wooden gate that was now opening. Who dared enter—

The Dragon Prince stepped inside. His smile lit the night. "Garnet," he said on a breath, coming close and kneeling near the edge of the spring.

"'Tis cruel, whoever you are, to come here looking so much like him."

"I am he, my love." The endearment had come to mean something during their time together, and she heard meaning in the way he said it now. "You brought me back." He gestured to the skies filled with ribbons of light, and then to the spring in which she sat. "I could see and watch over you, though I felt so helpless. I saw that you loved me, rather than merely tolerated me as I thought." He reached for her hand, his fingers closing

around hers. "Your love, along with the magick here, brought me back."

He was real. Alive, flesh and blood. Tears came faster now, free of the pain that usually accompanied them. "I didn't know I loved you until you were gone."

He tugged gently on her hand. "Let me see you. Both of you." He pulled her to her feet, his eyes taking in her face before moving down to the lushness of her pregnant body. "Amazing. Beautiful. A miracle."

When she looked into his face, he was gazing at her.

Chapter 22

———

Cyn's cell phone vibrated. "Jay," he whispered, and they left the viewing area.

"I'm here," she could hear Jay say as they walked down the path. "Cottage 14B."

"We'll be there in a minute."

Cyn grasped her hand as they took the trail down to civilization. She squeezed, reveling in the feel of it. She'd been daydreaming while watching the lights, giving Garnet and the Dragon Prince their happy ending. Now she wanted one, too. When she'd withheld her forgiveness, all she had was anger and bitterness. By forgiving Cyn, she'd gained so much more. And freed herself in the bargain.

As though he'd picked up on her thoughts, he lifted her hand to his mouth and kissed it.

In turn, she pulled the back of his hand toward her mouth. "I hope you can forgive yourself, too."

"I took away your parents. That you are the one woman

who touches me, who makes me feel something…
karma." She could see his wry smile in the dim lights.

She held their linked hands to her heart. "If I can
forgive you, you can sure as hell forgive yourself." She
bumped him with her hip. "Don't make me hurt you."

He rubbed his thigh, faux pain on his face. "You *have*
hurt me. Or have you forgotten that beating?"

Her cheeks warmed at the memory of her lost control.
"Emotion over logic. That's going to be a tough lesson.
But I'm sorry—"

He swung her around so that she faced him, pressing a
finger to her mouth. "Don't apologize." He took her hand
again and checked the number on the cottage just ahead.
"We're here."

The door opened, and a big, burly Deuce with mussed
dark hair and the beginnings of a beard stepped onto the
stoop. For someone who was close to her father's age, he
looked like he was in his twenties.

"Cyntag!" His voice was boomingly loud, which was
how she'd heard him so clearly on the phone. "Long time
no anything." He gave Cyn a back-slapping guy hug, then
turned to her. "Well, well, what do we have here?" He
thrust out his hand. "Jay Caruso. And you are…"

"Ruby Salazaar," she said as he enveloped her hand in
his.

"Nice to meet you." He waved them inside the warm
cottage. "Come in, make yourselves at home."

The place was cluttered, though not dirty. Papers and
whiteboards covered with calculations made her long for
her parents. Framed pictures of auroras adorned every
wall. Off to the side sat a huge backpack.

"Coffee? Tea?" Jay said from the kitchen, pouring

from a pot. "Something to warm you up?" He shivered. "Spending two days in the wilderness is a bit much even for my Alaskan blood." No wonder he smelled of fresh air and pines.

She rubbed her upper arms. "Coffee sounds great."

Cyn pulled her against his chest. "Got everything I need right here."

Jay gave him a speculative look. "I see that." He handed Ruby the mug and set out milk and sugar. Then he opened a wooden cabinet and poured out two shot glasses of whiskey. "Bet I can tempt you with this."

Cyn waved the glass under his nose. "You remembered."

"It was the only way I could regale you with my fascinating studies of the aurora borealis." Jay cleared off the couch and gestured for them to sit. "You said you're here because of Brom. So you know he called me about the *Deus Vis* fracturing in Miami that coincided with a vision he'd been having for years. Where is he? I haven't heard from him since his initial call to me."

Cyn and Ruby filled him in on what had happened, her gaze going to an aquarium on the floor that contained a prism instead of fish.

Jay finished off his whiskey, shaking his head. "Will he be all right?"

"Once we kill the one who summoned it," Cyn said. "We need to know what you found out."

Jay braced his elbows on his thighs as he sat forward. "When Brom had the first vision, Justin wouldn't tell us what element he was using to fracture the *Deus Vis*. He said no one knew but him, and if it was doing something dangerous, he wanted to keep it that way. I don't think he believed his father's vision yet. I told them how to make this, something I'd been working on for years." He tapped the aquarium with his foot. "Brom called and said they could see the fracturing. Justin's prototype pulled the *Deus Vis* ribbons so hard they completely fell apart. The solar storm we were experiencing at the time wasn't particularly strong, but it was enough to weaken the ribbons. That exacerbated the effect of the element Justin was using."

Jay went to the cabinet, took out the bottle of whiskey, and poured more in their glasses. "Brom called me back a few days later and said that Justin had obviously destroyed his device—and was killed for it. The good news was that the fracturing stopped. Then Brom came here, broken and catatonic. I tried to talk to him several times over the years he's lived here, but he wouldn't even see me." He gave a slow shake of his head. "He saved a lot of lives, but all he could focus on were the two he didn't. I think it made him crazy."

Ruby took a long drink of her coffee, hoping it would warm the cold that truth left in her heart. "Brom's vision of Black Doom came back."

"Yeah, and he came to me pretty freaked out, especially when he learned about the big upcoming solar storm. Apparently someone re-created your father's technology. But Brom had new information. He saw you trying to destroy the cause of the fracturing—and the device exploded. Not only did it kill you, but it also totally fractured the *Deus Vis*. And that narrowed down the element that Justin was using to a few choices. I got my hands on them, which wasn't easy, and ran some experiments."

Jay got up and dug through his backpack, extracting a glass tube. He killed the lights, grabbed a black light, and mounted it on clips over the aquarium. The ribbons were visible as they undulated in the water. He lowered the tube into the water, and the ribbons began to pull toward it. "This is a weak example. There are formulations that would need to be figured out to do it properly. But you get the idea."

"What's in the tube? It looks empty," Ruby said.

"*Deus Vis*. There's only a trace amount in the tube. *Deus Vis* isn't magnetic, per say, but it acts like one, drawing more of the essence toward it. Your father did it, Ruby. He found a way to free us, to make *Deus Vis* portable. He would have been a hero if it hadn't ended up being such a bad thing."

"How?" Cyn asked, studying the vial.

"It stems from hydrogen and helium," Jay began, "the two most basic—and prevalent—elements in the universe."

Ruby leaned forward for a closer look at the tube. She saw just the tiniest flicker of silver. A trick of the light or the *Deus Vis*? Hydrogen brought to mind water, H_2O. And helium. She thought of how she used to suck air out of balloons backstage at Mon's magic shows. Gosh, she really should've paid more attention during her tutoring sessions.

"Mundanes would kill for this technology," Jay muttered. He pulled the vial from the water and set it carefully on a towel. "To date, there is no practical fusion reactor in use. Justin discovered a way to harness the energy of these basic elements. No small feat."

"How does it work?" Cyntag asked.

"Hydrogen plasma is superheated. The isotopes collide and combine, then fuse. In labs, it takes massive electromagnets to confine the plasma. It took some time, but I figured out how your father did it. He used an orb."

Magick and science, a dangerous combination.

Jay ran his finger down the tube. "What I can't figure out is how the orb is maintained for any length of time. Eventually they disintegrate."

"The device we saw in Darren's lab was metal," Ruby said.

Jay tapped his temple. "Ah, titanium, maybe. It's one of the few elements that resists magick, meaning it can maintain the energy of the orb for an extended time. And thus the fusion process. The fusion draws in the *Deus Vis*, channels it." He frowned. "And that fits in with Brom's vision of doom. The process isn't stable. Think about it. This fusion is the same reaction that fuels stars. It's how our sun works. The fusion gives off massive amounts of energy and heat." Jay raked a hand through his hair. "Combine it with the upcoming coronal mass ejection, and we're talking the perfect storm, so to speak."

"Smith—Purcell used that phrase about the ejection," Ruby said. "What is it exactly?"

"That's the blast of charged particles that hits the Earth a couple of days after the eruption. It bombards our magnetic field, disrupts communications, and, unbeknownst to most of the scientists studying this, distorts our *Deus Vis*—"

"And a device that acts like a magnet for *Deus Vis* is going to draw all that instability into one place." Cyn's dark eyes were bleak.

"That kicks off a chain of events. If the *Deus Vis* within the reactor isn't dismantled, it will fuel a fusion process that won't stop. The heat and energy released will cause massive damage."

"Like killing every Crescent in Miami?"

Jay shook his head. "Beyond that. The blast will obliterate the entire state."

Ruby slapped her hand to her chest, Jay's words thudding heavily inside. "That can't be what Purcell's goal is. Otherwise he'd be leaving. And seriously, what would he gain by doing that?"

"He may not know that will happen. He probably has no idea what he's dealing with. This has got to be stopped."

Cyn pinched the bridge of his nose. "So how do we dismantle this thing?"

"Very carefully. Your inclination will be to destroy it with your Dragon fire, but you'd detonate it instantly. Which is what Brom saw."

Ruby snapped her fingers. "When Garnet defeated the monster, she didn't lob flashy orbs at it. She used a gentle, beautiful orb. Maybe Brom had the answer and didn't even know it."

After she explained who Garnet was, Jay said, "Yes, gently release the orb's energy, the way air releases from a punctured tire. You'll need something that's strong enough to penetrate the metal but leaves you with enough control to pull it back before crushing the tube."

Cyn bared his teeth. "Like a Dragon's fang, maybe?"

Ruby's mouth dropped open. "You're going to bite an explosive canister? No, I'm going to bite it. Because it's my destiny."

Cyn got to his feet, pulling her up with him. "We have to go."

Ruby wrapped her fingers around Cyn's arm. "When Brom was trying to talk, he said 'J-J.' We thought he was saying 'Justin,' but he was probably saying 'Jay.' If we hadn't come here, we would have blown the damned thing up."

Jay leaned back against the desk. "Should you approach the Concilium?"

Cyn's expression shadowed. "Purcell has connections in the Guard. I don't know who else might be involved."

"If the solar storm is the key factor, you only have until tomorrow to destroy this object. Is there anything I can do to help?"

Cyn clapped his hand on Jay's shoulder. "How long since you've fought?"

Jay rolled his eyes in thought. "Fifty or so years. But it's like riding a bike, right?"

How weird to hear guys talk about that kind of span of time so casually.

"You're out of practice dealing with demons and the like. But keep your phone with you. I may need your guidance."

Cyn called Grayson once they said goodbye. She packed her bag while Cyn retrieved his clothes. When he returned, he wore the black pants and white shirt he'd had on before. He closed the door behind him, but his gaze went right to her. To the way she was taking him in, no doubt.

"You're right, there is something magic here," she said, slinging the bag over her shoulder as she came closer.

He skimmed his hands over her shoulders. "Does that

mean you're going to go back to hating me when we get to Miami? I'm not sure I could bear that." He was serious.

"No, I meant that there's something magic...here." She gestured between them. "Us."

A sound drew their attention to the sight of Grayson appearing out of nowhere. Holy...well, not holy exactly. Black, ethereal wings shimmered. He took them in with a curious expression. "Your energy has drastically changed from a few hours ago."

She said, "It's called forgiveness. You should try it."

His eyes frosted over. "Holding on is a good reminder not to make the same mistake. Ready?"

All righty then. No forgiveness happening for him.

Cyn took her hand and led her over to him. "Let's go."

Seconds later, they were in Grayson's condominium. She couldn't stop staring as his wings shrank down to the tattoo on his back. His shoulders drooped, and he braced his hands on the back of his couch for support.

"Does Leaping take a lot out of you?" she asked.

He stepped away from her, bowing his head and running his hand back over his hair. "Leaping by itself is taxing. Bringing two people even more so. Twice in a short period of time...definitely." He looked at Cyn. "But if you need help—"

"I'll let you know. We've been having demon trouble. We've handled them so far. But be on call. And if you start to feel unusually fatigued, or fluish, get out of here. Tell the other Caidos. The clerk at Sanctum said the place was fully booked starting tomorrow, solar storm panic."

"I can already feel the difference," she said. "In Chena, the energy was alive. Invigorating. Not here."

The first faint hints of dawn lit the sky. They reached

the car, and she pulled out Brom's book as soon as they'd closed the doors. "There's a new entry. Hopefully something useful."

Her finger followed Brom's scribbled words. *Cyn dies. Ruby must Breathe his power. But enough to defeat???*

The words clutched her throat. "No." She looked at Cyn, whose face had gone pale. "No."

"The Dragon Prince died in Mon's story," he said in a low, careful voice.

"But that's because he hated you. He made it up."

"His stories were based on Brom's vision, Ruby. We can't ignore what's right in front of us." He tapped the picture. "This is why you need me. You will need my power to succeed."

She grabbed his arm, her fingers twisting the material of his sleeve. "Kade said visions were an approximation of what could happen."

"Maybe so, but everything Brom saw has come true so far."

"Cyn, you can't die. Not now that I…" Loved him? Isn't that what giving him her heart meant? "Not now," she finished.

His mouth turned to a wry grin. "Would have been easier if you still hated me." She could see his mind working as his embers became jagged sparks.

"Well, it's too late for that now, Cyntag Valeron. What I've given you, you can't give back."

"Your forgiveness?"

"My heart."

He reached out, his palm on her cheek. His mouth opened, but he seemed to struggle with the words. She suspected he changed them when he said, "Remember what I said about Breathing Dragon. Just in case," he added, when she was going to protest. "You'll see the Dragon's essence hovering above the physical body. It'll look like heat waves over sunbaked pavement. The stronger and older he or she is, the more power. I'm old *and* I've killed a lot of Dragons, so if you Breathe me, you're going to get overloaded. This is where you really have to put logic over emotion."

"Can't I heal you? Like you healed me?"

He shook his head. "You're not strong enough yet. If I'm killed or mortally injured, you have to Breathe me, Ruby. Because if Magda does it, you'll never win. Promise me."

She nodded, tears making her eyes tingle. She remembered feeling Garnet's pain at being so alone and lost.

"Afterward, you should be able to tap into my Obsidian qualities. But if you let your emotions drive you, you'll be killed. It's as simple as that. And if we both die, so do a lot of other people."

"But you're not going to die."

"I'll do my best." He rubbed his thumb against the side of her mouth. "Before you came into my life again, I didn't care about living or dying. But now I have a lot to live for. So believe me when I say that I'll fight like hell to stay alive, and to keep you safe."

She kissed him fiercely, her hands gripping his face. "Don't you dare die, Cyn. Don't you dare."

"No matter what happens, know that you brought me to life again." He rubbed away tears she didn't know she had shed.

She pressed her hand to his chest. "I want you to know something, too. You have a good heart, despite everything you've done. When I looked past my anger, I saw everything you really are. Not just a cold, badass Dragon warrior, but a man with integrity and a sense of right."

He curled his fingers around her hand. "Would it make any difference to tell you not to have those feelings about me?"

"No. You don't know the half of what I feel for you."

His fingers pressed against her mouth. "Don't tell me. It'll mess with my head, make *me* fight under a red haze of emotion. Let's find Purcell and finish this."

Chapter 23

Cyn called Fernandez. "Are you at home?" He didn't apologize for calling at one in the morning.

Ruby leaned close to his shoulder, listening in.

Fernandez's voice was low, hard to hear. "Yes. I'm with Celia. She's sleeping."

"I'm in your driveway now. Does she know what's going on?"

What you did for her? Ruby wanted to shout.

"No, I haven't told her anything. Not until I have to. I'll meet you outside."

Cyn disconnected, giving Ruby a nod. She leaned on the passenger door and watched between half-closed eyes.

Cyn got out as Fernandez approached the car. "I need to get Ruby to whatever this device Purcell has. Now. She's been feeling the effects of the fracturing, but now she's barely hanging on." She could hear his fear of losing her in his voice. "Purcell said to get in touch with you."

Fernandez glanced her way, though he could only see the top of her head for the most part. He pulled out his phone and started touching buttons.

Cyn rammed his fingers back through his hair. "I understand how you felt now, when Celia almost died a long time ago. And recently. I understand why you set me up to save her."

"I'm glad, because it was the hardest thing I've ever had to do." He focused on his call. "Purcell? It's Fernandez. The woman who was with Cyntag, she's very ill...Yes, I'll put him on." He handed the phone to Cyn. "He wants to talk to you."

Cyn took the phone, looking for all the world like a man distraught. "She started out feeling lethargic but went downhill fast. She...she can hardly breathe now. She hasn't eaten in hours. I've been keeping her alive by using my healing power, but I'm so weak I don't know how much longer I can do it. You promised if we backed off, you would save us...I'll be right there." He shoved the phone at Fernandez. "Thank you."

"Where is he sending you? Is it where we're all supposed to go?" Panic punctuated Fernandez's voice. "He won't tell me."

Cyn didn't answer, running to the car.

Ruby sat up as soon as they were out of view of the house. "What if it's a trap?"

"The vision says you have a chance to defeat the monster. The only way we're going to do that is to get to the reactor."

She didn't want to think about the other part.

"I think I was pretty convincing," he said.

"Very. You broke my heart."

"All I had to do was remember watching you walk away from me yesterday." He let those words settle for a moment. "Purcell wants to meet at a gas station north of here. We're to follow him. Remember, he can reach into your mind, so you have to think 'sick.'"

"All I have to do is remember walking away from you. As much as I wanted you to hurt…damn it, I was hurting, too."

He looked at her, his expression softening. "Ruby…"

"Don't say anything." She pressed her fingers to her temples. "It'll mess with *my* head."

Fifteen minutes later, he pulled up to the Chevron. It was closed, but the lights were on. Purcell waited by a Rolls-Royce, his arms loosely crossed in front of him. He approached the Thunderbird, and Cyn got out.

Purcell glanced into the passenger window where Ruby sprawled. "She seemed fine earlier."

"She's been complaining about stomach pains for the last day or so. I convinced her that you were telling us the truth. That we had to look out for ourselves. It was soon after that"—he pinched the bridge of his nose—"she got so fatigued she could barely move. I think it's hitting her hard because she's newly Awakened. Save her, and I'll do everything I can to help you."

She could hear the strain in his voice as he begged. Cyn was not a man who was used to begging.

Purcell said, "I will hold you to your word, as you hold me to mine. But I insist that once you are there, you remain until the fracturing passes."

"Whatever you say."

"Follow me."

Cyn got back in, closing the door with both hands, like he was too weak to do it with one. "We're on."

They wound through the city, busy even at this time of night. Ruby remained slumped but watched the buildings go by. Finally he pulled into a nearly empty parking lot. A sign pronounced the place closed for renovation.

"Where are we?" she asked.

"The Devil's Ray nightclub, one of the private clubs for Crescents only."

He parked near the entrance, going around to the passenger side and helping her out. She let her body go limp.

"In here," Purcell said, leading the way to the back entrance of the three-story building. "I've commandeered one of the clubs to gather the Chosen. You're the first to arrive."

Cyn pretended to stagger, though when Purcell put his arm out to help, he stepped back. "I've got her."

"Can you still become Dragon?"

Cyn sounded weary. "I doubt it."

He stepped into the cavernous space, and the door closed behind them. More ominous, she heard the locks click. She felt an immediate difference in the energy, similar to how Chena felt. The reactor was definitely here. She met Cyn's eyes, and he gave her a subtle nod.

Some lights were on, though they didn't illuminate the space well. She heard two men talking somewhere nearby. Stacks of cots lined the outer wall. So that part was true, anyway. Two bars flanked the large space, and in the back, an open space she guessed was a dance floor. This would be the place where the Chosen would hunker down while all the other Crescents died.

Bastards.

Purcell gestured, and a man rushed over and set out a cot.

Cyn laid her down, whispering, "You're going to be all right, baby."

Another man came over and both remained a few feet away from Purcell. No doubt security.

Purcell held out his hand. "I will require your cell phones. No one can have access to the outside once they're here. It's for your own safety. When friends or acquaintances call, panicked about how people are dying, some will weaken and give our location. We can't allow any more than are planned for."

Cyn slowly pulled his phone out. He wouldn't be able to call in Grayson.

"Hers, too."

She wasn't sure how he knew she had one, but Cyn dutifully dug into her pocket and retrieved it, handing both over.

"Stay with her," Purcell said. "I'll be right back."

Cyn knelt next to her, but he watched the man retreat. She couldn't see from her vantage point. They agreed that as soon as they were inside, they were completely in their roles. The two guards had remained, preventing even a subtle exchange.

Purcell returned and paused by the two men. "Where is Magda?"

Ruby's eyes widened at the name. Of course Magda would be here. She was Purcell's daughter-in-law.

One of the men said, "She went to gather some provisions."

Purcell stepped into view, taking a call on his cell phone. "Yes?... It's getting to be too much?... All right,

you know where we are. I'll see you soon. We're ready."
He disconnected, turning to the two men. "People will
start arriving soon."

Cyn stood. "Ruby needs healing now."

"The *Deus Vis* in the building should bring her
around."

"She's fading fast. If she dies…" He let the threat hang
in the air. They had a small window of opportunity, with
only a few men here and Magda out.

After a tense moment, Purcell turned and walked
away. "Bring her."

Cyn picked her up again and followed Purcell down a
short hallway where the offices were. Purcell opened the
door to the second room, allowing Cyn to carry her in.

In a wooden cabinet lined with black velvet sat a reactor roughly two feet long and six inches wide. Energy
pulsed all around it, as thick in the air as her pulse was
in her blood. Purcell took her hand and pressed it against
the smooth surface. Its energy charged through her so in-
tensely that she gasped.

He pulled it back. "Now, go back to the main area."

Ruby slid to her feet, not having to pretend to adjust to
the power rocketing through her. She and Cyn exchanged
a nod and Catalyzed.

Purcell used his magick to throw Cyn against the
wall, shouting, "Carew! Balston, get in here!" Purcell
turned to her, his eyes as wild as the aurora borealis. He
held out his hand, and she ducked as a fireball shot over
her.

She didn't see the second one that followed right behind the first. It hit her squarely in the stomach with a
fiery heat and hurled her to the floor. Cyn blew out a dark

cloud that surrounded Purcell, though he was using magick to dispel it.

Ruby grabbed the reactor and raced to the door as the two guards rushed in. She barreled into one, knocking him to the side. Cyn fought the other man, fangs against orbs.

Like a football player, she tucked the reactor against her chest with her chin and ran. That was the part of the plan she didn't like, leaving Cyn behind.

Because of Brom's vision.

So she would take it away, hide it, and come back to fight with him. Except the back door opened and Magda stepped inside, turned away as she argued with someone behind her. "You have no right to be here yet."

The man was saying, "I need to know where—"

She suddenly spun around to face Ruby. "I thought I sensed a Dragon." Her gaze narrowed in on the reactor. "Oh, no you don't." She Catalyzed, and the man behind her ran inside. It was Fernandez, who, unlike Magda, wasn't surprised to see Ruby. Because he'd no doubt followed them here.

Magda pointed at the reactor in Ruby's grip. "She's trying to steal the device that will save us! Help me stop her."

Oh, hell. Of course he would. Fernandez Catalyzed, too, a black-and-blue Dragon like Cyn. Ruby couldn't fight and hold the reactor at the same time. It slipped from her grasp. Fernandez went for it as Magda charged at her. Ruby tried to dodge, but like an oncoming car in a game of chicken, Magda changed angles and rammed her.

Ruby shattered the hostess stand when she landed on it. Before she could get to her feet, Magda pounded on her. Fangs glistened as they came at her. Ruby deflected, feeling them scratch across her scales with the ear-shattering screech of nails on a chalkboard. Ruby braced against the floor and shoved Magda off of her. She rolled, coming up on her feet, ready to attack again.

Where was Cyn? She could hear thumps down the hall. *Focus.* Fearing for Cyn's safety would not help her.

Magda advanced on Ruby, whipping her tail equipped with that fatal stinger. "You killed my husband."

Ruby sent a stream of spikes at her, trying to sever the deadly tail. "You killed my parents," Ruby said, her voice a snarl. "My uncle. And now I'm going to kill you."

Magda laughed. "You're a babe. Without your big, bad Obsidian Dragon, you're helpless." She pointed the black tip of her tail at Ruby, sending a shower of small flares at her. Three hit her, penetrating her scales and sending what felt like electrical shocks pulsing through her. The muscles in her right leg seized, cramping like the worst charley horse ever.

"The. Hell. I. Am." Ruby stretched her leg, trying to regain control of it. Magda lunged forward, and Ruby surrounded her with a firestorm the same way she'd done with the demon.

Magda screamed and shook off the flames. Before the last of them were out, Ruby sent fiery spikes at her face. Even temporarily blinded, Magda shot more of those damned darts, hitting Ruby's shoulders. Pain radiated down her arms and paralyzed her hands.

Purcell burst out of the hallway. "Where's the reactor?" he screamed.

Magda blindly pointed at the doorway as she kept her focus on Ruby. "That Guard Captain grabbed it when she dropped it."

"Who, Fernandez? He was here?"

Was, but not anymore. He was gone. And so was the reactor.

Magda screeched, "He must have taken it!"

Purcell raised his hand and began to create an orb. A green one, like the kind that killed Mon. Cyn dove out, knocking Purcell to the ground. The orb disappeared. God, Cyn was bleeding, the red of it streaking down his chest. A huge bubble orb surrounded Purcell as Cyn lunged forward to attack. Cyn bounced back from it, then inhaled and encompassed it in black smoke. Like a living thing, it squeezed the bubble.

Magda took advantage of Ruby's distraction and knocked her to the ground, landing hard on top of her. Magda lifted her tail, like a scorpion, and readied to lance her with it. Ruby could only reach Magda's arm, but she bit hard just as the tail was coming down. Magda screamed as scales broke and bones snapped. The tip still jabbed into Ruby's thigh, sending shocks through her entire lower half. A series of seizures overtook her body, smashing over her like wave after wave. Magda crept closer with a cruel smile to deliver the final blow. And damn it, Ruby couldn't move as her body convulsed.

Cyn threw himself between Ruby and Magda, lashing out at her with his talons. Using the element of surprise, he knocked Magda down and lunged toward her throat. A green bolt of lightning hit him in the neck, tearing through the scales and into muscle. It threw him back with a grunt of pain. He sent an arrow of black smoke hurtling back at Purcell. It speared his shoulder, making him stumble back.

The bolt raced back around again, aiming for Cyn. Oh,

God, it was those horrible moments at Mon's all over again. Cyn dodged the bolt and sprinted away from her, probably so she wouldn't get hit accidentally. He left a trail of blood on the floor.

Please let him be all right.

The wound looked severe, but it was already beginning to heal itself.

She saw no sign of the other two men, so she assumed they must be dead. From the corner of her vision, she saw Magda about to strike. Ruby whirled around and shot spikes of fire at her eyes. Several hit the vulnerable area Cyn had told her about, tearing away strips of skin. Magda roared, whipping her tail ominously as she circled Ruby. Hell, the aftershocks of the last attack still sparked through her.

Ruby could only see Cyn and Purcell from her peripheral vision as she faced Magda. The bubble around Purcell kept Cyn from doing much damage to him. He could hardly do much anyway as he fended off the damned star orb that was intent on impaling him. Killing Purcell was the only way to defeat it. And Ruby couldn't help with Magda deviling her, even with her destroyed arm. Now she needed to disable her tail.

Every time Ruby checked on Cyn, Magda took advantage and tried to attack. So this is where emotions weakened. Cyn kept pounding it in that Ruby use her logic instead of letting emotion drive her.

But wait. Ruby could use Magda's emotions against her. "Too bad you didn't have a man who would give you everything you wanted. Oh, how you must have hated when my father was the one who figured out the solution for portable *Deus Vis*."

Golden flames burst in Magda's eyes. "Shut up."

"I remember how sad you were when you kept miscarrying. I can imagine how hard it was when my mother got pregnant so easily. Did she rub that in your face, too, or did you just see her happiness that way?"

"You little bitch. How dare you—"

"And then the last thing your husband said was how women weren't worth sacrifice, how they—*you*, he meant—were insatiable bitches."

With a cry of rage, Magda stormed at her. Ruby twisted out of the way at the last moment. As Magda's tail whirled past, Ruby clamped onto it and bit down hard. Magda screeched. The tip thrashed, stinging Ruby's cheeks. She held on through the shocking pain, her jaw aching from exertion. More, more, more, and then she heard and felt the snap of bone. Magda's tail fell limp.

Ruby took advantage of her surprise and battered her with a stream of spikes. Sprawled on the floor, Magda grabbed hold of her tail with her good hand, probably intending to use it as a sword.

Be ready to kill, Cyn had said. She descended on Magda, everything in her ready to end it. "It's been lovely, but now I have to kill you."

Except the lightning bolt shot past her, snagging her attention. Cyn tried to evade it, but the bolt shifted and plunged into Cyn's chest. He went to pull it out but jerked his now burned hand away.

Magda smiled. "Now you know how it feels, you—"

Ruby sank her teeth into Magda's throat and tore away a chunk of flesh and scales. As Magda struggled to push her away with one hand, Ruby ripped at her again. She couldn't even feel the victory when the Dragon fell limp, emitting a pained cry as Cyn dropped to the floor.

Purcell burst out of his bubble and tore out the door.

Ruby sank down next to Cyn, tears blurring her eyes. "No. No!"

His voice was hoarse and low. "Good job on Magda. Go, Breathe her power, quickly. Then Breathe me, like I told you to do." His uninjured hand closed over her forearm. "Ruby, you must do it. You'll need all the power you can get to defeat Purcell."

She shook her head.

"Ruby, damn it, logic, not emotion."

How could she put aside her emotions now? Once again she was watching someone she cared about dying, helpless to do anything about it. She couldn't bear to look at the gaping hole in his chest, focusing on the gash in his neck instead.

He trembled, wincing in pain. "Go."

She got to her shaky feet and approached Magda. Ruby had to do it before Magda died and became human again. Had to...

To hell with logic. She was not helpless. She dragged Magda's body closer to his, kneeling between them. He'd told her to pull it deep within. A frenetic energy hovered all around Magda's body, her essence. Ruby Breathed but she did not pull it all the way inside her. Instead she moved close to Cyn, pressing her mouth over his, and Breathed out. Like he had done to her in that apartment to heal her. Maybe she didn't have enough power to heal him, but Magda did.

He thrashed his head, murmuring, "Ruby, don't take a chance."

She felt the same frenetic energy around him, too. "No! I will not lose you, Cyn. I can do this." She braced her hands on his cheeks, staring into indigo eyes with very few embers left. "You made me love you, you arrogant, hard-assed Dragon, so you *cannot* die on me!"

She didn't know if he'd heard because he seemed to sink into oblivion. She went back and forth between Magda and Cyn, trying to transfer her power to him. Magda Catalyzed to human in death, a naked, blood-covered woman sprawled on the black tile floor. The energy dissipated.

"Cyn, come back to me." Tears flowed down Ruby's cheeks as she pressed her face against his and whispered, "Cyn, please."

His chest was still rising and falling, but his exhalation was nearly imperceptible. Her finger, pressed against the scales at his neck, picked up hardly any pulse. She fought the tide of grief that threatened to drown her. She'd gone against his orders, risked everything, and failed.

Then she felt a change in his energy. She sat up as he Catalyzed to human. "No. No!" She shook his shoulders, willing him to return to Dragon where he had a chance of healing. She buried her face against his chest and gave into the grief for a few seconds. But wait. His heart was beating. She sat up and searched for some sign of life. His eyes were still closed. The wound in his neck...it was healing.

His eyes slowly opened; then he jerked upright, sending her tumbling back. He patted his chest, searching for his fatal wound, then took in the room, Magda's lifeless body, and then her. "What did you do?"

She Catalyzed, too, and smiled. He was alive, even if

he was peeved. "I Breathed Magda's essence into you. If there was a chance of saving you, I was going to do it."

He got to his feet, pulling her up with him. Now he surveyed her. "You're hurt."

She glanced down at all the scratches, cuts, and swollen places. "They're mostly healed. We have to get the reactor. Fernandez showed up. He must have followed us, desperate to find out where this place was. He grabbed it and ran. Purcell went after him."

"Fernandez probably took it back to his house. He's beyond desperate to save his wife." Cyn led her by the hand down the hall and stopped near of one of the guard's bodies. "We can't leave here like this. We'll have to borrow their clothes."

"Oh, yuck."

But she started wrestling with the man's clothing as Cyn did the same with the second man. He nearly burst out of clothing that was skintight. She drowned in hers. Barefoot, they ran to the entrance and headed to Fernandez's.

Chapter 24

Cyn had been surprised by a lot in the last thirty minutes: that Purcell got the better of him, that Ruby had risked everything to save him. He couldn't dwell on them now or anything else but what lay ahead. Because what didn't surprise him was finding Purcell's car at Fernandez's home.

They parked along the road and walked down to the entrance. Cyn automatically linked his fingers with Ruby's as they stayed close to the shrubbery. She looked ridiculous in the black dress pants and white button-down shirt that swamped her, and adorable, and vulnerable all at once. She had blood in her braid, which had half-unraveled. God, but he wanted to pull her against him, feel her body, her heartbeat. No time for that either.

Voices floated on the air from the vicinity of the backyard. He nodded to go around the right side, where he knew the bushes grew thickest.

"Give me the reactor, you idiot. You are not thinking

logically. Go get your wife, and we'll return to the club. You can't keep it to yourself."

They peered through the bushes, where Cyn could see the two men facing off in the glow of security lights at the corner of the house. Fernandez gripped the reactor against his chest like an infant. His face was a mask of pain and desperation, no trace of logic left.

"And *you* can't select who gets saved. Who made you God?"

"One of the gods did, as a matter of fact."

One of the gods? Was he serious?

Purcell lifted his face to the skies. "Fallon, show this pitiful mortal your face!"

Amazingly, a mist formed several feet above the ground, luminescent against the night sky. A man appeared, his face long and his eyes angry. "Release the reactor, Crescent. You know not what you do."

Cyn started stripping out of his clothes and leaned close to Ruby. "I'm going to grab Purcell and take him for a swim. Try to keep Fernandez calm and where he is."

She nodded, gripping his arm. "Be careful."

Fernandez held it closer to his chest. "I do know. This will save my wife, and her family. Our friends. *I* choose who lives! Me!"

"Kill him," Purcell said, pointing at Fernandez.

"No!" Ruby raced out of hiding. "If you shoot him with magick or fire or whatever, you'll detonate that thing." She slowed as she reached the three faces looking at her now. "It's a dangerous mix of magick and science, like a friggin' hydrogen bomb. What you're doing is going to kill thousands of Crescents. Why? Why are you doing this?"

Damn it, Ruby. Cyn started to follow but remained. No, he would let her do what she needed to do, which, he suspected, was enlightening Purcell.

"There are too many of you!" the god boomed. "You clutter the earth and suck all the energy away."

He hated them. Cyn could hear it in his voice.

She turned to Purcell. "And you're all right with this?"

Purcell was watching the reactor in Fernandez's hands, though he briefly met her gaze. "Fallon is right. You do clutter Miami, so many of you with your mixed bloodlines. I am merely facilitating a purge and return to simpler times." He searched behind her. "Where is your Dragon friend?"

"Did you know that the reactor could take out the entire state of Florida? Darren must have realized the risks."

"Fallon would not let that happen."

She glanced up to the god, who could probably detonate everything with a look. "You don't care, do you?"

"I care about regaining what was once mine."

Interestingly, Fallon wasn't detonating anything. Regaining what he'd once had...power? The gods hadn't interfered physically with this plane since Cyn could remember. Purcell was working on an orange orb behind his back. Time to move. Once Cyn ascertained the best approach, he Catalyzed and flew at him. His out-of-practice wings only kept him a few feet above the ground, but that was all he needed. Night vision made everything stand out in shades of gray and black. His talons reached out just as Purcell, either hearing him or seeing the shocked look on Fernandez's face, turned.

Too late.

The orb dropped to the grass as Cyn sank his talons

into Purcell and dragged him the few yards to the seawall. He dove into the water with the struggling man. Magick tore at Cyn as they descended down through the murky depths to the ocean floor.

A bubble of air formed around Purcell's head. Cyn poked it with a claw. Purcell tried again and again, and each time Cyn popped the bubble immediately. Purcell's magick ebbed as he placed breathing over fighting on his priority list. Cyn circled back toward the house, not wanting to venture too far from Ruby.

Purcell's essence waned, then disappeared completely as he stopped trying to pry Cyn's talons away. Cyn dropped him and watched his body drift down, no sign of a last-ditch effort to swim to the surface. After another few seconds, Cyn came up just behind the house. Ruby and Fernandez stood facing each other in the yard, tension in their stances. Human again, he climbed up onto the dock, leaving puddles as he made his way to them.

He spotted the mist, now higher in the sky, a sky that was becoming muddy with dark clouds. He flicked his wet hair from his face as he approached his former boss, who was still clutching the reactor. Cyn held out his hands. "Give it to me. The reactor is what's fracturing our *Deus Vis*. It's what's made Celia sick. We have to destroy it."

"No!" He held it tighter. "This healed her! I can feel its power!"

Fernandez darted to the house. Cyn shook his head and ran after him, shoving him to the ground.

"You'll have to kill me, Cyn. I won't give it up, not if it means losing my Celia. It doesn't have to go down this way. You and Ruby can stay here with us. We can ride this out together."

Rage welled up inside Cyn. "You're saving your wife at the expense of thousands of Crescents."

"I don't care." He shook his head violently. "I won't lose her again."

Could he kill his former boss and mentor? He wanted to kill Fernandez for his selfishness, his betrayal. But Fernandez was acting out of a fear of losing the woman he loved. Cyn could not kill him. But he would get the reactor from him. He hit him hard. Then again. Fernandez's head went slack, falling to the side. Thunder ripped through a sky that moments ago was clear. Forked lightning stabbed the ground only yards away.

Ruby crouched down and gently took the reactor from Fernandez's now slack hold. "We have to do this now. I have to do it."

Black clouds roiled above them—and only above them. Superimposed in the miasma was the face of a very angry god.

Ruby stripped out of her clothes and Catalyzed, then picked the reactor up again. It frightened him, her holding such an explosive device. He wanted to do it for her, but he stepped back.

A chair blew at them, and he yanked her out of its way. It tumbled to the dock and into the water. Palm fronds cartwheeled toward them.

"Peter?" Celia's called from the back door. "*Cyn?*" Then she took in Ruby, the red Dragon in her yard.

"Go back inside, Celia!" he called.

But she saw her husband lying on the ground and ran out into the rain. "Peter! Cyn, what have you done?" She knelt next to him, shaking him awake.

Lightning hit the ground inches from them. Ruby lifted

the reactor to the tip of her fang, grazing the metal surface. She closed her eyes and punctured it. Cyn's whole body tightened, ready for an explosion. Nothing happened.

Fernandez barreled into Ruby, sending them both crashing to the ground. Cyn grabbed him and jerked him off of her. While he held Fernandez still, he and Ruby looked at the reactor. As the volatile mixture escaped the tiny hole, the canister started crumpling in on itself. Fernandez watched, too, gasping, his frenzied motions coming to a standstill.

Celia ran forward, trying to peel Cyn's hands off her husband. "What is going on here?"

The storm abated, the clouds moving away in a preternaturally fast way. The thrumming energy dissipated. Ruby quickly dressed as Fernandez stormed toward Cyn, jabbing his finger at him. "He destroyed it!"

Cyn stood, pulling Ruby close. "Feel, Fernandez. Feel how the erratic energy has settled down."

Fernandez stopped mid-yell and took in the atmosphere. He grabbed his wife and started sobbing.

Cyn turned and walked back to where he'd dumped his clothes, now a sopping mess. He managed to get into them and walk to the car, Ruby's hand tight in his.

"Will you ever be able to forgive him?" she asked, when Cyn looked back at the house one last time.

"I have to." He pulled her close, wrapping his arm around her. "Forgiveness has been good to me."

She buried her face against his chest. "I just want to go home and sleep in your arms." She moved back a few inches. "We have to find Brom. In case he needs help with that demon."

"It should return to the Dark Side now that Purcell's dead, but demons...well, they're demons." As much as Cyn wanted to go home, he owed Brom. "Let's find him." He didn't let go though. Instead he squeezed her tighter. "Give me a minute to feel you. To know this is over."

Ruby had saved his life. She had given him her heart. She held on just as tight, her body shivering.

He lifted her chin to look on her beautiful face. And he spoke the word that thrummed through him. "Mine." Then he claimed her mouth. She kissed him back, and he felt everything in that kiss, all of her fear at losing him, of what they'd just gone through. He pulled away and pressed his forehead against hers. "We'd better go before I get all blubbery."

Ruby opened Brom's book as they drove to his house. Her fingers passed over the words. "There's nothing new. But we didn't fight a three-headed monster. So what did that mean?"

"Hopefully we'll get to ask him."

This time they pulled up his driveway, rather than sneaking in the back way. Cyn knocked on the door. He leaned closer to it. "I hear something. Like a struggle." He tried the knob, finding it unlocked, and they went inside.

Brom was, indeed, struggling to fight off the demon. He'd managed to pull out the "root" that had been buried in his throat. The demon turned and saw the two Crescents standing there. Its eyes widened.

"Your summoner is dead," Cyn said. "So are the other

demons he brought here. I strongly suggest you remove yourself from this man and go home."

It pulled out its other roots, slinking down to the floor.

While its attention was on them, Brom sent a blue orb at it, shattering it into smoke. "Damn, but I've wanted to do that for days now." He shook his hand, staring at it. "The thing disabled my abilities." Then he looked at them, his expression brightening. "You're alive."

"It's finished," Ruby said. "Purcell is dead, so is Darren."

"You did your part. But I saw a three-headed entity."

"Yeah, we wondered about that." Ruby leaned against Cyn, wrapping her arms around his waist. "Please don't tell me we have to fight two more heads. I can't take anymore."

Brom took them in, a soft smile on his face. "Your destiny has been fulfilled. There are others who are fighting for victory." Brom took Cyn's hand and linked it to Ruby's. "Now you must go on to fulfill the last part of my prophecy."

Ruby furrowed her eyes. "But there wasn't anything else in the book."

Brom's eyes twinkled. "No, I didn't put this one on the pages. You and Cyn will have to figure that out yourselves."

Acknowledgments

Nichol Huffman for giving the book an early read and your great feedback.

My fabulous street team, the Rushkies, for your support and book love.

To the folks at Grand Central Publishing for helping me to make this book the best and prettiest it can be, including:

- editor Alex Logan
- editorial direction Amy Pierpont
- art director Christine Foltzer
- publicists Jessica Bromberg and Marissa Sangiacomo

It's a fine line between love and hate.
Can two adversaries team up
to find the truth—

and defeat a powerful force out to
destroy the Dragon community?

Please turn this page for a preview of

Magic Possessed.

Chapter 1

⁓

The scream tore through the cypress trees and gripped Violet Castanega's heart like a strangler fig's roots. She dropped the amethyst and silver necklace on her worktable and ran out the open doorway of her workshop. Chumley, her tan hound, ran up beside her, her brow wrinkled as she stared in the direction from which the sound came.

Not good when a man screamed like that. Not horseplay or a foot being run over by a swamp buggy, but the sound of life being torn from a body. Her brothers and cousins flashed through her mind as she ran across the muddy ground, barefoot. She'd spent thirty years roaming the acres of her family's land, most of them without shoes. Rocks and roots dug in, but she knew instinctively how to shift her weight to soften the impact. Chumley ran beside her, his paws slapping the ground.

Another sound, lower and more guttural, squeezed her heart and damn it, she was already having a hard time breathing. She thought it came from the southern edge of the Castanega land. The stitch she usually felt when running pinched her side.

She emerged from the thicket of pine trees into the more open palm farm, running between the low rows of bushy sago palms and through the outer edge of thicker areca palms. Her pace slowed as she searched for whoever had screamed. She heard shouting. Others coming, too. She tried to pick out the identity of the voices that were filled with the same fear she felt, but they were too far away.

Her foot hit something. Grabbing on to the feathery palm frond didn't stop her momentum. She pitched forward, her hands sinking into the soft ground. Before she'd even scrambled to her feet, she found him, bloody and motionless on the muddy ground. God, not mud—blood. It soaked the ground around the naked body with a gash in the chest.

Even through the blood, she recognized Arlo's square face. "No, no, no." She dropped down beside him, clamping her hands on his cheeks. "Arlo!"

He was warm. Not cold, not stiff. He didn't respond. She searched for a pulse point at his throat, but her finger slid in his blood. His clothing lay shredded nearby. That meant he'd Catalyzed, turning Dragon so quickly, he didn't have time to disrobe. Which meant he'd been attacked. Her Dragon tingled with awareness, rolling through her cells like a wave of energy.

Two people ran closer, smashing through palm fronds. She opened her mouth to call for help but stopped. Maybe those footsteps belonged to her family and maybe not.

"I thought I heard Vee," a man said.

"But that scream...it wasn't her."

"I'm here!" she called, hearing her voice falter.

Her brothers burst into view, their wide-eyed gazes taking her in as they rushed toward her.

Illian and Jessup took in the blood, Arlo, and both went into defense mode, spinning around, their bodies rigid and ready to fight off an attacker.

"Are you all right, Vee?" Jessup asked, sliding his wary gaze toward her.

"I...yes. But Arlo..."

"Keep watch," Jessup told Illian, dropping down beside her. He assessed her with light green eyes that usually sparkled with mischief or flared with ire. Crescent Dragons had flames in their eyes, visible only to other Crescents, and Jessup's blazed with anger and shock. "What happened?"

"I...don't know. I heard the scream and came running, probably like you did. He was already...dead."

Jessup felt for his pulse, too, with a hand much steadier than hers. He spit out an expletive, his mouth tightening. His voice was a growl as he again surveyed their surroundings. "Someone came onto our land and killed him. Ambushed him, no doubt. How the hell did they sneak up on Arlo?"

He was the oldest of her siblings and had seen the most action during the centuries-old feuds between the Dragon clans.

"He was drinking," she said. "I smell booze on him."

He'd struggled with alcohol and drugs the last few decades, a dangerous combination when you were a Crescent. You couldn't afford to be out of control when your DNA held the essence of an ancient god, especially when you were a Crescent Dragon. The Dragon part took advantage of weakness, eager to manifest and play. Or kill. Arlo's very human addictions gave control to a magick beast that lived by its baser instincts.

Jessup lifted Arlo's body slightly. "Someone killed him for his power."

Violet sucked in a breath. The blue Dragon tattoo sprawled across his chest was gone. "He's been Breathed." Her Sapphire Dragon, wrapped all the way around her like a belt, vibrated in fear and anger.

Every adult Dragon wore their Dragon's essence on their body, a magnificent image that manifested during their Awakening ceremony when they turned thirteen. The fact that it moved and kept watch over its person was hidden from Mundane humans, who only saw a regular tattoo. When one Dragon Breathed in the power of another, their Dragon disappeared. Without their god essence, so entwined in their bodies and souls, Crescents died.

Illian stepped closer, still watching but taking in his brother's still form. "It's got to be one of the Fringe clans."

The Fringe consisted of the marshy land along the fringe of Florida City and Homestead, where several Dragon clans settled.

Violet came slowly to her feet. "It doesn't make sense. We haven't had any clashes or encroachments lately."

"The Murphys started an alligator farm, damned copycats. That's an encroachment. And the Augusts copied our tourist show."

"Both were years ago. And *they* copied *us*, so why would they come onto our land and attack?"

The fire in her brothers' eyes scared her. There had been relative peace—okay, more like the Cold War kind—for the last ten years. Nothing more than a few broken bones and torn flesh, disagreements settled at Ernie's. She craved that peace, being able to wander their land without fear of being attacked.

Jessup laid Arlo back down. "We need to kill someone." Heat radiated off him as his Dragon pushed to Catalyze.

"We don't even know who did it," she said. "Let me do some snooping, find out who's behind this."

Illian shook his head. "No, I think we need to kill someone."

"Stop." Her own impulsive nature, along with her Dragon, pushed hard to join in. "Give me some time to figure out who did this. If someone's got a vendetta against us, I can find out who it is. No doubt, he's been talking, bragging or bitching down at Ernie's."

Jessup's eyes flared in his bossy, big brother way. "You're not going to Ernie's by yourself. I—"

She pressed her finger to his collarbone. "You are not coming with me." She shifted her gaze to Illian. "You'll both barge in, banging heads together. And then you'll end up in the Conference Room, and it won't even be with Arlo's murderer. I can take care of myself. Haven't I had the best teachers?"

"Yeah, but—"

"Let me approach this logically. Once I get a lead, I'll let you know. Then—"

"We kill someone," Jessup said.

"Yes, we kill them." Violet met Illian's gaze. "We'll scrape out his or her eyeballs, cut them up, and feed them to the gators." The old Violet reared her head and bared her fangs. The one who jumped into a fight without thinking, who'd attacked an officer of the Hidden to defend Arlo, even when he was in the wrong. The Violet who'd become as hotheaded as the rest of her family. She took a breath. "But if you go off half-cocked and kill the wrong person, it'll start a war again. Dad died because of this damned feud business. So did Grandpa and Great Uncle Hank and . . . the list goes on. I don't want to lose you two. I'll find out who's behind this. I promise."

Illian looked at Jessup. "She is good at ferreting out information. She figured out which of the cousins was stealing our oranges. And the idjits who were digging up the royal palms at the nursery."

Jessup was still taking in the desperation in her eyes. She let him see all the hurt, just for a second. Any longer and he'd chide her for it. Castanegas didn't cry; they got revenge. That was their motto. But that motto would get them killed.

Jessup made a grunting sound. "All right, cupcake. You've got a day."

"Give me two."

He shook his head but said, "Then we start digging around ourselves."

Violet knew exactly what kind of digging he meant.

The sign on the roof of the ramshackle building read THE FRINGE. Couldn't get clearer than that who belonged, at least to the Crescent community. Ernie couldn't hang a MUNDANES NOT WELCOME sign, because regular humans didn't know they were called Mundanes by Crescents. They didn't even know there *were* Crescents, or a facet of their world called the Hidden that contained people who turned to Dragons, sorcerers called Deuces, and descendants of fallen angels called Caidos. Not to mention demons, Elementals, and other creatures from which nightmares were made.

The bar sat on the outer edge of Florida City, tucked back from the road in a grove of oaks dripping with Spanish moss. She parked beneath one of the old trees in the gravel lot and stepped out beneath its shadow. Only four other vehicles filled the lot, as she'd expect midday.

While Fringers weren't welcomed by Crescents, or even Mundane humans, the tables were turned here at the place they knew as Ernie's. Ernie had owned it for a hundred and eighty years. He belonged to none of the Fringe clans, which made him neutral—a status he held on to with calloused hands.

Her boots crunched on peanut shells as she walked into the gloomy interior. The main room was large, but divided up into separate areas to accommodate clutches of clan groups. Ernie demanded civility in the public space, banishing bar fights and those who participated.

"Violet, a surprise to see you in here." Ernie, with a face that looked as though he'd been crunched in a vise from top to bottom, set a bowl of peanuts on the bar as she approached. "None of your people are here."

She'd had to drag home a drunk brother and even her father a time or two. Sometimes they needed assistance, not because they'd had too much to drink but due to the activities in the Conference Room, where disagreements were settled in a way that required no civility. The door to it blended into the far wall, though every Fringer knew where it was. To any outsider, say, a health inspector, it was a pit where one could ride the mechanical bull surrounded by cheering crowds. Most of the time the bull was pulled aside and two Dragons, in full scale and fury, fought to the delight—and bets—of onlookers. All of her brothers had fought in there at one time or another, coming out broken and bloody. And that's when they won.

She glanced at the four men playing darts over in the corner and fought not to roll her eyes. Augusts. She clenched her fists at the sight of Bren, who was already giving her a cruel smile. As he always did, he made a V with his fingers and waggled his tongue suggestively in the crotch.

She stuffed her disgust, refusing to give him the satisfaction, and turned back to Ernie. "I'm here to see you."

His wiry eyebrows bobbed in surprise. "You know you're a bit too young for me."

"You're hundreds of years too old for me. So stop flirting and give me an AmberBock draft."

"You break my heart, you do." But he wore a smile as he pulled the draft into a mug.

Because of their deity essence, Crescents lived longer than Mundanes—and aged very slowly. Ernie looked to be in his sixties. At thirty-four, she was a mere babe in Crescent terms, and only looked to be about twenty-two. She idly cracked a shell and lined up the peanuts side by side on the bar.

He set the frosty mug on the shellacked bar top. "What're you after then, if not my buff, brawny body or rapier wit?"

So not in the mood for humor, such as it was, she swallowed back the grief that wanted to bubble out at the mere thought of saying the words, "Arlo's been murdered."

Ernie digested that, his wide mouth flattening even more. "Damn. What happened?"

She told him the scant details.

"Breathed." He shook his head but didn't look shocked.

"There's been talk, hasn't there? If something's going on, it usually starts here. This place is the hub of the Fringe." Finesse him, feed his ego. "Nothing gets past you."

He soaked it in, his shoulders widening. "I pick up tidbits here and there." Then he got onto her, the proud expression hardening. "But I stay out of it. Switzerland and all." No, he just collected on the bets.

"Ernie, I'm not asking you to take sides. Simply pass on what people have been talking about lately."

His gaze shifted to the men, who were glancing their way more than at the dartboard. "Fringers have been edgy lately. Restless and downright crotchety, breaking out in scuffles despite my rules. I heard there's a big solar storm erupting, and we're already getting the effects of the flares."

"It's not that and you know it. We've felt the effects of solar storms before, and it didn't make people kill."

He shrugged. "Supposed to be a strong one."

"Share." She crooked her fingers, ignoring her blunt, unpolished nails. At least they were clean.

He hesitated, then relented. "There's been murmurings, but not about your clan."

She took a draw of her ice-cold beer, feeling it tingle

across her tongue and down her throat. Damn. Clan problems again. "What about then?"

"Defensive, not offensive." He leaned across the bar, as casual as could be, and flicked the peanuts off the bar. "Arlo's not the first Fringer to be whacked lately."

This was getting worse. "Who?"

Ernie held out his squat fist and flipped out one finger. This was not going to be good. "Liam Peregrine, killed a week or so ago. Breathed." Another finger straightened. "They found something at the scene that pointed to the Wolfrums. So no surprise that Peter Wolfrum was Breathed two days later."

She pulled out her phone and put in the names. She had a photographic memory, but hearing information didn't imprint worth a damn.

He shifted his gaze to the men by the dartboard, and his voice lowered. "Larry's grandmother, Shirley. Six days ago. I don't know what they found, if anything, but two days later, Bobby Spear turns up dead. Breathed."

No, she didn't want to be in this place again of tension, hatred and constant fear. "Bobby is—was—a kid!" she hissed. "What, seventeen?"

Ernie nodded, his expression somber. "Good kid, too, for a Fringer, anyway."

She fought not to look at the Augusts and clue them in that they were talking about them. Another blunt finger on Ernie's hand flicked out.

Gods, no more.

"Dan Murphy, killed two days ago."

"Breathed?"

"Yep."

Her stomach cramped, like a demon had reached right

into her insides and twisted her stomach. A sensation she fortunately didn't know firsthand.

"With the history between your clan and theirs, could be they thought you did it. Maybe Arlo's death was an act of revenge, like some of the others."

"Did they find evidence?" She would not believe someone in her family would attack another clan unprovoked. Fringers always had a reason, or at least they believed they had one. She would know if there was a problem.

Ernie shrugged. "Haven't heard one way or the other."

She was cold all over but tried to reveal nothing of what she felt. "We didn't kill Dan or anyone else. Six murders in ten days. That's crazy. And scary as hell." She finished half her beer and set a twenty on the bar. "But I'm damned well going to figure it out."

As she strode over to the Augusts, their bodies snapped to attention and suspicion lit their eyes. The oldest son scanned her, clearly trying to assess her intent. *Come on, like I'm dumb enough to confront four of you?*

She kept a table between them and gave Larry, the oldest clan member present, her attention. "I'm sorry about your grandma."

Larry narrowed his eyes. "How'd you know?"

The second oldest stepped forward. "Ernie told you, didn't he?"

"I heard it through the grapevine and was trying to get him to confirm it before I approached you. The way that he tried to pretend ignorance told me it was true."

Larry stuck a wad of chew between his teeth and gum. "You wouldn't happen to know anything about it, would you? Through the grapevine?"

"She's not the only one." So they didn't know about Arlo yet. Or weren't mentioning it. The Fringers didn't go around advertising when they'd lost one of their own. It revealed that your family was now a little weaker. "Sounds like trouble's brewing again." She curled her hands over the back of a chair. "*You* wouldn't happen to know anything about Bobby Spears's death, would you?"

Dragon energy crackled off them all at once. Bren, the youngest, and unfortunately, the one she knew best, stepped forward. "Not a thing, sweetheart. Kid was a jerk. Probably into something or another." He came around the table and stopped too close for her comfort.

She didn't back away. "Why would someone kill Shirley?" The August matriarch was one of the few of their clan who didn't cause trouble. There was no love lost, but still, it wasn't right. "I'm not being nosy," she said when no one spoke up. "We've had peace in the Fringe for years now. Six murders in ten days…someone's trying to stir things up. I want to find out who."

That got a chorus of low chuckles out of them. Bren placed his hands on her shoulders, angling his hips closer. "Aw, Vee, you gonna make things right for all us Fringers? Get justice?"

She pushed him back. "You don't get to touch me."

He gave her a contrite look. "You liked when I touched you before. You used to sigh…"

She slugged him, which slammed his head to the side. The others stepped closer, their fists tightening as Bren caught his balance.

He laughed it off, even as his eyes still swam. "Damn, Vee, you still got a hard-on for me, don't you?"

"Stop calling me Vee, and I couldn't care less about you." She narrowed her eyes. "You do know women don't get hard-ons, right? Or are you getting the genders of your lovers confused?"

She wouldn't admit how much she hated him, wanted to cut off his balls and feed them to the raccoons, because that would reveal how much he'd affected her. He'd wooed her, saying all the right things. Not how beautiful she was, how clever or sexy, but how if they got together it would heal the rift between their families. Somehow he knew exactly what to say, and she'd let down her defenses a little and bought it.

Finally all his questions about their alligator operation, cleverly worded and coated in mild curiosity, burrowed down to her cynical senses. He was using her to get information about their farm and shows. Not long after, they'd opened up their own tourist attraction with alligator wrestling. She'd been so mad at herself, not because her heart had been broken. She hadn't given it to him. But her pride had taken a big hit, even to this day, and that was nine years ago.

She turned to the oldest brother. "Did the Spears kill Shirley?"

He hesitated, then said, "Yeah."

"How do you know?" She'd seen enough retaliatory murders based on nothing more than speculation.

Bren's expression changed to fierce. "We found that stupid skull handkerchief Bobby wears all the time about twenty yards from her body."

"How can you be sure it was his? He's not the only one who wears one."

"He's the only one around here who does," Bren said.

His eyes sparked, no doubt at his satisfaction over wreaking justice.

None of this felt right to her. Not that Fringe justice ever felt right. The Spears would rear up and strike back. And the wars would start once more.

Chapter 2

She was either making a huge mistake or saving her family. Too damned bad she didn't know in advance which it was going to be. Violet stood on the steps of the Guard's Headquarters. She'd heard that it was fashioned after the government buildings on the Crescents' ancestral island of Lucifera.

There was no written history of Lucifera, only legends handed down orally over many generations. As in many ancient cultures, Luciferians worshipped gods specific to the island. A fluke of nature allowed several gods to become physical on the Earth plane, where they fell to sensual temptations. Eventually, two disgruntled gods and one overly righteous angel decided procreation was a bad idea and instigated a war between their progeny. The war caused a violent schism that not only reversed the gods' physicality but broke the island apart, forcing the inhabitants to flee to Florida.

Etched symbols like hieroglyphics adorned the two-story columns along the front of the otherwise nonde-script building. Violet recognized several symbols, mostly the Dragon gods with which she was familiar. Some of her Crescent jewelry store customers requested pieces with the symbols for various gods. No one ever requested a necklace depicting the Tryah, the trio who started the war.

And we're on the verge of war now.

Maybe rage and violence was in the blood, the venge-ful tendencies just a throwback to the flawed beings that sired them so many generations ago.

Crescents knew the financial services firm was a front for the Hidden's police force. Couldn't go to the Miami police with a complaint that your neighbor's magick was disrupting your satellite signal. Or that your brother was murdered by a Dragon. The Guard's main focus was en-forcing Rule Number One: Crescents must never expose their magick to the Mundanes. Then there were Crescents who'd gone Red, their term for magick psychosis.

Violet betrayed her clan with every step she took to-ward those ultra-tall double doors. As much as she hated the idea of going to the Guard for help, she had no choice. There was going to be a lot more bloodshed if she couldn't convince them to intercede. She took a deep breath as she clutched the steel handle. *Act like none of your family has ever been on the wrong side of their ser-vices.*

Compared to the bright Miami sunshine, the lobby was dim and cool, dominated by shades of blue. Even the woman behind the reception desk wore a dark blue blouse.

"I need to speak to someone about a murder." That

last word caught in Violet's throat. When the receptionist asked her name, "Castanega" came out even hoarser. She had to repeat it, and the woman's eyebrows rose.

Yes, I'm one of those *Castanegas.*

The woman's previously placid expression soured. "Did you commit murder or are you reporting on behalf of the victim?"

"The victim."

She opened a drawer, pulled out four pieces of paper, and clipped them to a board with a practiced hand. "You'll need to fill these out."

Violet could only stare at the words DEATH REPORT at the top. Her fingers trembled as she reached for the clipboard. The woman jabbed a pen in her direction and walked into the back rooms.

Crescents in general had their prejudices against Fringers, viewing them with the jaundiced disdain bestowed to "hillbillies." Since Fringers didn't want outsiders poking into their business, they happily perpetuated the stereotype. Mostly it worked, and the Guard only stepped in when illegal activities might draw the attention of the Mundane police.

The joke was on the Crescent population, really. Fringe families had taken land no one else wanted so long ago and cultivated it. The marshes and swamp areas were the most beautiful, richest, and most private of all the inhabitable land in the area. To Violet, the busy, loud city was the unwanted area.

The receptionist returned a few moments later. "Someone will be with you shortly."

I bet.

She bet right. Once all the papers were filled out, with

the cold facts of her brother's life and death crammed into lines not nearly long enough, she spent the time checking e-mails on her phone and confirming a couple of appointments with jewelry stores. Finally she played a couple rounds of Angry Birds before a voice penetrated. "Miss Castanega."

A young man stood in the open doorway with that same sour look. He'd drawn the short straw, evidently. She was so sick of being judged by her name, her family.

She swallowed the weariness and plastered a professional expression on her face. He took the clipboard and said nothing more, just walked into a large room filled with desks. Expecting her to follow, she assumed. The Guard's officers wore business attire, not uniforms. She didn't need to see his magick tattoo identifying him as the lowest officer, an Argus. The fact that he led her to one of the desks crammed into the center of the room said as much. There were only two types of officers in the Guard, Arguses and Vegas, who handled the higher-level issues.

Several other officers sat at their desks, both men and women. Most were engaged with a complainant, and she heard snippets of conversations about the crazy neighbor releasing orbs from his roof and Aunt Betty running naked down the street. Those officers not busy watched her openly, as though they were ready to be amused. Someone whistled the banjo theme from *Deliverance*.

Idjit. That movie was set in Georgia, not southern Florida.

She gripped her alligator purse handle tighter. The skin came from their farm, the purse from the company that fashioned them into four-hundred-dollar bags and belts. She wanted to tell these people that their operation used every part of the gator so nothing went to waste. That the income from their various enterprises provided well for the families it supported, far better than the Guard probably paid their employees. They also ensured that the alligator population thrived, that the nests in the wild were protected.

Violet met a few curious gazes, most giving her a dose of a sneer. Her Dragon rolled over her senses, bringing everything into hyperfocus. She felt its heat as it pressed close to the surface.

Back. Not a good place to show yourself. You'll—we'll—be pounced, blasted, and incinerated before we can blink.

She pushed it back deep inside her and found the more tolerable sight of paintings situated between doors, done in various mediums, styles, and probably eras. Depictions of the gods, even the ones who fell. For younger generations, the gods were mythical, part of distant history. Her clan descended from Mora, Dragon goddess of creativity and beauty. Here she was illustrated as a gorgeous green Dragon surrounded by flowers and butterflies. She was about to snap her fangs around the neck of a bird with bright plumage.

The man led her to a female officer's desk. "Here, K, this one's all yours." He shoved the clipboard at her. "I've got better things to do."

Mia Kavanaugh, according to her nameplate, gave him an acidic look but turned to Violet. "Please sit." Her gaze skimmed the top of the report, and Violet could tell the moment her last name registered.

Mia's moss-green eyes took her in, swirling with trademark Deuce mist that, like Dragon's flames, could only be seen by Crescents. She seemed surprised by something, maybe that Violet could wear something other than torn blue jeans and swamp waders or that she had all her teeth. Nah. She hadn't smiled to show them.

Mia set the clipboard down and met her gaze. "Ms. Castanega, please tell me your family hasn't killed the Mundane who is screaming to the world that there's a dinosaur in the swamp."

Dragonfire, that's where she was going to go? "Even though Smitty's always sneaking around on our private land with his video cameras, we have refrained from harming him. This has nothing to do with him."

"You piqued his interest. One of your family members obviously revealed your magick. Which makes you a reckless element—"

"This has nothing to do with that idjit, and we are not reckless." Well, most of the time. Wild, daring, and a little bit crazy, yes, but all aware of the punishment for breaking Rule Number One: death. "The murder I'm here to report is my brother's."

"Details?"

Don't cry. You're good at that, years of being teased by three brothers...now two...

She swallowed back the rest of her thoughts and the sob that threatened to erupt. "My brother Arlo was murdered yesterday by a Dragon who Breathed his power. He was attacked on our property without provocation. But—"

"You know the Guard doesn't interfere with the swamp clans' feuds." Mia lifted the clipboard, her face relaxing as she thought her job here was done. "We will, of course, file the proper paperwork."

So his death would be filed with the government but

not the suspicious nature of it. No need to involve the Muds—the Mundane police force.

"I'm not just here because of my brother's murder." Violet pulled out a piece of paper and laid it on the desk. It contained the names of five other Fringers. "Swamp trash," she knew they were called more often than the Fringer moniker they'd given themselves long ago. "As I was about to say, there have been five similar murders in the last ten days. All Breathed. If you'll look up these names, you may find that their deaths were all obscured, the same way you're going to obscure Arlo's murder. Surely the Guard has put together that something's going on here. Someone's inciting the feuding clans."

Mia barely glanced at the list. "The feuding clans are inciting the feuding clans. That's what you do down there."

"We've been at peace for the last ten years. There has been no provocation, no stirrings or burglaries or anything. But there will be. My family is ready for blood. I'm sure these other families are, too. That's how it works: someone's killed for 'good reason' and there's a retaliation murder, and then another." The Garzas were completely wiped out. It pained Violet to know her family was responsible, even if the Garzas deserved it.

Violet pointed to the list of names. "I bought time in my family by doing this research to show a pattern. They're only going to hold out for so long before they start looking for justice. Justice the Guard can't—or won't—provide." She met her gaze. "You can prevent bloodshed by finding out who's behind this. A teenage *boy* died."

Movement beyond the woman caught her eye. One

of the office doors opened, and a man walked out. Her Dragon snarled at the sight of him, the Vega who had tangled with her family on several occasions in the name of the Guard: Kade something or another. The one she'd attacked, *but let's just forget about that, shall we?* His green-eyed gaze homed right in on her. Something fiery sparked between them, surprising her because she didn't know what it was exactly. *Sure as hell wasn't* that. She turned back to the Argus. "Will you investigate?"

Mia shook her head. "I'm sorry, but this looks like typical Fringe infighting, and we are way too busy to deal with that particular kind of crazy right now. Maybe it's the effect of living on the edge of the Field. Who knows what the lack of full *Deus Vis* does to you after a while—"

"We get plenty of *Deus Vis*." Latin for "god force," it was the essential energy that fed Crescents' deity essence. The supernatural energy emanating from the crystal makeup of the island was behind the electromagnetic energy found in the Bermuda Triangle that threw off ship and airplane instruments. The Field of *Deus Vis* extended in a crescent shape into the Miami/Ft. Lauderdale area, fading at the edges. The Fringe lay at the southern curve of that edge.

"But how would you know? I don't mean to sound derogatory, but to give you an example, if you grow up crazy, that's your norm."

If Violet cared to consider it, maybe it made sense. The Fringers *were* on the edge, in more ways than one. But she didn't care to consider it, not now or ever.

Violet stood, snatching up her paper. Her cheeks burned when she saw those who had been listening, smirks on their faces. Kade's expression, as he paused outside the door from which he'd come, held curiosity, as though he were trying to figure out who she was. The last time he'd seen her she was grimy with mud, having just come from feeding the alligators.

On the door of the office Kade stood near, a brass plate read LT. ALEC FERRO. Maybe he would be more open-minded. She aimed for Kade, pasting on a docile expression.

Kade wasn't buying it, not by the way he shored his shoulders and shifted his body to face her. The jerk was a waste of honey-colored hair and a mouth made for sin. Too bad a scar marred his gorgeous face, though the waves of his hair partially hid it. She remembered when the wound was fresh, bleeding like a bitch down the side of his face. His mouth curved in a smile. He was looking forward to tussling with her.

Double jerk.

She feinted left at the last second, pushing open the door and approaching a middle-aged man whose fire in his eyes indicated he was Dragon like her. Good. He stood immediately.

"I'm sorry to barge in on you, but your officer isn't taking me seriously. My name is Violet Castanega."

A hand clamped onto her arm, followed by the scent of sandalwood. Kade took her in with a surprised expression. "You're *Violet Castanega*?"

Yeah, the one who jumped on you. She tried to yank her arm away and focused on Ferro. "I need to talk to someone reasonable."

"I'll escort her out, sir."

Kade started to pull her away, inciting her Dragon.

Getting into an altercation with a Vega at the station—or Catalyzing to Dragon—was only going to prove how uncivilized Fringers were. Or crazy, as the Argus implied. She would not prove them right.

"Dragons are being killed." She kept her gaze on Ferro as Kade pulled her toward the door. "Someone is targeting the Fringer families, starting a war…"

Ferro held up his hand. "Wait, Kavanaugh."

She'd been out the door, but Kade stopped at his commanding officer's order. Ferro crooked his elegant fingers, indicating that Kade close the door once they were back inside. Several officers, including Mia, hovered, ready to tackle her.

Mia Kavanaugh. Ah, the two green-eyed jerks were related. Even though Kade looked to be in his late twenties or early thirties, he *felt* old in a way she couldn't pinpoint. Mia was probably younger than Violet.

She focused on Ferro, who felt much older. He was distinguished and poised, the benefit of having lived a long life filled with privilege and pride. Behind him, a large, gilt-framed portrait showed a Dragon incinerating a village. The plate mounted on the bottom of the frame read DRAKOS. Dragon god of peace and war, and one of the Tryah. This man apparently idolized him. Maybe not so good.

Ferro said, "Finish what you were going to say."

Her control had paid off. She pulled free of Kade's grip, handing Ferro the paper on which she'd outlined the timeline of deaths. "Someone is killing and Breathing Dragons, and they've chosen the Fringe clans because they know the Guard will figure it's us misbehaving. First, one of the most vengeful families was targeted.

An unprovoked attack on the Peregrines guarantees back-lash, so who in their right mind would do it? Then the Peregrines killed one of the Wolfrums, their biggest and closest foe."

Ferro leaned back in his chair, perusing the list. "Sounds like the typical barbarian activity we've seen before."

"But the initial attacks weren't provoked. You hear things in the Fringe, at the least, rumors. Three people were killed, so the victims' families felt they had reason to take revenge. We don't kill without reason. Someone wants war. I'm asking you to find out why."

"What would one hope to gain by inciting the clans?" Ferro rubbed the gold pendant he wore, a symbol that looked like curled whiskers. The same one in the Drakos painting.

"That's what I'm hoping you can find out. Being the authority, and outsiders, maybe you could ferret out more information than I can."

"Fringers aren't exactly cooperative where the Guard is concerned. Which, frankly, is why I'm surprised that you've come to us. Does your family know you're here?"

She almost snorted. Thankfully she held it in. "No. We don't have a cordial relationship with the Guard."

Kade did snort. "If only you would stop breaking the law..."

She flashed him a flame-eyed look, even if he was right. The Fringers, her clan included, had a long history of flouting the law. When they claimed the land at the edge of the Field over three hundred years ago, they decided they also lived on the edge of the law.

She continued. "If the Guard intercedes and conducts an investigation, the clans would back off." She hoped.

Ferro glanced at her list, then at her. "I know it's upsetting to lose one of your family members, but these feuds have been going on for... well, since Lucifera. I remember the warnings about wandering into the pirate clan territories."

He *remembered*? "You were there? On Lucifera?"

He gave a curt nod. "Even then the Castanegas and other clans had a reputation. The island's *Deus Vis* drew ships to it like a magnet, trapping the inhabitants the way we are trapped here. Some were pirate ships, crewed by barbarians. Those pirates were already enemies, and their hatred for each other erupted into battles. They were banished to the far side of the island, and carved out territories adjacent to one another. Interestingly, they did the same thing here."

She craved more information about the island and the legends. None of her living clan members had been on the island. "How old were you when the island sank?"

"Eight."

The oldest Crescents were only ten. "So you remember the war?" She nodded to the painting.

"I remember fighting, but the Tryah were scapegoats." He gave her a tight smile. "At least that's my opinion. But you're not here to discuss Lucifera."

No, she wasn't. "This isn't about the feuds." She pressed her hand to her solar plexus. "I feel it here. Something isn't right."

"I think it's probably a combination of the temperament down there, plus the unusually strong fluctuations we've been seeing from the impending solar storm."

That again. "We've felt the effects before, and they've never incited anyone to murder."

"I would suggest you weather the storm and stay out of trouble."

He was dismissing her.

Violet's gaze went to a map of Miami on the wall behind him. Went, in fact, to a red pin at the western edge of her clan's territory where Arlo had died. She took several steps forward, Kade shadowing her. She pulled up the memory of the map she'd made at home. Six red tacks that matched where the murders had happened. This map had some yellow ones, too.

"You know about the murders. What are the yellow pins for?"

Ferro moved to block her view of the map with his large, muscular body. "We are investigating, Ms. Castanega. As you can see." Those words grated out. "But I cannot discuss the details of the case."

This didn't make sense. He was dismissing her, yet he knew about the murders. "Thank you for your concern," he said. "I'm sure it took a lot of courage for you to come here." He looked beyond her. "Escort her out."

Okay, *that* was a dismissal. Kade put his hand on her back to guide her out the door. The prickles that zinged through her at his touch were as odd as what she'd felt when their eyes had met. She involuntarily jerked away from him. He grabbed her arms and shoved her against the wall, pinning her wrists and flattening his body against hers.

"No fast moves," he said, his voice a growl in her ear, his breath hot on the back of her neck. "Or I'll remove you from the premises bodily."

Bodily. Which meant, his hands on her body. The idea crackled across her skin like the heat flush she got when she had to go into the alligator pens. Except Kade smelled a hell of a lot better.

"Going for another cheap thrill?" she rasped, her cheek mashed against the wall.

"What?"

She lowered her voice to a near whisper and turned to look at him. "You grabbed my boob on our last tussle."

"That was an accident, and you know it. Come on, you think I need to cop a feel on a suspect to get off?"

No, she supposed not when he looked like that. Arrogant son of a bitch.

In her peripheral vision, she sensed other officers at the ready, but Kade's body heat enveloped her, overwhelmed her senses—and had her Dragon panting. "I was moving away from you. Your hand on my back, specifically. I don't like being touched. If I promise to be a good girl, will you let me go?" Contriteness saturated her voice.

The fog in his eyes swirled provocatively. "*Can* you be a good girl? Is that even possible?"

"Try me. After all, you have plenty of backup."

"I don't need backup."

What were they talking about? Oh, Heathe, Dragon goddess of sensuality, were they . . . flirting? No. Not possible. Why did her body tingle then? Why was her Dragon shivering with a lust she hadn't felt in forever?

Enemy! Stop that. I know it's been a while, and then only with boring ole Mundanes, but really.

Kade released her, and she rubbed her shoulders where he'd held them. "I can find my own way out."

"Sorry, policy." His fingers settled on her mid-back

again as he guided her toward the door. "I have to escort you."

She heard someone whisper, "Wouldn't want her to go bat-shit crazy in here."

Her mouth tightened in response, the only one she would show.

Another man murmured, "Kade said she's as nuts as the rest of the Fringers. I wouldn't mind her going nuts on me."

Several men chuckled, the thick sound of innuendo charging their laughter.

Kade lifted his hands, not looking the least bit contrite. "You did go crazy. Jumped me, tore a chunk of my hair out."

"You were beating my brother to a pulp."

"He deserved it. I came to arrest him. He should have gone peacefully. Instead he Catalyzed and went all scales and fangs on me."

She swallowed back the angry things she wanted to say as the memory of that terrible day returned. She eyed the fine line that lanced Kade's right eyebrow and across his temple. "Nice scar."

He paused at the door that led out to the reception area, drawing his finger across it. "Yes, it is. Scars are a badge of honor in the Guard. Arlo did me a favor." He arched that eyebrow. "And the ladies like it. Gives me a dangerous look."

"How'd that shiner work for you? Did that make you look mad, bad, and dangerous, too?"

A black guy who reminded her of Wesley Snipes hovered nearby, amusement on his face. "Kavanaugh, you didn't tell us this little girl gave you that shiner." He eyed her up and down, the kind of survey that made her feel marginalized. His taunting gaze remained in place as it shifted to Kade. "You must be getting soft."

Now it was Kade's mouth that tightened into a line. This was not friendly camaraderie, especially since the black guy was jabbing Kade in front of her.

Why the hell she had the insane urge to defend him, to say that he'd fought...well, like a tiger, she had no idea. No, take satisfaction at humbling him in front of his colleagues. And umbrage at the Wesley guy calling her "little." Not at five foot seven.

Get me out of here. She turned the door handle.

It wouldn't move. Damn. She wanted to get out of there. Now.

Kade leaned close, pressing a series of buttons and pushing the door open for her. "Allow me."

She gave him a look that, while it may not kill, hopefully would singe him. Except, no...he gave her a bemused half-smile. She stalked out. Behind her, she heard the muffled laughter of the people who had no doubt heard every word of their exchange.

THE DISH

Where Authors Give You the Inside Scoop

♥ ♥ ♥ ♥ ♥ ♥ ♥ ♥ ♥ ♥ ♥ ♥ ♥ ♥ ♥

From the desk of Jaime Rush

Dear Reader,

DRAGON AWAKENED and the world of the Hidden started very simply, as most story ideas do. I saw this sexy guy with an elaborate dragon tattoo down his back. But much to my surprise, the "tattoo" changed his very cellular structure, turning him into a full-fledged Dragon. I usually get a character in some situation that begs me to open the writer's "What if?" box. And this man/ Dragon was the most intriguing character yet. I had a *lot* of questions, as you can imagine. *Who are you? Why are you? And will you play with me?* This is the really fun part of writing for me: exploring all the possibilities. I got tantalizing bits and pieces. I knew he was commanding, controlling, and a warrior. And his name was Cyntag, Cyn for short.

Then the heroine made an appearance, and she in no way seemed to fit with him. She was, in the early version, a suffer-no-fools server in a rough bar. And very human. I knew her name was Ruby. (I love when their names come easily like that. Normally I have to troll through lists and phone books to find just the right one.) The television show *American Restoration* inspired a new profession for Ruby, who was desperately holding on to the resto yard she inherited from her mother. I knew Ruby was raised by her uncle after being orphaned, and he'd created a book about a fairy-tale world just for her.

But I was still stumped by how these completely different people fit together. Until I got the scene where Ruby finds her uncle pinned to the wall by a supernatural weapon, and the name he utters on his dying breath: Cyntag.

Ah, that's how they're connected. [Hands rubbing together in anticipation.] Then the scene where she confronts him rolled through my mind like a movie. Hotheaded, passionate Ruby and the cool, mysterious Cyn, who reveals that he is part of a Hidden world of Dragons, magick, Elementals, and danger. And so is she. Suddenly, her uncle's bedtime stories, filled with Dragon princes and evil sorcerers, become very dangerously real. As does the chemistry that sparks between Ruby and Cyn.

I loved creating the Hidden, which exists alongside modern-day Miami. Talk about opening the "What if?" box! I found lots of goodies inside: descendants of gods and fallen angels, demons, politics, dissension, and all the delicious complications that come from having magical humans and other beings trapped within one geographical area. And a ton of questions that needed to be answered. It was quite the undertaking, but all of it a fun challenge.

We all have an imagination. Mine has always contained murder, mayhem, romance, and magic. Feel free to wander through the madness of my mind any time. A good start begins at my website, www.jaimerush.com, or that of my romantic suspense alter-ego, www.tinawainscott.com.

Jaime Rush

♥ ♥ ♥ ♥ ♥ ♥ ♥ ♥ ♥ ♥ ♥ ♥ ♥ ♥ ♥ ♥

From the desk of Kristen Ashley

Dear Reader,

I often get asked which of my books or characters are my favorites. This is an impossible question to answer and I usually answer with something like, "The ones I'm with."

See, every time I write a book, I lose myself in the world I'm creating so completely, I usually do nothing but sit at my computer—from morning until night—immersed in the characters and stories. I so love being with them and want to see what happens next, I can't tear myself away. In fact, I now have to plan my life and make sure everything that needs to get done, gets done; everyone whom I need to connect with, I connect with; because for the coming weeks, I'll check out and struggle to get the laundry done!

Back in the day, regularly, I often didn't finish books, mostly because I didn't want to say good-bye. And this is one reason why my characters cross over in different series, just so I can spend time with them.

Although I absolutely "love the ones I'm with," I will say that only twice did I end a book and feel such longing and loss that I found it difficult to get over. This happened with *At Peace* and also, and maybe especially, with LAW MAN.

I have contemplated why my emotion after completing these books ran so deep. And the answer I've come up with is that I so thoroughly enjoyed spending time with heroes who didn't simply fall in love with their heroines. They fell in love with and built families with their heroines.

In the case of LAW MAN, Mara's young cousins, Bud and Billie, badly needed a family. They needed to be protected and loved. They needed to feel safe. They needed role models and an education. As any child does. And further, they deserved it. Loyal and loving, I felt those two kids in my soul.

So when Mitch Lawson entered their lives through Mara, and he led Mara to realizations about herself, at the same time providing all these things to Bud and Billie and building a family, I was so deep in that, stuck in the honey of creating a home and a cocoon of love for two really good (albeit fictional) kids, I didn't want to surface.

I remember standing at the sink doing dishes after putting the finishing touches on that book and being near tears, because I so desperately wanted to spend the next weeks (months, years?) writing every detail in the lives of Mitch, Mara, Bud, and Billie. Bud making the baseball team. Billie going to prom. Mitch giving Bud "the talk" and giving Billie's friends the stink-eye. Scraped knees. Broken hearts. Homework. Christmases. Thanksgivings. I wanted to be a fly on the wall for it all, seeing how Mitch and Mara took Bud's and Billie's precarious beginnings on this Earth and gave them stability and affection, taught them trust, and showed them what love means.

Even now, when I reread LAW MAN, the beginning of the epilogue makes my heart start to get heavy. Because I know it's almost done.

And I don't want it to be.

Kristen Ashley

♥ ♥ ♥ ♥ ♥ ♥ ♥ ♥ ♥ ♥ ♥ ♥ ♥ ♥ ♥

From the desk of Kristen Callihan

Dear Reader,

In SHADOWDANCE, heroine Mary Chase asks hero Jack Talent what it's like to fly. After all, Jack, who has the ability to shift into any creature, including a raven in *Moonglow*, has cause to know. He tells her that it is lovely.

I have to agree. When I was fifteen, I read Judith Krantz's *Till We Meet Again*. The story features a heroine named Frederique who loves to fly more than anything on Earth. Set in the 1940s, Freddy eventually gets to fly for the Women's Auxiliary Ferrying Squadron in Britain. I cannot tell you how cool I found this. The idea of women not only risking their lives for their country but being able to do so in a job usually reserved for men was inspiring.

So, of course, I had to learn how to fly. Luckily, my dad had been a navigator in the Air Force, which made him much more sympathetic to my cause. He gave me flying lessons as a sixteenth birthday present.

I still remember the first day I walked out onto that small airfield in rural Maryland. It was a few miles from Andrews Air Force Base, where massive cargo planes rode heavy in the sky while fighter jets zipped past. But my little plane was a Cessna 152, a tiny thing with an overhead wing, two seats, and one propeller to keep us aloft.

The sun was shining, the sky cornflower blue, and the air redolent with the sharp smell of aviation gas and motor oil. I was in heaven. Here I was, sixteen, barely legal to drive a car, and I was going to take a plane up in the sky.

Sitting in the close, warm cockpit with my instructor,

I went through my checklist with single-minded determination and then powered my little plane up. I wasn't nervous; I was humming with anticipation.

Being in a single-engine prop is a sensory experience. The engine buzzes so loud that you need headphones to hear your instructor. The cockpit vibrates, and you feel each and every bump through the seat of your pants as you taxi right to the runway.

It only takes about sixty miles per hour to achieve liftoff, but the sensation of suddenly going weightless put my heart in my throat. I let out a giddy laugh as the ground dropped away and the sky rushed to meet me. It was one of the best experiences of my life.

And all because I read a book.

Now that I am an author, I think of the power in my hands, to transport readers to another life and perhaps inspire someone to try something new. And while Mary and Jack do not take off in a plane—they live in 1885, after all—there might be a dirigible in their future.

[signature]

♥ ♥ ♥ ♥ ♥ ♥ ♥ ♥ ♥ ♥ ♥ ♥ ♥ ♥ ♥

From the desk of Anna Sullivan

Dear Reader,

I grew up in a big family—eight brothers and sisters—so you can imagine how crowded and noisy, quarrelsome and fun it was. We all have different distinct personalities, of course, and it made for some interesting moments. Add in a couple of dogs, friends in and out, and, well, you get the picture.

I was the shy kid taking it all in, not watching from the sidelines, but often content to sit on them with a good book in my hands. Sometimes I'd climb a big old elm tree behind our house, cradle safely in the branches, and lose myself in another world while the wind rustled in the leaves and the tree creaked and swayed.

Looking back, it's no wonder how I ended up a writer, and it's not hard to understand why my stories seem to need a village to come to life. For me, the journey always starts with the voices of the hero and heroine talking incessantly in my head, but what fun would they have without a whole cast of characters to light up their world?

The people of Windfall Island are a big, extended family, one where all the relatives are eccentric and none of them are kept out of sight. No, they bring the crazy right out and put it on display. They're gossip-obsessed, contentious, and just as apt to pick your pocket as save your life—always with a wink and a smile.

Maggie Solomon didn't grow up there, but the Windfallers took her in, gave her a home, made her part of their large, boisterous family when her own parents turned their backs on her. So when Dex Keegan shows up, trying to enlist her help without revealing his secrets, she's not about to pitch in just because she finds him…tempting. Being as suspicious and standoffish as the rest of the Windfallers, Maggie won't cooperate until she knows why Dex is there, and what he wants.

What he wants, Dex realizes almost immediately, is Maggie Solomon. Sure, she's hard-headed, sharp-tongued, and infuriatingly resistant to his charms, but she appeals to him on every level. There must be something perverse, he decides, about a man who keeps coming back for more when a woman rejects him. He enjoys their verbal sparring, though, and one kiss is all it takes for him to know he won't stop until she surrenders.

But Maggie can't give in until he tells her the truth, and it's even more incredible—and potentially explosive to the Windfall community—than she ever could have imagined.

There's an eighty-year-old mystery to solve, a huge inheritance at stake, and a villain who's willing to kill to keep the secret, and the money, from ever seeing the light of day.

The Windfallers would love for you to join them as they watch Dex and Maggie fall in love—despite themselves—and begin the journey to find a truth that's been waiting decades for those with enough heart and courage to reveal.

I really had a great time telling Dex and Maggie's story, and I hope you enjoy reading about them, and all the characters of my first Windfall Island novel.

Happy reading,

Anna Sullivan

www.AnnaSulivanBooks.com
Twitter @ASullivanBooks
Facebook.com/AnnaSullivanBooks

Introducing
TINA WAINSCOTT'S
JUSTISS ALLIANCE SERIES

Five ex-SEALs are on a mission to find
purpose, honor, and love.

Wild Hearts
Coming January 2014

After a Navy SEAL Team mission goes awry,
these ex-SEALs must decide if they want
to take their next mission with the Justiss
Alliance.

Wild on You
Coming February 2014

Rick Yarbrough is taking on his first civilian
mission: to serve as a bodyguard for a general's
daughter, an animal activist who crossed the
wrong people. Only he has the expertise to
protect her—and the passion to win her
heart.

And look for

Wild Ways
May 2014

Wild Nights
November 2014

For contests, sneak peeks and more,
visit **TinaWainscott.com**

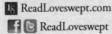

ReadLoveswept.com

ReadLoveswept

Find out more about Forever Romance!

Visit us at
www.hachettebookgroup.com/publishing_forever.aspx

Find us on Facebook
http://www.facebook.com/ForeverRomance

Follow us on Twitter
http://twitter.com/ForeverRomance

NEW AND UPCOMING TITLES

Each month we feature our new titles
and reader favorites.

CONTESTS AND GIVEAWAYS

We give away galleys, autographed copies,
and all kinds of exclusive items.

AUTHOR INFO

You'll find bios, articles, and links to personal websites
for all your favorite authors—and so much more.

GET SOCIAL

Connect with your favorite authors, editors, and
other Forever fans, and share what's important to you.

THE BUZZ

Sign up for our monthly romance newsletter,
and be the first to read all about it.